Praise for *A Good Hou*

"A feminist gothic that evokes Shirley Jackson's *The Haunting of Hill House*."

—*New York Times Book Review*

"The dream house in the country is a fictional standard for illuminating the realities of women's domestic life; when the dream turns to nightmare, it's the perfect setting for horror.... Atmospheric and beautifully written, *A Good House for Children* builds slowly but surely into a terrifying ghost story."

—*The Guardian*

"[Will] go down a treat for all of those (numerous) readers with tastes straddling what passes for 'literary fiction' and good old deeply satisfying horror. It has a little bit of all things not very nice that make up a page-turning popular novel, without resorting to moral simplicity or predictability. It's a highly readable book that still inspires more questions than it answers—which is impressive, for being so rare.... More than once, I was put in mind of *The Turn of the Screw*."

—*The Irish Times*

"Collins skillfully intercuts the two story lines, making clever use of structure to maximize tension, resonance, and fright, while the familiar setup fools readers into thinking they know what path the plot will follow. A moody, evocative, close-third narrative underscores the keenly rendered characters' mounting distress and claustrophobia. A harrowing slow burn with feminist undertones."

—*Kirkus Reviews* (starred review)

A
Good
House
for
Children

A Good House for Children

for Children

A Novel

KATE COLLINS

MARINER BOOKS
New York   Boston

A GOOD HOUSE FOR CHILDREN. Copyright © 2023 by Kate Collins. All rights reserved. Printed in the United States of America. No part of this book may be used or reproduced in any manner whatsoever without written permission except in the case of brief quotations embodied in critical articles and reviews. For information, address HarperCollins Publishers, 195 Broadway, New York, NY 10007.

HarperCollins books may be purchased for educational, business, or sales promotional use. For information, please email the Special Markets Department at SPsales@harpercollins.com.

Originally published in Great Britain in 2023 by Serpent's Tail, an imprint of Profile Books Ltd.

A hardcover edition of this book was published in 2023 by Mariner Books.

FIRST MARINER BOOKS PAPERBACK EDITION PUBLISHED 2024.

Library of Congress Cataloging-in-Publication Data has been applied for.

ISBN 978-0-06-329103-4

24 25 26 27 28 LBC 5 4 3 2 1

For Shirley and Phil,
best beloved

Budding

—

Awake, arise, pull out your eyes,
And hear what time of day;
And when you have done, pull out your tongue,
And see what you can say.

English nursery rhyme, traditional

1

2017

——

IT'S POSSIBLE TO LOVE SOMETHING too much. It's even possible to love something to death, and when Sam was seven weeks old and screaming himself scarlet with an existential fury particular to small babies, Orla McGrath stood over his cot and thought, *I love you so much I could kill you.* It was only a quick thought and it passed into that humid night soon enough, but from time to time over the years she would remember that she had once had it, and adrenaline would race up her spine.

As Sam grew older, he grew less angry, and, gradually, silent. His early infant babble never really formed past a few words and soon those sounds, too, ebbed away out of his red mouth full of pearl-barley teeth, until one day, when Sam had just turned three, it occurred to Orla and Nick that their son hadn't spoken a single word for almost a week.

"Should we take him to the doctor?" Orla peered into his mouth as he stood obediently in front of her in the kitchen.

"I don't think there's anything *wrong* with him, really." Nick, arms folded, leaned against the oven and looked interested but not exactly worried.

"Sam, darling, can you tell me if your throat hurts?" She cupped his cheek in her palm. Sam shook his head. "Do you mean you can't tell me, or that it doesn't hurt?" Sam nodded. Orla sighed, frustrated, and pulled her son onto her lap so that his little head rested against the hollow between her breasts and she could feel the heat of his blood through her shirt.

"I suppose an appointment couldn't hurt," Nick said. "I'm not here much next week, though; I probably won't be able to come with you."

When Orla was pregnant with Sam, heavy and slow and cow-eyed, she developed a thirst that couldn't be put out. She drank no more than usual, but would descend into a panic if she found herself without water to hand, and so she developed a habit of collecting. Her nightstand became a fortress of half-filled tumblers, the boot of the car perpetually weighed down by cases of bottled spring water. Liters of sparkling water filled the cupboards, gathered dust stashed neatly behind the toilet cistern, rolled about beneath the sofa. Outside, buckets and pots stood in rows to catch the rain and slowly turned green. Sometimes, when she felt the thirst, just looking at her water suppressed the need for it, and she'd smile and touch the bottles lightly with her fingers. The biggest saucepan was called into service as a doorstop holding open the French doors from the living room into the kitchen, full of beautiful water and serene as a mirror.

Her mother-in-law came to visit during this time, saw the depths of Orla's sickness and took her to the GP to test for gestational diabetes. Nothing—she was perfectly fine. Her GP, a kind man who looked a little like a heron, held Orla's hand and said, "If it makes you feel better, you may go on collecting." Orla smiled and was grateful.

When Sam came, tearing his way into the world, Orla and

Nick brought him home to their house full of water, where Orla saw it all and decided she didn't need it anymore. Out it went—the buckets splashed into the grate in the garden, the endless green bottles in their creaking plastic cases given away to neighbors. Orla stood with her son in her arms and emptied all the places in which she had collected herself.

Bridie, three years later, was an easier pregnancy. She was such an undemanding fetus that Orla occasionally forgot she was pregnant at all, especially in the early months, and when she finally delivered a hefty baby after a gasping ninety minutes of labor, she was almost startled by the appearance of a living thing. Although Bridie was a more relaxed baby, Orla found her less rewarding than Sam had been at that age. Nick said it was only natural, that first babies were always special, and Orla nodded along.

Orla worried that Sam might take against the new arrival—she'd heard enough horror stories of toddler siblings putting babies into the washing machine on the spin cycle, or pushing them out of prams. But Sam was enchanted by his sister—by her dark duckling fluff and satin lips and the way she lay curled up like a wood louse on its back. He stroked her toes when Orla bathed her in the sink and insisted that he be the one to hold the bottles when Orla finally gave up on breastfeeding, after six exhausting weeks of underproducing a thin and unsatisfying milk.

The GP, after a thorough examination through which Sam sat patiently, declared that he couldn't see anything obviously out of the ordinary and referred them to a child psychiatrist. Orla and Sam endured three sessions, during each of which Sam grew more and more cross, until Orla put an end to it. The woman sent them away with a diagnosis of "selective mutism" and a shrug: "Honestly, I can't find anything wrong. Most children who are silent around strangers are rather chatty at home. That's not the case here, but I can't see any reason for it."

Orla looked at Sam, sitting placid on a chair in the waiting room, swinging his legs. "So, what do we do?"

"Not much, really. At the moment. For most children, it's a manifestation of severe anxiety. I see no evidence of that in Sam."

"I thought perhaps, with the new baby—"

"How does he seem with her?"

Sam adored his sister. He communicated with her without words—he dressed her carefully and picked up her abandoned socks and petted her cheeks while she slept. Sam appointed himself Bridie's faithful custodian and loved her beyond language, and Orla was faintly jealous.

"He's been great with her, honestly. But, you know, the disruption."

"Perhaps. But in my opinion? It seems to be entirely stubbornness. Likely he'll grow out of it."

"What if he doesn't?"

"Mrs. McGrath, there's nothing physically wrong with your son and you should be grateful for that, at least. Right now, I suppose he just doesn't feel like talking."

So Orla was left to wonder, and she watched her son with an intensity that made them both too aware of each other and a friction developed between them. Only a slight rub, but it was there. She was conscious that her hovering and worrying was exacerbating the problem. She couldn't help but encourage him to use words when he wanted lunch, rather than patting the fridge, and would hold up his bright T-shirts in the morning out of his reach, so that he'd have to tell her which color he wanted to wear that day. Stubbornness, indeed. Orla, privately, thought of it as a "mute-iny." Sam sailed on his beatific silence; he pointed and smiled and circumvented Orla's attempts at conversation with a wry ease that made him seem much older than three.

On a Tuesday night, while Orla rinsed the plates from dinner, her husband seated himself on a kitchen chair and said, "I'm worried about Sam."

"What?" Orla stripped off her rubber gloves and turned to lean against the sink.

"It's not getting any better."

"Nick, we just need to give him time. Give him space."

"Exactly."

"What?"

Nick popped the caps from two bottles of Italian beer and handed one to his wife. "Space. I've been thinking—how would you feel about a new house?"

"What?"

"Stop saying *what*. A new house!" He grinned, excited.

"Do we need a new house?"

"I think so. I've been thinking about it for a while."

"Why?"

He took a couple of long swallows. "We've always talked about moving to the coast. Nearer my parents. I think maybe it's time. The business is doing well, we can afford it. And I want the kids to grow up like I did. Free, you know? Country-side, all that. My parents would like it; you know they want to be closer. And Sam loves it down there—we all do."

His parents lived in Dorset, not far from Poole, and their family did love it down there. The rocky coves, the scallop-edge of hidden beaches. She liked Nick's parents, too, and how easily they'd folded around her and brought her in. Eva had been so kind to her when she was pregnant with Sam. It was Eva who held her hand in the doctor's waiting room, Eva who admonished Nick, gently, when he shouted at Orla for

spending almost fifty pounds in one go on cases of bottled water: Orla would always be grateful for that. And Sam loved his
grandparents so much, Bridie too, in her limited way. Who was
she to stand in the way of so much potential happiness? Orla
recalled the rule-bound household of her own childhood, the
constrictions that had choked her.

"Are you sure it would be the right thing?" Orla framed her
opinion as a question, because she knew that Nick would have
an opinion of his own. Nick's opinions were never compro-
mised by question marks.

He stood and put his hands on her waist. "Definitely. Sam
needs it, I think we all need it. I don't want to be in town
anymore."

They spent a few companionable evenings on various
property websites, teasing each other about their differ-
ing priorities, setting the upper price limit at outrageous
amounts. One million, one point five, two. Of course, they
weren't really going to end up somewhere like that, but it
was fun to look; even Orla had to admit that. And Nick was
right, there were some beautiful properties up for sale. Orla
thought about gold summers and turquoise beaches and relaxed into the inevitability of moving, decided that she probably didn't mind after all.

A benevolent summer turned gracefully into a warm autumn,
and when Nick came home one day and told her, smiling,
that he'd found them a new house, Orla was feeling generous
enough to listen properly. The sun had made her limber, relaxed, and she'd spent a happy day in the garden with the children, watching Sam dig for worms and Bridie kick her fat feet
under the shade of the parasol clipped to her pram. It was as
if Nick knew that her day had been nearly perfect, and that
in turn this was the perfect time to announce change. He'd

always had a good read on her moods, although lately he'd used that to his advantage rather than hers.

"Right in Dorset. Like we talked about." Nick sat back in his chair and took a long mouthful from a gin and tonic. He'd brought one out for her, too, with a segment of grapefruit, the way she liked. The citrus oils from the fruit sparked against the gin and turned the tonic cloudy.

"Which part?"

"About three miles east of Lulworth, just outside a village called Holmesford."

"That's far." She drove the route mentally, looping around Bath across the downs, the straight shot south into national parkland, past the Regises and the Minsters and the Magnas.

"I saw it on the way back from Mum and Dad's. Remember I went down the other week? Got diverted on the way back and saw a sale sign, so I thought it would be worth a look. Orla, this place. I'm telling you, it's the one. Absolutely gorgeous, right on the top of a hill. Amazing views and honestly not half bad, price-wise. We've got a viewing at the weekend, thought we could make a bit of a holiday out of it. Leave the kids with Mum, go and have a look around." He waved his hands in the approximate shape of a square. "It's huge—amazing for the kids, and you'll have so much room to paint. Great local primary."

It startled her that they would soon have to think about primary school. They'd never put Sam into nursery—at first because what was the point? Orla was at home anyway, so why spend the money? And then because of his speech: they didn't want him to feel left out or teased, and so the need to protect him within their family circle outweighed any benefit gently hinted at by the psychiatrist, who made a pointed little aside about socialization in their final session. Orla took him to various activities and classes instead, and hoped that was enough.

Nick pulled up the property listing on his phone and cupped

his hands against the screen so she could see. "And the garden! Sam's going to get such a kick out of it. And maybe, you know, a change of scenery—" He gestured toward their son, sitting on his haunches and peering intently at the grass. Sam was turned away from them, his face shadowed by a blue sun hat with a brim. For a moment he looked alien to Orla, as though he could be any child.

"He's not broken—he doesn't need you to fix him. Moving house isn't the magic answer, Nick." She hated having to defend Sam against his own father. Nick's main concern always seemed to be what other people thought of Sam: how they responded to him, how they would treat him. Sam didn't seem to mind much, he adored his father, but Orla minded on his behalf. She understood that Nick saw their children as an extension—*reflection*—of himself, and that deviation from expectation troubled him.

"I'm not saying it is. Christ, Orla, why does everything have to be an absolute with you? I didn't say it was the miracle cure, I just think it'll help." He smiled and touched her arm across the table. "Will you at least try to like it?"

"Of course." Orla drained her gin. "I'm sorry. I can't wait to see it."

Did she want this new house? Perhaps. She mulled on the topic with the same amiable ambivalence she once gave to getting pregnant. And because she didn't know, she was happy to be led. Nick had so much purpose, so much focus, that she allowed him to gently position her as she ought to be. He turned her this way and that, looking toward or away from the things he decided were worth it or not, and she was grateful for it. Most of the time. Orla knew, really, that the decision had already been made.

She shrugged out of her old life, skinning herself, and slipped into the new.

2

2017

———

THE REEVE. THE NAME WAS engraved into a plaque of limestone on the pillar at the front gate and repeated above the expansive doorway of the house itself, along with the date of construction: 1812. The driveway looped in a semicircle to the front of the house and the front lawn stretched almost thirty feet down to a low brick wall. Beyond the wall was a sandy footpath and then, abruptly, the cliff edge.

Orla had been put in the back of the car and was largely silent while Nick chatted with the estate agent up front about local house prices, the logistics of their move, further plans to buy a small flat back in Bristol after their old house was sold. That was the arrangement they came to: Orla would be alone during the week and Nick would return for weekends. She'd been apprehensive about this until Nick reminded her that he left before the children were up anyway and was rarely home for bedtime. She wanted to ask, *But what about me?*

She watched the hedges weave past, watched as the land grew greener and emptier and lonelier. They'd come up the hill road from the village, rather than the main road that cut through the fields to the rear of the house, and Orla was pleased to see that the village looked large and lively. One nice-looking restaurant, a library, even a small gallery. A few tourists strolled about with optimistic ice creams, but the summer season was coming to an end and the air through the car window smelled of leaf rot and salt.

When they pulled up to the house, Nick reached into the back seat to squeeze her knee and transmitted, in that one brutally simple gesture, how things were to be.

"It's been empty for about five years." The estate agent shut the car door with a thump and peered up at the house. She shielded her eyes with her palm, as if to better take in the sheer scope of the property, and Nick did the same. Orla climbed out and moved away to look at the view out over the cliff edge.

"Yes, the girl on the phone mentioned that when I first called—but we don't mind a project." Nick pulled at Orla's jumper. "Come here." He slid an arm round her waist and turned her to face the house. "The previous owners died—they were quite old, I think—and the estate passed to a nephew. He'd been trying to off-load it for ages, and that's when we came along."

The estate agent nodded. "This could be a great deal, Mrs. McGrath. He's already haggled us right down." She winked at Nick, who laughed. Orla looked at the sapling growing out of one of the chimney stacks.

"Room for a double garage, if you take down that lean-to." The estate agent pointed at the decrepit shed. On the gravel in front of the doors lay a small bird, brownish. Its body was collapsed and awkward, flesh long gone, just feathers on bone.

"Plenty of space on the drive, though," said Nick. "If you get rid of the grass."

The front lawn was overgrown and patchy, dotted with fierce dandelions that grew unchecked and daisies scattered like snow. The gravel was of the same pale, honeyed stone as the house, although it too was sparse and threaded with weeds.

The entrance was recessed enough to allow for a small porch area, in which stood two iron boot-scrapers and a rusted metal rake. Gossamer spiderwebs trailed from the glass carriage lamp that hung from the ceiling. The porch was laid with large gray flagstones, polished by two hundred years of feet and worn in divots.

The front doors, a double behemoth of aged oak, curved upward into a graceful arch—a strangely Gothic touch to a Regency house. Orla wondered who had designed them; they were a quirk of personality, a raised eyebrow on an otherwise serene face, and she liked them for that.

And then the windows. Orla had never seen anything like them, and they made the doors look almost sheepish by comparison. Two enormous picture windows at double height, one on each side of the front doors, that began on the ground floor and spanned up to the first. They matched the sash windows that covered the rest of the frontage in width, but the height was substantial and they were shaped to follow the curve of the doors. Iron frames painted white held the glass in place, cut in that incongruous Gothic arch. Original windows: they must have been enormously expensive at the time.

The slate roof, pitched at a gentle slope, housed four small dormer windows like narrowed eyes. A dead wisteria stretched itself across the frontage from the left, planted somewhere behind the high brick wall that led to the garden, and a narrow wrought-iron gate showed a glimpse of the wilderness behind the house.

"North-facing back garden," said the estate agent. "Bit of a shame, but I suppose they wanted the sea view more."

Inside, light and symmetry abounded; Orla imagined a split peach, a halved apple. The house seemed like something whole that had been bisected and then butterflied; incised and opened up.

The rooms were arranged around a vast entrance hall the full height of the house, capped with a clouded dome of glass and iron, splashed here and there with dead leaves and bird droppings. The light filtering through it was muted and warm, even on that gray day, and cast long shadows from the prominent lintels above each door on the first- and second-floor landings, giving them a glowering sort of look. It felt to Orla like the decks of a ship; the landings formed a horseshoe above the stairs and ended up against those great tall windows at the front—a cathedral to look out over the sea.

From the front doors, a long stretch of tiled hallway veered upward into the sudden vertical of the stairs, which swerved off into a perfect left and right along the first-floor landing. The left flight led up to the master bedroom, nursery, and ensuite, while the right-hand side trailed along past two further bedrooms, a family bathroom, and a large and dusty airing cupboard. All of the windows on the first floor were dressed with old-fashioned wooden shutters, precarious now but still pretty, although of the two sets in the master bedroom one shutter lacked its companion, and made the room look like a mouth missing a tooth.

The second floor was accessed by two further flights of stairs at either end of the first-floor landing. These stairs were narrower and carpeted with the same moss-green as the landings, splattered here and there with cheap white undercoat paint and thick with dust. Orla thought about the hands-and-knees job of pulling up all that fusty carpet and felt very tired. This floor was home to two smaller bedrooms, a toilet and shower room, and a nothing-y sort of room that contained a door hiding the attic steps.

Orla trailed after Nick, who strode ahead of the estate agent and flung open doors in what Orla felt was a proprietary and off-putting manner.

Nick caught her expression and asked, "Are you okay?"

"Fine, just thinking."

"She's a big thinker, my lovely wife." He smiled at the estate agent and squeezed Orla's arm.

The agent continued, "There is internet, the previous owners had it put in, but you're quite far from the exchange up here so, to be frank with you, it's pretty patchy. You might want to call around, price up a new line." She pointed to a couple of LAN sockets screwed into the wall above the baseboard.

They moved together into the sitting room and Orla let Nick and the woman go ahead of her. They admired the original cornicing and the wide oak floorboards. Orla saw the woodworm and the rot and the dust, but she didn't want to intrude on their mutual excitement. She stayed in the doorway, surveyed the proportions of the room, and let herself imagine a life here. Nick had made all this possible, she couldn't forget that.

When they met, Orla was a young painter already gathering a solid following, and Nick had just dropped out of university to start his own programming company. She'd been struck by him immediately, in the back garden of a friend's student house. The barbecue had gone out and Nick was kneeling on the concrete and fiddling with the gas pipe, laughing as he pretended to drop a lighter next to the leak. He was tall, funny, already balding but entirely unconcerned by the fact, younger than her by a margin that seemed faintly scandalous.

Nobody tells you how claustrophobic it is to fall in love at first sight. Balanced consideration must be abandoned, to turn away seems an impossibility. You are bound to a future you may not have imagined, or intended, and the idea that you might walk away from it is only a little more painful than accepting it. Nick decided he was going to marry her and Orla felt both imprisoned and breathlessly ecstatic at how certain he was of their future.

Nick gathered it up wholeheartedly, never questioned it—but Orla, who was seeking a certain kind of wildness, turned it over and over in her mind as she lay in the dark next to the man who had already claimed her possibilities. She loved him very quickly, and it altered the course she'd been charting.

Orla's parents, back in Ireland—evangelical, worn, horrified—wrote her a furious letter when she moved into Nick's studio flat. But Orla had already lived their life, and decided she wanted to live her own. And if sometimes she wondered whether Nick's certainty about who he was and where they were going was comfortably familiar to her parents' fervent rigidity, she tried not to think about it. His success had delivered them a comfort she would likely never have achieved on her own, certainly not as a jobbing artist.

After Sam, Orla produced work only sporadically, and after Bridie she stopped altogether. Nick didn't exactly consider her painting to be work—even the paid commissions made him slightly fretful that she might not have enough time left over for him. Sometimes she wondered where she had agreed to all this, at which point she had placed her finger on the map of their lives and said, *Yes, here we are and here is where we will go.*

Orla hadn't ever minded, until now it occurred to her that she should have minded, or watched closer for the losing of herself. Unnoticed, she'd slipped into a life that she'd never intended. Her blossoming career had been subsumed beneath Nick's choices. It was an unspoken pact, what she was asked to give up in return for a measure of financial freedom. Increasingly, she didn't feel so free.

"Well?" Nick turned to Orla in the bare and echoing drawing room, after the estate agent removed herself discreetly into the orangery. The set of keys dangled from his fingers; the red plastic tag looked too bright, too modern, in this old, old room.

The drawing room, spare and lovely, was dominated by an impressive fireplace topped in marble. On the other side of the house, the sitting room resembled a humbler cousin, a snug companion. The kitchen ran along the whole back side of the house, boxing in the two front rooms at their rear, and the French doors out of the kitchen led into an old-fashioned orangery with vaulted windows in iron frames. The kitchen was rather dated—there were no fitted cabinets, just scarred oak counters sitting above shelving units fronted with little curtains on wire runners. An AGA squatted at one end, recessed under a weathered beam, and Orla bit her cheek at the thought that she would have to learn how to use it. A stained Belfast sink sat between the counters on the orangery side, giving the washer-upper an uninhibited view of the walled garden. The fat brass taps had turned green, and looked obstinate.

"It's really beautiful. You were right, about the pictures."

"Size of that garden. It'll be brilliant for the kids."

"Yes." She hesitated, opened the door and closed it again, listened to the hinges. "Are you sure? I mean, we don't have to. If you've changed your mind."

"I haven't. I don't think we can stay where we are—do you? Like we said, Sam needs it."

"It's a big change."

"You know what Sam's like, he'll take it in stride." Nick looked at his wife. "How do you feel about it?"

Because she had only ever known half of herself, Nick had taken advantage of that. He'd pushed at her weak places, and hadn't she followed him? She was complicit, she knew. Happy to be led, content with half-closed eyes. So sure, so confident, he made the world fit round his shape. But Orla had spent a lifetime contorting herself, trying to understand how she slotted into the landscape of her present.

To ask her now how she felt—the time for that had come and gone and she hadn't spoken up because she never did, and Nick knew that. Whose fault, then?

"It's done, isn't it?" she said.

He leaned back against the tall frame of the sash window. The way the light came in from behind made him look dimmed, unreadable. "You said you liked this house."

"It's not really about the house."

"I thought I was doing the right thing. I thought if I could just find the perfect place you wouldn't have to think too much, that it would be easier—" He turned and the light caught his face and he looked so deflated.

"I really like the house. I do. It needs work. Quite a lot, I think." She paused. "I just want us to be sure."

Nick opened his arms. "Well, I'm sure enough for the both of us." He pulled her close. "Don't be cross anymore, Orla. It'll be good for you."

Would it be good for her? To be so isolated, cast adrift out here on the top of a cliff? Perhaps. As a person who felt very keenly the weight of other people's expectations, and their demands on her time, there was something pleasurable in the notion of surrendering to this new life. To be freed of obligation, to be cut loose from book clubs and playgroups and

awkward brunches at which she had nothing of note to report; perhaps she could live quite well out on the edge of the
world.

And didn't the house suit her? Quiet, enigmatic, active
under the surface. It held its own secrets, showed only frac-
tions of its nature. It was like her, wasn't it? She listened to its
sounds—the clicks of tree branches against the sash windows,
the distant dripping of a tap somewhere on the second floor.

Orla invited herself in, and the house woke up.

3

1976

———

LYDIA DREAMED OF LONDON, STILL, even after all these months. She only ever dreamed of the nice bits, and not the awful Tube or the beggars or the men who leered or the crowded pubs or the blind, thin cats that haunted the street behind her flat. She didn't dream about the rancid, vegetable smell of London summers, or the persistent damp that crept up the kitchen wall behind the oven.

When she woke, she made herself remember that she'd chosen to come here because she loved the children and because Sara was so sad, all the time, and because it sounded better than sharing her space with three other girls in a tenement flat in Holborn, better than laddered nylons hung over the bath and overflowing ashtrays balanced on dirty windowsills and pathetic attempts at growing geraniums in a window box choked by the diesel buses and a yowling record player that none of them could afford to replace.

But there were things from London she missed, of course there were. She missed the bakeries and the Chinese food and drinking with the girls on the grass of the Heath in the spring and the nice nightclubs, the ones with proper stools lined up along mahogany bars and alcohol that hadn't been watered down.

Lydia thought about Danny and his print-stained fingers and the way he made Brandy Alexanders just how she liked, and how good the sex was when he was being kind. She tried not to think about how bad the fights had been, or the sneering way he made her feel smaller than him, just because she didn't have a degree. But look where he'd got to—he never earned much more than she did and once, during an argument, she'd told him that he thought he was so much better than her because he worked for a newspaper but he only set the type, he didn't even write the fucking articles, *so who was the idiot now?*

Danny hadn't liked that at all, and it turned out to be one of the last fights they'd had before she moved to Dorset with Sara and the kids. Lydia wondered if she should telephone him. She'd thought that a lot recently, but never did.

It was too hot up in her attic room. The windows didn't open and beamed the sun directly onto her bed. Although it was only the middle of May, the weather had turned summer-hot about a week ago and hadn't let up. She had sort of assumed, when they arrived, that the twins would share a room and she would get a bedroom with a window that opened. But the girls insisted on being separate and so Lydia got shoved up here, like an old-fashioned servant. There wasn't even enough room for a wardrobe, not with the way the roof sloped. It had been bloody cold over Christmas, too, and she was having to use battery-operated camping lamps at night. Sara promised she'd get it wired soon.

Lydia rolled over when she heard feet slapping on the stairs and pulled on a dressing gown.

Philip appeared at the door that connected the first attic room to her bedroom. "Hello, hello, are you awake!"

"Yes, I'm awake—look, I'm sitting up and talking to you! Could I do that if I were still asleep?"

Philip jumped onto the end of her quilt and bounced on his knees. "Maybe, if you were a sleepwalker, or a ghost. Mummy said that some people talk in their sleep, so maybe you talk too."

Lydia laughed and reached out to tickle him. "I don't talk in my sleep! Right—breakfast. Shall we have toast?"

"No, thank you. I want a banana."

"We can have bananas."

Philip hopped off the bed and tugged on the belt of her dressing gown. "I like you being with us all the time. It's better than when we were in London, and you had to go home every day. It's like we're having a sleepover, isn't it. And you make me nice breakfasts, Mummy used to make me eat Weetabix and I don't like that."

"You know I still make you eat Weetabix sometimes."

Philip disappeared down the stairs in front of her and called back, "Yes, but not every day. I don't like it every day."

Lydia still marveled at the scope of the house. It made her feel both insignificant and superior to descend that grand, wide staircase every morning, to go in and out of the magnificent arched doors, to light a fire in an actual drawing room.

Sara hardly seemed to notice the house; Lydia often thought it was just a place for Sara's body to exist while her mind went somewhere else. She'd always been like that, though, even before Doug; her face carried a permanent expression of mild bewilderment, as though she was constantly surprised to find herself wherever she was. Sometimes it irritated Lydia, who was of a more pragmatic bent.

Lydia had lived all her life in London, and when she told her mother she was leaving for an elegant country house in Dorset, her mother laughed and then coughed and Lydia heard her spit into a mug, heavy smoker's phlegm. She had met Sara, once, when she came to the house to deliver a bag of Lydia's clothes, and after they'd shaken hands and Sara had gone back inside, her mother grinned and called Sara an "uptight" cunt. Her accent had made it sound like "can't."

On the telephone, three days before Lydia took the train south, her mother had said, "You'll be back soon enough," and hung up. Sometimes Lydia felt guilty about how infrequently she went home, back to the chill public housing flat in Lewisham, but her mother never invited her and Lydia never proposed it. Her brother almost never went home, and Lydia thought that her mother was rather glad to be rid of them both. When they were together, Lydia felt judgmental, Protestant, and made curt comments through thin lips at her mother's fondness for the *Racing Post* and a seemingly endless parade of much younger boyfriends who worked in the bookie's, or drove grimy cabs through the neon circus of Piccadilly at night.

Philip took two bananas from the big wooden bowl on the Welsh dresser. "Can I eat these outside?"

"Yes, I suppose. Where are the others?"

"Mummy has Owen and the twins are in the garden."

Sara came in from the sitting room, carrying the baby. "Morning—tea on the go?"

"Just put the kettle on."

"Can you have a word with the girls, please, Lydia? They were running riot all last night, kept me up." Sara dropped an armful of laundry into the hamper in the kitchen, shuffling in her slippers, and handed Owen to Lydia.

Lydia hadn't heard a single sound from the floor below during the night. What was Sara on about? "Sorry, what?"

Sara yawned. Philip slid off his kitchen chair and went to

put an arm round his mother's hip, but she stepped sideways, out of reach. "I could hear them, all that whispering. You've got to break them of that habit, I don't like it. Banging on the floor, sounded like a herd of elephants up there."

Lydia jiggled the baby. "Right, sure. I didn't hear anything, though, are you positive?"

"Keep them in check, please. It's your job."

Sara turned and left, never acknowledging her eldest son. Philip watched her go, eyes on his mother all the way down the hall. "I don't think she likes us very much, Lydia."

"Who, duckie? Me and you?"

"No, me and Tabs and Clover. Maybe Owen. I think she still likes Owen."

It pained Lydia to know that Philip saw and understood his mother's indifference. "You mustn't say that. She's your mum, she loves you. She likes you! She's just been working a lot, you know. She's tired." Lydia sat down at the table. "It's not her fault. There's been a lot to do."

"I think even before, when Daddy was alive, she didn't like me as much as the twins." He said this baldly, a fact. "They're better than me."

"Better?"

"Funner."

"More fun," said Lydia. "Funner isn't a word."

"All right." Philip nodded.

"And it's not true. You're just different. Tabitha and Clover are their own thing, you know that. I bet Owen will grow up and be just like you." She smiled, wanting to cover over the wound in his little heart with loving hands. "And besides, I like you very much."

Before Doug died, Sara used to make fun of Philip with her husband. About how he didn't like to be dirty, how he always finished his crusts, how carefully he combed his hair. Doug would joke that Philip was more like a girl than the girls, and Philip would writhe with distress and Sara would laugh. Lydia hated them for it, but she herself despaired at Philip's propensity toward tears. He could stand to be a little tougher, Lydia thought, but it wouldn't do any good to make fun.

She went out through the orangery and called across the lawn to the girls. A moment later, breathless and with green knees, the twins stood frantic at the kitchen door.

"Morning, girls. Toast?"

"We aren't hungry, Lydia."

"You have to have something, you can't be out playing with no breakfast. You'll run out of energy and faint dead away and then we'll have to revive you and none of us have the time for that." Lydia winked at Philip. "Here." She broke another two bananas off the bunch and handed one to each child. Owen wriggled in her arms and leaned toward his sisters. He loved the girls, even if they were mostly indifferent to him and used him primarily as a prop in their games of house or school or exploring. Sometimes he was their recalcitrant pupil, sometimes he was a dangerous hippo on the Zambezi, and once Lydia had found him staked to the lawn with a leather belt tied to his foot, which the girls explained was necessary as he was a circus elephant and mustn't be allowed to escape. Owen bore all of this with gratitude.

She murmured nonsense to the child and bounced him on her hip. Owen waved his arms and caught her cheek with his christening bracelet, all gold and sharp edges. Lydia tightened it round his plump wrist and thought again what an unsuitable item it was for a small child. All the children had one, gifted from Doug's parents, who were wealthy and rather old-fashioned. The girls' were silver, and Owen and Philip had gold, but the twins hadn't worn theirs for years. It wouldn't be long before Philip grew out of his entirely, which he lamented. Such a sentimental child.

Poor Philip, in the middle, stuck close to Lydia. The girls considered him to be both too much of a baby to be amusing and too old to be useful like Owen. He spent a lot of time alone, or with Lydia while she mended torn socks for the twins or wrestled Owen in the bathtub. He missed the routine of school, particularly, and Lydia remained unsure of Sara's sweeping decision to "give them all a year off," as she'd put it. Tabitha and Clover had always been half-feral, even in London, and they reveled in the freedom of the enormous garden and the beach and the woods. But Philip—studious, empirical Philip—missed his teachers and his homework and the familiar rhythm of Monday mornings.

Lydia had tried to talk about it to Sara, once, but was put aside. "It'll be good for them. Total freedom. It's why we moved out here, isn't it? I think a different life might be nice for a bit. There's enough time for them to be stuck in school next year."

"What about just Philip, then? He keeps asking."

"Tell him they'll all go back next year, but for now we're having a holiday."

Lydia hadn't pushed. She'd watched Sara nurse and then lose her husband; she knew better than most what had been taken through that endless, wretched year of sickness and drawn curtains and bone broth and silent children and the smell of it, sticking to everything in the house. When Lydia left each day, she stripped bare in the tiny bathroom of her flat, convinced the odor of dying clung to her skin.

It hadn't surprised her when Sara decided to move out to The Reeve. Doug had bought it as a second home, about a year before he got so thin it looked like he was haunting his own clothes, and they'd intended to use it in the summers, mostly. When he died and the house in London spilled over with grief and anger and the cloying, damp fug of decaying lilies, Sara moved them all out here, where the sea would wash away her loss and the air would bring color back to her children's faces. They needed the money, too, she said, and the London house fetched a good price.

Lydia had been invited, and Sara made it plain that, while she would be grateful if Lydia came with them, they would be leaving with or without her.

Lydia shifted Owen on her hip and picked up the banana peels from the kitchen table, where the girls had left them. She stepped into the orangery and watched Philip tail his sisters, desperate to be involved but too proud to ask. Within moments, all three were out of sight among the sunny thicket at the bottom of the garden, underneath the tall oaks that bordered the pond.

When they'd first arrived, Sara had taken them all down to the pond and given them a stern lecture on not venturing near it, or trying to paddle in it, or even throwing stones in. Philip had nodded, solemn, but the girls bounced on their toes and eyed the monkey puzzle for climbing and only half-listened to their mother.

The pond had iced over in the depths of January, and the twins had begged and begged to be allowed to skate on it, but Sara held firm. Lydia hadn't realized that the world could be so cold, like a shock every time she went outside—born and raised in London, under its warm fleece of pollution, she'd lived with a permanent sniffle for the first four months after moving out here to Dorset.

Now, the garden was all sunlight and bright scents and the patio stone was warm under her feet. She opened both sets of windows in the orangery and left the patio doors standing wide. As she stepped onto the grass, Lydia hesitated at the thin sound of a baby crying from deep inside the house, a faint noise like the rise and fall of a London ambulance in the distance. But Owen was in her arms, reaching out for butterflies, and after a moment the cries died away.

A few cabbage whites bobbed in the lavender beds that bordered the patio, and Lydia shivered and was grateful for the heat.

4

2017

———

"NEXT YEAR—DOUBLE GLAZING, I PROMISE." Nick held his wife's hand in bed as they watched condensation run down the bedroom windows. Orla had padded the windowsills with rags to soak up the moisture; they were already sodden.

"We have to, Nick. We can't put it off."

"I know, I honestly didn't think it would be this bad. We'll fix it." He paused, weighed her up. "Listen, I had Mum on the phone the other day and I invited them here for Christmas."

"Here?" Orla sat up.

"That's all right, isn't it? I know we've always gone there, but they're so keen to see the house and we've got so much room, I thought it would be nice. Take the burden off Mum a bit. And I'll be home, I'll help."

"No, of course. It'll be grand, it's fine. I'm just surprised, I thought we'd be going there. And it's far away, yet. I didn't think we'd decided."

A moment that might have turned into a quarrel was settled by the appearance of Sam, who flung himself dramatically onto the end of the bed and crawled toward them. Orla caught him and swung him into her lap, kissed his silky hair.

Sam wriggled away and bounced between them. He knelt and pulled a face, hands in front of his chest like claws.

"A lion?"

Sam shook his head at his father.

"A rat?" Orla knew, he'd been making this face all week.

"Rats make squeaking sounds, you know," said Nick, pointedly. "Maybe if you made rat sounds it would help me guess."

"Don't, Nick." Orla touched his face. She wanted to sound kind.

"Fine. Fair enough."

Bridie shouted from the nursery and Nick made a face. "Your turn, I've got to get in the shower. I'm already late, traffic's going to be a nightmare going up." He disappeared into the bathroom and Sam bounced into the warm spot left behind.

The corner of the master bedroom was connected to the nursery by a short corridor—what would have originally been a small dressing room—with a door at each end. The door into the master bedroom opened freely, but the second door out into the nursery was either locked or stuck fast, they couldn't tell. Nick had looked everywhere for a key, had even called the estate agent, but no luck. He'd tried shouldering it open, but all that achieved was a bruised arm and a crack in one of the panels. A comment was made about a locksmith, but somehow Nick never got round to it.

Tall cupboards lined the passageway and Orla used these for storing sheets and towels and summer clothes. It was a useful space, if a little annoying that it could only be entered from one side. The angle of the doorframe against the old floor was such that the door would often swing open if it wasn't closed tight, so she'd got into the habit of locking it shut every night, with the small iron key that lived on Nick's bedside table. Sometimes, if Bridie cried loudly, the sound reached Orla in a strange way down the corridor, as if Bridie was sitting right on the other side of the door.

Out on the landing, Orla paused to stand in the light streaming in from the cathedral windows. A hard, bright sky reflected jade in the sea, small skiffs of creamy foam capped the waves. The front lawn and cliff path were dusted with a quick frost already melting in the sun, diamonds in the light. Already she longed for the reprieve of spring—Christmas was always hard.

Each year, Orla sent a brief but warm Christmas card to her parents in Ennis, and each year it went unanswered. She understood they were making a point, and for several years in a row Nick had encouraged her to do away with the tradition of punishing herself. But she never could—the invisible thread that sews a child to their parents remained intact.

When Orla left her parents' Church she understood that she was sacrificing many of her relationships, but she hadn't thought her parents would be among them. The disgrace of her subsequent lifestyle dogged their reputation. Imagine, a child born before a wedding. *Heathens. Pray for them.* Her choices tainted her parents, although she hadn't known that then, and they had never forgiven her. The things she wanted, the life she wanted with Nick—although so conventional in many ways—was an affront to them, a rejection of the values they had chiseled into her.

They had never sent the children a birthday present, a Christmas present. No new baby gifts, no Easter cards, and only a cool acknowledgment of their existence in the first place. A short and labored phone call—*So, it's done then. Are you both healthy? Good. Goodbye.*

Nick's anger at her pain only worsened it. He might have forgiven them Orla's joyless childhood, but he couldn't bear the slight to his own children. So thank goodness for his parents, really, that comfortable haven of English middle-class normality. The first time she met them, Eva and George were so kind to her that she cried over dinner and Eva turned pink with confusion and pressed paper napkins to Orla's face. They were faintly bewildered by their daughter-in-law, they never understood her all that well, but they made an effort to love her and Orla loved them for that in return.

Orla carried Bridie back into the bedroom and plopped her onto the bed to change her. Sam, wrapped in the warm sheet, danced his fingers across Bridie's nose and cheeks to make her laugh.

"Will you phone from the office?"

"Course, always do." Nick lifted a tie from the drawer and shoved it into his pocket. He kissed Orla full on the mouth and turned Sam upside down by the ankles and then he was gone, his mind already halfway to the city. She heard him banging about in the kitchen, scooping up laptop bags and car keys, and then the slam of the front doors and the pop of car tires on the gravel. She'd dropped hints about perhaps getting a second car—it was a pain to be left without one during the week, especially with the children—but the decision had been made to wait until the new financial year.

Orla took the children down for breakfast, to find that the kitchen, usually so warm from the heat of the stove, was really quite cold. The door into the orangery stood open, and the patio doors, too. Two windows in the orangery were unlatched and banged back and forth in the wind. Orla pulled them shut and wondered why Nick had been in the garden.

Although it was eight o'clock, it felt much later. Orla had noticed that time felt slightly wrong inside the house—either later or earlier than it really was. Likely something to do with how the light came in, distorted by all those enormous windows. She found herself waking at two, three, four in the morning, convinced it was nearly nine and that the children would be hungry. Or going to chop vegetables for dinner and discovering that it was only one in the afternoon. She'd never had the habit of wearing a watch—too often her wrists were covered in paint and white spirit—and the only clock was in the kitchen.

And Sam—her beating heart—was so quiet. She'd learned to listen for the sounds he produced from elsewhere: the scratch of a brush on paper, the click of Lego bricks. Little feet in small tennis shoes, running.

When the house phone rang, thin and shrill, she started and knocked her hip bone against the porcelain sink.

"Hello?"

"Orla?"

"Yes?"

"It's Helen!"

"God, Helen, hi!" Orla pulled out a kitchen chair and sat, relieved to hear another voice. Helen was her oldest friend, made at college, and she'd known Orla before Nick, before the children, before life had become something entirely different from what she and Helen had dreamed up in their basement flat.

"Got your email, thought I'd call and see how it's all going! I tried your phone a few times but just got voicemail?"

"Yes, sorry, reception here is shite. Landline is best, probably."

"Did I get you at a good time?"

"Yes, yes, absolutely. How are you?"

Helen laughed. "I'm fine, you know I'm always fine! I want to hear about this brilliant house."

"It's great." Orla paused.

"Okay? I mean, it sounds great. How is it?"

"Honestly, Helen? It's absolutely fucking massive and the thought of getting the Hoover out makes me want to throw up."

Helen screamed. "Oh my God, you're an ungrateful bitch."

"I'm not!" Orla started to laugh. "I promise I'm not! It's just really big, Helen. Seriously. I'll send pictures. There's so many rooms!" She tried to make a joke out of something that had kept her awake at night. The house seemed immeasurable, unknowable, hiding itself away among all these corridors and landings and doorways that defied counting.

"I can't believe you're complaining about your mansion, Orla."

"It doesn't feel like one. You should see the state of the place—no wonder it was cheap. Everything's single-glazed, too—it's freezing. I've two jumpers on."

"And the kids?"

"Fine, good, actually. Sam likes it a lot, the garden's huge."

"Any luck, you know?" Helen hesitated.

"Nothing, yet. We do think it'll help, eventually."

"Well, if there's anything I can do . . ." Helen trailed off.

Everyone wanted to help, everyone tried their best. In the early days, when they'd first received the diagnosis, family and friends were full of suggestions for encouraging Sam to talk. Sticker charts! Rewards! Children's yoga! Music therapy! Nick and Orla discounted some outright, but she did take Sam along to the music thing. Never made any difference, although he enjoyed himself. In silence.

"Thanks, Helen."

They made noises about another call and hung up. Helen was a partner in a large law firm in Birmingham, and Orla struggled to recall the last time they'd actually seen each other.

The absence of Helen's voice amplified the stillness of the house. The easy silence of the morning had turned brittle, watchful. Orla had always been so happy in her own company, but this morning she wanted the solid comfort of another adult body in this space. On the kitchen table, her mobile phone lay useless. The signal inside the house was dreadful; only in the occasional, inconvenient spot did any of the bars flicker into life. She'd once got a text from Eva while she was on the loo, which made her jump, but there didn't seem to be a reliable place and so she'd taken to leaving her phone in the fruit bowl among the jumble of keys and baby socks and Sam's colorful marbles, retrieved constantly from under the sofas and the fridge.

Orla thought about what she'd said to Helen and knew she was right. This house was too big. It was so much more than she'd imagined, than she'd ever have guessed from the pictures. It was grand in a way that would never diminish, no matter how the carpets rotted or the ivy took hold in the mortar, in that soft flesh connecting the elegant bones of the house. It demanded so much of her, and there was still so much left to do.

Playroom, studio, nursery, kitchen—Orla did like the Rubik's Cube nature of it, how all sides presented a different view and offered the challenge of fitting them together. To the back, the walled garden with its two tall oaks and angular monkey puzzle rising deft above a flurry of orange maples and an elegant flowering magnolia that dominated the view from the orangery. To the front, the strip of scrubby lawn before the cliff that cut abruptly into the endless sea—the sharp intake of breath before a long sigh.

The sides of the house were taken up mostly by tall chimney breasts that allowed a fireplace in almost every bedroom— Orla hadn't lit any of these yet; they were still waiting on a sweep to come and clear the flues. The chimneys branched off at various intervals and hadn't been cleaned in years; it was going to be an expensive job.

The master bedroom and Sam's room were fairly livable, and although a whole new kitchen would be needed in time, the ground floor wasn't too bad, either. She and Nick had spent a whole weekend painting a foul-smelling woodworm treatment onto the floorboards in the drawing room and the sitting room—she wasn't sure this would fix the problem but at least it wouldn't get worse. Really, it needed a joiner to come and have a look at what had to be replaced, but that could come later.

They'd put curtains up in most of the rooms—crucially, the nursery—and Bridie's room was looking rather charming. The squashy green armchair from their old conservatory was moved into the nursery. Sam had bounced around in it, watching his father put shelves up, pleased to be involved.

One of the second-floor bedrooms would become Orla's studio: the one at the back, facing north. The light in there was clean and cool, perfect for her work. The other bedroom would be Sam's playroom, a repository for the endless boxes of children's toys. The third room, which housed the attic stairs, might make a nice library. The attic remained unexamined thus far.

Orla led her son up the stairs and reached for him when he stumbled on the uneven treads. Sam went up on all fours, an eager puppy, and she watched the light shift and change from floor to floor, filtered through the banisters.

"What do you think then—your own special room?" They stood in the doorway of one of the second-floor bedrooms. Sam had his back to her, looking out of the window down into the garden. "We can put your things up here, Daddy will set the cars up for you, and the marble run, and we'll put all your drawings on the wall.

He nodded, serious. Wallpaper the color of pale honey and dotted with tiny brown birds lined the room, faded squares showed where pictures had once hung. The floor was of wide, bare boards—the rooms on this floor had never been carpeted. Autumn light illuminated the dust and turned the room to gold.

"Do you like it?"

Sam smiled and kissed his fingertips. Orla laughed—he'd picked that up from some film a few weeks ago and now used it to show his approval. Sometimes he added a hand on a cocked hip or an extra flourish of the pinkie finger to make her smile.

"Good. And I'll have my room right next door, won't I—so we'll be neighbors. We can tap on the wall to say hello, or when it's time for lunch."

Sam beamed. He put his knuckles to the adjoining wall and rapped twice, then pointed to the door.

"Shall I go next door to make sure I can hear you?"

In the first bedroom—her new studio—Orla put her ear to the wall that connected to the playroom and knocked. Two sharp taps came back, and she knocked again, three times. Four times Sam answered, and Orla laughed. He appeared in the doorway, her beautiful, strange son.

On their way back downstairs, Orla checked on Bridie in the nursery, where she'd been deposited earlier in the day for a nap. The baby had been fussy all morning, crying sharply at intervals as the wicked little points of new teeth cut through tender gums. When Orla reached for her daughter in the cot, a faint but persistent noise came from behind the blackened boarding over the mouth of the fireplace. At first it seemed like nothing, just an echo of the breeze.

And then again—insistent, regular. Orla hesitated, Bridie kicked the air, and Orla set the baby down and knelt on the hearth.

Again—there. Scratching—mice? At the edges of the board, right where the metal tacks held the wood in place. Louder this time, and quicker. Orla put her ear against the wood and held her breath.

The wind rattled in the flue, she smelled coal dust and damp. The hearth tiles froze under her knees, sharp cold that spiked right through her thick jeans.

Something scrabbled against the wood. It sounded intent, purposeful, wanting to get out. Mice, surely. But the sound came from high up, at the top of the boards. Birds? But there were no sounds of distress, no fluting calls. Just rough scratching from an unseen place, so quiet she almost hadn't heard it.

She picked up Bridie and left the room.

Later in the evening, when the wind had risen in the trees and the children were in bed, Orla ventured to the apex of the house. As she climbed the main stairs, the radio in the kitchen faded away, falling silent as she reached the second floor and the funny little corner room tucked away at the side of the house, hiding the attic staircase. The door was a latch affair, old but serviceable and solid on its brass barrel hinges. The slip of her fingers left clean lines on the grimy metal.

The steps up to the attic were thick with dust; Orla's tread on the wood was muted and soft. Yellowed scraps of paper littered the stairs, bits of string and a few rusty old nails signaled the long sleep of this part of the house.

The stairs jagged left, sharply, and turned Orla out onto the main attic floor, which ran the full length of the house and at one point had been clumsily divided into two by a flimsy plasterboard wall and a connecting door. A single iron bedstead had been dismantled and propped up against the wall, almost touching the lowest slope of the vaulted ceiling.

Each side of the attic contained two of the four dormer windows at the front of the house, small windows in leaded frames that didn't open. The walls up here were bare plaster, a poor contrast to the lavishly papered rooms below. There must have been servants up here in the past, hidden away at the top of the world. Two tin trunks were stacked on top of each other in the corner over by the makeshift door, shut tight with rusted locks. Yellowed paper tags read *L. Price, Flat 42a, Caraway Close, E13 8PN*.

A very old can of paint sat beneath the far window on the

cover of a *Woman's Weekly*, faded and brittle with age. When Orla picked up the tin, it brought half the cover with it, the other half drifted to the floor.

From what she could see of the roof joists, they were in good shape. Woodworm, of course, but no rot. Huge iron nails studded the crossbeams—the house had been built solidly and well, constructed to withstand the sea and the sky.

Orla moved to the end of the attic and laid her palm on the chimney breast that rose through the roof. No fireplaces up here, although the occupants must have benefited from the heat radiating through the chimney bricks. She imagined the network of flues and crossings that lay beneath the stone and brick, the hot veins of the house. Down near the floor, in a spot just above where she knelt in the dust, someone had scratched a tiny cross into the plaster. Very simple, just two lines, and underneath the letters *P R*.

Outside, the day died away, long shadows drew closer in the attic and Orla wished she'd brought a flashlight—there were no electric lights up here. She put her finger on the letters and thought about who might have made them.

When one of the windowpanes shattered, she turned instinctively. The wind hummed around the jags of broken glass hanging from the iron frame. The last of the light turned the blood to rubies and the bird at her feet made no sound. Its belly was torn clean open, pearl-pale bone glistened through the mass of purple gut. Disemboweled by the window, it must have flown in at such speed, betrayed by the reflection of the rising moon on the glass.

Rivulets of the bird's blood made tracks along the floor. Orla thought, madly, of a documentary she had seen once about a drought in Africa; when the rain finally came to fill up the river, it had looked just like this as it flowed along the cracked earth, a torrent of blood gathering dust as it went.

5

2017

———

ORLA SLEPT BADLY, dreamed of the bird and the glass. The distaste she'd felt as she wrapped the broken body in a plastic bag stayed with her through the night and colored her sleep. Twice she woke and touched her face where she could feel feathers against her cheeks, but of course there was nothing. Each time, her fingers fluttered to her ears, her hair, panicked by the thought of sharp claws and beaks tangled up next to her eyes.

Bed was abandoned when she woke for the third time to a sky clouded in mist and the music of rain on the windows. Down in the silent kitchen, she filled the coffee pot and lifted the plate cover on the stove. She would know when Sam was awake because she'd hear his feet—small and deliberate—on their way to the bathroom. The rhythm of his day was as familiar to her as her own; together, she and Sam played their own symphony of sound. Orla's vocals never changed; Sam's echo never came. "Did you sleep well, darling? Isn't it a good day for painting? Will we get the Legos out? Can you fetch me the wet wipes, please?" No answer required, all received in loving silence. Her little helper, her silent shadow, her beloved companion.

Out in the garden, the trees moved together in dark conversation. They leaned, eager, toward one another to listen, jumped back in surprise. The maple was particularly expressive on this sullen morning. Wet grass shone in streaks of moonlight, bordered by the thicker shadows of the tangled brambles and roses. The view seemed limitless, expanded. Orla could barely make out the retaining walls, and the dead thicket stretched endlessly away from the house, a rotting ocean.

A shadow flicked between the oaks. Something with more depth than the trees, something deliberate. Quicker than the waving grass and gone out of her sight as fast as it appeared. Small, like an animal, but upright.

In the orangery the wind was louder, insistent as it pushed through the gaps in the old windows and rattled under the glass doors. Orla strained to see to the end of the garden, down among the sentinel trees that watched over the house. Only the movement of the bushes in the wind, nothing else; no animals, no birds, no small form. She went back into the kitchen, and when she looked at the clock mounted above the heavy oak sideboard littered with papers and tiny toys and stacks of junk mail and bills, she saw that it was exactly half past three. Not breakfast time, not even close. The coffee had burned and smelled acrid. It wasn't the right time for coffee at all.

Bridie sang out from the floor in the sitting room, where she'd been left after breakfast to amuse herself with a cardboard box full of wooden bricks. She made turtledove noises to herself, stuck her hands in her mouth, toppled over gently with the force of her own waving arms. Sam sat apart, concentrating hard on his own set of Lego. Bridie pointed to the ceiling and laughed, delighted, and when Sam followed her gaze upward, he smiled.

Orla watched her children and noted how much taller Sam seemed. It was unsettling in a way she couldn't identify, how his legs had lengthened and protruded from shorts that were now far too small, how his limbs looked too long for his little body. She thought that if she couldn't stop time entirely, or even slow it, then she could at least fix Sam in amber, just a little. She had never painted the children before, perhaps they were too young—their faces changed too often and truthfully all babies looked alike to Orla. She often confused photographs of Bridie for Sam at the same age, although Nick could tell them apart easily and would tease her for being a terrible mother.

"Sam, my love, will you help me with something? I want to make a painting of you—won't that be fun! So can I borrow you for a little while?"

He rested the Lego bricks in his lap and tilted his head to look at her.

"It won't take long, honestly, I promise—just a few minutes while I sketch you."

Sam folded his arms and frowned. Orla was surprised: he was usually so eager to please her.

"Please, Sam—just for a bit? We'll go to the village afterward—we'll have an adventure! Maybe we'll find an ice cream?" Orla herself wanted out of the house, away from the long, dim corridors and the invisible but heavy presence of the bird in the bin, shrouded in white plastic.

Sam shook his head.

"All right, but can I take some pictures? Just a couple? And then I promise you won't have to do anything else."

He nodded and Orla grabbed her Polaroid camera. She

chose the drawing room for the quick studies; she liked the grandeur of the background, and the autumn light coming in from the tall sash window was particularly lovely.

Sam sat by the window, tense, and watched her work with an intensity that disturbed her. The second she put the camera down, he ran.

Orla stood alone by the window and watched the Polaroids develop in their enigmatic way, the images appearing as if through a clearing mist. Digital may have been sharper, but she generally preferred the texture of Polaroid, how it made everything look both blurred and hyper-real. She'd captured Sam three times—each picture showed only a minimal difference but it was there, in the angle of his shoulder and the line of his mouth. Twice he had turned to look at the room behind him; the second picture caught him just as he turned back to face her.

In the pale light of the afternoon, the photographs looked washed out, sickly, removed of the usual rich vitality imparted by the color film. Orla noted that they seemed somehow faded, as though they'd existed for months rather than minutes. She left the room to gather the children, and after a moment a draft from beneath the sash window caught the photographs and lifted them, briefly. Sam's face—white, solemn—slid to the floor and came to rest against the baseboard.

The path to the village was closer to the cliff edge than Orla would have liked and she made Sam stay close. Hardy grass grew in tufts and bright gorse sprang up at intervals. The path was littered with tiny shells; Sam stopped every few seconds to stow a few away in his pockets. Imprisoned within a nylon hiking pack on her mother's back, Bridie babbled happily, and the salt wind whipped Orla's hair across her face. From up here she could see the village quite clearly, tucked away at the bottom of the hills. The cove was small, the beach almost the shape of a perfect C. A few dog-walkers dotted the sand; Orla watched their tracks appear, only to be erased by the tide. The water in the bay was flint and iron, spiked with white waves, and the green cliffs stretched away in the distance toward Lulworth.

Down in the village, bunting fluttered in rows across the main streets—it had obviously been strung up some time ago, but the effect was still jolly and the muted reds and pinks added a carnival air. Some of the more niche shops had already closed down for the winter season, the ones selling tourist bric-a-brac made of seashells and woolen scarves in heather-purple and bottle-green, but plenty of others were still open. The streets were pretty—old-fashioned and winding—and most of the buildings had retained their original frontages dominated by plate-glass windows. Ornate iron streetlamps bore hanging baskets of trailing ivy and dying petunias, and down one of the quieter side streets Orla recognized the gallery she'd seen on her first visit to the house.

Double-fronted, the shop housed three generous walls of local artists on one side and a café, she realized, on the other. The windows were steamed and ran with condensation. Orla could barely make out the paintings displayed on the gallery side.

Inside, Sam went immediately to the counter full of cakes and made begging eyes.

Orla laughed. "Show me which one, then—and if you choose it you have to finish it all!"

Sam took a step back to better observe the selection. A man came out of a back room, holding a cardboard box full of takeaway cups, and smiled at Sam. "Afternoon—help you with anything?" He was in his fifties, Orla estimated, on the heavier side, with a rough brown beard and a completely bald head. He leaned forward onto the counter. "I can certainly recommend the chocolate brownie. You seem like a fellow who enjoys his chocolate."

Sam nodded and reached for Orla's hand. The man looked up at Orla and asked, "Shy?"

"He doesn't speak. He can—he just doesn't. It's nothing personal, don't worry. It's what you prefer at the moment, isn't it, sweetheart." She looked down at Sam, who pressed his face into her leg.

"Well, that's perfectly all right—people round here talk too much, if you ask me; you can never get a word in edgeways. Better to listen than to talk, you see more that way." The man tapped a finger on the counter. "Right, lad, tell me which one it's to be. The brownie?"

Orla was grateful to this stranger. Children never seemed to mind that Sam didn't speak—his friends at playgroup back in Bristol had always included him, and Sam was deft at demonstrating his thoughts and feelings using only his little hands. Adults found it much harder to deal with, usually. Although Orla had been keen on teaching Sam sign language, Nick had never encouraged it—he thought it would be too easy for Sam, too easy for this to slip into their life permanently. Orla wondered if perhaps Nick wasn't punishing the both of them.

Sam shook his head and pointed to a butter-yellow wedge of lemon cake, crusted on top with sugar and leaking syrup onto the plate.

"Excellent choice, made fresh today. On the house, I think, as it's your first time. And for Mum?"

"Oh, it's fine, I'm happy to pay."

"Absolutely not. It's the last slice and we're nearly done for the day, in any case. Anything to drink?"

"Coffee would be lovely."

Orla seated Sam at a small pine table next to the counter and unbuckled the hiking pack to set it on the wooden floor.

Bridie, drowsy from the heat of the café, relaxed on Sam's lap. They were the only customers.

The man put the slice of cake in front of Sam with a flourish and lifted Bridie up and into his arms as if she belonged to him. Orla was moved by the intimacy of it, the ease. He motioned to Orla to taste her coffee, which was dark and bitter and smelled of something like clove, something savory and foreign.

"This is delicious. Thank you so much."

"Now then, I've not seen you before, but someone said a young lady with two babs moved into the big house, so I'm thinking that'll be you."

"Yes, about three weeks ago. This is the first time we've come down into the village, actually—it's lovely."

"It is that. Just you, then?"

"My husband is back at weekends, he's working in Bristol. It's been grand so far. Nick, I mean—he's Nick. I'm Orla."

"Claude." He sat and shifted Bridie in his arms. "Alone in the week? Sounds tough. You getting on all right?"

Orla returned his concern with a smile. "I'm good in my own company, not much of a talker. And I've the children, too."

Only recently had she realized how isolated they had become. She hadn't been back to Bristol since they moved, and Nick had been too busy with the business to arrange their usual calendar of dinners with friends. Helen hadn't yet offered to visit and Orla hadn't asked. Eva called sometimes for a chat—she was good at keeping in touch like that—which Orla appreciated. She sent her own parents a postcard of the cove with their new address, but they never wrote back. She called, once, and was met with the answering machine. She hung up without leaving a message.

"Well, there's always company for you down here if you need it. Big old place to be knocking around on your own. People don't tend to take well to that house, never stay long."

"Don't take well? How so?"

"Reckon it's just a bit too out of the way." He frowned. "Not really part of the village, no view but the sea. Bit much, for some people."

"Why?"

Claude sat back in his chair and bounced Bridie on his leg. "There's a lot of empty space in that house. That can be— unnerving? I suppose? For some. People tend to fill it up with their own ideas. About what the house is."

Orla rubbed cold hands on her jeans, disinclined to hear more about her new house. "Well, it's bigger than we're used to. Have you lived here for a long time?"

"About ten years. Seems like a lifetime, but we're still the new folk round here. We came from Poole, so I'd consider that local, but most people here were born in the village and they'll die in it, too."

"It's a beautiful gallery." Orla turned in her chair and gestured toward the opposite wall, full of seascapes and intricate sketches of birds and fish. A few vibrant watercolors of cows in outrageous colors filled the back wall, and two enormous oils of stylized waves hung on wires in the front window.

"We put the effort in—we do well. Alice, my wife, she does events and so on. Evening shows, drinks things, you know."

"I do know—I'm a painter myself."

"You never are!" Pleased, his smiled widened. "Anyone we'd know?"

"Probably not, I've not been active for a while. Orla McGrath?"

"I do know you! Landscapes, am I right? Big pieces—oil?"

"Yes!" She was gratified and surprised to be known all the way out here. "And a few portraits, privately."

"So nothing new recently?"

"Not as much since she came along"—Orla nodded at her

daughter—"but the views from the house are so incredible that I've been restless a bit recently. I'm keen to get back to it."

"Are you showing anywhere at the moment?"

"Not really—there's a gallery back in Bristol that has a few of my older things knocking around, but they don't seem to be getting rid of much." She sipped her coffee and waited for the question.

"Do you want to put anything in here? We'd love to have you, we've got the room. And our commission is a bit lower, forty-five percent, as we're on the small side."

"I don't have a lot on the go, nothing worth anything, really—but, if I get my act together, I could have something in the new year?"

Claude smiled and held Bridie a little closer. "We'd love to show you. Alice would want to make a thing of it, I'm sure."

Orla stayed up for a long time that night, until well after the children had been put to bed and she had drunk and refilled two tumblers of wine.

Alone at the kitchen table, she considered Claude's words. Hadn't she made the same complaint to Helen—too big? Too empty, the house turned each of its inhabitants into something solitary. The family orbited one another like lone stars, passing by only briefly, touching only gently. Only now did she feel how alone she truly was out here, away from the village. How small she was within the wilds of the house.

Orla put her head in her hands and pressed the hot skin of her forehead against her palms. It felt as though she was running a fever, but she'd been perfectly well all day. She phoned Nick.

When he picked up, Orla talked and talked. She sounded manic, she realized, as she rattled on down the phone about Bridie's teeth. "I just feel so bad for her, you know? Poor baby. Can't do much about it, either. I stocked up on Calpol, but we just have to wait it out—makes me feel helpless, when she cries. I feel so *guilty*—"

"Poor Bridie—remember how bad Sam was?"

She heard Nick take a long swallow from a glass bottle, the wet pop of his lips round the neck. "Listen, Nick, you know when you bought the house? Did the estate agent say anything about it?"

"Like what?"

"I don't know. Just—anything odd. Unusual."

"No, just that it had been empty for a while." Nick cleared his throat. "She was pretty keen to make sure we knew the work that had to be done. Why?"

"Nothing, really. Just, someone in the village said something about it, about people not staying long here. I just wondered if the estate agent had mentioned anything to you."

"No, nothing like that. But look at you, making friends already."

"Right. But, you know, it doesn't make up—" Orla paused, reconsidered. "Look, I was thinking. Why don't you take a few days off? I'd really love to have you home. Things have been a bit—"

Nick took another pull from the bottle. "A bit what?"

"Just a bit much, you know. The kids, the house, usual stuff. Bridie—she's not been sleeping, I'm whacked half the time."

"Of course I'll take the time. Absolutely." He sounded like he meant it.

"That would be amazing. The kids will love it. Thank you." She hung up, loose with relief, and swept aside papers and orange peel to clear the table. The peel in her hands smelled citrus-sharp, clean and sweet.

Orla washed up and watched her reflection and stood by the window until the sky had turned from cobweb to slate to ink. The wind died and the trees stilled, and after a while the clouds cleared enough to show the stars. The garden, which had returned to its regular, familiar size during the day, once again stretched out preternaturally. She knew it was just an illusion, that it only seemed that way because the back wall was no longer visible in the dark, but she still found it unsettling. It made her feel marooned, stranded in a strange place.

And she was watching for something else. The small, quick thing that had shown itself so early that morning. Of course it wasn't real, or else it was a cat or a fox. She knew that, and didn't allow herself to think about its upright stance or the way it had turned, sly, toward the house, as if listening.

6

1976

——

THE RAIN HAD KEPT THEM all inside for two days. A large packet of files arrived with a courier from London and Sara shut herself away inside her office. Sara was an accountant before she met Doug and had picked up some work in the last year to supplement what Doug had left behind. Sometimes she went back to London to see clients, and Lydia resented being left alone in the house. Lately, she'd felt uneasy during the evenings when the children were in bed, as though there were some task she'd forgotten about and left undone, but couldn't recall with any clarity. She found herself going in and out of rooms, hoping to jog loose a memory that wouldn't come.

The only television was in Sara's office, brought from the London house, and the children complained bitterly at being deprived of *Doctor Who*. Lydia was secretly put out by Sara's new rule of "no television, creative play only," and when she was gone to London, Lydia would sneak in and put the volume on very low. The signal was terrible and she spent most of the time holding the rabbit ears at strange angles with her face very close to the glass.

Lydia stood in the doorway to Sara's office and watched the rain turn the tall sash window to a silver pool that reflected her own hazy face. "Just for today—let me bring it down. They've been so good." This was a lie, but Lydia wanted to sit slack-jawed in front of the television for a while, too. A brief reprieve.

Sara shook her head. "You know how I feel about it—I want them to use their imaginations. Be wild, you know? Free. Healthy."

"I understand—really, I do. It's just that we've sort of run out of ideas and the twins are getting a bit stir-crazy and there's a film on later. Thought it might be nice."

But Sara wouldn't be moved. This notion of them being "wild and free" wasn't new, but it had been heightened in this house. Sara blamed London when Doug got sick, blamed the smog and the fumes and the proximity of too many unwashed people. Coming out here hadn't just been about finances; she was conjuring a ring of protection around her children—a spell drawn of hawthorn blossom and clean water and lots of fruit and living, Lydia thought, like a bloody Enid Blyton family. She half-expected Sara to pull up any day now with a border collie in the back of the car.

"Sorry, you lot. No dice." Lydia closed the sitting-room door behind her.

Clover threw herself back against the sofa cushions. "I'm so *bored*, Lydia! What are we going to *do*?"

Lydia sat on the wooden arm of the sofa and swung her feet up to push her toes in the soft chenille of the cushions. "Dot will be here in a bit. We could bake? Fairy cakes, or something?"

"Won't that be too much sugar?" Philip looked worried. He knew Sara's rules.

Dot arrived just after lunch, shaking bright rain from her mackintosh like a seabird. She kicked off her wellies in the hall;

they spun and slid away from her on the wet tiles and Philip put them side by side, neatly, on the mat.

"Shit, I'm soaked." She laughed and ran her hands across her hair, tied back in two fat braids.

"Language, around the kids." Lydia knew she sounded uptight but she couldn't help it. She'd never considered herself a prude, but next to Dot she became stiff. Dot made her feel buttoned up; Dot, with her louche, curvy frame and countryside, no-nonsense air toward sex and men, who filled out every blessed inch of sunburned skin, plump and healthy in the way of someone brought up on four eggs a day and full-cream milk. Dot, who had scrunched up her face when Sara called her "Dorothy" on her first day and begged them, please, *never* Dorothy.

Tabitha slid toward them on the wet tiles and caught hold of Dot's leg. "Dot!"

"Tabs!"

"Lydia says we can do fairy cakes—can we? I want to do the icing, will there be jam?"

Dot hooked two fingers underneath Tabitha's dungaree straps and laughed. "Let me get my bloody coat off, then we'll see about the cakes. Come on, give me a hand."

Lydia followed Dot and the children into the kitchen, warm and steamy from the heat of the range. Rain battered the orangery and slid in under the door, trickling along the terracotta tiles.

"Make us a tea, then, Lids."

Philip seated himself at the far end of the kitchen table; he was slightly afraid of Dot, who came Mondays to Fridays and was in charge of laundry, cleaning, and most of the cooking. She couldn't sew worth a damn, though, so Lydia kept the job of mending and hemming. Dot's family was large and overbearing and she had nine—*nine!*—brothers and sisters still living at home, so she was glad to get out of the house, she said. Lydia crossed her legs at the thought of anyone giving birth nine times over.

"Right, what do these horrible children want?" Dot took the mug from Lydia and wrapped it in two hands reddened from the cold.

"We thought we'd do a bit of baking, if you're up for it. They're bored, figured they deserved a treat." Lydia poured a mug for herself. She was glad of Dot, glad of another adult today.

Dot blew on her tea. "Still no TV, then?"

"No! Mummy won't let us!" Clover, incensed, pulled two wooden spoons from the striped jar next to the range and handed one to Tabitha.

The children set to work and soon flour lay in drifts across the long wooden table, the girls up to their elbows in ceramic mixing bowls of batter. Underneath the table, two broken egg-shells leaked mucus onto the floor.

"Dot says I can do the icing!" Tabitha crowed, triumphant, and smacked her sister hard on the hand with her wooden spoon.

"Hey, now—neither of you can do it if I see bad manners." Dot took both spoons. "I'll give the job to Philip if you're going to be little horrors. God, Lids, you're a bloody saint to put up with this all day."

Lydia winked at Philip, who looked pained by the criticism. "They're not so bad."

Evening put its hands around the house. Lydia sat with Dot in the kitchen and watched the garden fade into twilight. She'd woken several times in the night, starting from sleep convinced that Philip had crawled into bed beside her, that she'd felt the mattress sink, the tug of the quilt. But when she woke she was alone and, despite the batteries, she'd kept the lamp on until morning.

Dot put two wet hands into the paper sack of meat on the end of the kitchen table. Her elbows protruded, the skin pink and taut. A few damp curls clung to her forehead and she raised her shoulder to her cheekbone to wipe away the sweat. "Too buggering hot in here—tell Sara she needs to get me a gas oven. Can't be doing with that range on all summer."

She slapped the joint, slick and purple, as if it were a plump behind, and tipped it into a roasting tin. Lydia watched Dot strip the membrane from the lamb neck, stretched white and fibrous. A little watery blood trickled into the bottom of the tin. Lydia felt ill.

"Might go for a lie-down, while Owen's asleep."

Dot pushed the tip of the knife into the meat, and the blade sounded thick and wet as it sliced. "You do that. Dinner in about an hour."

Lydia dozed on the sofa and half-listened to the twins whispering together in front of the fire. Philip sat on her feet and read a book, Owen dreamed in his playpen. Lydia sank in and out of an elusive sleep colored by the cooking smells from the kitchen and the strange sounds from the twins. They had their own language, an ill-formed assembly of sibilant nonsense words and throat noises; sometimes she caught them, foreheads pressed together, hissing at each other with glee. Poor Philip was left out, as usual.

The rain beat at the windows. Sparks from the fire cracked on the hearth stones. Philip shifted occasionally, and Lydia felt the bones in her feet slide over one another under his weight. She breathed in the dust from the sofa cushions—London dust. Petrol and soot and brick and grass. She would go back for a weekend, maybe. Stay with the girls again. Lydia hadn't taken a holiday since they'd moved, even at Christmas. Her brother had invited her down to Rye, but he had three kids of his own and Lydia knew that his sour wife wanted her only for babysitting. So she declined, and stayed in the house with Sara and the children.

It had been somber, muted with grief. Lydia had wondered if it was better or worse to have the first Christmas without Doug in a house devoid of anything of him, or his life, or the way he had loved his family. Would it have been easier to get through if they'd been in London, in the house full of his smell and a sofa that still bore the indent of his buttocks and back? Maybe, maybe not. Sara wandered through the day in her satin pajamas, carrying a bottle of Madeira from room to room. Lydia hadn't said anything, even when Sara spilled Christmas gravy all over the drawing-room floor and laughed and laughed as she tried to pick it up with her hands and made a joke about *poor dead Daddy*. Philip spent the day with a distraught expression and put himself to bed at seven o'clock.

Sara came down from her office for dinner. "This is great, Dot. Thank you." She looked pale and weary and rolled her shoulders to ease the knots. "Stay for dinner?"

Dot nodded and reached into the drawer for another knife and fork. "Thanks."

"Good day, then, Lydia?"

Lydia leaned over and wiped Owen's sticky fingers with a dishcloth. "Fine. He had a couple of good naps. Philip finished his book." She smiled at Philip.

"Well done, Philip. Tabs? What did you do today?"

Tabitha shrugged her shoulders and rolled a potato across her plate.

"Answer me, please, Tabitha."

"Nothing. We didn't do anything. We never. Do. *Anything*."

Clover nodded in agreement; Sara sighed.

The children got like this when Sara had been gone too long or spent too much time up in her office. They had been used to a good deal more of her attention when Doug was alive and struggled with this new, absent version of their mother. Sara was much more involved in their lives back in London. She often came with Lydia to swimming lessons and ballet lessons and organized the birthday parties and never failed to turn up for a parents' evening.

Lydia wondered sometimes if the children's "year off" wasn't as much an excuse for Sara herself to opt out of all of those things, to opt out of parenting in a way that only served herself. No school reports to tackle, no recitals to attend, no homework to help with; these feral children laid no claim to Sara's hours. Owen, who didn't talk back, was an easier task and Sara continued to nurse him at night, far beyond necessity. Sara interacted with her older children only as she pleased, and Lydia wondered if they knew how much of the affection they received was given only on their mother's terms.

Lydia stacked empty plates. "I'll wash up, Dot. What time tomorrow?"

Dot stood, covered the remains of the joint, and rummaged in the boxy yellow fridge to make room for it. "Usual, probably."

Sara handed her plate to Lydia. "It's still raining—it's filthy. Come on, Dot, I'll give you a lift back down."

Lydia watched them leave through the sitting-room window—indistinct shapes among a world made of water. Soft headlights swept through the rain as Sara reversed out of the drive and away down the cliff.

Lydia had never learned to drive; there was no need for it, in London, and it wasn't like she could have afforded a car, anyway. Sometimes she was jealous of the freedom it afforded

Sara, particularly out here. Lydia was confined by the distance she was willing to walk, but Sara could go anywhere. It was something Sara took for granted, too. Sometimes she would say, "Oh, Lydia, if you're heading into the village, just take the car. Maybe bring some shopping back?"

And then Lydia would have to shake her head and shrug in a way that meant, *No, thank you; you know I can't drive, you know I never had the money for lessons*, but Sara wouldn't notice, and so Lydia would fetch the shopping up anyway and pretend to Sara that she didn't mind, and the heavy bags of potatoes and laundry detergent would cut into her fingers and leave purple lines.

"Right, Philip—hands, face, and teeth, please. Girls, I want you out of those dirty clothes, you can leave them over the banister for me."

Philip, always so obedient, left the table and headed upstairs. Clover protested immediately. "But I want to wear this tomorrow! It's my most comfortable dress—it's my climbing one."

Lydia felt very tired. "Don't care, it's filthy. You promised me—*promised* me—that you'd let me have it today to wash and mend. Poor old dress."

"But—"

"No, I don't want to hear it. And if you're climbing, then you really should be in trousers anyway. Like Tabs."

Tabitha, who lived in corduroy dungarees, looked smug. "Yeah, no one wants to see your horrible knickers when you're up a tree." She reached over and forked up Clover's last slice of tinned peach, which dripped syrup all over the table.

"It's not because of knickers," said Lydia, brisk. "It's to protect your knees."

Children's toys and shoes and half-eaten biscuits littered the sofas and the stairs, and Lydia's final job, at the end of each day, was to gather up the remnants of a family who spent too much time inside the house, eternally on top of one another. She picked up a full pack of crayons that lay scattered across the drawing-room table, two grass-stained socks from the landing on the first floor, a half-drunk glass of orange squash from the second-floor flight of stairs, and, inexplicably, a bone-handled knife that she found lying outside Sara's office. It was an odd shape, the blade flat and tapered to a point, dappled with hard flecks of dried blue paint. It looked like a letter opener and Lydia supposed it had come from Sara's desk, so she returned it to a drawer.

The grandeur that she had enjoyed when they first arrived now felt like emptiness rather than generosity. Lydia knew that there were no more stairs now than on the day they moved in, but didn't it take her longer to climb the staircase these days? Sometimes, when passing down the landing or through the kitchen, she found herself turning very quickly, as if her subconscious had registered a disturbance. But there was never anything out of place.

Later, she poured herself a sherry from Sara's cupboard and sat alone at the kitchen table. Sometimes Sara joined her, sometimes she worked late. Lydia liked the nights when Sara came down from her office, when they shared a cigarette and a drink and Lydia told her about Danny and about Brian, before, and Sara laughed and called them *arseholes* in a way that made Lydia feel adult and wealthy and equal. But tonight Sara had come in, wet from the rain, and disappeared upstairs without a word to anyone else.

On her way up to bed, so late that it was really tomorrow, Lydia checked on Owen in the nursery. He stirred in his cot and whimpered when she stroked his head. His cheek was cool to the touch and she pulled the blanket up to his chin.

Doug never met Owen, never saw him born. Lydia remembered Sara, huge, at the funeral, draped in black like a horrible tent. At the wake, when she'd gone to the toilet, she found Sara crying in the bathroom of the church hall.

"I look like a fucking pantomime cow, like there's two bloody people under here." She wiped at her face with cheap toilet paper and smeared mascara over her temple.

Lydia, who had never heard Sara swear before, wanted to make her feel better and said, anxiously, "Well, there sort of are two people under there."

Sara had laughed, then, properly laughed, for the first time in ages, and held on to the edge of the sink with one hand and held Lydia's hand with the other while she laughed so hard that she started to cry again.

Lydia looked at Owen and thought that he had been born with a heavy burden—to scrub away Sara's grief and make a family happy again. He didn't even know the awful load he carried, and Lydia felt sorry for him. She leaned over the cot to kiss his soft cheek and heard the dry sound of something scraping against stone, against iron, from somewhere up inside the chimney breast.

The open mouth of the fireplace sat dark, but not silent. Scratching, inside the chimney, like a bird was trapped up there. Little claws against the brick. Lydia crouched on the hearth and held on to the mantelpiece for balance, with her head right in the opening. When she looked up, she saw only faint black. The scrabbling noise came again, closer to her face and louder, but she still couldn't see anything.

On her knees, she shuffled forward to turn her face upward. The chimney smelled of old rain, of forgotten decay. After a moment, she lost her nerve, and, as she retreated, something thudded against the brick, up high, struck the stone above her head as it fell, and thumped into the iron grate in a cloud of soot and grime.

Lydia leaned back onto her heels and brushed, frantic, at her clothes that were frosted with soot. On a soft mound of brick dust and ash in the grate lay the body of a small bird—a young thing, all brown fluff, dead yet perfectly clean. Lydia picked it up with two fingers.

Behind her, Owen stirred in his cot and cried out. Lydia dropped the bird and fell backward and winced when her tailbone hit the floorboards. But Owen didn't wake.

Cold sweat prickled her back. The mouth of the fireplace yawned, too large in the small room. It looked sullen, almost sly, as if it were about to produce more awful things, like a horrible trick. But the only thing that came down was a thin wind that wailed through the flue.

The draft from the chimney ruffled the bird's juvenile down and parted it a little to reveal gray skin. The beak was shut tight, the head lolled to one side. It didn't look as if it had been up the chimney at all; other than where her sooty fingers had picked it up, it was pristine. Lydia took it outside and put it, with reverential distaste, into the tall metal bin behind the garden gate.

7

2017

———

NICK HAD, EVENTUALLY, FOUND SOMEONE to deal with the sprawling, treacherous garden and the multitude of outside jobs. A local farmer's son, apparently, and Orla imagined a thin seventeen-year-old staring with dismay at the iron-hard branches to be lopped and burned. When he stuck his hand out to greet them on the dirty gravel driveway, Orla was relieved to see that he wasn't a slender teenager after all, but a stocky young man in his twenties.

"Toby. Tradgett."

Orla liked him. He had a wide, open face and windblown hair the color of otters. "Tea? It's cold—why don't you come in."

He shook his head. "I'm all right—thank you, though. I want to get on. Show me what I'm here for?"

Nick stepped out of the front door and took Toby to the high iron gate in the side wall. They disappeared round the corner of the house and Orla was faintly disappointed, although she couldn't have said why. Sam appeared in the doorway of the drawing room, eating a broken digestive biscuit.

"Who gave you that?" Hands on her hips, matriarchal, Orla knew she sounded like her own mother. Sam swallowed, greedy, and pointed to the floor. *I found it!*

"You can't be eating biscuits off the floor! Horrible child!" She lifted him and threw him over her shoulder and pretended to bite his legs, enjoying the vibration of his silent laugh.

In the kitchen, Bridie was slapping a piece of toast against the plastic tray of her high chair. Orla lowered Sam to the floor and he tapped the table—*More breakfast, please.*

"If you're still hungry, then you need to ask, properly, please."

Sam put his chin on the table and pulled a sad face to make her laugh.

"No, I mean it. Tell me what you want."

Sam pointed to the paper bag of crumpets on the counter and disappeared into the sitting room.

Orla put a crumpet into the toaster. Claude had told her about various activities for children at the local library, including a music morning, and she thought it might be helpful. Sam used to love to sing, and even though now he only swayed in time with the beat, she hoped that some gentle encouragement might produce results. And he'd been fractious, too—trapped in the house by her commitment to the new paintings and then by the weather. She had forgotten what it was like to be so consumed by her work and felt guilty.

She put the radio on, loud, for company. Delicate piano music like water sounded through the kitchen; she had always liked Debussy's trailing, ethereal arrangements. "*Feuilles mortes,*" apt for an autumn day like this, when dead things littered the ground.

Outside, Nick pointed to the trees, Toby shrugged. Nick swept his hand around at waist height and Toby nodded. They shook hands. Nick came in through the back door.

"Good lad. He'll sort it. It'll be nice for you, as well, having someone around during the week. Tuesdays and Thursdays—I thought that would probably be enough."

Orla buttered Sam's crumpet. "Oh, come on, I know you like the thought of the three of us holed up here like little castaways."

"I mean it, I don't want you to be lonely. I feel a bit bad, I know I've been away more than we'd thought—"

She knew her lines. "Nick, it's fine. Really, it's fine, we're doing great. Sam loves the house, and the new pieces are going so well, I can't wait to deliver them. You were right about that room—lovely light." Nick looked pleased.

Three large canvases now took up most of the space in the studio. The same scene from different angles—the sea, the air, the sky. Sketches and studies lined the walls and she'd put down linen sheets to protect the floorboards that now bore the splashes and stains of her frantic activity. Her paintings eliminated the front lawn and the wall and the cliff path, and showed only the endless iron of the water and the muted skies. Her style was abstract, verging on impressionistic, and the canvases seemed alive with oil. Thick strokes gave green depth to the sea, purple moods to the clouds.

Over and over, she passed along the landing and the stairs from her studio at the rear of the house, down to the windows at the front. Back and forth she went, sometimes to take Polaroids in the changing light, but mostly just to look, and to watch the beckoning motion of the waves and how the blues and blacks of the deep water shifted and rippled. Something about the view compelled her to witness, to be a part of it, as if the tides pulled her in and she herself was a tethered moon, pale and in love with the sea.

And she was pleased with the work, she knew it was some of her best. Inspiration had come quickly, and while she'd always been fast, the rate at which she could turn out the bones of a piece seemed accelerated up here in this small room, filled with cool north light. She'd noticed, recently, that the work seemed to take more out of her than it had before, that it was harder to come back to the world once she lost herself in a canvas. Like an addict, she wished she could spend longer under the spell of her own hands, and each resurfacing cost her a little more.

Bridie whistled peacefully through the baby monitor propped up on the table. Orla doused a rag with white spirit and began to clean her hands, scrubbing at spots of black paint flecked along her wrists. She thought of Lady Macbeth and smiled as she worked the rag under her nails and between her fingers.

Her oldest palette knife—trusted companion throughout her career, bone-handled, rusted at the joint—had disappeared in the move. Distressed, she'd searched for it among the boxes, could have sworn it lay in its usual prime position on her trestle, but no luck. Even Nick had helped, but Orla supposed it had become a casualty of moving. She'd made do so far with an inferior one, but it wasn't the same.

The library was warm and fairly empty; only a few other parents had bothered to come in on such a horrible afternoon. The children's area was kitted out with squashy, lime-green beanbags and a bright rug with ladybugs on it. Larger chairs were arranged in a semicircle for the adults and two tall urns of coffee stood off to one side on a tall table. The space was friendly and comforting, as all libraries should be, and Orla took a chair in the middle. Sam was already away with a stack of books to a beanbag—he was almost reading by himself, although his writing was underdeveloped for his age.

"New?"

"I'm sorry?" Orla turned to the woman approaching her with a clipboard.

"New? Are you new?"

"Oh, yes, sorry. Yes, new!"

"Which one's yours, then?" The woman took a quick scan of the room.

Orla pointed. "Over there, dark hair. Sam, he's mine. And this one, too, of course, but she mostly just eats the books!" She bounced Bridie in her sling, but the woman didn't return a smile.

"Right—and you are?"

"Orla. I'm Orla." Although the library itself was inviting, this woman really wasn't.

"Fine, good. It's three pounds a session, tin's over there." She pointed with her pen to a biscuit tin on the coffee table and moved off.

Orla dug in her pockets for change and another woman moved in front of her to drop coins into the tin.

"Hi, hello. New?"

"Hello—yes! First time today."

They shook hands awkwardly across Bridie, who shouted and reached out her chubby fists to make a new friend.

"She's a lively one!" The woman laughed, and tickled Bridie under her wet chin.

"God, she really is. Absolute terror at home."

"Just the one, then?"

"He's mine, too." Orla nodded toward Sam, engrossed in a *Where's Wally?* "Four next year, and off to school. I can't bear it, really, I'll miss him so much."

"I'm Rachel, I've got two." She gestured toward one of the big plastic tubs full of toys, at two small, identical girls of about three, who were rummaging intently through the naked baby dolls and headless plastic dinosaurs. "Didn't think I'd seen you before." It was said with a smile, but had the edge of an insider querying a possible outsider.

"Yes—we moved here in the autumn."

"Oh, lovely; local then. Welcome!" Rachel offered to fill a cup for Orla, who accepted gratefully. Other parents began to filter in, clearly longtime participants. Orla was glad to have met Rachel, who put her things on the chair next to Orla's and introduced her to a couple of the other mums. All mums, in fact, Orla noticed. At Sam's old playgroup there had been a few dads: one single, a couple of stay-at-homes. But here, not a father in sight.

"We'll come more often, I think. Just haven't got round to it yet, you know how it is, doing up a house." Orla leaned in to Bridie and inhaled the scent of her baby hair.

"Too right, it's taken us about five years just to put that bloody conservatory on." A mother across the room rolled her eyes and the others laughed. "A year, Andrew said, just put up with it for a year and then we'll have this wonderful space! Right, sure. Bastard." It was affectionate, though; Orla had the impression that this was a stock complaint amplified for amusement.

"What about yours, then?" the mother continued. "What state are you in?"

"It's been a lot, actually. I didn't quite know how much there would be to do, when we moved, but it's getting there."

"Where in town are you?"

"Oh, we're not in the village. Up the hill—The Reeve?"

The talk around the circle died. Rachel sat back in her chair. "That's you, then? Up there? I heard it had sold, didn't know who to."

"Yep, that's us! We haven't done much villagey stuff yet— my husband is away during the week, so it's just me and the children." Orla looked at the strange faces. "I've met a few people, though. Claude and Alice, you know, at the gallery? They've been very kind. And Toby, Toby Tradgett."

"Don't know him." Rachel looked at Bridie. "So it's just you—with the children? Just you and them up in that house?" She sounded accusatory, almost angry.

"Yes, but we don't mind. I know it's big, but we—"

"It's not about the size," Rachel interrupted.

"Sorry, I don't quite—" Orla put out her hand, awkward.

The woman who had complained about the conservatory sighed, shook her head very quickly. "It's not somewhere you'd want to keep a family, is all."

"Why not?"

"It's a bad house. It's a bad place." She turned her mouth down.

"It's not safe," said Rachel, clipped. "It's not right."

Orla laughed. "I'm sorry?"

But the librarian clapped her hands and everyone turned toward the toddlers arranged in the center of the circle. The music was too loud, too brash, drowned out the questions Orla tried to ask. She held Bridie tight; no one else met her eye and her confusion at their obvious judgment made her anxious and hot beneath her jumper.

When they left, Orla wanted to say goodbye to Rachel, but by the time she'd returned Bridie to the carrier and Sam had his coat on, Rachel had gone. Orla stood alone for a minute or two, smiling at the others, and then slipped quietly out.

"Orla! Hi, hang on one minute." Sounds of shuffling papers, the creak of a chair.

"Are you working? It's so late, Helen." Orla looked out at the shadowed garden, held at bay by the light spilling from the orangery.

"Yes, of course. I'm always working!" Helen laughed. "You okay?"

"I'm fine, just wanted a chat, really."

"Ah, you're a soft old thing, Orla McGrath."

Orla smiled. "I'm working, too."

"Painting? You never are!"

"There's a little gallery here, down in the village. I'm working on some pieces for them. They want to show me."

"Orla, that's brilliant. I'm happy for you, really. It's been too long."

"Thanks, Helen. It feels good."

"How's the mansion, then?" Helen laughed derisively.

"Still too big. And a bit—"

"A bit what?"

"Well, a bit weird, honestly, Helen."

"Weird? How so?"

Orla jabbed at the kitchen table with a knife, worrying at the wood. "Been hearing a few weird things. And we get a lot of birds flying into the windows; I know it's because we're up high, but it's awful when it happens." She laughed and it came out like ice. "The people here, in the village, they think the house is bad. Cursed? I don't know. Christ, I know how this sounds."

"It sounds a bit mad, Orla, honestly."

"I know. God, sorry. It's just that a few people have said things to me. Nothing specific, just little comments, you know? Like—like it's bold of us to live here."

"Don't apologize." Helen sighed. "It's been a big change, you know? And fast, too. I know you're fine with it now, but the way it happened—well. You know what I think about that."

"I really am fine with it, now," said Orla, gently. "The thing is, I was wondering if you'd do me a favor. No rush, just—would you see if you can find anything out, about the house? I've had a quick look online, but there isn't much, just previous property listings. I thought you'd be able to find more, hotshot lawyer."

Helen laughed. "I'm pretty good."

"I know you are. That's why I'm asking."

"No problem. I'll see what I can find." Helen paused, suddenly serious. "Are you sure you're all right? I really don't think your mansion is cursed, but you don't sound yourself. You sound tired."

"It's been harder than I thought. Nick's gone a lot, I'm on my own most of the time."

And although that had been the plan, and she had consented, only now did she allow herself the luxury of resentment. Only now, when reality smacked up against the ideal like a wave breaking on glass, did Orla allow that early promises had been broken. Or, perhaps, worse: that promises had been withheld.

"Well, you know you can always call. I'll give you a ring when I've got something."

Late that night, much later than Orla knew, she woke abruptly from a dreamless sleep and reached out a hand to Nick, who wasn't there. The room came into focus, faint in the darkness, waiting to be seen. She examined the shadowed ceiling, the moonlight sliced by the shutters.

The door from the master bedroom into the nursery passageway stood open and beyond was only the vivid dark of the corridor. Orla hadn't opened the door in days, it had been locked for almost a week. Down the passageway, the connecting door to the nursery was invisible, still shut tight.

Her T-shirt stuck to the skin between her shoulder blades, wet with sweat. She flicked the lamp on, stood in front of the black passageway and turned the knob of the door a couple of times. Her hot hand left a damp print on the cold brass.

Everything was as it should be; the catch turned and released. She tried the door to the nursery—nothing. Still stuck. She waited for her heartbeat to slow, then returned to the master bedroom, closed the door, put the little iron key in the lock and felt the mechanism turn smoothly. She pulled on the handle, just to make sure; the door stayed firmly within the frame.

Orla went back to bed and fell asleep, a long while later, under the light of the lamp.

For a week, Orla worked almost exclusively on the portrait of Sam. Other things were put out of her mind: the seeds of disquiet that had been planted by people who knew her house better than she did.

It became important to set Sam down onto canvas, an act of preservation for the child he was now. She studied the Polaroids and noted the way his face lengthened and narrowed, the creep of age in the shadows beneath his eyes.

Radiant in a shaft of sunlight, Sam sat alone on his little wooden stool. She painted him in light, bright colors in contrast to the shadowed room behind him; she liked the effect, as though he was leaning forward out of the canvas. Deep earth colors for the background: purples, browns, even black. It was quite different to her usual gray-blue landscapes, different enough that Nick would later remark that he found it "unsettling." Sam's face glowed pink and cream, almost fevered, above a loud yellow T-shirt.

When she'd painted portraits previously—only a few, but accomplished enough to draw some commissions—she liked her subjects to be looking away. It gave them a wistfulness that Orla enjoyed, an abstract kind of mesmerism. Gazes through a window, a small smile aimed at hands folded in a lap. But Sam was staring straight ahead, eyes shining, right at you. He was confrontational, direct, demanding to be looked at. So unlike Sam's personality, really, but Orla liked this version of him. She'd painted his mouth half-open, as if he were about to speak.

But Sam's face was too unnatural, the skin too sickly, no matter how Orla mixed the colors. She wiped a smear of oil on her jeans, frustrated, and licked the residue from her thumb. Some days were like this, especially recently, and so Orla wrapped her palette and conceded defeat.

She called out for her son on her way down the stairs, anticipating the silence in return.

The wind rose and screamed around the house; the glass panels of the orangery windows rattled in their iron frames, mournful cries spilled out of the unlit fireplaces in the sitting room and drawing room. The ivy that grew so heavy over the back of the house slapped wetly against the kitchen window; the overhead lights flickered a couple of times but stayed on.

Orla cleared one end of the table of breakfast plates and phone chargers and Sam's heap of drawings, which seemed to grow by the hour. She flipped through the sheaf of papers, the enormous orange cats and something else that might be a pirate; several purple fishes and multiple repetitions of what looked like the house—spiked windows and vast lawns. The house was colored all grays and greens, so different from the vivid colors of the others. Sam had drawn the garden, over and over, surrounded by its high wall, a little wobbly in places, and the tall oaks. Under the trees, several gray figures floated on a wide green lawn. Three pictures in a row depicted this same scene, although sometimes there were four people and sometimes only two, and they were drawn carefully, much smaller than the trees: child-sized.

Intrigued, Orla laid the drawings on the table and put aside the fantastical cats and fishes to examine closer the repetitions of the house and the children.

One of them, the littlest one, appeared only once, at the feet of the others. The final drawing showed the gray people arranged around a flat blue circle—a pond, or a lake.

Sam appeared in the doorway of the kitchen, carrying a fistful of Lego bricks and patting his stomach to show her his hunger. Orla held out the drawings.

"These are wonderful, Sam. Will we stick them up in your playroom?"

Sam shook his head, quickly, and put out his hand for the pages.

"What's wrong? Don't you want to show me?"

Sam looked at her and at first Orla thought he might speak. He pursed his lips, opened his mouth.

"Who did you draw?" She pointed to the little people.

Sam took the papers and held them close to his chest.

"Are these your friends?"

Sam nodded.

"What are their names? Do they have names?"

Sam sighed, nodded again. Orla was testing his patience, she knew. "And where do they live, your friends?"

Sam frowned, confused, and pointed at the kitchen floor. *Here.*

Ripening

—

Awa' birds, away!
Take a little, and leave a littler,
And do not come again;
For if you do,
I will shoot you through,
And there is an end of you.

English nursery rhyme, traditional

8

1976

———

IT SURPRISED LYDIA HOW THE evenings crept in, how the days turned from bright to black almost without her noticing. And sometimes the night would arrive in the sitting room while the garden was still lit gold at the back, as though the house itself divided the light.

Beneath her room were the twins in their adjoining bedrooms that faced out onto the garden. Underneath the twins were Sara in the master bedroom and Owen in his nursery next door, and Philip, at the front, looking out over the sea. The back bedroom on the first floor was turned into Sara's office, and she worked with her back to the ivy-covered window, often with the door propped open with a wedge of paper to hear the baby. Sometimes Lydia was grateful not to be on the main floors, tangled up with the rest of them. And sometimes it made her feel othered, outcast, the stranger in the attic.

The house always felt more relaxed with Dot in it—her relentless good humor wore away at the rigid unease that dogged Lydia now, a constant companion since she'd found the bird in the fireplace. As though the house had known she was there, crouching and listening, and had sent her a message. She tried to avoid the nursery as much as possible, and disliked turning her back to the chimney.

As the sun set across the garden, the trees and the pond disappeared gradually into the evening. Dot hefted a basket of clean laundry onto the kitchen table to fold small clothes with deft hands and pestered Lydia, again, to come out with her, down to the pub in the village on one of her Friday nights off. "Come on, it'll be a laugh. You hardly ever leave the house, you deserve a night out."

"Who else will be there?"

Dot laughed. "There's some good-looking lads in the village, you know, but if that's what you're worried about I'll tell them to stay away. Tell them you have a piece back in the city." She winked, salacious.

"It's not that! And I don't. Have a piece—you know what I mean. There was someone, you know that. But not for a long while."

"Why did you finish?"

Such a simple question, but Lydia found that she had no answer. "I don't know. I suppose I moved here."

"He didn't fancy moving as well, then?"

Lydia was faintly shocked. "I couldn't have asked him to do that."

"Why not?"

Why hadn't she asked Danny about coming with them? They could have rented a house in the village together, made a life. Why hadn't she said? Why hadn't *he* said? "I suppose I didn't think I was allowed."

Dot threw her head back, strong teeth gleaming. "What do you mean, 'allowed'? Haven't you ever just asked for what you wanted?"

"No. No, I don't think I have." And Lydia laughed, too, at the utterly ridiculous notion that she could ever be a person to ask for what she wanted, and at the following absurd realization that not being that person could very well mean a life of never getting what she wanted. How odd. How funny.

"Will you come, then? There's usually a crowd of us; you won't stand out."

"I don't mind standing out, Dot. I just don't want to not know anyone, I don't want to be a lemon."

"But, once you've actually met everyone, then you *will* know them. Right?"

Lydia had always enjoyed being persuaded. "Sure, all right. I'll come."

After Dot had left and the children were in bed, Sara motioned for Lydia to follow her into the kitchen, where she hunted in the cupboard for two clean glasses, switched on the radio, and kicked off her shoes under the table. She lit a cigarette, tapped the packet, and winked.

"How are they getting on, then?" Sara flicked ash into the saucer on the table. She really only smoked inside when it was warm enough to leave the doors open; during the winter, Lydia often spotted her hunched against the orangery, grinding the ends into the patio slabs. Once, coming back from the village up the cliff path, she crested the hill and saw Sara sitting out on the drawing-room windowsill, wearing two coats, framed by the bare wisteria branches and wreathed in blue smoke.

"Fine. All right. Philip asked me to set him maths homework yesterday."

Sara shook her head. "Just like his dad—what a little swot."

"Shall I?" Lydia took a cigarette, even though she didn't really want one.

Sara stretched her arms above her head and yawned. Wisps of residual smoke curled from her nostrils on the exhale. "Don't see why not. If it keeps him busy. Do you think the girls need it?"

"Do you think they'd do it, even if I set it?"

"Good point." Sara leaned over and topped up Lydia's wine. She'd donated their set of wedding crystal, never used, after Doug died, and replaced it with fashionable green glass dotted with artistic knobbles. Lydia didn't like the new set much; it made her think of warty toad skin.

"Thanks." Her mouth tasted of ferment and ash.

"Debussy."

"What?"

"The radio—Debussy. 'Feuilles mortes,' I think. French, means 'dead leaves.'"

"Oh. It's nice. Relaxing."

Sara sat back in the chair and pulled her knees up so that her feet rested on the edge of the seat. They looked like a bird's feet, like talons curled under. "I know you don't agree with me."

"What?"

"About school. About all this—taking the year."

"It's not that I think it's bad, I just wonder if—"

Sara interrupted. "I understand that it's not exactly what Philip would prefer. I know it suits the girls better. I just want them all to have a bit of time together, a bit of time off real life, before we all have to start again."

"No, I do understand. I know it's been hard. After."

"You know more than anyone, Lydia, what we all went through. And I know it was hard on you, too—you were a lifeline. I'm glad—really, I am glad—that you came with us. We wouldn't be able to do this without you. It's so important for the children to have something constant, especially now that I'm working. We all need to be together."

"I know. And I'm glad you asked me." Lydia felt the praise like alcohol in her blood. The warm rush of it made her want to do anything Sara asked.

When they'd hired her, Doug and Sara asked, tentatively,

how much they should pay her. Lydia had been astonished, opened and closed her mouth like a fool and stared at them across the coffee table in the parlor. "Ah, I'm not sure? It depends, I think—what do you want me to do? Weekends, and so on—it's different with every family."

"Right, yes, of course." Doug looked at Sara, who shrugged, and then proposed a figure that wasn't incredible, but wasn't insulting, either. Lydia knew they could probably have afforded more, but she'd never been much of a negotiator. Sometimes, when she was counting out coins for the gas meter, she thought about the enormous cupboard under the stairs in Doug and Sara's house, fitted with multiple racks to store wine that Doug didn't drink, but instead "invested" in. Sara sold it when he died; a short man in brown overalls came with a clipboard and made a list and the next day it was hauled away in packing cases stuffed with straw and hessian, and loaded into vans. Lydia watched it leave the house in a similar way to how Doug had left, in the end: upended, in a box.

Sara kept a few of the cheaper bottles and once in a while she would open one in the evening and tell Lydia to sit with her. Lydia loved those times best, when Sara invited her into a different life. They would talk about their parents, and about old boyfriends, never really about the children. They never talked about Doug. Sara would ask her about her friends, and going out, and nightclubs, and sometimes Lydia invented wild stories of being offered very expensive drugs by very unsuitable men and Sara would scream and open another bottle. It was something approaching a friendship—the only one Sara really had, out here in Dorset.

But as the months went on, those evenings became more and more infrequent. Sara would excuse herself after supper with a headache, or a pointed comment about the work she had to do to sustain them all in the house, and Lydia would feel guilty for wanting her time. She had to make the most of the moments she did get with Sara, tried to cram in conversations about the children when they had five minutes together. Sara had said that coming out here was about being together, but they all saw less and less of her.

Sara drained her glass and yawned. "Lock up, would you?"

Up in the black attic, a pile of magazines toppled over and slithered onto the floor as Lydia groped in the dark, trying to find her pajamas and the battery lamp. She swore, quietly and with feeling, when she knocked her forehead against one of the low beams and sighed when her hands finally found the lamp. A moth fluttered against the plastic and Lydia shook it off and smothered it with a tissue. The idea of it landing on her face while she slept made her feel panicky and ill.

Lydia thought again about Danny. She'd given him the address and phone number of the house, but he hadn't used them. Maybe he was punishing her for leaving, maybe for something else. Danny was usually punishing her for her transgressions, real or imagined. She never knew what would rile him up—he'd sometimes find it funny how other men came on to her when they were out, and then whip round and tell her that she couldn't possibly go to the supermarket in that skirt, it was far too short. He dazzled and enraged her equally and she felt tired when she remembered him, and how often she fell short of the requirement to keep up with his lightning moods and unspoken expectations.

She turned off the lamp. Sara had made a point of telling Lydia that she was buying rather a lot of batteries, and Lydia had thought, *Well, maybe you should put electrics up there like you promised?* But she didn't say it.

Something moved in the dark below.

Lydia lay very still. The door to the attic steps was closed, and although there was a hook-and-eye catch on the inside, Lydia never latched it, to allow the children in. The connecting door between the attic rooms was also closed—Lydia couldn't sleep in the face of an open door. Her bed and one of the dressers occupied the room at the far end, the one that contained the rise of the chimney breast, and the first room she used for the rest of her clothes and boxes of books and shoes.

Faintly, she heard the attic door open, and then very soft footsteps on the stairs. She wondered if one of the children had come up looking for her—but generally the children raced up the stairs like a herd of goats, stamping and biting. These footsteps came even, slow, measured. Louder now, as they crossed the attic. Lydia opened her mouth to call out, and then closed it again. The sound stopped at the door.

A heavy thump on the glass of the dormer window made her cry out; she put a hand over her mouth. She was so frightened she felt queasy and the back of her neck left a wet patch on the pillow. She was cold now, but didn't want to move to retrieve the quilt—the bedstead was old and squeaked viciously. She turned her head on the pillow and stared at the pale shape of the door. The lamp was on the floor, too far to reach without making a sound.

Lydia lay and watched the door for a long time. After a while, she closed her eyes. *Just to rest them, just for a moment.* Still no one came through the door, but she hadn't heard the footsteps leave.

Lydia fell asleep with her face toward the door, and when she woke in the hot light of the early morning she saw that the door at the bottom of the attic steps was open, pushed right back against the wooden paneling of the corner room that Sara used to store old toys and junk and boxes of things from London that they had no use for in this new life. The dormer window shone oily, streaked with dirt where the bird had hit it.

Downstairs, she made a pot of tea and took it out to the picnic table on the patio. Sara appeared almost an hour later, still drowsy from bed. Lydia tasted the old tea, coppery and thick, and poured out the last drops for Sara.

"Children aren't up yet, then?" Sara reached across for the milk bottle, warm from the morning sun.

"Haven't heard anything; I'm enjoying the peace!"

Sara laughed and sat back in her chair, closed her eyes, and tilted her face to the sun. "Such a beautiful day. I feel so lucky to be out here, you know. I can't imagine being in London in this heat."

Lydia remembered the hot, gritty air of the Tube in summertime, the crush of sweaty bodies, and the rank stink of the river. Sara never really took the Tube; she and Doug hailed black cabs everywhere they went. And their house had such a lovely garden, with smart outdoor furniture and a perfect lawn. If Lydia wanted to escape the gasping heat of her flat, she had to make do with the dusty scrub of the Heath.

"Sara—did you come up last night, to the attic?"

"What? Why would I do that? This tea is stone-cold, Lydia, did you know that?"

"Yes. So you didn't come up to my room?"

Sara took the teapot and called out from the orangery, "No—was it one of the children?" She disappeared into the kitchen.

Lydia took in the gleaming lawn, the flawless sky. She turned in her chair and shielded her eyes from the sun and looked to the very top of the house, where her bedroom squatted under the violent point of the roof.

The pub was too warm for a summer evening like this one, crammed with Friday-night locals. The low ceiling was stained with nicotine and soot from the open fire that was, inexplicably, going full-tilt in the old inglenook fireplace, and tarnished horse brasses hung from the wooden beams propping up the bar. It smelled sharply of stale beer and sweat and too much perfume.

Dot waved toward the back exit; Lydia left her ordering at the bar and went out to the beer garden to snag one of the few remaining trestle tables. A fragrant haze of cigarette smoke hung over the tables crowded together, and Lydia wished she'd swiped a packet of Sara's before leaving the house.

Dot appeared with two very full wineglasses and two very tall men, who sat down across from Lydia with such enthusiasm that the table rocked and Lydia slid forward on the bench.

"Shit, sorry!" The men laughed, and the taller one put out his hand. "Lee. Lee Barrow."

"Wheelbarrow." The other one smiled at Lydia. "That's what we all call him, since school."

"Hi. Hi. I'm Lydia?"

"Yeah, we know, Dot said." Lee tapped his packet of cigarettes. "Want one?"

"God, yes. Yes, please."

"She's keen!" Not-Lee winked at her, and Lydia flushed.

"Shut up, Freddie. Sorry, Lids. I promised you nice boys, but I could only find these two fools."

Lee smiled at Dot, and Lydia knew immediately that, if she stayed, she'd end up stuck with Idiot Fred, who had dirty fingernails and a hole in the collar of his shirt.

"How're you finding the big house, then?" Lee reached over and lit Lydia's cigarette for her. He struck the match against his thumbnail and it flared blue then orange.

"Fine. It's good. I like it out here, I like it more than London."

Fred waggled his eyebrows and gulped at his brown pint. "Seen the ghosts yet?"

"What?"

Dot flicked an old cigarette end at Fred. "Fuck's sake, Fred."

Lydia leaned forward. "What do you mean, 'ghosts'?"

Lee rolled his eyes. "It's nothing, just stupid stuff folk round here say. Lot of people have come and gone from that house, no one stays long. People joke that it's because of ghosts. Really, I think it's just a bit of a shit house."

"A shit house?"

"Just because of where it is." Dot sipped her wine and made a face. "Christ, this is awful. Well done asking for the red, Lids, this white tastes like piss."

"Oh yeah, and you'd know, would you?" Fred stuck his tongue out.

"You're disgusting."

Lydia asked again, cold now even in the heat of the evening, "Why is it a shit house?"

Dot sighed. "You know, it's big. Expensive. Bit isolated, out on the cliff, right out of the village like that. People like the views, then they realize they don't actually like living in it. Gets cold up there, with the wind, especially in winter. You know that. If we get a load of snow, you can be really cut off."

"Right. Yeah. So no ghosts, then?" Lydia laughed, and it came out too high, too fast.

Lee shifted on the bench. "I mean, there have been a few accidents up there, and so on. But, like, years ago. Not recent. Right, Dot?"

Smoke streamed from Dot's lips. "Not recent, no. My mum talks about a little girl that died there, but ages ago."

"A kid? When?" Lydia reached over for another cigarette, the packet jumped away when her fingers touched it.

"Years and years ago, before my mum was even born. Before the war—first, not second. My grandad remembers it, he went to the funeral. All the village did, for things like that. Drowned."

"At the beach?"

"No, up at the house. The pond." Dot inhaled. "My grandad said she was missing for a few days, so everyone was searching, but she'd got tangled in the weeds. So when she came up after a week—not pretty. An accident, though. Sad, but things like that happen."

The silver foil from the cigarette packet fluttered on the table for a moment and was whipped away by the salt breeze from the cove, only a few streets away from the pub. Lydia reached for her wine and finished it very quickly.

Dot continued, "Anyway, we've never seen a ghost, have we, Lids?" She laughed and dropped her cigarette butt into the creamy dregs of Fred's pint, and the three of them moved on to something else.

9

2017

—

THE HOUSE HUNG ON THE EDGE of the cliff in a swath of gray mist, hidden from view by silver clouds of shifting rain. Water ran down the chimneys and pooled in the fireplaces; the ivy on the back of the house rippled like the sea and clung fast to the stone.

Toby knocked on the kitchen window and beckoned Orla outside. "Mrs. McGrath—will you come out?"

Poor Bridie was having a rough day with her gums and whined terribly anytime she was left alone, so Orla fixed her daughter to her front with a cotton jersey sling and ignored the throb that began in her lower back. She felt like a cow or an ox, weighty and animal. Having children made Orla feel biological in a way that continually ignited discomfort; their need for her body—her smell and her touch and her lap—reduced her to something bestial, foreign even to herself.

Coming out through the orangery, arms round her daughter, she caught sight of herself in one of the long, arched windows. The mist pressed up against the glass and turned the window into something like a mirror, and she saw her own ghostly out-line shudder from pane to pane as she moved.

When she looked again, faltering on the step, the child in her arms was not Bridie. Reflected back at her was a different child altogether—Orla's face was her own but she carried a lit-tle boy, bald-headed and sleeping in an old-fashioned romper with wooden buttons at the neck. It was a brief flash only, a momentary waver in reality. She looked down—Bridie lay snug against her chest, entirely herself.

Orla put a hand to her eyes. She'd had so little sleep—they'd all had so little sleep. She touched a finger to the window, leav-ing a mark in the condensation.

Orla stepped onto the patio and shoved her hands deeper into the pockets of Nick's coat. Droplets of her breath beaded the collar that she'd turned up to protect her cheeks from the cold. She followed Toby down the length of the garden.

He called over his shoulder, almost running. "The pond!"

She caught up with him beneath the oaks. "What do you mean, 'the pond'? We don't have a pond."

"There used to be a pond up here. Got filled in years and years ago, I think. It was big, from the looks of it. That's why everything here is growing in a bit of a dip, why there's no ma-ture plants. See this whole section, just here?" Toby pointed, pleased with himself. "You don't see it, do you?" He laughed and patted her arm. "Not to worry—but you'll need to decide what to do about it."

"Why? Can't we just leave it?" Orla slipped a little and clutched at Bridie's sling.

Toby touched her elbow. "Not a good idea, Mrs. McGrath. Doesn't look like it's been filled properly—it's boggy as hell, all lumpy. You'll just end up with a swamp if you leave it, sinkhole type of thing. May as well clear it and fill it right, or you could make a pond out of it again, if you wanted to?"

"No. I don't know." Sam had drawn a pond, hadn't he? Here, in their garden, surrounded by little people. Orla wondered what Sam saw when he looked out of the windows, if he saw the same house that she did. A coincidence, surely. He couldn't have known.

Toby looked at Orla. "Well, listen, I'll dig it out for now. Have a word with Nick, decide what you want to do. But it needs to be filled right and that means I've got to dig it out first. You don't know what else might be down there."

Orla recalled the darting shadow she'd seen—the furtive movement between the trees. The garden still seemed so vast to her, an unconquerable space; she couldn't seem to fix the proportions in her mind and could never quite remember if there were two oaks or three, or the exact placement of the maples, or where the patio ended in relation to the rickety old shed propped up against the east wall.

Toby crouched on his haunches and prodded at the soil with a trowel. He'd put up a rough circle of stakes, and orange string marked out the original edges. "You can see how big it was." He nodded toward the staked-out area, which occupied a decent portion of this section of the lawn. "Found a statue as well."

"What, in it?" Orla said, stupidly.

"No!" Toby laughed. "In the undergrowth, over there, right under that oak. Been there a while; it's half-buried. Broken, too, I think, looks like it's missing a head."

"A head? What is it?"

"Some sort of cherub, maybe a fairy, something like that. Very traditional, just plain old granite. Not worth anything, mind."

"Should we keep it?"

"I don't know, Mrs. McGrath, do you want a statue of a headless fairy in your garden?"

Orla frowned. "I really don't."

"No bother, then; I'll shift it. I found something else, too. Come and see this." He squatted next to a length of the orange string and turned over a piece of earth with the trowel. Orla stroked Bridie's leg.

"What is it?" She stepped carefully across the slick grass.

"Jewelry, I think."

"Seriously?" She tightened the sling round her waist and knelt next to him to peer into the hole. Toby dug at the mud with the point of the trowel and carefully worked something loose. She heard the metal scrape against small stones embedded in the dirt and watched the thing come out into the light.

It looked like a bangle, a solid circlet, but very small. Toby tipped it into his palm and brushed away the wet soil.

"I think it's gold." He spat on his thumb and rubbed at the metal, which came up gleaming. "Yup. Gold, see? No tarnish. I wonder how long it's been down here." He pulled his T-shirt out from the hem of his thick cotton jacket and cleaned the tiny thing, leaving dark stains on the fabric. The gold was engraved with a sort of floral pattern, like vines, bisected by a sliding catch to either expand or contract the circle.

"It's a christening bracelet." He looked surprised.

"A what?"

"A christening bracelet. That's why it's so small—this was for a baby. See how you can make it bigger, for when they grow." He pulled on the catch and it slid a little way then stopped. "Stuck, though."

"How do you know that?"

"It's traditional, but you don't see them much anymore. I had one, from my grandparents. But mine's silver. My nan keeps it in her jewelry box."

"Are they expensive?"

"I don't think so, there's not much to them. Feel this, it's so light." He hooked it on the end of her finger.

"Why would it be out here?"

"You know what kids are like, Mrs. McGrath. Running around losing things, dropping things. Pretty cool, though. Are you going to keep it?"

"I don't know—it doesn't belong to us."

"I'd say it's pretty old, I don't think it belongs to anyone anymore. You could put it on this one. Look." Toby took the bracelet from her finger and tugged Bridie's fat wrist from the sling.

Panicked, she grabbed Toby's sleeve. "Don't!"

Toby dropped the bracelet, startled, and looked hurt.

"I'm sorry, I'm sorry. I just—it's not right. It's not hers. I don't know who it belongs to, we don't know where it came from. It's not clean—" She hadn't meant to be so ungrateful, but the thought of that dirty little bracelet touching her daughter's skin made her want to retch. Her jeans were soaked through at the knees with muddy water.

Toby picked it up from the grass. "That's all right. I'm sorry if I overstepped—"

For the first time, Orla thought, she and Toby were awkward together. "No, you didn't. I'm sorry, Toby, I'm not quite myself today." She smiled, but it felt painful on her face. "I thought I saw something, back at the house. Just now, I mean. I know it wasn't anything, but it gave me a fright, there."

"What did you see?"

"Honestly, it'll sound stupid."

Toby lifted his shoulders. "I don't mind."

"It was just Bridie's reflection in the window. For a second, I thought she was someone else. It just—it didn't look like her, that's all. Sorry, I know how that sounds." She touched her fingers to her mouth.

He frowned and looked back across the garden at the house, which stood implacable, blameless. "That's old glass, you know, it's really warped. It's not flat, so it sort of distorts things. I get that it gave you a shock, though." He swiped his hands on his jeans. "You okay?"

"Sure. I'm fine." And she laughed when he put a solemn hand on Bridie's head. "Really, we're fine."

"This bracelet, then, technically it does belong to you now. What do you want to do with it?"

"I don't know. Clean it up, maybe? Sell it?"

"Here." He pulled a handkerchief from his back pocket, pale-blue check, wrapped the little bracelet tight, and handed it to her.

"Thank you."

She left him prodding at the earth at the bottom of the garden and made her way toward the back door. The house looked so beautiful from down here. Pale and soft, it rose into a cloud-streaked sky, skirted bountifully with bare trees the color of mice. The view of the house from this distance never failed to impress Orla, never failed to make her feel small and thin and *pinned down*. Like a butterfly on a board.

Scattered windows shone with lamplight, the orangery glowed and beckoned beyond the lawns. Despite the light and the warmth, Orla stood out on the patio for a long time, until Bridie whimpered and kicked her cold feet.

So beautiful and yet so relentless; the peeling wallpaper and stubborn plumbing and pits of shadow unbowed by modern lighting. And not just those things, either, not just every other renovator's complaints about botched jobs and insufficient damp-proofing. Those weren't the things that made Orla reluctant to be alone inside, hesitant to go to bed each night in a room that contracted and suffocated her while she slept.

"Right, we'll start at the top and work down."

In the morning, the sweep she'd booked weeks ago finally arrived, and now heavy cloths lined the floors and the stairs.

They came early, with two vans and a couple of lanky young men in coveralls, and started loud. Orla expected sets of sooty brushes and was startled by the appearance of what looked like industrial vacuum cleaners with long, flexible hoses.

"Sounds fine to me, do you need help?" Orla stepped back as one of the boys elbowed past with more hose attachments. It was raining and his wet boots left ashy prints on the canvas cloths.

"No, no. Best if you're out of the way." The sweep tapped his canines with a pencil. "Should have done this in the summer, really, you know. Shouldn't have waited so long."

By suppertime, the sweep and his crew had cleared the fireplaces in the three second-floor rooms and moved on to the first floor. Orla left the children in the kitchen with jam sandwiches and made her way upstairs just as they were starting in the nursery.

"What's behind here, then?" The sweep rattled the door to the passageway and turned to Orla.

"It's a little corridor, it connects the nursery to the master bedroom."

"That's pretty handy, then."

"Would be, if the nursery door opened. We can't find the key." Orla shrugged. "Not the end of the world."

"Right, so today we'll finish up in here and we've probably got time for one more, maybe the spare room? And tomorrow we'll do the rest."

"Brilliant, thank you so much."

He knelt in front of the hearth and took a short iron crowbar to the board that covered the opening to the fireplace; the wood cracked and bowed as he worked it loose. Orla listened to the footsteps of the men on the floor above as they gathered up the drop cloths and hauled away the machines.

Clouds of dust erupted from behind the board each time a nail was popped out, and the sweep coughed into his elbow.

As he pulled at the final nail, the wood split in half right down the middle and one whole side came free and fell sideways onto the drop cloth.

The sweep leaned forward and put his head up into the opening. "Looks clear enough. Hang on—shit." He withdrew and put a hand to his face.

"Are you all right?"

"Something hit me." He groped around in the hearth. "This, it fell." He put the object in his lap and brushed at his overalls, now bloomed with dust.

Orla crouched next to him. "Oh, God. What is that?"

The sweep picked it up and held it to the light. "It's a shoe."

"A shoe?"

"Yep. Old, probably belonged to a kiddie."

Crudely constructed of small leather panels, the shoe had been roughly stitched together with tough thread, snapped in places. It didn't look much bigger than one of Bridie's and fastened across the top with a leather loop and toggle. The shoe was aged black, mottled in places with white mold and streaked with ash.

"What was it doing in the chimney?"

"You do find it, sometimes, in old houses. Tradition."

"Tradition?"

The sweep turned the shoe over in his palm to examine the sole. A thin crack ran down the middle. "It's for protection. People stash away all sorts of things in various places to protect against bad spirits. Old-fashioned thinking, obviously. We find a fair few when we're called in to a renovation, or just an older house. Sometimes people would put a little jar of nails up in the rafters, or a scrap of cloth in the walls. Shoes are common, children's shoes. Like I said, for protection."

"That's—well, it seems a bit horrifying, honestly."

"Not at all, don't fret yourself." He laughed. "It's a custom, same as a horseshoe for luck, you see? Although—" The sweep raised his hand to his face and peered closely at the shoe.

"Although?"

"Well, you'd usually do it during the build. Makes sense, you can stash it in a good secret place. Away from the witches." He made his eyebrows jump to demonstrate the joke, but Orla didn't laugh. "And then the next family would come along years later, do the same thing. And so on. But this is old—very old. Much older than the house. Older than anything I've come across. I wonder when it was put up there?" He leaned forward to look up the chimney again.

Orla felt faintly sick. "How old, do you think?"

He shrugged. "I'm no expert, love. But, to me, it looks medieval, honestly. You could take it over to Poole, if you felt inclined. There's a museum there, they might be able to tell you. This house is, what, eighteen hundred?"

"Eighteen twelve."

"It's certainly older than your house, then." He turned the shoe over between his hands and passed it to Orla—a little reluctantly, she thought. "A mystery for you."

Late in the evening, Orla sat alone in a pool of light at the kitchen table and unwrapped the handkerchief containing the bracelet Toby found in the soft earth of the old pond. She had stuffed it away in the back of her knicker drawer, but, although it was out of sight, it had pressed on the front of her mind for days. The bracelet sat sourly on the linen square, still streaked with earth and shining in the places polished by Toby's spit.

She placed the shoe next to it on the handkerchief. The leather was brittle with age, hard to the touch, like the bark of a tree. The stitching, done with a human hand too many years ago to count, made her feel ill when she thought about it. The split in the sole ran from toe to heel. Another hand had touched this, across the years, another hand that left oil and prints on the leather.

On the fridge, Sam's careful drawings of those small, gray people. His steady hand that drew with such precision this arrangement of figures around a flat expanse of blue pond.

They live here.

His *friends*. At his insistence, she'd stuck them to the fridge with bright magnets shaped like pieces of fruit. But, in truth, she hated looking at them. Sam couldn't have known about the pond, of course he couldn't—none of them knew about it.

More pictures lay scattered on the table, done in violent pencil and lacking the care of his earlier efforts. Multiple children, now, the same collective depicted several times on each sheet. Some of the pencil people were girls, Orla could see that from the jagged sticks of long hair that spiked out from their heads. Two at a time, holding hands, repeated over and over. A smaller bundle with a wide, loud mouth that could be a baby, if you squinted. And a little boy who looked a bit like Sam, in short trousers, with lopsided arms. The boy's tongue stuck out, enlarged and grotesque and scribbled over with red. Orla had the fleeting thought that if she touched it, it would be wet.

Who else had been in her house? She thought about who might have come and gone over the years. Who else had slept under these ceilings or stood at these uncanny windows? Countless people, she supposed, lifetimes of human hearts beating and ceasing in these rooms.

Orla folded up the handkerchief and left the awful parcel in the middle of the table. She emptied an old bottle of red that had been open on the sideboard for too long, tipped the last of it into a mug and took it to the sofa.

The wine ran warm in her blood. She tucked her feet underneath her on the deep, sagging sofa and listened to the sounds of the house as the velvet night folded in. The wind had picked up and sang through the sash frames, now cradled by heavy drapes.

Nick had promised to come home every weekend, and even as she looked at his face while he was saying it, she'd known it was a lie. And so it fell to Orla to continue with the sorting and the cleaning and the enraging job of attempting to steam rotting wallpaper from the drawing-room walls, only to find another wretched layer underneath. On the day she discovered that the carpet covering the two flights of upper-floor stairs had been cut into sections and nailed down on each individual stair, rather than laid in one long strip, she knelt among the dust and the rusted tacks and put her bleeding hands up to her face and wept silently in the dead light of the early evening.

That vile green carpet was finally gone, heaved into Toby's Land Rover to be taken away and burned. Both reception rooms now had furniture, even if a great deal of it was second-hand and mismatched. Most of the rotten wallpaper was off and the old plaster was breathing and drying out. Small patches of faded paper remained and she liked the aesthetic of them against the soft, aged plaster; it made the rooms look elegant in an artistic, faintly Parisian way.

Curtains were hung, two enormous Turkish rugs lay in state in the drawing room and sitting room. Side tables and cushions had found their way out of storage. But the balance of Orla's affection for the house swung daily between a determination to appreciate its loveliness and an embryonic sort of fear, a fear that if she made the mistake of acknowledging would climb up her throat and put its hands over her eyes.

Orla woke when she felt the liquid seeping into the crotch of her jeans, a maroon and livid wound, and for a moment she thought she might be dying.

"Shit."

In the kitchen she pressed an old tea towel against her thighs and watched the wine seep into the fabric.

Orla locked the front doors and then found herself checking twice more, rattling the heavy handles loudly in the oppressive silence of the hall. Afterward, she paced the lengths of the first and second floors to check each window, pushing at the brass catches and pulling the sashes down farther against the sills. The thought occurred—creeping and unwelcome—that perhaps she shouldn't be so concerned about shutting something out. That perhaps she ought to concern herself more with what she might be keeping in.

The dome above her was dark, opening out to the black sky, and she imagined a great eye pressed against the glass. She felt cold and exposed and took the stairs two at a time and left the silent hall behind her.

She looked in on her studio before heading down to bed. The moon through the window caught the large, beautiful sea-scapes and hung them in night light. They shimmered in the dark; when Orla looked at them, she could almost hear the sea. The oils were good, she knew it. It had been a long time since inspiration had taken hold like this, a long time since she'd last given herself over completely to the work. Where light touched the canvases, ridges of new paint shone. They were mesmerizing, fluid. And there were details in them now that she couldn't recall adding—the largest one contained blurred shadows that could be fish, rippling between the waves. A few careful flecks in the third one, down in the bottom corner, looked a little like eyes. If you tilted your head, though, the eyes slid away.

On the opposite side of the room sat Sam's picture, propped on her largest easel. It cast a long shadow; the piece was too large—it crowded the studio and seemed to absorb the glorious light that Orla loved, leaving the room flat and gray. Beside the portrait, her seascapes were diminished, made small and feeble by the dominance of Sam's shining face and the livid black of the room behind him.

The Polaroids taken as studies, tacked up on the wall next to the easel, had faded even further. Parts of the images disappeared entirely behind blooms of leached color, and the white borders had yellowed to deepest cream, as if they had faced the sun for long decades.

Orla stepped back to examine the portrait and saw that it was changed. Sam looked even brighter and the room behind him darker. It gave the effect of distance, as though Sam had been pushed forward as the room retreated. The perspective was slightly off, the lines were no longer true. Everything in the painting was askew by a few unsettling millimeters. The window was smaller, the floor longer, the walls had narrowed.

To anyone else, the painting would probably look no different, but Orla saw it and she knew it was changed; her gift was for the detail, for the small things. Sam stared out with flat, fixed eyes. Orla knelt in front of the painting in the dark and touched her son's face—his eager, ravenous face.

10

2017

———

WINTER ASSAULTED THE REEVE FROM all sides. Battle lines were drawn in frost, traps were set in ice on the front steps. Those large flagstones in the porch, so beautifully smooth, wore their treachery as a slick cloak and Orla fell more than once on her way out to the bins or the village. The back patio was almost impassable until Toby heaved a bag of salted grit out of his Land Rover and liberally blessed the ground.

A thick hoarfrost captured the garden and held it hostage for almost two days. It was impossibly beautiful to look at in the sun, sharp and ethereal, and then the sea mist rolled in and took back the land with its warm breath.

Sam loved it, though, the cold, and spent a great deal of time outside with Toby, finding and shattering ice puddles with his red wellies.

Orla tried to lose herself in work. As much as it was a compulsion, it was also an escape, a process that offered a reprieve from the increasing pressure of living in a place that did not feel as though it belonged to her. She had become a reluctant archaeologist, uncovering relics to which she had no claim and did not want. The bracelet and shoe remained shoved away, buried in her dresser. At least once a day, she opened the drawer and reached to the back and felt with her fingers, making sure the parcel had stayed where she put it. The undulating glass of the orangery had stayed reassuringly ordinary, too. Still, Orla didn't like the potential for trickery that lurked within the wall of repeating windows, and consciously averted her gaze whenever she passed through into the back garden.

Sam's portrait occupied most of her time; Orla spent more hours with the painted child than the real one. The mood wasn't coming out quite how she wanted it. Every painting has a feeling to it, a proprietorial energy that makes each piece unique. A lot of her landscapes were pensive, melancholy; some even felt like anger. Her critics accused her of despondence, and this was largely the same interpretation as that of her admirers. Orla had learned very early on that her worth was not fixed and intrinsic but precarious, and entirely a matter of perspective.

But this painting of Sam had a furtive vitality to it that verged on feral. It was so unlike her other work, even her other portraits, and no matter how she scraped and repainted and mixed her colors, she couldn't rid the piece of its strange personality. She had intended it to feel joyful, bright, something like spring—but each stroke of the brush only intensified its peculiar vigor. Orla was affronted, as though the painting was playing a joke. *Febrile* was the word that sprang unbidden whenever she thought about it. Infectious.

"Sounds interesting, love, if you ask me. You going to keep it?" Claude set down a pot of tea and two mugs, with a plate of shortbread for Sam. She'd told him about the shoe, unsure how to explain the way it made her feel.

"For now, I suppose. Don't know what else to do with it, really. It's just, just *horrible*. I hate the thought that it's been in my house this whole time. Makes me feel like, what else am I going to find?"

"What are you expecting to find?"

"I don't know." She took a piece of shortbread and crumbled it between her fingers onto the plate. "Claude, when I took Sam to the library a while ago, I got talking to a woman from the village. And she asked where I lived, of course, and when I told her, she said that our house, it isn't safe. That it's bad. And, honestly, I think she's right." She looked at her son, who was focused on fixing a jetpack to a small plastic astronaut. "It's been hard living there. It is hard."

Claude didn't seem at all surprised—in fact, it felt to Orla as though he'd been waiting to have this conversation. He shook his head. "Your house has itself a bit of a reputation. You know it does."

Orla pressed on. "This is different. What you said, just about people coming and going, I could bear that. Because you're right, it is a big house. It's not an easy house. But this is something else—she said it's a bad house, Claude. That children shouldn't be there."

Claude sighed and passed a hand across his beard. "It's all gossip, mind. Foolish talk—me and Alice have no time for it. Toby, neither. Just superstitious stuff, nonsense."

"Really? Just nonsense?"

"Now, listen, it's an old house—plenty of people have died in it and plenty lived, too. It's the way of old houses. Don't go taking any notions." Claude leaned across and tapped a finger on the table.

"Claude, please. What do you know?"

He picked up his tea and stared into the cup. "Few kids lost themselves, from families that lived there. But it's passed through so many hands, that house, nobody stays long. So I say, of course there have been a few unfortunate incidents. Kids get sick, they have accidents—right? Number of families in and out of that house, it's bound to happen. Even here, right, the café? Our flat upstairs—some poor old bugger offed himself up there, years ago. Doesn't trouble us none, you can't go making an enemy out of death. Comes for us all. So—don't be worrying about what people say."

Orla thought of the house's generous scope for harm—the wide and uneven staircase, the splintered floorboards, the thin and brittle windows. The long drop from the landings to the expanse of floor below. "Claude—what sort of accidents?"

He hesitated and looked at Sam. "You sure you want to know this?"

"Please."

"There was a little girl, long past. Early part of last century. Drowned in the pond—used to be one up there. Terrible, of course, but an accident. Only a wee thing, took them a while to find her. So, you know how people get. Ghost stories and so on, and that made a good one. Family shut the house up and went back to London. A few people came and went, never stayed long.

"Then, in the seventies, the same thing. A drowning. Something happened to one of the children, can't remember rightly which one, now. There were a few up there, with a nanny. Twins, too—a biggish family. Pond was filled in, after that. Not many round here remember the details of why, anymore. So the house got itself a reputation, but there's nothing to it. Not as far as I'm concerned, anyway. People can be small-minded, you know that. Once an idea takes hold, it's hard to shift it."

"Why didn't you tell me any of this before?"

"And what would you have done if I had?"

A good question. Would it have put them off buying, if they'd known the history? Orla knew that Nick wouldn't care, it was all so long ago. And would it have changed things, if she and Claude had had this same conversation on her very first visit? They wouldn't have turned round and sold again, she knew that. There wouldn't have been a way out and Nick would have admonished her for looking for one. What did any of this matter to them, to their family?

Claude continued, "Nothing to be done, if you ask me. It's just stories."

"Toby found the pond. Well, where it used to be. He talked about putting it back. I said no." At least that was something about the house that she could control, even if she couldn't alter its history or her own future there.

He laughed. "Sounds nice. Everyone likes a water feature."

"Claude. Come on. I don't want that in my garden, not where people have died. It's not right, it's not *safe*—"

"Why would you be worried, love? None of that's got anything to do with you. All in the past, that stuff."

"You said people don't take to it well, and I always wondered what you meant. The woman, too, she tried to say—"

Claude raised a hand and gestured out of the window to the street. "People here are superstitious, woolly-headed. It's just that kind of town. It's the Dorset way. We love to see things that aren't there." He frowned. "You'll be fine."

Children had lost themselves. Such a strange way to phrase it, as though they were active participants in their own ends. Erased by a decisive hand. Such a thing to imagine, losing yourself. Setting out to be lost, turning yourself around and around so that when you opened your eyes, everything was tilted and nothing was familiar. Doing it on purpose, disappearing *yourself.*

Claude stood to deal with a customer and patted Sam on the head. "It's a God-given house, Orla—you're very lucky."

Toby cut reams of ivy from the garden, and Orla spent the afternoon outside with him, working them into long, trailing garlands. One over the fire in the drawing room, one over the fire in the sitting room, a loop suspended above the AGA, and several more to wrap round the banisters on the main stairs and the first-floor landing. Nick helped her fix them with strings of fishing wire, and the effect really was grand—delicate stems of green ivy, soft against the polished wood. Heavy twists of mistletoe, ripe with fat white berries, hung in each doorway, and Nick made a point of kissing them all, laughing, anytime he passed by.

The garden was run over with the stuff; it grew rampant through the oaks. The oldest relationship in the world, Toby said, oak and mistletoe. The greed of the vine drinking up the strength of the trees: another of those symbiotic cruelties that occur so often where green things grow and gasp and die.

Orla knelt next to Toby on the patio and twisted ivy branches, her hands made clumsy by heavy gloves. "I saw Claude the other day."

Toby smiled. "How's he getting on? Haven't been down for a while."

"Good. Fine." She sat back on her heels. "He told me about what happened here, about the pond. The deaths. Did you know?"

Toby shrugged and fixed his eyes on his hands at work. "My nan told me some stuff, but honestly I never took much notice. She used to be here a lot, she said, when she was young. Knew a few things. But it was a long time ago, all that. Didn't think it mattered much."

"It matters to me. It's something you should know, about your own house."

"Does it bother you?" He handed her a length of wire.

Orla looked out across the lawn. "Yes. Yes and no, I think. It's not a nice thought."

"No, I suppose not. Sorry, I really didn't think it was worth mentioning."

"That's all right. You weren't to know. But, listen, won't you come for drinks? We'd love to have you, honestly, Nick's parents are dying to meet you."

"Now then, have you been telling people about me, Mrs. McGrath?" He smiled and waggled his pruning shears.

"I mean it, really—won't you come?"

"That's very kind of you, honestly it is, but we've family over ourselves. You know how it is, gets busy."

"I do know. Well, that's all right. Another time?"

Toby turned away from her and bent his head to his work. "Maybe. Sure." He seemed distracted, concerned, and Orla didn't press him further.

Christmas Eve, cocooned in white, dawned blinding and breathless. It had started the evening before, the snow, and continued on through the night, falling reckless and thick.

Drifts slumped against the house, the lawns and gravel were quilted silver and ice. The oaks hung heavy with their load, the magnolia strained toward the sky, pushing skeletal fingers up out of the snow that threatened to envelop it entirely. The pond at the bottom, half dug out now by Toby, was reduced to a soft divot rather than a hard gouge. Orla hated looking at it and avoided that part of the view from the kitchen. Since her conversation with Claude, she had become acutely aware of the unknown quantity of the place in which they lived.

Orla lit the fires in every room and, for the first time since the weather had turned, the house felt warm, even comfortable. The sweep had been right, too—the consistent heat of the drawing-room chimney finally killed off the little sapling growing from the stack, and, although she checked obsessively several times a day, Orla heard no more birds.

"Mum! Hi, hi, come in—bloody hell, freezing, quick." Nick, the generous host, flung open the front doors to greet his parents, who entered in a flurry of bags and coats and snow. George bent to pull Sam into his arms.

"Now then! Now then! Who's this big fellow!"

Sam, upside down in his grandfather's arms, tugged on his jumper to stop it riding up and exposing his stomach, which was being tickled by his grandmother.

"Oh, look at this tummy! Just see how delicious it is! I think I'll have this for my Christmas dinner!" Eva landed a wet kiss on Sam's torso and he reached out to pat her hair.

"Orla! My goodness—what a house!"

Orla leaned into her mother-in-law's embrace and caught the scent of Clarins perfume and petrol fumes from her camel coat. Orla was moved but embarrassed by her in-laws' geniality—she welcomed it, but was also made a little reticent by it. She was never quite sure how much of herself to give in turn.

"Thank you, yes, isn't it!"

"Beautiful, beautiful," said George, as he handed his coat to his son and looked skyward, up to the great glass dome sheathed in snow. Orla, out of nowhere, thought of wood lice under a cloche.

"Nick sent pictures, obviously, but it really is something else." Eva put her hand on Nick's arm.

"We love it here, don't we." Nick beamed at his wife.

"We do—Sam loves it. The garden is wonderful, you've to come back in the summer, when everything's up." Orla picked up Eva's bag and started up the stairs. "Right, you're next to Sam; there's a lovely guest room. Looks out over the sea—you'll like it."

Such a beautiful Christmas.

It was perfect. The dinner, the wine, the gifts. The house shone, it preened. Beautiful old thing, center of attention, glittering bride to marry them all to their future. Nick was elated, expansive. Sam was spoilt and adorable, Bridie was cheerful and captivating.

Orla stood, occasionally, in the doorways, just to watch. This life she'd built, this family she'd been absorbed into, sometimes seemed removed, as though she experienced it from behind a tissue-thin sheet of glass. Present, yet separate, and no one else could see the divide. Her response to their happiness, her love for them, arrived a beat behind. There was always an infinitesimal pause between Orla's observations and the reaction; it was what made her such a good artist—the ability to inhabit that brief space in which she decided how to feel before she felt.

The house seemed to enhance the separation, as if it was the fifth member of the family and demanded her consideration also, so that her focus was frequently split. Orla was suspicious of this version of her house, the one that shimmered with festivity and expanded itself to make room for guests and turned only its most lovely aspect outward. It gathered up its secret corners and rotting walls and hid them away, and drew an organza veil over a scarred face.

The Reeve was limitless in its capacity for illusion. Usually so temperamental, over the last few days the heating had regulated itself reliably and the locked doors stayed locked and the dead things stayed outside. To be in the house now, one could almost believe that it had been like this since the first day, and might forget the bleeding hands and the scattered mouse shit and the dreadful, intermittent thumps of tired and desperate birds flinging themselves into those merciless windows.

This house, this temporary and celebratory house, encouraged a keyed-up festivity in its occupants. They'd never eaten so much, drunk so much. Cut off as they were by the snow that fell ever thicker, obligatory thoughts of Christmas services and carols down in the village church slipped away and the family turned inward, and opened more wine. Decorum suffered; George wandered about in a thick jumper and pajama trousers, and Orla caught Eva feeding Bridie trifle for breakfast.

Late on Christmas night, Orla found herself slumped in an armchair, half-asleep, with an empty brandy snifter in her hand. Nick, seated on the floor, reached over to take the glass, kissed her fingers, and smiled up at her. He stood with an exaggerated groan, made a joke about getting old, and went off into the kitchen to fetch more wine.

George and Sam, heads bent together, tinkered with some sort of plastic board game involving catching magnetic fish with a pole. Eva watched them, eyes fixed on Sam. She turned to Orla.

"So, how has it been?"

Orla tucked her feet under her thighs. "How so?"

"You. The house. It's really very beautiful."

"It is, isn't it. Bigger, I think, than what we'd talked about." Orla wasn't sure if Eva knew about the careless, authoritarian way in which the house had been bought, and she'd never welcomed criticism of her son.

"But perfect, really. Room to grow. Room for Sam."

"He seems to like it here. I think he does. He hasn't told me different."

Eva stiffened; she didn't like it when Orla talked about Sam like that, as if he'd said real words. "And does he tell you much, these days?"

Orla knew what Eva was asking. "Same as ever, really. The psychiatrist we saw gave us flash cards for things, but that's not really helped. He knows the words—that's not the problem. He just won't say them."

"Aren't you doing anything?"

Orla opened her hands. "There really isn't much we can do at this stage, Eva. That's what the woman said. Just encourage him, let him know it's safe. Being cross with him won't help. It'll come at his own pace. For now, it's just part of who he is."

Nick returned with a bottle and two glasses. "He's doing great. We're really hopeful. It's fine, Mum."

Eva took the wine from her son. "Well, I suppose you know best. He's so like you." She clasped his wrist and laughed. "Such a clever little boy."

Orla received Eva's pointed message with perfect understanding. It sailed right over Nick's head, of course, the sharp edge of female competition beneath Eva's concern. Eva needed to believe that Nick was right about everything, that it was Nick who held their family together with his strong, decisive hands.

Orla's head ached, the room was overly hot, and she wanted to be between cool sheets in a silent place full of open windows. She stood up and stepped quietly across the hallway, heading for the stairs. As she left the sitting room, she heard Nick and his father laughing, Eva cooing at the baby. She heard the crystalline kiss of the neck of a wine bottle against a tall glass, the dull retort of her father-in-law slapping his knee at a joke. She wondered what Sam's voice might sound like, how long it might be until he joined in.

At the top of the stairs, Orla turned right, down the landing to Sam's room and the guest room. Few of the ceilings had been wired for overhead lights and so most of the illumination came from strategically positioned lamps. When night came, the family were left to make their way from room to room via a series of golden pools, a little like stepping-stones. The hallway was so vast, the landings so long, that one could spend a second or so in darkness before approaching the next island of light. Orla had left Sam's night-light plugged in and it glowed a sickly orange. The door to the guest room was open a few inches, showing only darkness.

She went in and turned on a bedside lamp, shook down the duvet, and smoothed it out. The curtains were open and she drew them tight against the night.

Small feet, running; a little shadow past the door.

"Sam! No running upstairs, you know that." She heard him go into his room, the thump as he discarded his slippers on the floor. Orla sighed.

She heard Sam leave his own room and start, loudly, toward his parents' bedroom.

"Oh, Sam, come on—" Orla stepped out of the room and caught the turn of his thin shoulder and the white flash of his leg as he slid from the solid darkness of the landing into the dim light of her bedroom.

"Sam, stop it—you know it's time for bed. Come here, please."

A beat of silence.

"Sam!"

She set off after him and knew that she was too tired to deal with him in her usual equable manner. She didn't want to be cross with her son on Christmas Day, but she feared she might not be able to help it.

"Orla!"

At Eva's call, Orla stopped and turned to where her mother-in-law stood at the foot of the stairs in a river of mellow light spilling from the open door of the sitting room. Eva, pink-cheeked from white wine, hair escaping its tortoiseshell clip.

Eva, afloat on those mesmerizing black-and-white tiles, holding Sam, asleep, in her arms.

Orla opened her mouth. She put out her hands.

Eva held her grandson close. "Sam's here, Orla. He's down here, with me."

Orla came down the stairs on legs that felt too easily buckled. "How long has he been asleep?"

"Orla, what's wrong?"

"Jesus, Eva, just answer me."

"He fell asleep when you went upstairs. What *is* it? You look dreadful—are you ill?"

Orla put her hands on the banister. "No, no, I'm not ill. I'm all right. I'm—Has he been with you? He hasn't come upstairs?"

"No, I told you, he's been with me. Sit down, sit."

"I thought I saw him. Upstairs. It must have been something else." She shook her head.

Eva shifted Sam in her arms. "What?"

"Nothing, it's nothing. I'm sorry, I think I'm just tired."

Eva stepped past her and disappeared up to the first floor. Sam's white feet dangled over the crook of her elbow and Orla pressed her lips together to hold back the sudden and frantic compulsion to call out for her son, to make Eva bring him back, *bring him back!*

Instead, she sat alone on the stair and listened to Eva's footsteps above. After a moment she rose and pulled hard at the cold brass handles of the front doors. Locked—of course they were. She'd locked them herself, hadn't she? She felt the weight of the house at her back, the whole house, waiting for her to turn so that it might embrace and swallow her—as though it were a living animal, ready to bite.

11

1976

———

LYDIA DIDN'T FORGET WHAT FRED had told her. She had laughed, at the time—everyone had. Ghosts! What a foolish notion. But, increasingly, it didn't feel so foolish. Although on the surface nothing changed about life within the house, Lydia began to feel a low pressure, a murmur of something not quite right. No one else felt it, as far as she could tell. The twins carried on with their games, Dot baked as many cakes as she ever had. Even Philip seemed perfectly cheerful, and he was usually so inclined to melancholy.

It was unsettling to watch the others exist within the house, sailing on in their routines with no acknowledgment of the shadows that swam beneath the surface of their lives here. It made her feel separated, and alone.

Out in the garden, in the hot sun, the twins had been gone for almost an hour. Philip was easy enough to find, huddled under the yew bush, his red T-shirt visible through the branches. But Lydia hammed it up for his benefit, stalking around and around his hiding place and saying out loud, "My goodness,

Philip is such a good hider! I wonder where on earth he could be! Perhaps I've lost him forever!"

Her distress unnerved him so much that he crawled out and grabbed her ankle. "Here I am, Lydia, I'm here! It's me!"

"Good grief! Where on earth did you come from?"

"I was right there—right there, just by you!"

Lydia held out her hands for a high five. "Such a good hiding place; aren't you clever?"

"What about the twins?"

"Hmm, no sign yet. But you can help me look."

Philip knelt to tie a lace. "I bet they've gone to the woods, that's where they always go when they want to leave me out."

"I did say to stick to the garden, that the woods would be cheating. They'll be here somewhere."

They wandered together down to the bottom of the garden, where the tall oaks cast long shadows across the lawn and the monkey puzzle leaned temptingly over the pond. The deep water shone jade, a few insects zipped across the surface. The stone cherub, alone in the middle, wore a cloak of green moss and cried bird-dropping tears.

Something surfaced and submerged again, creating a silky ripple and a noise like a pebble thrown in.

Philip took her hand. "What was that?"

"I think it was a frog—or maybe a newt?" There were no fish in the pond, she knew; it had been left for the wild things. For Tabitha and Clover, she would have made up something about a shark, or the Loch Ness Monster's cousin, but she didn't want to give Philip nightmares.

So when she came up after a week—not pretty.

Philip put his hand to his brow like a small sailor and said, "Well, I don't think they're down here."

"No, I don't, either. Maybe they're under the elderberry."

The tree burst with wide lacy flowers, cream-colored and fragrant. It had grown rather unruly, and Sara kept saying she'd get out with the loppers and trim it back, but hadn't yet. Dot spent a morning when the blossom first came making cordial, gathering and infusing flowers until the house was steeped in the heady scent of elderflower. She'd let the children decant the gold liquid into the glass bottles and lick the crystallized sugar from the rims of the little metal funnels.

Lydia and Philip pushed aside the trailing branches that swept the lawn. It was dim and aromatic under the boughs of the tree. The grass was damp, scattered with fallen blooms. But no children here, either, just Lydia and Philip standing silent in the green shadow.

"Maybe they're inside?" Philip looked worried, but then Philip always looked worried.

Lydia was also beginning to worry. "Maybe—shall we look? You do downstairs, I'll do upstairs." She left him going through the kitchen cupboards, very methodically.

The hallway was hot and bright with sun trapped beneath the glass dome, like a greenhouse. The wood of the stairs ticked gently a couple of times, expanding in the heat. Little fingerprints dulled the shining banisters, beeswaxed monthly by Dot.

Lydia went all the way up to the top of the house, to her own room, silent and stuffy and distinctly lacking any children. Clover's bedroom was dusty, empty, and, as Lydia turned to leave, a tapping noise caught her ear. A small sort of noise, like fingernails drumming on a notebook in a warm classroom on a summer afternoon.

Lydia stood very still, held her hands close to her chest. There it came again, faint, from the other side of the wall, from Tabitha's room.

"Tabs?"

Three more quick knocks, down low, near Clover's dresser.

"Tabitha!" Lydia left Clover's bedroom and opened the door into Tabitha's room, where the sunshine illuminated nothing at all. Tabitha's bed lay unmade, books and coloring pencils littered the floor, and the only thing out of place was Lydia's own frightened face in the oval mirror above the bookcase, her open mouth reflected again and again in the beveled edges.

Lydia dropped to her hands and knees to look under the bed, pushed aside abandoned shoes and hair clips. A splinter caught the skin of her bare knee and drew blood. She smeared it away with the flat of her palm.

"Hello? Girls?"

Lydia sat back on her heels, felt the hot sweat gather under her arms and in her hair, and her breath came shallow and dry.

She headed for the main stairs, unable to shake the feeling that something was coming down behind her. But nothing did, of course.

Sara was in her office, with Owen in his travel cot on the floor by her desk. Lydia put her head round the door. "Girls in here?"

Sara laughed. "I should hope not. Haven't seen them all morning. Why?"

"Hide-and-seek. They're getting too good at it." Lydia closed the door gently. She leaned against the wall and waited for her heart to settle.

Philip's room was empty and perfectly tidy. His books were arranged by color in his bookcase, clothes all put away in his chest of drawers. Tartan blanket folded precisely at the foot of his bed, stuffed animals in a row along the top of his wooden toy chest.

In Sara's bedroom, Lydia put her hands underneath the bed and went right to the back of the wardrobe, breathing in the musty smell from two hanging fur coats and cardboard boxes of shoes. Sara didn't really wear her nice clothes anymore, what Lydia thought of as her "London clothes." Since coming out here, Sara had retreated into a staid rotation of poly-cotton trousers and turtlenecks in somber, country colors. Lydia touched one of the dresses—her favorite, and one she hadn't seen Sara wear for a long time. Crushed velvet in chartreuse, floor-length, with tiny buttons all the way down the front and a low, low neckline. Long bell sleeves ended in narrow, buttoned cuffs, embroidered with periwinkle flowers. The colors made Sara glow, the perfect complement to the ribbon of dark hair that snaked down her back.

The first time Sara wore it was for a Christmas drinks party at Doug's firm. She'd paired it with staggeringly high gold platforms that made her taller than Doug, who'd laughed and spun her round on the pavement outside as the taxi pulled up. Lydia had been so jealous that it made her almost sick.

Lydia backed out of the wardrobe and shut the doors. She hadn't checked the nursery yet, and put her hand on the door to the passageway that connected Owen's room to Sara's.

A whisper, a little noise that came through the keyhole. Lydia knelt and put her eye to the lock. In the dim light of the passageway, two small figures, sitting. The door to the nursery was ajar, dusty summer light illuminated the twins. They faced each other, swaying a little, singing in their made-up language. First one, then the other picked up the rhyme and carried on. It sounded a little like "Row Your Boat," Lydia thought, the way the verses overlapped. Tabitha put out her hands and Clover reached up to meet them, palm to palm.

Sweet voices sang out:

Tom-a-lin and his wife and his wife's mother,
They went over a bridge all three together.

The bridge was broken and they fell in;
"The devil go with all," said Tom-a-lin.

The twins clapped their hands together at the end of each line. It wasn't a rhyme or a tune that Lydia was familiar with. She thought about opening the door, calling out, *I found you!* But this was a communion, a private thing that she wasn't supposed to see. She felt grubby, voyeuristic. The girls carried on, unaware of being watched. Their singing sounded low and older and not of themselves, as though other voices came through their mouths.

They stopped and turned together, facing the keyhole. Lydia stood up quickly and went back into Sara's office.

"Found them! All fine—not to worry." Her underarms prickled with sweat.

"Great. Great." Sara wasn't paying attention.

"Listen, Sara—Sara? I was thinking, might be nice for us to get out of the house. I could take them to the beach, it's so warm today. Good for the girls, let them blow off some steam."

Sara frowned. "Maybe. I do like having them here, though. It's nice to hear them out in the garden while I'm working." She paused and looked down at her ledger. "Makes me feel less alone, I suppose."

"We don't have to be gone long, just so they can have a swim. It's so hot." Lydia balked at the idea of keeping the children home just so Sara could enjoy listening to them. And bringing Doug's death into it like that—Lydia felt both sorry for Sara and irked at the transparent manipulation.

"I'd rather you didn't, on balance. Besides, three children on your own is a lot. Maybe another time. We'll see."

Doug had always been the strict one, the immovable parent who set the lines in the sand. Kind but firm, forceful yet empathetic. The twins bit against his rules like two wild horses, but Philip flourished under his father's regime. Sara was the light, the fun, the gleeful encourager of mutiny and rebellion, and Doug would sigh, exasperated, and then finally turn up the corners of his mouth and laugh out loud at whatever rambunctious rule-breaking Sara had permitted. It had been a good balance, and now Sara struggled to occupy the bleak space that Doug left behind. Authority didn't come naturally to her, it made her miserable to impose on her children, and so she ricocheted between her old self and her new obligations, so that none of them ever quite knew what Sara would think about things, or what she might do. Philip took to biting his nails, and the girls ran riot.

"That's fine. I'll find something else for them to do."

Lydia felt suddenly very tired. To amuse three small children and a baby on a stifling summer's day in the same space they'd all been in for months was no small task—the same collection of worn board games, the same toys, the same faces. To be confined here on a whim, confined by Sara's selfishness, was almost an affront.

"Thank you, Lydia. I do appreciate it, the effort you make with them. We're all lucky to have you." Sara smiled, and Lydia felt guilty.

Out on the landing, Lydia stood silent at the top of the wide stairs. No sound from the nursery, no sign of the twins. A cloud moved across the glass dome and shadowed the hall.

Philip met her at the drawing-room doorway.

"Well, I found them!" said Lydia. "They've been playing upstairs, forgot all about our game. Rotters."

"Does that mean I win?"

Lydia clapped her hands. "Definitely! Shall we celebrate? What would you like for your prize?"

Philip hesitated. "What am I allowed?"

Any other child would have asked for sweeties, or a for-bidden treasure—a prize worth getting in trouble for. But not Philip, who was always so very concerned about doing exactly as he ought and liked Lydia to report back to Sara how good he had been, every day. Philip never wanted praise—he wanted reassurance. His need for full marks was born of fear, not superiority. The line between his eyebrows made Lydia's heart hurt, and sometimes when he was sleeping she would smooth it out with her thumb before turning off the light.

"Anything you like. You won't be in trouble, I promise. It's a treat."

Such cautious pleasures for Philip. Lydia sliced strawberries and snowed them with sugar. Her hand shook as she waved the spoon, heaping uneven drifts onto the fruit that bled into the dish.

When Philip took his fruit outside, Lydia sat uneasily on a dining chair and watched the muscles of Dot's back shift under her blouse as she washed up.

"Dot—you know what Freddie was saying? About the house?"

"What?" Dot, distracted, scrubbed at the burnt sides of a battered loaf tin.

"About it being haunted."

Dot turned off the tap and shook her hands. "Lydia, you shouldn't listen to a word that idiot comes out with."

"But why would he make it up?"

"To scare you? To be a prat? I don't know why he does half the things he does." She squirted more Fairy into the greasy water.

"Do you think he might be right?"

"Why?"

"I don't know, I just wondered." Lydia chewed on a hangnail.

"Lids."

"I thought I heard something."

Dot looked at her. "What did you hear?"

"Promise you won't think I've lost it?"

"You know I don't make any promises." Dot winked, to make Lydia laugh.

"I mean it."

"Well, get it out, then."

"I thought I heard someone coming up to my room. A few nights ago, before we went to the pub. Someone walked up the stairs and then stopped, and I didn't hear them go back down. Sara says it wasn't her."

Dot shrugged. "You know this house makes all sorts of noises. Especially at night. Creaks like hell in this heat."

"But after what Freddie said—"

"I really do think it's just the house. Old wood, old beams. Happens in our house, in winter, you know. When the doors get hot they start to crack, it can be really loud." Dot put a wet hand on Lydia's shoulder. "And what else would it be—a ghost?" She laughed, but without much humor.

Later, when the children were asleep and Sara had disappeared with Owen into her own room, Lydia sat alone in the kitchen and smoked two of Sara's cigarettes, a subversive act. Then she went into the hallway, cool and shadowed, and stood in her bare feet next to the telephone table by the front doors. She touched the handset, gently, and put her finger into the dial and swung the numbers round and round to telephone Danny.

How strange, she thought, *that I'm reaching all the way to London with just my finger*, as if she had stretched her arm long enough to touch his face. She held the receiver to her ear, heavy and loud, and sat on the hallway floor and listened to the line ring out.

Lydia replaced the handset. The gasping silence made her want to cry. It was only ten o'clock, Danny never went to bed before two. Maybe he was out. Maybe he'd moved. She'd given him the new address before she left, written carefully in capital letters on a piece of notepaper, and stuck it to his fridge with a magnet in the shape of a pint of beer.

"You'll come and visit?"

"Of course." He rummaged through the magazine rack full of vinyl, on his knees on the thin carpet with his back to her. Autumn was already beginning; the flat was damp and cold and her legs pricked with gooseflesh.

"I mean it—listen, will you?"

"Jesus, Lydia. I said I would, all right? Sounds nice, anyway, bit of a holiday on the coast. Leave it, yeah?"

"You haven't even asked about the trains." She folded her arms, hurt like a child.

"I'm a big boy, more than capable of figuring out a National Rail timetable."

But of course he wasn't, and he hadn't. She'd worn a scandalously brief pair of linen shorts the last time she visited him—pea-green, high-waisted, with a line of gold buttons right down the front. She wanted to make him angry, to make him shout, *Did you wear those on the Tube? Christ, Lydia! Do you want people to think you're a slut? A whore?*

And when he'd let her into the flat and hadn't even noticed the shorts, hadn't even looked closely enough to be jealous, she'd known then that he was lost to her. Maybe he was already fucking someone else.

Cross-legged on the cold black-and-white tiles, she picked at the chipped varnish on her toenails. Shell-pink, summery, weeks old. The twins had begged to be included and so she'd done their fingernails to match. They'd crowed, delighted, and immediately smudged it all over the sofa, and Dot had cut it out of the tufts of chenille with a pair of nail clippers, laughing, while Lydia apologized.

Up on the first-floor landing, a door closed. She looked up. Only stillness, the quiet night holding them all in its warm mouth. The wisteria hung generous with purple flowers in front of the drawing-room window, which was still open and allowed for the black air to wind its way into the house, bringing the smell of the blooms with it. Lydia closed her eyes. She was very tired.

Another sound from upstairs—running. Small feet close together, that heavy-footed tread of little children—quick but clumsy. Lydia stood and peered up into the darkness, saw only a swift shape move against the darker shadow of the wall. Sara's door remained resolutely closed, no stirring from the girls on the second floor or from Philip, either.

She felt, very keenly, the smooth tile under her feet, the sweat beginning at the small of her back. The weight of her hair in its ponytail, the chapped skin of her lower lip that was so satisfying to peel away between her front teeth.

From darkness at the top of the stairs came a sound like typewriter keys, brittle clacking coming toward her faster and faster, picking up speed as it approached. She opened her eyes wide, futile, to see this invisible thing that would not show itself but grew louder and louder in its repetition, a tortured, fragile sound that might split apart at any moment, might crack and break open and release the awful thing that waited for her.

The marble bounced down the last three stairs, skittered across the tile, and came to rest against her instep.

On the landing above, a white leg flashed between the banister railings, the upper part of the body obscured by the handrail. The leg winked in and out of the light and disappeared into the bathroom.

Lydia stepped toward the stairs, hands outstretched in supplication, in begging. *Please.* For what, she didn't know. For respite? For reassurance? The stairs ascended into a black mouth, newel posts at the top like receding fangs in the dark, lamps on the landing like the dimmed eyes of a fading animal.

She picked up the marble. It was warm in her hand, as if it had been held tight in another palm. At the foot of the stairs she waited a moment, and when she saw nothing else she climbed them slowly. Her head came level with the landing and she stopped again—all doors closed, all children in bed. Clover, who had narrow sinuses, snored sweetly.

No child, no pair of feet in the gloom.

We've never seen a ghost, have we, Lids.

12

2018

———

DURING THE BLACK HOURS of the night, Orla would wake alone in a place that she did not recognize. When dawn slid under the shutters and brought with it the reprieve of the light, she could hardly stand the relief.

Mornings are a promise, afternoons are a heartbreak. Evenings are sly, and they deliver you into the thin arms of each dark night. But mornings hold such possibility, the tangible weight of better: *today will be different*. When the evening comes (such dreadful hours), the promise of the day has been broken because nothing is different—you are still yourself. To return to that, every day, to return to the truth of who and where you are, is more than a person should have to bear.

Orla had always measured time not in minutes but in light, and so the early evenings were painful. This winter, she raged at how the world took longer to wake. She came to loathe the dark with a clenched, ragged hatred.

The solitude she had welcomed so readily when they first moved, the isolation that she had held both arms out to embrace, now threatened to overwhelm. She had always been so perfectly complete in her own company, but since Christmas it was almost unbearable to be here alone. Orla went through the house several times a day to close any open doors—she could not stand an open door. The possibility of what she might see through it, what might catch her unaware, was too much. This house had too many corners she could not monitor, too many fertile rooms that might birth something horrific the moment her back was turned. She made a great effort not to think about the double-child she had seen, nor the kick of a leg as it disappeared through a doorway.

Orla retreated from the wilds of the house to the confines of her studio. Sam followed her up each day and stayed next to her while she worked, silently painting his own versions of the world. His muteness was amplified in the expanse of the house, his habitual noises distorted by the vast spaces.

Three quick knocks pulled Orla from her focus. She resented the interruption—time was tight to deliver to the gallery. A few of the smaller pieces were already complete, and she was rather proud of a series of miniature oils on board depicting abstract, rainy windows. Two larger landscapes of the back fields were nearly done, but the main focus of her return to work was the trio of seascapes that still needed attention.

She stretched on her stool and noted how the day had slipped away, far beyond the trees. The fields to the back of the house ran all the way to the horizon, expanses of frozen, desolate soil. Some of the hedgerows kept their stubborn green through winter, but for the most part the land was bare and brown and tired. Bridie stirred in her carry-cot in the corner of the studio; they'd had such bad nights with teething that she was sleeping too much during the day, but at least it meant more time for Orla to work.

The knocks came again and Orla stood. "Sam? Are you hungry? What will we have?"

Sam rounded the corner, paint all over his face, and she saw bruised shadows beneath his eyes. He shrugged and wiped his hands on his T-shirt.

"Don't do that, my love; keep it nice, please."

All through lunch she was distracted—poor Bridie waited patiently for her next mouthful of yogurt, while Orla stared out of the window and held the spoon a few inches away from the baby's face. Sam finished his sandwich and Orla didn't even notice when he left the table and went back up to his playroom; she only realized he was gone when she heard his footsteps on the stairs.

In the afternoon, Toby enlisted Sam to help him plant spring bulbs—pink ranunculus and delicate lily of the valley—and Sam knelt and put his hands in the soil as Toby explained how it would work, how the bulbs would sleep under their blanket of earth until they were woken up by the sun.

Orla left Sam outside with Toby, put Bridie down for an afternoon nap, and returned to the studio; the unfinished paintings nagged at her. On her way upstairs, she closed the doors to the spare room and the family bathroom—two doors she knew were shut when she had come down for lunch. She paused in front of each one and closed her eyes as she reached for the handles and pulled the doors to.

From the studio window, she watched Toby and Sam make their way along the flower beds with the bulb planter. The baby monitor sat silent on the trestle table; Bridie occasionally whimpered in her sleep like a puppy.

The scents of linseed oil and turpentine filled the room; Orla loved the sharp, chemical smell. Gradually, as she slipped deeper into concentration, all sounds fell away and all Orla heard was the beat of her own blood inside her head. Time stilled, became irrelevant. The light inside the room trembled and changed; she barely noticed when the sun turned from pale lemon to deepest gold and took with it the meager warmth.

When her back began to bother her and the good light was gone from the room, Orla put down her brush and rolled her neck a few times, cracked her knuckles and stood up. Sam would be wanting supper—she could hear him next door, the mechanical music from his kid's "computer" came faintly from the playroom. A Christmas present from Eva and George, it had been a big hit, and although Orla knew they'd bought it because they hoped it might encourage him to speak, she didn't really mind. Sam was too clever to be tricked like that.

Orla wrapped the larger brushes in cling film and was startled by how dark the colors had come out. These three seascapes had begun in the palest of blues and grays; along the way she'd added touches of deeper color, but she hadn't intended to make them quite so moody. The sea in front of her was bottle-green, the sky almost navy. Streaks of orange shone in the waves, like harbor lights reflected, and the overall effect reminded her of dark, dangerous water at night. She hadn't quite noticed what she'd done, so absorbed was she in the texture of the surface and the movement of the knife.

Bridie was half-asleep when Orla retrieved her from her cot, floppy and weighty and warm. Orla started down the stairs and almost fell when something large thumped into one of the cathedral windows. It hit high up, near the apex of the window, and dropped quickly out of sight. Then another, shaking the glass in its frame, on the other side—a slender, black bird. She watched it break its neck and tumble. Another followed, then two more in quick succession; each bang sent a shock of adrenaline down her spine and Bridie was howling and the dying birds left oily smears on glass that was aflame with the setting sun.

More birds followed, too many to count; one by one they

threw themselves against the windows, those enormous, beautiful windows that snatched each bird and tossed them, broken, to the ground: tall nets of glass to catch death from the sky.

Toby was already running across the driveway, Sam close behind but struggling to keep up and distraught. "Don't come out! Stay there!"

Orla stayed in the shelter of the porch and listened to the noises, the sickening smacks of more birds against glass. The birds were long and delicate, something like a swift or a swallow.

Sam was crying, tripping, flailing at his head with his hands. "Bring him in, for God's sake, Toby—bring him here!"

Toby picked up the child beneath the wheeling mass of birds and darted into the porch. Orla took Toby's hand and felt the calloused warmth of it; she was glad to be with him, relieved not to be on her own beneath the hurricane of dying birds. He jerked his hand from hers, scratching her palm with a rough thumbnail.

They stood together and watched the birds swarm. She imagined what this must look like from the air: the house, reduced, alone on the hill. The sweep of green lawn, patched with winter decay. The empty sky, lit by a fading sun. A swirling flock, moving apart and then coming together again, each blindly following the last toward death. And farther out still, a tiny house on a narrow cliff, facing a vast sea, surrounded by birds as small as insects.

One final thump signaled the last of the birds; the thick glass had held, but was streaked with feathers. Toby left the porch and stared at the ground; Orla followed. Birds were everywhere, littering the gravel with their soft, broken bodies and smashed beaks, their claws that curled against the ground. Sam wept, silently, against her leg. Orla put her arm round his shoulders and pressed him to her. Bridie was finally quiet, the neck of her sleepsuit soaked with tears.

"There must be close to a hundred—Jesus." Toby stepped back. Bones cracked under his boot. "Oh, God." He looked sick.

"What happened? Why would they do this?"

"I think the flock just follows, I think the ones at the front just flew straight in, you can hardly see the glass in this light, and I think the rest just followed."

"What do we do?"

"Take the kids in, I'll get a sack. I'll burn them, back at the farm."

"Oh, God. God, how awful. Thank you, Toby, I'm so sorry."

"It's all right, it's all right. I don't mind. Nick can buy me a few beers." He laughed, and there was no heart in it.

"I'm so sorry—"

"Don't, Mrs. McGrath, it's fine. You get them inside, now."

Orla thought of the bird in the attic, fooled by the windows, fooled by the house. That bird had met its end because it thought it was coming to a place of rest but instead it suffered and died because it couldn't see what was real.

And the birds outside, confused and stupid and eager. None of it made sense, none of it was natural—even out here in the countryside, where little deaths happened in a thousand small ways hundreds of times a day. It was the wrong time of year for swifts, still much too cold, and their approach upon The Reeve had felt panicked and inevitable, as though they'd been pulled in, helpless, by unseen hands.

From the sitting room, Orla watched Toby, in a pair of heavy gloves, pick each dead and dying bird from the gravel. Occasionally, he used two hands to snap tender necks.

I want to leave.

But how to put that to Nick? Nick, who had worked so hard for this house, who had gifted them all this life?

Children lost themselves.

A heaving, unacceptable thought. Death in her house—death that she and Nick had purchased and painted over and, eventually, dug up. At the back of her mind, a picture began to form. Vague, for now, just outlines and wild spaces. She didn't want to examine it, wouldn't look at it. Unbidden, her subconscious began to weave a story from all the threads she had picked up with her fingers but refused to knit together.

Orla waited for Nick to come home. In the shadowed living room, she pushed her knees up under her chin on the sofa and listened to the sea through the windows, away down over the cliff edge.

When he finally came through the front door, a mess of bags and suit jackets and old Thermos cups collected from the car, Orla came out to meet him.

"Hi, sweetheart. Kids in bed?" He sat on the bottom stair and prized off his shoes.

"Yes, ages ago. You're late."

"I know. I'm sorry." He handed her his keys and tie.

In the kitchen, she retrieved a bowl of salad from the fridge and handed him a fork and a beer. "I'm glad you're home. I don't much like being here on my own."

"What?" Nick was tired, only half-listening.

Orla hesitated. "I'm not sure about this. About the house, about being here."

"What? Where's this coming from?"

"I've been feeling it for a while—since Christmas, really. This house, it's too much for me."

"Too much?"

"Too big. Or—not that. It's not the space, I don't think. It's the feeling. I just don't feel quite right here. And I keep finding all that shite." He knew about the shoe, but was largely un-moved when she'd shown him.

"Orla, it's a really old house. There's bound to be all sorts of stuff knocking around, hidden away. You know that."

"I don't feel right here. Don't you feel it, too?"

"No," said Nick, and touched his fingers to his mouth. He paused for a moment and said, again, "No. I like it here."

"Do you? Actually? Because it seems like you go to fair lengths to stay away."

Nick put his fork down on the table and looked at her; she avoided his eyes and stared out toward the dark garden. "Look, I get it. It is big, and it's old. I'm sure you hear things, but it's nothing out of the ordinary. You should be used to it, right? You grew up in an old house." He leaned back in his chair.

Her home in Ireland—her parents' leaden house—was an ancient farmhouse with stone walls two feet thick and win-dows that shivered in their frames and decor that had barely changed since it was built. But that house was heavy and plodding and unchanging. The Reeve was different; it was like an infection in the blood—hot and quick and hidden, and it took you by surprise every moment. It was just like Nick, she thought, to decide that every house built before 1970 would feel exactly the same inside. He never did have any imagi-nation for things he'd never directly experienced, and who was he to preach to her now, from the safety of a childhood spent in a 1960s cube with gas heating?

He tipped the chair forward and it rocked against the tiles. "We chose this house, Orla."

"Not really. You know I didn't. I want to talk about moving."

Nick sighed. "There'd be a penalty to pay on the mortgage;

it's too soon. We can't afford it, Orla, honestly. We'd lose a lot."
He swallowed another mouthful and said, "Are you really that
unhappy here? Is it really that bad?"

He expected her to adjust in return for this idyll that he'd
gifted her. Imagine—having to learn to love Paradise. Nick
said he adored the house and the wildness of the garden and
the stinging air. But he didn't have to be here all the time and
he could choose to leave—that was the difference.

Nick finished his supper—they sat together in fraught
silence—and when he left the table to take a shower upstairs,
Orla poured another glass of wine and dialed Helen's number.

"Orla?"

"Helen! Hi!"

"How are you?"

"I'm all right. I just wanted—I wanted to see if you'd found
anything. About the house, you know."

The sound of paper rustling. "Actually, I have. It was just a
quick scan, really, of the records we have access to. Land Regis-
try, a few things from the county council archive, the usual."

Orla closed her eyes. "And?"

"It's been sold a lot, but nothing really unusual there. A few
deaths. Was that the kind of thing you were after?"

"I don't know. I suppose so. Maybe."

"Orla, that's nothing out of the ordinary. You know that,
don't you? In a house that old?" Helen's voice was gentle.

"Tell me, Helen."

"Nothing horrific, if that's what you're worrying about. No
unsolved murders." Helen laughed. "When the house was being built, a laborer's son was caught under a beam that fell.
Took both legs clean off, he died of an infection. He was only
twelve. Very sad, but I imagine that kind of thing was pretty
common back then."

Orla heard pages turning.

"The next one was at the turn of the last century—a little girl. A drowning accident, in the pond. I think you said it's not there now? So, nothing to worry about on that front."

"I know about that one. About the little girl, I mean."

Helen said, "Right, okay. Here we go. Next death was back in the seventies—a male child."

"A child? Another child?" A long pause. "Helen?"

"Sorry, just finding the right page. Yes, a child. But then another death, too, same time. An adult woman. Drowned—accidental, according to the cert. They moved away not long after."

"Shouldn't they have told us this when we bought the house?"

"Not really, Orla. It was a long time ago. And it's not like it was a murder or anything, just normal life. Sad, but normal. Did you really think, in a house that old, that there wouldn't be a few of these?"

"I never really thought about it. You know, until. Until it was happening."

"That's all I could find, really. There's been nothing since. People don't stay for long, it looks like, and the previous owners were adults, no children. They moved out when the husband went into a home. But that's all, Orla. It's what you already knew. And it doesn't seem like an unusual history, honestly."

Orla put a hand over her eyes; the phone against her cheek was wet with tears. "I don't know what to do."

"Don't cry, Orla, please. Have you spoken to Nick?"

"No. God, no. Not about this. He'd think I'd lost it."

"I really do think it's fine. There's nothing out of the ordinary that I can find in any of the searches. Maybe you just need a break? Are you all right, Orla?"

"Fine. Fine." She thought to herself, *You're a liar, Orla McGrath.*

She considered their old house in Bristol, and those last few weeks before they'd arrived. They seemed like different people to her, now. A different family, utterly unconnected to their present selves. Nick had decided that they would all be happy here, but she hadn't been unhappy in Bristol. Neither had he, she thought. He'd never stopped to ask, and she'd resolved a long time ago not to let that little detail fester, but here it was again, a splinter of resentment trapped beneath calloused skin.

Orla wished she hadn't spoken to Helen, she wished she'd never brought it up. Those nights spent wanting to know more, thinking that it would help her understand—how foolish it seemed now. So easy for Helen to dismiss, but impossible for Orla to forget. All of it coalesced into a rancid fear: the nasty little objects that kept turning up, the awful incident at Christmas.

And so the joy she had always felt in solitude, in the spacious luxury of being alone with her own mind, was lost in the thin current of anxiety that seemed to run through everything she did. A black crevasse of unease that opened up a little more with each day that passed.

13

1976

———

DOT ARRIVED EARLIER THAN SHE usually did on a Friday, just after ten, with a large plastic tub full of strawberries under one arm and a carton of a dozen eggs under the other. The weather was glorious, fine and warm, and the breeze coming in off the sea was gentle and fresh. A few fishing boats glinted on the bay, red and cheerful against the water. The garden thrummed with bees.

Lydia, usually up so early, had lain awake all night and only slid into sleep when the light crept into the attic. She'd sat up in bed, waiting for footsteps on the stairs that never came. Over and over, she pictured the feet on the landing, the swing of the bathroom door. At nine o'clock, Sara came to rouse her, irritated that Lydia had missed breakfast with the children.

"Are you unwell?" Sara stood in the doorway, silhouetted against the bright morning.

"Sorry, Sara. I'm really sorry. I didn't sleep—" Lydia struggled upright, but Sara was already away down the stairs.

Sara had gone to every floor of the house and opened all the windows, even made Philip take off his jumper. Sara was like that; she would look at the children and declare them too hot or too cold depending on her own temperature. She never listened when they told her that they were *perfectly fine, actually.*

Exhausted, Lydia worked through the morning to tidy up after the twins and to amuse Philip, who hadn't slept well, either, and clung to her and complained. She quashed a brief resentment when Sara appeared for lunch with Owen on her hip and declared herself officially "on holiday" for the weekend. "What's the point in being here if I can't enjoy it with the children?" She kicked off her sandals and stretched her legs out on a patio chair, face half-hidden by an enormous pair of tortoiseshell sunglasses with twisted gold arms. A nice little relic of her London days, they made Sara's country outfit look even more drab. Owen wriggled on her lap and shouted cheerful nonsense. "Might do some baking with them; haven't done that for a while."

"Sounds like a nice plan, Mrs. Robinson. Let me know if you need more eggs." Dot set a plate of sliced ham on the patio table.

But when Lydia went to fetch her, later in the afternoon, Sara looked up from a ledger and took off her glasses to rub her eyes and shook her head.

"Sorry, tell the children I'm sorry. Not today. Too much to do, you know how it is. I'll be up all night with it."

"Again? You've been working at night a lot, recently. I wonder if—"

"I can't just leave it, you know that. I'm responsible."

"Right." Lydia stopped in the doorway. "It's just, Philip was asking for you. I know he's missing—"

"You don't need to make me feel bad about it, Lydia. I already feel guilty enough, thanks."

"Sara, sorry, I don't mean it like that. You know I don't, I'm just saying."

"Well, don't. Don't *just say*." Sara uncapped her pen. "Can you close the door on the way out? Thanks."

Lydia rounded up the children for supper and found Philip cross-legged on his bedroom floor, doing very precise coloring inside the lines.

"Dinner in a few minutes, okay? Will you come down?"

Philip nodded, focused entirely on his pencils.

The stairs shifted under her feet, warm and slightly gritty with summer dust. Lydia paused on the first landing and eyed the bathroom. The door was ajar, the room full of yellow light, and silent. Lydia pulled the door shut.

Tabitha's room was on fire with setting sun, reflected in the honey wallpaper. Clover had chosen new paper for her room, but Tabitha loved the pattern of tiny brown birds on buttery yellow so much that Sara had allowed her to keep it, even though a few of the corners peeled and cracked.

The vast wheat field behind the house rippled softly in the sea breeze, stretching away to meet the dying sky. Lydia put her hands on the windowsill and looked out across the lawn, the pond, the oaks that shifted in the wind.

Two little girls, running, black against the blue-green of the young wheat. Only their heads and shoulders rose above the plants; Lydia thought they looked like swans, necks bobbing and feet pounding madly. They were close to the high brick wall at the end of the garden, pelting toward the house, knowing they were going to be late for supper, pushing each other to avoid last place.

Lydia watched their shining gold heads, like seals in a river, rising and falling among the wheat. She would go down and meet them.

Dot handed Lydia a gin and tonic at the doorway to the

kitchen. "Right—supper's out, Philip's laying the table. You all right? You look a bit shit, to be honest, Lids."

"No. No. Not really." Lydia took the glass and drained it. The gin helped, a little.

Dot frowned. "What?"

"Right, so last night, I was the last one up, and I went to use the phone, to call Danny—"

Dot shook her head. "Jesus, Lydia, honestly—you *know* he's not—"

"Yeah, *yeah*, I know—I do know. I don't know why I did it. I think I was lonely—everyone else was asleep and I'd been thinking about what you said, you know, why I never asked him to come? So I thought, well, maybe I should just talk to him, see where we stand.

"Anyway, I called and he didn't answer, and I felt a bit sad, but mostly sort of relieved, because I didn't really know what I was going to say. And when I hung up, I heard someone upstairs."

"You mean, like, one of the kids?"

"No, the girls were asleep. Philip, too—you know how he is. Sara was in bed. It sounded like a child, running really fast up and down the landing."

Dot rubbed her arms. "Spooky."

"I know? And then it stopped and I thought, well, I was just hearing some other sound. But when I looked up, I saw something."

"What did you see?"

"Well, nothing, really. Like a shadow. I don't know."

"Not a kid, then?"

"No, not like that. Just sort of a shape. At first."

Dot picked up the scouring pad and made a face at the threads of old meat caught in the wire. "Probably just your eyes, playing tricks. It was dark, right? You said you haven't been sleeping that well."

"But that wasn't it. After I heard the noise, I went and stood at the bottom of the stairs. And this marble came absolutely flying down—like someone had thrown it. You know the way the kids do, with the marbles? It was like that, like someone had sent it down the stairs."

"Okay, that is weird."

Lydia looked at Dot. "I know—really weird, right?"

"Yeah. But maybe the marble was already on the stairs? The girls are always leaving stuff lying around—maybe it was already up there and just fell." Dot's face was round and hopeful.

"Maybe. I mean, that would make sense. But when I went upstairs, where the marble came from, I saw—" She stopped and put the glass on the table, clumsy, and it rang out against the wood. "I saw a little kid. A child, upstairs."

Dot looked confused. "Which one?"

"Not one of ours."

"What?"

"I just saw legs, running. And I went after it and there was no one there, Dot. The kids were in bed."

Dot sat on a chair next to Lydia. "That's *horrible*."

"I know." Lydia paused and scratched at an insect bite on her shin. "Do you think I'm going mad?"

Dot laughed. "Maybe, a bit. But no, not really. I don't know what to say, though. It's a bit much."

"You know I've heard things before. Someone coming up to my room. I am frightened, Dot. I don't know what to make of any of this. Do you think I should say something to Sara?"

"What would you say?"

"I don't know. I don't know."

All through dinner, Lydia was distracted. She ignored the

twins when they asked for more bread, didn't even hear Sara ask her for the butter. Afterward, she sat with her chin on her knees and listened to the sounds of the house. Sara padding gently above, tucked away in her office. Far-off shouts of the twins outside, barefoot on the brittle grass, hunting for interesting butterflies as the night drew close. Dot hard at work over the sink, the noise of the hot water in the pipes. Lydia was listening for the minor note, the discordant sound, among the living music.

The twins hated being bathed, only rarely could Lydia convince them to submit, but Philip insisted on it daily. Mostly she didn't mind, but on an evening like this, when the air was too hot and she was too tired, too shaken by this wretched house, the thought of leaning over a tub full of steaming water and entertaining a child made her weary.

The house beyond the kitchen was dim and cool, and she stood for a moment under the stairs and enjoyed the silence. Philip's face appeared between the banisters on the first floor.

"Shall I have my bath now, Lydia? I don't want it too hot, please."

"Five minutes, duckie." She made her way slowly up the stairs and down the darkened landing toward the family bathroom, past Sara's office, door shut firmly against her own family. There, coming low and delicate through the evening: music. Very quiet, but audible in the silence of the first floor. Lydia put her head over the banister, heard only silence from below. The sound came again—*singing*—from the bathroom, from the end of the corridor.

The bathroom door was closed, shadowed. The sound was very faint, rising and falling behind the door. Lydia pressed her ear to the warm wood. A woman's voice, soft. Lydia couldn't hear all of it, only the odd word, in a voice that dipped low and slipped out of hearing and rose again so sweetly.

Blood hummed in her ears, turned her face hot. Lydia touched the door, gently, and it swung back to reveal nothing but the familiar, mundane family bathroom. Striped towels, cracked soap in a shell-shaped dish, an unruly regiment of toothbrushes jostling in a painted mug that proclaimed *Happy Easter!* in jaunty script.

The open window swayed a little in its frame, back and forth on the summer breeze. Scents of shampoo and floral soap in the air, that particular smell of damp and drying towels.

The inside of the bath was wet and the last trickle of water ran toward the drain, where it disappeared down the plughole. It carried with it a few strands of long hair, like river weeds in the departing water.

Lydia caught the hair in her hand and wound it round her fingers, held it up to the light. Not Sara's, too light. Not her own, much too dark. Not the twins', who were pale as wheat.

A few suds stuck to the side of the bath and Lydia wiped them away. She wrapped the hair in a twist of toilet paper, flushed twice to make sure it was gone, and ran her hand under the hot tap of the bath until it turned red.

Afterward, Philip waited for her in bed, damp hair parted carefully to one side and his pajama jacket buttoned neatly. He'd laid out the book he wanted her to read—a very old copy of *Paddington*, with a Christmas inscription from his parents on the flyleaf. *Paddington* came out whenever Philip was poorly, or upset, or especially tired.

"You feeling all right, duckie?" Lydia sat on the edge of the bed and touched his hair.

"Yes, thank you, Lydia. I would just like some *Paddington* today." His face was lit softly by the bedside lamp, a little refuge of light keeping the shadows of the room at bay.

"Well done on tidying up your room—it looks lovely."

Philip frowned. "I *keep* it tidy, Lydia. It's always tidy."

She laughed. "You're quite right."

"Lydia?" Philip folded his hands on top of the blanket. "Who is the other little boy?"

"What's that, love?"

"Is he from the village? The twins won't tell me."

"Is who from the village?"

Philip sighed. "The little *boy*, Lydia. The twins are with him, sometimes, in the garden. They play games and they climb trees and they leave me out."

"I don't know, Philip. I didn't know they had a friend." She searched his face and saw only glass-like honesty, bright and transparent. "When does he come?"

"He's always here. Well, outside. He won't talk to me."

A little boy—another child. Lydia had never seen another child here, but then realized that wasn't quite true. She cleared her throat to remove the tremble from her voice. "Shall I ask the girls?"

"Yes, please. It's not fair if they won't let me play. I want a friend."

He looked so sad. Darling Philip, her favorite. She tried not to let it show, but suspected the girls wouldn't care either way. He'd been undone by his father's death, a complicated grieving that reared its head at strange moments. So stoic through the funeral, and when they'd come home and Lydia put him into the bath, he laid his head on the enamel edge and wept, his little body shaking.

Sara had remarked on how quiet he'd been at the church, noted the absence of tears afterward. A pointed, reproachful comment, as if Philip was defective, or felt it less. But Sara hadn't seen him in the bath and didn't know the way he said good night to his daddy when Lydia switched off the lamp every evening. Very rarely would Sara put any of the children to bed—she removed herself from that tender time when children are half-asleep and honest and sweet. They'll say things in the dark that they'd never tell you during the day, their little hopes and triumphs and fears and worries, when their cheeks are pink and their breath is shallow and you make them feel so, so safe just by sitting on the edge of the bed with your hand on their warm hair. Lydia cherished that moment with them, especially with Philip, who was so lonely, now.

"I'm your friend, sweetheart. I'll always be your friend."

"Will you stay until I fall asleep, Lydia?"

Lydia, cold with fear, said, "Of course," and opened the book.

14

2018

———

ORLA ROCKED BRIDIE BETWEEN HER knees in the bath. Sam watched them from the wooden chair in the corner, cocooned in a towel. He'd been so quiet all evening, quieter than usual, but seemed pleased to help her with Bridie. He soaped his sister's downy hair and splashed her squashy stomach, which made her laugh. Orla shivered in the cooling water and cleaned behind Bridie's ears with a soft flannel.

Friday now, Nick returning. He'd been gentle with her recently and had even come home on Thursday last week, just like he'd promised. Sometimes, she turned to find him watching her, and she would feel as though she had his attention the way she used to when they first met. As though she was being examined.

"*I see the moon, the moon sees me, God bless the moon and God bless me. There's grace in the cottage and grace in the hall, and the grace of God is over us all.*"

She sang to her daughter and stroked her wet hair. Sam swayed on the chair and smiled, opened and closed his silent mouth along with Orla's singing.

"*I see the moon, the moon sees me . . .*"

Sam pulled his knees up under his chin and closed his eyes. Orla smiled, Bridie smacked her fat hands on the surface of the water and yelped, delighted, babbling nonsense sounds.

"Are you cold, sweetheart?"

Sam nodded.

"Hang up the towel, then, and put your pajamas on. I'll be done in a minute."

Sam slid off the chair and disappeared.

When Nick finally arrived home, he was late and tired.

"Fuck, that was such a shitty drive. Bloody tourists, honestly, I think the traffic is getting worse." He leaned against the AGA and rubbed his eyes with the heel of his hand.

Orla was so glad he was home that she'd almost wept when the car pulled up, even though it was three hours later than he'd said. "Four whole days! What luxury." She rested against his chest and pushed her nose into his shirt. He smelled so comforting, like laundry and sweat. "I hate being here on my own."

"Haven't you been going into the village?" Nick untangled himself to get a beer from the fridge.

"Not much, recently. Been so busy with the work."

"Mm, how's it going?" He yawned. She knew he was only asking to be polite, but she didn't mind; she was glad he had asked at all.

"Okay—still a lot to do. You know how I get." She recalled the early years of their marriage when she was still actively working; the accolades, the separation, the long nights where he waited for her to come to bed, fruitlessly, and fell asleep alone in the early hours of the morning. She knew he resented her, resented that she was distracted and shutting herself away to concentrate on something that wasn't him. She'd kept her maiden name, too—the name she'd built her career on—and Nick had never quite forgiven her for that.

"You should stop, if it's too much. They won't mind if you're a bit later than you said."

"I mind, though. They've got the date set for the first showing, you know I don't like to think I've let people down."

Nick unbuttoned his shirt and flung it into the washing machine. "Still, don't push yourself. It's your work, you do it on your terms." He took her cheeks in his hands and searched her face. "Are you all right? You look tired."

"I haven't been sleeping. Not well, anyway. And Sam, he's not been himself."

Nick shrugged. "Kids. You know what they're like."

"It's a lot to manage, you know. Being here with the kids all the time and trying to sort the house. It's a bigger job than we'd thought—I'm worried that it's too much for me."

"Come on, I've got faith in you."

"Nick, I'm serious. I don't know if I can cope with it all." She shook her head, frustrated. "Can we at least talk about maybe selling? Please?"

"Fuck, Orla. Really? Again? I'm too tired for this." He moved away.

Orla put her hand on his hip. "Maybe we could look, together? Something smaller?"

"I thought you wanted the space?"

"You wanted it, I was perfectly fine where we were. And you keep telling everyone how great it is here but you're hardly ever here. I don't think you like it as much as you say you do."

"I'm not here because I have to work, to pay for all of this."

"I don't believe you."

"Believe what you want, but you're just going to have to get used to it. You know we can't go, not yet. And even if we could, I don't want to. We've put too much into it. I don't want to hear this." He left the room.

When Nick came to bed, he reached out for her—intimacy as silent apology. Orla surrendered, half-asleep already and grateful for the comfort of another body beside hers, inside hers. But she felt far away from him, even as he was as close as her own shape would allow, as though she was watching them both from a distance. She heard his intake of breath, the ecstasy in that brief silence, and her own pleasure was dulled by the uncomfortable feeling of separation.

That night, Orla dreamed that she went through the whole house, room by room, touching each door and window and wall. Taking an inventory, fixing in her mind the spaces she inhabited. As if waking, the house shifted and turned under her hands. She breathed in the dust and still air, noted the width of each floorboard and the exact spots on the stairs that produced creaks. Top to bottom she went, passing her palms along picture rails and old, silken wallpaper, kneeling to touch the cool tiles of the kitchen floor.

But when she woke she was in her own bed, with Nick, and only minutes had passed since they'd fallen asleep. Orla rubbed her legs together under the duvet and felt the dust slough off the soles of her feet.

"Orla, please. I'm exhausted." Nick turned his back on her in bed and pulled a pillow over his face. Although he'd come home, he hadn't really come back, not yet. He'd begged for peace, respite from the noise of the children. But hadn't he had peace all week?

"I'll take them out, then, will I?" She touched his shoulder and he sighed.

"If you would. I'll be myself by lunchtime."

She slipped out of bed and left him in the gloom.

The sea was a dog, loud and rough. Heavy tongue lapped at the cove, white waves with cold teeth inside them nipped at the curve of the shore. It shook, sent salt sprays into the air. Sam ran ahead down the cliff path. Softer wind picked up tiny drifts of pale sand and a few seabirds hovered above where the sheer rock met the water. Bridie, who absolutely would not consent to being trapped in her carrier, took tentative footsteps between Orla's spread legs.

Occasionally, Sam returned to show his mother a good shell, or an interesting insect, and Orla noted how loose his sweater hung on his shoulders and the protruding bones of his ankles above his shoes. He'd lost weight; his appetite had waned lately, no matter how she tempted him with forbidden treats and little rewards for *just one more bite, please?*

The café was busy when they arrived, loud with tourists— no room for a quiet coffee today. Orla waved at Claude across the room and smiled at Alice as she wrapped a print in tissue paper for a customer who looked impatient. Sam tugged at his mother's hand and they left.

The beach was almost empty in the chill air. A few dead jellyfish broke the line between the sand and the sea, the color of beef broth and pancake-flat. The tide was out; forests of seaweed lay uncovered and gulls swooped low to pick at the skittering crabs exposed by the retreating water.

"Orla!" Alice came toward them across the beach, face almost obscured by an enormous red scarf, holding two paper cups and smiling broadly. Orla liked Alice, very much. She was the louder of the pair, energetic against Claude's more relaxed demeanor, with long gray hair worn in an unruly twist and a lively taste in patterned blazers.

Orla waved. "Hi!"

"We saw you, before—you didn't stay?"

Orla took the proffered cup of coffee. "You both looked so busy, we didn't want to be a nuisance."

Alice laughed. "Never! You never are. Claude missed you." This last comment was directed at Sam, who patted Alice's knee. "You're always welcome, you know that."

Alice took Bridie's other hand and she tottered along between them, heavy-footed and ecstatic. Sam jumped in and out of the lapping waves at the edge of the sand and found bigger stones to throw in, ones that made a satisfying thumping noise.

"You all right, love?" Alice let go of Bridie to touch Orla's hand, cold in the wind.

"Alice, Claude told me about our house. About what's happened up there, you know."

Alice closed her eyes, briefly. "He said you'd had a chat about it. It's really nothing to worry about."

"Right. It's just that there have been a few things. Bad things." She stopped, felt foolish.

"What sort of things?"

"Just—I don't know, really. At Christmas, I thought I saw something. Heard something. It looked like—Alice, it looked like another child. Not one of mine. And Sam, he hasn't been himself at all. So quiet—more so than usual, I mean. And the birds—I told Claude about the birds."

Alice frowned. "I heard about that. Nasty."

Orla nodded. "Isn't it? It's as if the house attracts them. Like a magnet. I know how that sounds."

"Honestly, Orla? I think you're just alone up there an awful lot. It's such an old house, and it's not been taken care of. Bad plumbing, old beams. You know how it is." Alice sounded so kind, so concerned, that Orla wanted to cry.

"I know about the children, the ones who died. I thought that maybe—" And she stopped, because it sounded so mad, so absurd, and she laughed.

Alice laughed, too. "What, Orla? Ghosts?"

"Honestly, Alice, I don't even know. I don't know what I'm trying to say."

"That's nothing, it's just history. Claude has his own ideas, you know that. He's more willing than me to entertain the odd notion about things left over. But you know it's not real. You're fine. Sam's fine." They watched him dance at the edge of the waves. "There's the showing—that'll be great. I know how hard you've been working to get finished, it'll be done soon and you can take a break."

Orla knelt to adjust Bridie's coat and looked up at Alice. "I told Nick that I wanted to move."

"Surely not? That would be such a shame, you've only just arrived!" Alice seemed surprised, and not a little disappointed in her friend.

"Alice, honestly. It's too much. I can't—I can't manage."

Alice put her hand out to touch Orla's face. "Orla, love—"

Orla, so used to turning inward for her own comfort, unburdened herself with desperation. "But Nick said we can't go, not yet. Financial, apparently. And anyway, he wants us to be here. So I'm stuck." She smiled, but it was tight and sharp across her face and the edges of her mouth cut into her cheeks. A brittle smile, precarious and breakable.

In the kitchen, Orla stripped Sam in front of the heat of the AGA. His clothes were crusted with sand and seawater, hands and face cold to the touch and streaked with grime.

"Disgusting, filthy! Horrible child!" She tickled him to make him smile. Bridie, delighted, squealed from her high chair.

Nick appeared from the sitting room, looking rumpled but happier after his lie-in. "Nice time?"

"Lovely—we saw Alice. Went to the beach."

He looked confused. "When did you get back?"

"Just now, a couple of minutes ago."

"You didn't come back then leave again?"

Orla bent to fling Sam's clothes into the washing machine. "No, we've been out for a while. Why?"

"I thought I heard you come in. Talking." He shook his head. "Can't have been."

"Who was it then?" He turned away and opened the fridge door. "Nick?"

"Nothing, Orla. I was half-asleep." He shook his head. "A dream."

The family ate dinner together with the news on the radio, soothing, in the background. The evenings were lengthening out, dying a little slower, and Orla was grateful. The last of the day turned rosy in the kitchen window as she fed the baby and nudged Sam to finish his green beans, while he stared out at the garden. He'd been out there all afternoon, down among the old trees, while Nick shoveled old gravel from the driveway into rubble sacks to make ready for the new paving that Toby had agreed to lay for extra cash.

"Right then, my darling—bedtime."

Sam pulled a face and held out his hands—*Not yet, Mummy? Just a bit longer?*

"We can have a story. Would you like that?"

Nodding, pleased—*Yes!*

"You put your pajamas on and I'll put Bridie down—all right?"

She followed Sam up the stairs with an instruction to brush

his teeth, please. Bridie wriggled in her arms, overtired and fighting sleep. When Bridie was changed and swaddled and drowsy, Orla sat in the squashy armchair and held her baby against her body. She appreciated Bridie more as Sam continued to grow; her daughter demanded less of her as Sam demanded more; it was a relief not to be quite so needed. With Bridie, she failed a little less.

When Bridie was asleep, Orla tried the handle of the door into the passageway. She touched the handle, tentative, and noted how cold the metal was under her hand. She twisted hard, but it wouldn't open. Obstinate, the door remained locked.

She kicked off her jeans and pulled on a pair of pajama trousers, ready to read to Sam, who was listening to a children's tape in his bedroom on an old, yellow cassette player handed down from Eva. It was a tune she didn't recognize; low and repetitive, it sounded more like speaking than singing.

On the landing, she stood to listen. The house was very still; night arrived through the tall windows and velvet shadows grew along the stairs, behind the doors. The hallway sank and receded. The central heating wound down and the radiators hummed and ticked as they cooled, and the door to the nursery moved ever so gently in its frame, rocked by the draft that came down the chimney.

Over the top of the tape, above the strange singing, Orla heard Sam's voice. Changed now, a little deeper, but she knew it was him. He sang in time with the music, leaving pauses that made it sound like a conversation.

She moved closer to his door, her breath so shallow that she began to feel light-headed.

The words were unintelligible, a choir of monotonous hissing, voices rising and falling, singing what sounded like a round—each verse beginning over the top of the previous one

in a continuous cycle. Sam returned the lines at regular intervals. The voices made no sense, the words slipped in and out of
one another like currents in a river.

Orla realized she was sweating, her palms on the bedroom
door wet against the wood.

Sam knelt on the floor with his back to the doorway, facing the window out to the back garden. His hands were on his
knees, head tilted to the side. His shoulders rose and fell in time
with the music—Orla saw the muscles of his back working as
he sang. His voice was low and hoarse, he hadn't spoken for so
long, and Orla imagined the tendons and muscles of his throat
stiff as dried fish, sinewy and lean.

She stepped closer to hear.

". . . *The bridge was broken and they fell in* . . ."

Orla cried out, Sam turned, his mouth snapped shut. The
music stopped, abrupt.

"Sam—was that you? What were you singing?"

He shook his head and put out his arms to be lifted, like a
baby. Orla stared down at him.

"Sam, what were you singing?"

Sam shrugged. *Nothing.*

Orla pulled her son close and held him so tight that she felt
him struggle, but she didn't let go. Her fingers twisted in the
collar of his pajamas, her breath came short and shallow, and
soon Sam's hair was wet with her tears.

Outside, the wind rattled the tops of the trees and shook
loose a couple of tiles from the roof. The garden writhed and
shuddered and surrendered to the encroaching night and re-
linquished the house to the dark.

Blooming

—

Hush thee, my babby,
Lie still with thy daddy,
Thy mammy has gone to the mill,
To grind thee some wheat,
To make thee some meat,
And so, my dear babby, lie still.

English nursery rhyme, traditional

15

2018

———

"THESE ARE REALLY SOMETHING, ORLA." Claude considered the three largest pieces propped against the counter of the gallery. "Beautiful—just beautiful. And so different to your previous work, no? Much darker."

Orla nodded. "It wasn't intentional—it just sort of happened. I try not to overthink the color, I use what feels right, but these are harsher than I'd realized. I like it, though—don't you?"

"Oh, indeed. They're striking—quite remarkable."

Alice handed Orla a mug of tea. "Almost fifty sent RSVPs. I don't expect all of them, but that should be plenty for a good show. Nice to get your name back out there."

The first showing was always for the industry types—the gallery owners and private buyers—and Orla was eager to try on this part again: Orla the Artist. Her burgeoning career had taken a left-swerve she'd never envisioned when she met Nick, and sometimes she thought, *What if, what if*. What if she'd met him later, or never at all.

There were times it made her queasy how swift the sea-change of her mind could be, sliding from firm fixity in her life as it *is* to a delicate treading on the skin-surface of something else, just out of reach, something that *might be*, were she to turn from the sink, or the child, and take the path out of the front door away down to the road. The abundance of possibilities evoked something like arousal; the ways in which her future could change spread themselves out beside her, trailing veins of lifeblood to be gulped and snatched at.

And then, as quickly as it came, the feeling would ebb and she would return to herself and turn off the tap, or wipe Sam's face, and of course her future was as set as her past, and she would chide herself for being so foolish as to ever have thought otherwise, even if it was only for a moment.

Today was hanging day: Alice had rehung everything else in the gallery to give Orla's pieces prominence at the front and on the largest wall. Orla left the children with Nick (a decision she was oddly unsettled about), and Toby brought her down in his Defender, full of feed sacks and old tennis balls furred with dog hair. Now, he made a face at Claude's strange coffee and kicked open the stepladder.

"Right, what's first?"

Orla looked to Alice to decide—she was good at leaving this part to the experts. Alice, confident, gestured toward the large bay window.

"Those three there—Claude put the wires up last night, so that's good to go. I want the window studies on this wall here, in a line, like this"—she ran a pointed finger down the wall—"and then this batch here, this batch here, and we'll need extra tacks for the information plates."

Toby shook his head and pulled a drill from the bag at his feet. "Right, you'll have to go through that again at about half the speed."

Orla sat on the café side with her coffee, at a wobbly pine

table turned copper by the sun, and watched them work. When was the last time she had done anything at all without the children? She couldn't remember.

Talent was something she had always taken for granted—although she worked at it—and the forced hiatus imposed by motherhood had removed a facet of her essential self. Her art was a conversation, it was the reciprocal method by which she made herself whole: she painted to fill the spaces inside and outside herself. The process of it took from her and restored her also; stepping away from that vital renewal had left her reduced. These paintings—this show—would rebalance her most fundamental obligations; too long had she been only a mother.

By the time she left the gallery, each piece was in place and Claude had swept up. Toby packed away his tools and Orla and Alice stood side by side and watched the seascapes sway, so gently, on their wires.

"They really are something. You'll have a lot of interest."

"Have I reentered the art world with enough of a splash, then," Orla joked.

"I'm serious, I've got my little red stickers ready to go." The older woman touched Orla's arm. "They're wonderful, really. So vivid. A bit frightening, actually."

"I never set out for that. It happened along the way—it's the house, I think."

Orla thought about her paintings and the frightening, eerie splendor of them. How to explain that the house seemed to color her paints with black and blue and how the unease she felt—the constant, low unease—came right out of her fingertips and moaned into the canvas? How easily it had come, the pounding inspiration. What sort of bargain might she have struck without even knowing it?

"How are you feeling about it, now?" Alice asked. "The house? Still thinking about moving?"

Orla shrugged. "I suppose. Nick really doesn't want to."

"I have something for you. Just small, to mark the occasion." Alice put her hand into the pocket of her blazer and pulled out a crude sort of necklace—a lone piece of ceramic on a long leather loop.

"Alice, it's gorgeous. Where did you get it?" Orla saw that what she had mistaken for porcelain was in fact a polished stone, no bigger than a large coin and shaped a little like a halved pear, with a hole in the middle. It shone prettily in colors of jade and navy.

Alice tucked a strand of Orla's hair behind her ear and hung the necklace carefully round her neck, where it came to rest on the flat of her breastbone. The stone was cool to the touch, the leather new and fragrant.

"I made it for you. It's a hag stone. Sometimes they're called witch stones, or adder stones. But my mother always called them hag stones. Like an amulet—old magic. Any stone with a natural hole, that's a hag stone. Mostly sea stones, or river stones. I found this one down on the beach the other week, after low tide. Lovely colors, aren't they?" Alice smiled. "Apparently, if you look through the hole, you can see things that aren't there. I've never seen anything, though, and I've looked plenty of times. People used to think they could ward off the dead, heal the sick—that they could protect against curses. Hag stones come from the water, and spells don't work on moving water."

"Do you think I need protecting, Alice?"

Alice touched the stone and stroked her fingers along the leather where it lay against Orla's bare skin. "Not like that, no. But there's power in knowing that you have friends here, that you aren't alone. I thought this might be a reminder for you, when you feel like you want to leave. That there's a life here for you."

Orla reached for her friend's hand. "Thank you, Alice. Really—thank you."

Nick had come home from Bristol a few days early especially for the showing, and Orla made an effort to show her gratitude, even though he reassured her that he didn't mind, *really, he didn't mind.*

He'd helped her pick an outfit for the evening, shaking his head among the heap of rejected clothes on their bed.

"You'll look great whatever you wear, I can't even believe you have this many clothes! So that's where my money's going." The joke carried a measure of accusation.

"You don't want people thinking you've got some baggy old woman for a wife, do you? I can't remember the last time I wore something that wasn't jeans, or covered in porridge. Come on, what about this one?" She held up a long silver dress, satin and backless. When she tried it on, she saw how much weight she'd lost. Alice's hag stone lay heavy on her chest, the blues in it flashed against the mercury wave of the dress.

"Beautiful. Honestly, it's perfect. Can we stop now?" He put a hand to his brow in mock exhaustion.

Nick had been strangely unmoved when she'd told him that she'd heard Sam speaking, that she'd heard him singing, even when she appeared downstairs, rattled and with tears fresh on her face. He didn't seem particularly surprised that their son had finally started to use his voice. Of the two of them, Nick was the one so keen for Sam to return to "normal"—Orla had hoped that Nick would seize the opportunity to investigate a little further.

"You don't think it's odd, then? That I heard him speaking and he pretended like it was nothing, like it hadn't happened?" She stabbed an earring at her lobe and missed the hole.

"Are you sure it was even him?"

"I swear it was him—I promise, Nick."

"Don't be upset, sweetheart. I thought you said it was a tape?"

"I didn't say that, I said he was singing along with a tape."

"Well, which tape?"

"What?"

Nick stretched out on the bed and folded his hands behind his head. "If we have the tape, we can play it and you can see if what you heard was actually Sam, or if it was just part of the soundtrack—right?"

Orla felt tripped up. She hadn't even looked for a tape. The music had stopped when she came into the room and she hadn't really thought about it since. Only about Sam's low, hoarse singing and his flat refusal to speak again.

"Good point. I'll look for it."

"Look, I'd be the first to be thrilled if he was talking again. You know I think it's gone on long enough." Nick stood to hunt in Orla's jewelry box. "Are my cuff links in here?"

"You know what the psychiatrist said—"

"I know—he'll talk when he's ready. What if he's never ready?"

Orla worried at her earrings. "He'll grow out of it, that's what they all said."

"Got them." Nick adjusted his sleeves in the mirror. "It's been almost a year and not a bloody word. What if he doesn't grow out of it?"

"He has to, he will."

"I suppose school will help. That's something to look forward to."

"I don't know. I wonder, should we hold him back a year?"

"Why would we do that?"

"Maybe this September is too soon. I just worry so much." Orla put her hand across her eyes.

"You can't coddle him forever."

"I'm not coddling him. He's not even five yet, Nick, he's still a little boy. We'll make it worse if we push him, if we make him feel bad about it."

Nick picked up her shoes by their delicate straps and held them out. "Come on. We'll fight about this another time."

In Sam's room, she made sure he was asleep and knelt in front of his bookshelves to rifle through the rows of children's tapes that were Nick's as a child. "Nellie the Elephant," various storybooks on audio, music from *Fireman Sam*. Nothing she didn't recognize, nothing in any other language. She popped the deck out of the plastic cassette player. Empty.

Outside, she heard Nick start the car.

Orla stood on the landing in her silver dress, in the hushed grandeur of her house, and considered the nature of silence. How quietness came about, what it meant for a place to be perfectly mute. Silence meant stillness, emptiness. It was the opposite of presence, surely? Silence was born of absence.

The quality of this silence—here, inside this house—was not empty. Not at all—The Reeve spoke to her. It had caught her in a conversation on the first day she ever came here, and only now did Orla understand that she had been communicating in turn all this time, without even knowing it. The house asked and Orla answered—how much of her own energy and blood and care had she put back into this house? She imagined a helpless, hapless blackbird mother feeding a giant, greedy cuckoo hatchling. Never full, never satisfied.

Eva, thrilled to be asked to babysit, sent them off from the house with a wave and encouraging words.

"Right, okay, got all your bits?" Nick tugged Orla's coat tighter round her and buttoned it up to her chin.

Orla shivered inside the car. She felt anxious and excited and slightly queasy. She knew Alice had invited a few press— no one of any real importance, just a couple of art correspondents for the local lifestyle magazines. But there were some gallery reps coming, too, and Howard, the manager from her old gallery up in Bristol. She wanted a drink, very badly.

The gallery was bright and hot and the windows had completely steamed up. Claude went over every few minutes with a cloth to wipe down the big bay window, so that the paintings could be seen from the outside.

Alice handed Orla a cold glass of cava. "No one here yet, but it's only half seven. You know they'll all be tastefully late." She touched the hag stone. "Suits the dress."

"What time is kickoff, officially?" Nick drained his glass and reached for another.

"Eight—not long to go."

Orla left the others and stood alone to study her work in silence. The cava helped her relax, cold in her throat and then hot along the muscles of her shoulders. The pieces looked so different under the halogen spotlights. Some of the depth was lost, some of the dreamlike fascination she'd worked under while she created them. In here, they looked ordinary.

By nine o'clock, pretty much everyone had arrived and Orla was on her fifth glass of cava. The gallery was unbearably warm and Nick shoved a couple of the leaflets that Claude kept in the café, about the mining museum and nature walks, under the front door to wedge it open.

Orla had lost track entirely of who she had already spoken to—every face blurred together and every compliment sounded the same. And how thick they came, all those kind words. All the admiration she had hoped for, all the praise and interest.

"I wanted to buy it, you know, but this miserable old shit beat me to it!" Howard caught her by the arm and waved his glass at one of the magazine people. The other man laughed and stuck up his middle finger.

"I'll paint you another one—sure, I'll paint you twelve!" Orla laughed, made generous by the wine, and Howard flung his arm round her shoulders.

"Good girl, bloody well done!" Howard kissed her face. He smelled of booze and cigarettes and sweat and she ducked under his arm to find Nick.

By eleven o'clock, every piece had a little red dot on the information panel and Alice was delightfully drunk.

"Every single one—every single one! You've got the magic touch; these are *magic* paintings." Alice wagged her finger in Orla's face.

Orla, no more sober herself, basked. "I could go full-time again, you know, Sam's almost in school. Do it properly." She stumbled and caught Alice's shoulder.

"You should—you *should*. Yes!" Alice swiped two more glasses from Claude's tray as he passed by.

No one seemed to want to go home. Every guest who had arrived in the early evening was still here, several ties hung off the counter in the café and Nick had pushed all the tables up against the wall to create a small and crowded dance floor. Mellow jazz had been replaced with 1980s hits and Howard was embarrassing himself in the middle of it all. Nick licked up the attention, bellowing about his talented wife.

Orla swayed under the heat of the spotlights. She'd taken off her shoes—no idea where they were now—and turned away from the party writhing on the other side of the room.

The gallery side was empty, littered with bags and coats and smudged glasses. She took a half-full bottle of cava from an abandoned tray and made her way over to her paintings in the window; the wine was tepid and nearly flat, but she drank it anyway.

The seascapes were the real hit of the evening and had sold very quickly. Orla had been pulled over to meet an unknown couple from London, clearly wealthy, who had taken them immediately at list price. She was grateful, of course, if a little resentful that her work would be hung in private, in a home that was likely empty for most of the week. Her seas wanted to be seen, they wanted to be swam in and swallowed.

Orla moved in front of the canvases, suspended on slender wires, and put her fingers against the paint. She closed her eyes and touched her forehead to the canvas, splayed her fingers wide and rubbed her palm against the rough surface. She took another drink from the bottle, nearly empty now, and pushed the sweaty hair from her face.

On an impulse, she lifted the hag stone on its leather loop to her eye. The world narrowed and stretched, contained by its blue-black depths. Her roving, blinkered eye caught a quick movement over by the main wall. Almost invisible, a minute interruption of her limited vision. And then, as if a hot mouth was right up against her ear, a shrill whisper of unintelligible sounds. Orla turned too quickly and dropped the bottle, which exploded on the floor. It went unheard beneath the thumping music. The necklace fell against her chest. Something had moved in the largest landscape. The brown field, the grim sky, and two small figures running across the winter-hard furrows, small as children. Impossible—Orla stepped forward onto shattered glass and felt only the dullest sort of pain when the broken neck of the bottle rolled under her foot and sliced her sole open from toe to arch.

With the hag stone pressed to her eye socket, she knelt in front of the canvas and scrabbled at it with her nails; great flakes of paint came away under her fingers as she dug to root out the source of the infection. *Something* was trapped inside, under the layers of oil and lacquer, a wrong thing that had crept in and shouldn't be there.

"Orla, Jesus!" Nick grabbed her arms—the bruises would stay for weeks—and pulled her backward, away from the wall. She fell and hit her tailbone on the floor, and saw her own dark blood mixed with the spilled cava.

"Claude, Claude, get the first-aid kit—shit—" Alice was shouting over the music, Claude didn't move; he stared at Orla, white.

"Someone turn off that fucking music," Nick roared over his shoulder. The room fell quiet, all eyes turned toward Orla, bleeding on the floor, and Nick, furious, holding her leg at an angle. The hem of her silver dress was heavy with blood and wine. Nick's hands slipped as he tried to close the gash in her foot.

"Right, okay, we've had a bit of an accident, it's all right, though, thank you for coming, we'll be in touch about the sales, thank you—out, out." Alice was babbling, pushing people toward the doors and sweeping up handbags and jackets. Howard tried to wave to Orla—she watched him leave behind the rich London couple, who looked ill.

Claude crouched next to them with a green-plastic first-aid box. Nick snatched a thick wad of gauze and pressed it against her sole.

"I saw something—in there." Orla pointed to the landscape, to the gouge she'd made in the barren field.

"What?" Claude rubbed a hand across his eyes.

Orla waved her hand, impatient. "In there, in the painting, there was a person in the field. Two persons. Little people." Her head rolled back and she almost vomited.

"Where, Orla? Show me?" Claude knelt in front of the painting and took it from the wall. He moved his hands over the paint, searching. "I can't see anything." Blood pooled along the edges of the dismembered canvas. He looked at Nick in distress.

"Orla, what the fuck. You're drunk, stop it." Nick signaled to Alice to fetch their coats.

"I'm serious, I *saw* it—Claude, you have to look, underneath the paint—" Orla reached out a hand to Claude. Nick stood and swung her up into his arms to carry her out; Orla writhed against his chest, dripping blood from her dress, and turned to the few guests who remained, standing silent and shocked. "Please, don't sell that one, it's wrong, I've made it wrong— please, *please!*"

16

1976

——

IT STARTED WHEN PHILIP WOULDN'T get out of bed. Lydia didn't realize until later that it was because he couldn't.

"Come on, everyone else is up. Lazy bones." She reached under the covers to tickle him and felt his sodden pajamas, the hot skin of his back. Philip muttered something and pulled his knees up to his chest, facing the wall.

"Philip, come on. You're much too hot under there, time to get up."

"No, thank you." He was still caught in sleep, eyes closed.

"I shan't tell you again."

He sighed. "My throat hurts. And my head."

Lydia put her palm to his forehead, flushed and too warm. "Your throat?"

"It's scratchy. I want to go to sleep."

In the family bathroom, Lydia pulled the medicine box from the Formica cabinet mounted above the enormous, clanking radiator. She rummaged among the sticking plasters and aspirin packets for the thermometer, bulky and sinister inside its beige plastic case.

Lydia snapped the case shut and looked at the bath, the dry

enamel, and the slightly rusted chain of the plug. No trickling water, no distant sound of water draining. The room was quiet. She hadn't heard the voice again, although she had listened out for it. Something would have to be done, someone needed to know what was happening to them here in this house. She made a list in her head—the sounds, the marble, the woman. The singing, the inexplicable running feet. And the time was coming to tell someone (who? *Anyone*), but this must be dealt with first, and then she could think.

She held the thermometer out to Philip. "Right, just sit up for a minute, my love. I'll take your temperature and then I'll bring you some barley water, okay?"

Philip opened his mouth obediently, drowsy and pink. Lydia stroked his damp hair. The color in his face alarmed her: high bright spots of pure red along his cheekbones and under his eyes. When she pulled the thermometer from his mouth and saw that the mercury rested against the tiny black numbers saying *100*, she shook it vigorously and went to find Sara.

"Sara? Sorry—I think Philip is poorly. I think he's quite poorly." Sara looked up from feeding mashed banana to Owen on the wicker chairs in the orangery, still in her own pajamas.

"Like a cold?"

Lydia gestured toward the hallway, impatient. "No, not like a cold. Can you come, please? I'll take Owen."

Sara handed her the baby and Lydia followed her up the beautiful staircase, shining in the bright summer sun.

Philip had fallen asleep again, sitting upright against his pillows. The curtains were closed still, which made the room feel like a sick bay, but it seemed wrong, somehow, to open them. Lydia stood in the doorway with the baby in her arms.

Sara put a hand to her son's forehead. "Did you take his temperature?"

"Yes—one hundred exactly."

"Oh."

"That's why I came to get you."

"No, that's the right thing. Doctor time." And Sara went off to telephone the surgery in the village.

Lydia called to Philip across the shadows of the bedroom. "Do you want anything, my love?"

No answer; Philip slept on.

The doctor, a harried and very thin young man, who spent only a few brief moments examining the patient, advised them to keep an eye on him and telephone again if the fever rose. "Probably a summer bug, something flu-like. Loads going round at the minute. Keep the other children away from him for now, plenty of fluids, lots of sleep. One paracetamol every four hours to help with the temperature. Really, only one of you should be going in and out." He looked at the two women, who looked at each other.

"I'll do it," said Lydia.

Sara smiled. "Thanks."

The doctor didn't look back toward the house as he climbed into a rusted Morris Minor and disappeared.

"Well, he was no bloody use." Sara laughed, but Lydia heard the strain in it.

"Nothing we didn't already know, right?" Lydia tried to sound reassuring.

"Are you sure you're okay playing nursemaid?"

"Of course—and it makes sense. Don't want Owen getting it, or the girls. Much better if I do it."

"Thank you, Lydia. What would we do without you?"

Lydia could tell that Sara was relieved—she was never very good with illness. In those final, abject weeks at home with Doug, Sara pretty much came undone. She was handed the role of grieving wife, nurse, priest; compelled to listen to Doug's last ramblings, his thoughts and wishes made inexplicable by drugs and pain. He'd confessed to Sara about an affair, very early on in their marriage and never repeated, and she was obliged to offer him absolution. Sara said to Lydia that she had a feeling Doug only told her about the affair because he thought she was someone else.

Doug insisted on being cared for at home—no rancid hospice for him—and Lydia wondered if he knew what he was asking of Sara, and, if he did know, why he was punishing her.

Sara's distaste for Doug's decaying body ate away at her as she washed and fed her husband, as she held the bowls for his vomit and stripped him of stained underwear. They hired a nurse to help, and she was wonderful, but she wasn't there for the evenings or for the early mornings, when Doug was sickest. He wanted his wife, only.

Lydia watched all of this from the periphery. She held the children's hands and distracted them from this most grotesque of endings, shielded them from their mother's bitter despair and their father's selfish dissolution. Even on his deathbed Doug was in charge, and Lydia hated him for it.

She left Philip sleeping and went out through the orangery to find the twins in the garden. "Tabs! Clover!"

White legs flashed against bark as they scrambled down the monkey puzzle tree. She knew they wouldn't mind so much about Philip, they'd be happy to stay outside. They hopped about in front of her on the back patio, chafing against the notion of standing still.

"Listen, girls—I said *listen*, Clover, will you pay attention for one minute, please? Your brother isn't well, he has some sort of bug. So you're not to go into his room, is that understood?"

"Why would we want to go into Philip's room?" Clover picked at a scab on her elbow.

"I'm just telling you, don't. We don't want you catching whatever it is that he has, all right?"

Tabitha waved her hands, impatient. "*All right*, Lydia. Can we have a snack?" They pushed past her toward the kitchen.

"There's digestives in the tin, you can have two each. No more until lunchtime. And another thing—I want to hear about your friend."

"What friend?" Clover wrestled with the biscuit tin. The lid fell and clattered against the tiles.

"Philip said something about a child that comes here, that you play with. Who is it? Is that who taught you the song?"

Clover knelt to scoop up shattered biscuits. "What song?"

"Give those to me, please, the floor is dirty. The song about the devil, I heard you singing it. Where did you learn that?"

"Don't know."

"Yes, you do. Give me that—*give me that*. Disgusting. Don't eat off the floor."

Tabitha rolled her eyes. "We dreamed it."

"You dreamed the song?" Clover nodded and Lydia took the tin and replaced it on a high shelf on the dresser. "You didn't learn it from the little boy? Philip said you have a friend, that he comes here and you play in the garden."

"Philip is telling *tales*."

"No, he's not telling tales, he feels left out. Tell me about your friend, please, I need to know if there's extra children to take care of. Your mum wouldn't want you playing with strangers."

"He's not a stranger." Tabitha crammed the other half of Clover's biscuit into her mouth. "He lives here. He lives in the garden. We play hide-and-seek."

Lydia rubbed the back of her neck, tight with fear. "Well, he can't live in the garden, no one lives in the garden. He has a house somewhere."

Clover shrugged. "He says this is his house."

"What's his name?"

The twins looked at each other. "We don't know."

*

For three days, Philip lay in bed and sweated. Sara helped Lydia bring up the cushions from the stiff corduroy couch in the drawing room to make a bed on Philip's floor, and for three nights Lydia lay in the dark and listened to the breath whistling in and out of him, and the cries when he woke in the night and thought he was alone.

Philip's bedroom smelled of cut grass and hot breath and sweet child sweat. He lay very still under the covers, and Lydia set the box of paracetamol and glass of barley water down on the nightstand. He moved a little when she sat on the edge of the bed, and he put his hand out of the blanket to take hold of hers.

"My mouth hurts."

"I know, I've brought you some nice barley. That will help."

He refused to swallow the paracetamol directly, claiming that his throat had grown much too small, so she dropped the tablet into the glass and stirred with her finger until it dissolved into a gritty powder. Philip drank rapidly, and lay back down and stared up at the ceiling.

"Am I going to die, Lydia?"

"Of course not, don't be silly." It came out harsher than she intended, so startled was she by Philip's morbid query.

"I'm not silly. Daddy died."

"Your dad was very sick for a long time, it was very serious. You just have a little bug, that's all."

"I'm not poorly like Daddy was?"

She stroked his hair and pulled the blanket round him. He shivered. "Not at all, you'll be fine. I promise."

The air in the kitchen hung ripe and heavy with acrid plant smells; boiling water steamed in two vast saucepans on the stove and in the sink an armful of blowsy elderflower lay sodden. In Dot's linen apron, barefoot on the tiles, Sara rinsed the stalks under the tap. The counter was piled high with wet flowers, fat and creamy and fragrant in the sunlight pouring in from the orangery.

Sara didn't turn when Lydia entered, and barely seemed to hear her name being spoken.

"Sara? I said, have you seen the girls?"

Sara sighed, busy with her task. "No. Not for a while."

"What are you doing?"

"I'm making tea. For Philip."

"Tea?"

Sara turned off the tap and shook her fingers over the sink. "You sound a fool, Lydia. Repeating after me like that, like a parrot. Yes, *tea*."

"What kind of tea?"

"*What kind of tea?*" Sara laughed, but it was short and brittle. "What kind of tea does it look like? Elderflower."

"Right. Did Dot help you?" Lydia examined the heap of plants and prodded at the pile. The blossom had an oddly green tinge in the tiny whorls of white, and purple spots punctuated the long stems.

"No, why would she? I picked it myself—I'm perfectly capable of boiling some flowers in water, Lydia. I thought it would help his throat. I know the children like Dot's elderflower cordial." The muscles in Sara's arms slid beneath pale skin as she stirred the flowers into the hot water, and a bitter cloud rose and filled the kitchen. "Should I put some sugar in, do you think?" She wrinkled her nose. "It doesn't smell very nice, does it."

"I suppose. You could ask Dot—she'd know what to do."

The saucepans remained on the stove until suppertime, when Sara peered into the pale-green liquid and declared it *perfect*. She upended a snowfall of sugar from its paper packet and closed the plate cover. Lydia, who was laying the table, disliked the abstract look on Sara's face as she hunted in the dresser for a suitable mug.

"Can we have some, Mummy?" Tabitha pushed her plate away and looked to Lydia, who shrugged.

"No, my darling. This is for your brother because he is poorly."

Tabitha frowned, but Clover didn't seem too put out. "It smells like the bathroom. I don't want it anyway."

Although they had agreed that Lydia should be the one to nurse Philip, Sara vanished upstairs to pour her tonic down the throat of her eldest son. Nature, surely, would cure him, Lydia thought sourly. She clattered dirty plates into the sink and wished for Dot. Philip's sickness seemed to have sparked something in Sara, some poisoned memory of caring for Doug, and it had made her difficult and distracted. Lydia knew it was caused only by fear, but it remained unpleasant. The girls stayed out of her way.

"Ungrateful."

Lydia looked up, surprised. Sara had reappeared silently in the kitchen, and tipped the mug of tea straight into the sink, across Lydia's outstretched hand holding forks under the tap.

"Wouldn't even touch it. Said it smelled horrid—horrid!"

"I'm sure he didn't mean—"

But her voice followed Sara out of the kitchen as she retreated back up the stairs and into her office, where the door shut with a thump. Lydia looked at the two pans of Sara's tea on the stove, the spill of leftover flowers drying on the windowsill, and sighed.

In the morning, when Dot arrived with her eggs and good cheer and Lydia could share the burden of being the only truly present adult, she recounted Sara's efforts with an edge of humor that she hadn't felt at the time.

"Doesn't sound like Sara, she hates cooking." Dot tipped half a dozen eggs into the wire basket shaped like a chicken and lifted the lid from one of the saucepans to peer in. She sniffed deeply and turned to Lydia. "Did you say this was elderflower?"

"Apparently. She brought in a huge load, there's bits of it everywhere."

"Where's the rest?"

Lydia motioned to the windowsill, where the remaining blooms had curled and shriveled overnight. Dot picked up a few of the stalks and rubbed them between her palms.

"Lydia. *Lydia.* This isn't elderflower."

"No, it is, Sara said she picked it."

"Picked it where? Where?"

Lydia took a step back. Her hip hit the countertop. "The garden, I suppose? Dot, that's elderflower, it looks exactly—"

"I know what it looks like, but it isn't. Lydia, this is hemlock. It's poisonous, really nasty stuff. *Really* nasty. Has anyone else touched this?"

"No, no, just Philip." A great weight compressed Lydia's chest.

"How much? How much did he have?"

"Almost none, I told you—Sara was so cross because he wouldn't drink it."

Dot tugged at the ends of her plaits. "Help me chuck this out."

They took a pan each, liquid slopping over the sides, and carried them out onto the patio.

"Can we just tip it out here?" Lydia nodded toward the lavender border.

"No. No, it won't be good for the plants. We'll sling it into the pond."

Lydia emptied her pan, gently, at the water's edge. Dot threw hers outward with great force, and the arc of the poison caught the sun like a bridge made of glass.

When they returned inside, Sara was open-mouthed and

red with annoyance. "What do you think you're doing? What's going on? I made that, you know."

"I know, Mrs. Robinson, and I'm sorry." Dot didn't look her employer in the eye, and took the other pan from Lydia to put them in the sink. "I know you think that was elderflower and I don't blame you at all because they do look similar. But that was hemlock—poisonous. None of you want to be eating that stuff, or drinking it, neither."

"How do you know?" Sara twisted her fingers in her cardigan, buttoned up tight despite the warmth of the morning.

"Different flowers. Different stalks, the colors and all. You can tell when you get up close. Didn't smell like elderflower either, did it."

Sara had to concede that no, it hadn't.

"Where did you get it? Surely not from the tree?"

"No, not from there. Down by the pond, there was a huge clump of it. And I saw it and thought it would be perfect. So I cut it all."

Dot shook her head. "If you want to make something for Philip, like an infusion, I can help you?"

"No," said Sara, faintly, "no, it's all right. I don't know why I thought—" She trailed off.

"Well, there you are, then. But look, no harm done, right?"

Sara looked out over the garden, into the bright morning, and a shadow of something that Lydia couldn't identify crossed her face. "No. No, I suppose not." She left them both in the kitchen; they heard her hollow steps heading back up the staircase.

Dot looked at Lydia. "You want to watch her. Something's not right there."

"I know."

On the fourth day, the thermometer said *103*, such spiteful little figures, and Sara telephoned again for the doctor. They waited, and Lydia sat with Philip on top of his quilts and rocked him while Sara stood in the doorway with her arms folded tight against her stomach. After a long moment, during which neither woman spoke, Sara left to shut herself in her office.

They hadn't mentioned the hemlock episode again—Lydia understood that Sara was embarrassed by it and therefore angry, and Sara didn't bring it up, either.

Philip talked nonsense words about the moon and a cottage and how it was *too bright now and would they all live on the moon together?* Lydia fed him more barley, and when she took the glass from his lips the liquid was pink with coils of blood, like smoke in the water. Inside his mouth, Philip's tongue was swollen scarlet and white, and blood blistered on the insides of his cheeks.

When she stripped him of his wet pajamas, she saw the livid welts all over his chest and legs—tiny red marks like nettle rash, like scarlet bites. As if someone had pinched him all over with mean little nails.

"Am I brave, Lydia?"

"So brave, my love." She wiped sweat from his hairline with her thumb.

"I want to be brave. Like how Daddy was."

"I think you're the bravest person I've ever met."

Dot appeared and gestured to Lydia. Very gently, she turned Philip over and laid him on the pillows.

Lydia stepped out onto the landing and pulled the door to behind her. The house was much too bright, and even though the front doors were open she felt suffocated in the dense, pollen-heavy air. "Everything all right?"

"Sure, sure. Everything's fine, just thought you might like some tea."

"Girls all right?"

"God, they're fine. They turn up for lunch and then bugger off again—you know how they are. Let's go outside for a bit."

Dot had picked up a lot of the slack with the twins over the last few days and Lydia was grateful. Sara was, too, and slipped an extra wedge of cash into Dot's weekly packet. She'd blushed and waved her hands when she felt the extra weight, but Sara insisted.

Blond light washed the back patio and Lydia's eyes stung. "It feels strange to be outside."

She took a seat at the picnic table and Dot handed her a mug. Too much milk and too much sugar, that was how Dot made tea, but Lydia didn't mind; it tasted like pudding.

"Yeah, I bet. Those sofa cushions don't look comfortable, either."

"My back is killing me."

Dot laughed. "That's because you're old."

"Careful, this'll be you one day."

"Don't I know it. My mum keeps asking me about Lee, you know? *Shall I book the church, Dot? Shall I fetch out all my maternity things, Dot?* She's unbearable."

"Well, should you book the church? You'd best let me know, I'll have to ask Sara for the day off." Lydia wiggled her toes against the cool stone slab under her chair.

"Christ, don't you start."

"He seems very nice. Polite."

"Freddie liked you." Dot slipped the tip of her tongue between her lips, salacious.

Lydia laughed.

Sara came out of the orangery, pale and anxious, and handed Owen to Dot. "Lydia? The doctor's here. He's up with Philip. I thought you might want to hear what he has to say."

They stood together on the landing outside Philip's bedroom to watch the doctor as he leaned over Philip and did something vague with a stethoscope. When he came out, he said, "Bathroom?" and Sara pointed down the landing. He returned carrying the hand towel, which he passed to Lydia, absentmindedly.

"Hospital time, I think. Scarlet fever."

Sara took hold of the banister. "Now?"

"Yes, now. You can follow me. I'll take him in. He needs antibiotics and a drip. He'll be fine, but it's got onto his lungs and it needs sorting. Mum only, I'm afraid." He nodded at Lydia. "If the rest of you haven't caught it yet, then you're not likely to, but it can be contagious, so best to be safe."

Sara turned to Lydia. "What shall I do?"

"I'll pack his things, clothes and so on, don't worry. You just go with Philip. I'll stay here with the rest. Don't worry, we'll be fine. You go. Go on, now." She pushed Sara toward the stairs.

Lydia undressed Philip to put him in fresh pajamas. "You're to be very brave now, all right, duckie? Just like we said. Your mum is taking you into hospital, for some different medicine. And I can't come with you, but I'll pack *Paddington*, is that okay?"

Philip sat quietly as Lydia fetched a clean pair of pajamas, eyes half-closed and marbled with fever.

"What about the little boy?"

"What's that, my love?"

"I want the little boy to come, too."

"Who's the little boy, sweetheart?" Lydia threaded one slack arm through the pajama jacket.

"You know him, Lydia. From the garden." Philip yawned and rubbed at his chest, where the rash flared against his skin. "He lives here. He lives with us."

He says this is his house.

Lydia watched the convoy leave from the tall windows—the doctor's Morris first and then Sara in her white Capri, dusted all over with pollen and sand, Philip rolled up on the back seat in his tartan blanket.

Then they were gone.

17

2018

———

ORLA CAME TO INHABIT A world that was only children—even in the old house there had been neighbors and the postman and the odd friend round for lunch. Up here, she'd go days without an adult conversation other than the occasional delayed text from Nick's mother or Helen, much too busy to visit, but concerned enough to check in sporadically. A few times a day she would stand out on the driveway and wave her phone in the air, feeling foolish but desperate for it to vibrate in her hand.

Sleep eluded her. She slept in fits and starts, no more than an hour or so at a time, and the days stretched out and she was tired—so tired, all the time. She dreamed of the house and the garden. In sleep, both were larger than they had any right to be, and she herself was diminished. Sometimes she dreamed that she, the size of a doll, was climbing the stairs, and it was like scaling Everest. Up and up she went, laboring breath, and to climb but two stairs was an unending task.

Or she might be running in that desperate, heavy way that one does in dreams, on leaden legs that take her nowhere. In her dreams she was alone in the house but not alone—the children were never there and nor was Nick, but someone else was, an unseen person Orla knew but couldn't name. And when she dreamed of the garden, she was always lost, pushing helplessly through brambles and tangled grass toward the house. But the house was never where it ought to be—she couldn't find it. The anchor to her life and to her children slipped away until she was devoured by the trees.

Her dreams left her bruised. The sleep was deep, but the further under she went, the harder the waking, the gasping swim to surface. The image that crept into her brain most often during those interminable night hours was the Fuseli painting of a squat, monkey-like demon, crouched with glee on the chest of a sleeping woman. *The Nightmare*: it had frightened Orla terribly as a child, and thrilled her, too. The possibility of a forceful, illicit visitation from another world—she loathed it and obsessed over it equally. And, in the background, the pale-eyed horse, watching.

Orla had tried to paint since the disaster of her opening, though only sporadically, and for the first time in her life she didn't know where to start. For hours, she sat in front of blank boards and empty sketch papers, with her hands in her lap, unable to quell the raging fear that she had lost something vital to herself, that something had been taken.

The hag stone remained round her neck; it was comforting to pass its solid weight back and forth through her fingers and she had taken to worrying at it with her thumb, endlessly turning and polishing the smooth stone with restless hands. A couple of times she had lifted it to her eye, tentatively, but the world remained unchanged and Orla wondered what she had really seen through it.

When she thought about that night, it was blurred by a

haze of alcohol and fear. She couldn't entirely remember what had happened, she only remembered how afraid she'd been of something she couldn't recall with much clarity.

Nick had apologized for scaring her, said he was just drunk and frightened.

"You shouted at me." Orla was reproachful, disappointed.

"I know. I'm so sorry, Orla. You were just acting so weird and there was so much blood—it was terrifying. Honestly, it was awful."

"I was frightened, too, Nick. It didn't help."

Alice and Claude had been extremely graceful about the whole thing; Orla offered to come in and help them clean up, but they insisted she shouldn't. She likely wouldn't have been much use anyway—the gash in her foot was deep and required stitches, done by a silent nurse in the surgery in the village. It had left her hobbling; only now could she put her full weight on it. The cut healed to a ragged purple line that bisected her sole.

A week later, Alice called to ask what was to be done about the ruined landscape. "I'm so sorry to have to ask, Orla—it's just that the buyer wants to know. They haven't actually paid yet, so we can just say it's no longer available. Or you could paint another—I don't know what you want to do."

"God, Alice. I don't know. What do you think?"

Alice hesitated. "Well. I don't think it can be repaired—it's pretty well done for."

Orla looked out of the window at the violet clouds that sailed across the bright sky, driven by the high wind like sheep before a barking dog. An image filtered through—the little figures, running, black and furtive in the desolate field.

"I'm sorry, Alice. I don't think I can paint another."

"I thought that might be the case—please don't worry about it. I mean it, you mustn't."

"But the buyer—"

"Don't even think about it. I'll deal with them." Alice sounded so certain, so maternal, that Orla wished for one painful second that Alice was her mother.

"Christ. They'll all think I've lost it."

"Honestly, Orla, everyone else was so drunk, I doubt they even remember what was going on. They just think you cut your foot and it was all a bit dramatic."

"I hope so. I'd hate to have hurt your reputation—you know, the gallery."

"You haven't—it's been brilliant, having your stuff. Haven't had that many people come to a showing for a while. Everything sold, that's the point."

Orla pulled out the sofa and adjusted Toby's stepladder. She wanted Sam's portrait here, in the sitting room, above the sofa. Not too intrusive, but present.

It had never come out quite as she wanted—the colors still looked odd to her eye and the proportions were still wrong. She spent weeks trying to fix it, with no further improvement, and in the end gave up, which was unlike her. But she was tired of working on it and the unfinished quality of the painting wore on her nerves. Once it was hung, she might finally accept that it was done.

Sam didn't seem too fond of his painting, either. He mostly ignored it and wasn't at all interested in the fact that it was him. It was as if he didn't recognize himself, and Orla supposed she couldn't blame him for that. It was Sam, but not Sam—a Sam doubled and altered. Now, the painted boy looked more real to her than the live one.

When the nail was in the wall, hammered deep into the soft plaster, Orla took the canvas by its lower corners and balanced it on it. She pushed the sofa back and admired the effect—the

deep colors of the portrait complemented the maroon uphol-
stery and the Turkish carpet. When she sat down, she imagined Sam watching her, surveying the room.

Orla went out onto the patio and handed Toby the folded-
up stepladder. "Thank you, Toby."

"No bother—get your job done all right?"

"Fine, all good. Tea?"

He smiled. "Love one, thank you."

Inside, Orla flicked on the kettle and watched him work.
He'd made such progress in the last weeks, as the weather
warmed further. New grass seed was down and already a scattered bloom of tiny green shoots made the lawn look bright
and promising. Today he was burning dead foliage in an old
drum over by the east wall. The air sparked with heat, ash fell
like snow. Toby fed the fire gently with old, gray wood and
bundles of yellowed ivy.

If she couldn't leave, if she couldn't take her children away,
she could at least try to keep them safe. From her dresser
drawer, she fetched the handkerchief and unwrapped that
horrible little shoe, holding it between finger and thumb as
though it was rotting before her eyes.

Outside, she handed Toby a mug of tea and opened her
palm to show him her rancid treasure.

"Thanks." He pulled his gloves off with his teeth and dropped
them onto the grass. "What's this, then?"

"The sweep found it in the nursery chimney. It's a shoe."

Toby nodded. "Yeah, bit of a thing round here."

"I hate it."

He looked surprised. "Why? They're for good luck, like a
charm."

"I know, but it doesn't feel like good luck. It feels bad, I knew
it the moment I saw it. I want to burn it."

"Mrs. McGrath, I don't know if we should—"

"Please, Toby."

He rubbed a hand through his hair and shrugged. "All right. Go on, then."

She leaned into the white smoke that twisted above the burning coils of ivy and dropped the shoe straight into the drum. It landed between two branches, stuck fast, just out of reach of the teeth of the fire. They watched it curl slowly in the heat and begin to catch.

"Thank you." Already she felt easier, as though she'd regained some control over this house and what it saw fit to deliver. The hag stone lay cool against her chest. Although the leather loop softened and warmed with the heat of her body, the stone itself seemed always to remain cold.

"No Sam today? You can tell him I've got jobs for him."

"Napping—Bridie's not sleeping much at the moment and she's waking Sam up, too. It's been a while since he's napped during the day, but it's like he just can't stay awake."

"Ouch." Toby made a face.

"I worry about him. You know, being on his own up here with just me. Although I suppose everybody worries about their children, don't they." She surprised herself, speaking so candidly to Toby like this. But hadn't he always been something of a comfort, when she was alone so much, too? "I'm worried he gets bored with just me."

"You're a great mum, Mrs. McGrath." Toby became suddenly serious, and turned away from Orla to look down the length of the garden. "The kids, they're brilliant. That's because of you. Honestly. They're lucky to have you."

Orla, who had never received such an explicit and genuine compliment for her parenting, didn't know what to say. "Thank you, Toby. Really—that's such a kind thing to say. But it's a team effort, really, I'm lucky to not have to do it on my own."

Toby handed her the mug and turned back to the fire.

The shoe was gone now, licked into nothing by the flames. "Don't you?"

Orla put the children to bed early. Poor Bridie, one of her top teeth was struggling to come through and her little face was red and swollen with irritation. Orla dosed her with Calpol and held her until she fell asleep—a terrible habit, really, but the child was inconsolable. Sam stood in the doorway to the nursery in a pair of dinosaur pajamas that were too short in the leg, and watched them.

"Do you want to come up for a cuddle? Come on, there's lots of room." Orla held out an arm and Sam climbed up. She held both of her children tight and listened to the waves out beyond the front window.

They'd been so tired, all three of them, Sam had almost nodded off into his pasta and Bridie whined with exhaustion. When Orla took off her watch to set it on the nightstand, she saw that it was only seven o'clock. She was too tired to question why on earth she felt as though it was midnight, and why even her energetic son had been so desperate to sleep.

The next morning was mercurial—bright sun came and went beneath a sky laced with heavy clouds that threatened rain, the wind got up and rattled the old windows in their shabby frames. Toby left to buy more compost and a sack of slate chips for the lavender beds and Orla was alone in her quiet studio. After a time, Bridie woke, cried, Orla was summoned: *Ma ma ma!*

She rapped a knuckle against the wall to the playroom for Sam—*shave and a haircut, no legs!* The little rhyme had tickled Sam when she first sang it and she liked knowing that she was making him smile on the other side of the wall.

Two taps came back—quiet, almost hesitant.

"Sam! Lunch! What shall we have, then? Bridie's awake!"

Three knocks, louder.

"I'm coming, Sam! You know I have to tidy up."

A shrill whistle came from the baby monitor, the volume such that Orla dropped the wet brush she was wrapping and splattered paint all over the floorboards. It sounded like a high-pitched whistle, and then she heard a woman's voice say, "Yes!" and Orla skidded out of the door and down the stairs.

She nearly fell on the landing outside the nursery, and when she opened the door she was almost savage with fear, her throat was tight and nausea roiled in her stomach. But no one was there—just Bridie in her cot, sobbing now, reaching out.

No woman, no noise. Orla rattled the door into the passage-way, but it was still locked, and she picked up Bridie and went into her own bedroom and then Sam's and then finally the guest room, but there was no one, nothing. Just her own harsh breath and Bridie crying in her arms, angry at being held much too tight and afraid of this frantic, desperate mother.

And Sam—Sam was nowhere.

In the kitchen, a few drawings lay half-finished on the table, the same brown and gray children in among green grass. Orla went to the foot of the stairs and called for him, but she knew as the words left her mouth that he wasn't in the house. She would feel it—feel *him*—if he were here.

She took Bridie out to the patio—through the orangery, warmed by translucent sun and made fragrant by two loads of laundry hung up. Outside, the wind ruffled the daffodils that hunched in clumps along the east wall and thumped against the old shed doors. "Sam?"

Bridie, slung across her mother's shoulder, shouted with joy—with recognition. She squealed and wriggled and reached out, and Orla had to catch hold of a plump leg to steady the child. Orla turned, expecting to see Sam, but, although Bridie was smiling wide, she was reaching out to an empty room.

At the bottom of the garden, where Toby had cleared so

much already and the edges of the dug-out pond shone bright in the cloudy afternoon, a little figure stood underneath the oaks. Sam, in his socks on the wet grass. He hadn't seen them, hadn't heard his mother call.

He circled the oaks slowly, looking around him all the time. At intervals, he darted behind one of the solid, mossy trunks— Orla saw his quick, dark head pop out once, twice, to look away down to the west wall. He moved his body round the trunk, slowly, staying close to the tree. And then he ran in double-quick time to the remaining thicket of yew and dogwood, flourishing now in the green space created by Toby, where he disappeared.

Orla saw that her son was playing hide-and-seek. She stepped off the patio onto the lawn.

A flicker over by the shed, right on the edge of her peripheral vision, caught her eye as it crossed the grass. Something small, no bigger than Sam, skirted the largest maple and vanished. And another, down by the oaks, down next to where Orla pictured Sam crouched on cold earth in socked feet. Nothing more than a gray shadow, but moving with purpose and intent toward Sam's hiding place.

Orla scanned the lawn for more little shadows, but there was nothing. "Sam!" She took two more steps toward the oaks and stopped. She didn't want to go any farther; she watched the yew bush with hot, acidic loathing. The tangle of maples shook, out of time with the wind, and harder, too.

There was something other than Sam down at the bottom of the garden, hiding itself in the rotted tangle. She knew now that it wasn't a fox, or a cat. How to warn Sam, how to bring him back to her? She couldn't shout—the wind was too high, he wouldn't hear her, not from all the way back at the house. Orla understood she would have to go and fetch him herself, and the realization brought a strange inertia.

She stood on the edge of the lawn with the house to her back and her invisible son somewhere out in front. To rescue him—and she didn't dwell too long on how her mind had chosen the word *rescue*—she would have to wade out there and put her arms into the trees and the long, thin vines and the decay and pull him back to the world: a forced and savage repatriation.

And around them, the unknown. The limitless, deceitful garden, the sweep of shifting, undulating lawn that made Orla feel seasick just to look at. But Sam needed her, there was no room now to recant motherhood and step back to the safety of the patio.

The ground was very soft under her feet, boggy with a week's worth of rain and cunningly slick. She couldn't leave Bridie behind, and the baby kicked against her ribs and protested. Together they moved across the grass, urged on by the feral wind that yipped and shrieked.

Flurries of browned blossom, swept from the trees by the wind and rotting in the grass, rose and fell in violence as Orla carried her daughter farther down the lawn. Clods of new soil clung to her shoes, she trampled over the delicate grass seed just beginning to take root. She looked across the garden, sickened, and waited to see something dart from behind a tree, or out from under the elderberries. But she was terribly, terribly alone. She couldn't stand the weight of the fear that hung in her chest—a dark animal—at the thought that she would have to go in among the inscrutable trees to search for her son.

And as Orla approached the yew bush, deaf to Bridie's urgent whimpers and with fear clawing, red, at her rib cage, she heard Sam clap once and call out. Her son—unequivocally. Not whispering, but *speaking*. Forming real, intelligible words with his husky, rusty voice, speaking out loud, and *excited*.

"*You found me!*"

18

1976

———

"LYDIA. LYDIA? I'M LEAVING. Back later, usual time." Sara fixed her hair in the small mirror that hung above the telephone and put her sunglasses on. This had been the routine for the past four days: Sara spent all day at Philip's bedside, with balance sheets on her lap and a stack of files at her feet. Even in terror, she couldn't bring herself to abandon her work.

Lydia followed Sara out to the car. "Shall I save some dinner?"

"No, don't worry. I'll get a sandwich at the hospital." Sara wrinkled her nose.

The car sputtered out a wave of blue smoke and sent the gravel flying as Sara spun out of the driveway. Doug had always told her off for reckless driving, but the girls loved going in the car with Sara—she drove fast and put the radio on loud.

Tabitha and Clover appeared from the side gate, bored and mutinous.

"Girls—shall we have a snack?"

They shook their heads and looked out across the front lawn and down to the sea.

Lydia wanted out of the house, too. "Beach?"

"Yes! Yes! Right now?"

"In a minute, let me pack some stuff—I have to get the baby's things."

"Can we go ahead?" They bounced on their toes, greyhounds at the starting gate.

"Absolutely not—you can wait for me and Dot. Go and get your costumes."

Sara hadn't expressly forbidden them from the beach, but Lydia suspected she might not approve if she knew. And Lydia couldn't say why, either—Sara's decisions had lately grown rather unpredictable, unburdened by logic.

They made their way down the cliff steps in the wonderful morning; Dot carried the basket and the girls carried towels and bags of fruit, and Lydia carried the baby. Summer wind whipped round their legs and filled their hair with salt and sand.

Dot handed Lydia an apple. "You all right?"

"Yeah. No. Just worried. Poor Philip." The halter strings of her bikini top pulled on her neck, dug into the flesh. She was relieved to be gone from the house—to be out of sight of it felt like a respite.

"He'll be fine. You know what Sara said: he's doing a lot better. He'll be home in no time." Dot pushed her sunglasses up from where they'd slid down her sweaty nose. "You should get some more sleep."

"It's so hot up in the attic. Makes it hard. I wake up a lot."

Dot shrugged. "Have Philip's room."

"What?"

"Until he's back—have his room. I'm sure Sara wouldn't mind. At least you'll get some sleep."

"That's actually quite a good idea." Lydia thought about the tall sash window that looked out over the sea, the cool breeze, the thick curtains to keep out the summer sun.

"I'll make the bed up for you later. I've always thought it was stupid that you got put in the attic—it's not even a proper room."

"I don't mind, usually. It was cold in winter, though."

"Of course it was fucking cold, Lids—it's the attic. She should have put the girls in together and given you a real bedroom, with actual lights and curtains. She still could."

Lydia wondered if she should have pushed harder for those things when they all first moved in. "Maybe I'll ask her about it. When Philip's better."

At the beach, they spent the day stretched out on two rough bath towels with Owen dozing beside them. Tabitha and Clover shrieked in the sea, which was only tepid on the top and still spring-cold underneath.

Owen squirmed in Lydia's arms back up the cliff path, hungry and shouting about it. The twins trailed behind, bare feet slapping wetly on the stone steps. They climbed and climbed; Lydia's breath came short, Owen weighed heavier on her hip. Even Dot fell silent as they approached the top.

As they reached the summit and followed the sandy path toward the house, Lydia lifted her chin to admire the glorious frontage, the beautiful honey stone and the abundant wisteria and the sweep of expensive gravel. Late-afternoon sun turned the two enormous vaulted windows to mercury: magnificent mirrors. And, behind the glass, on the landing above the sitting room, Lydia saw a person. Long hair, long limbs. A woman—wearing jeans, staring out at the sea. Lydia saw the pale oval of her face look toward the path and back again, and then she was gone.

"Dot?" Lydia pushed the girls ahead of her along the path. "Did you see a woman?"

Dot hitched the basket in her arms, clumsily. "What?"

"A woman, in the house just now? In the window?" Owen fussed and pulled at the neck of her dress.

"Lids, I didn't see anything. I can't bloody see anything, look at all this stuff I'm carrying." Dot's face was red from the sun and the effort of climbing the steep cliff steps.

"I saw someone standing on the landing, at one of the big windows."

"Sara?"

"Car's not here. She's not back."

Lydia ran ahead and nearly slipped on the hall tiles. Owen laughed with delight in her arms. The house was cool and silent.

"Hello? Hello!"

"Who are you shouting at, Lydia? Mummy's not here." Clover threw her wet towel onto the telephone table and made for the back garden. Tabitha followed suit.

Lydia flung open the doors to every room on the second floor, stamping along the landings.

Dot shouted up from the hallway, exasperated. "Lydia, for God's sake!"

"I saw them, Dot! There's someone here!"

But, of course, there wasn't. No one in the girls' rooms, and she even carried Owen all the way up to her own attic bedroom only to find it empty. Dot met her on the landing outside Tabitha's bedroom on the way back down.

"There's no one here, Lids. The back door was locked, I had to open it for the girls. And you had to unlock the front door, right? I know you think you saw—"

"I *did* see them. I saw a person."

"Right. What I'm saying is, it could have been anything. Trick of the light, weird reflection. But there's no one else in the house."

*

Dot made up Philip's bed before she left and Lydia brought her own quilt and pillows down from the attic. She opened the window as wide as it would go and stuck her head right out. So much cooler in here, maybe she would finally sleep.

They hadn't spoken much at dinner. Whenever Lydia lifted her head from the plate, Dot was looking at her.

"I'm fine, Dot. Really."

"Are you sure?"

"Like you said, probably a reflection of something else. And there wasn't anyone here, was there. So I can't have seen anything."

Dot gathered the plates from the table. "I'll stay until Sara gets back."

"Thanks."

Sara seemed pleased to find Dot still in the house when she returned from the hospital.

"You two having a girls' night?" She dropped her handbag onto the armchair by the sitting-room door and smiled.

"Something like that. Listen, Mrs. Robinson, I hope it's all right but I made up Philip's bed for Lydia. Just until he comes back—I think the attic is a bit hot at the moment."

"Oh, right. Yes, I suppose that's all right."

Lydia thought Sara might protest, might think it an overstep, but she didn't really seem to care where Lydia went. "The girls are fine, by the way," she cut in. "We took them to the beach."

Sara looked startled, as though the existence of her daughters was a sudden surprise. "Oh, right. Great, thank you. That was nice."

Lydia leaned across the table and put out a hand to Sara, who ignored it. "How is he? Is he feeling better?"

"No change, Lydia. No change."

*

Tabitha's bedroom was dim and suffocating and Lydia opened the window wide for the cool evening air. She turned on the bedside lamp, smoothed her hands over the rumpled quilt, and knelt to pick up a second wet swimming costume from where it had been dropped, carelessly, to stain the floorboards with seawater.

She had turned to leave when the knocking sounds stopped her at the door. Seven raps in quick succession, the old rhyme—*shave and a haircut, five bob*. Lydia held on tight to the doorframe. Quiet. She shoved Tabitha's dresser from against the wall and knelt next to the baseboard. On her hands and knees, she knocked back, twice, very softly.

Nothing.

Lydia knocked again, three times, loud enough that she startled herself.

The door to Clover's room slammed shut. Something heavy landed on the stairs and disappeared. Lydia fell sideways and skinned the heel of her hand on the bare boards. Beads of blood welled in the graze and salt water from the swimsuit stung the wound. She crouched on her hands and knees and stared at the landing. Sweat prickled her palms.

Down on the first floor, Sara chatted to Owen in the nursery—she liked to nurse in the early evenings. Lydia opened the door and watched as Sara cradled her son in the wooden rocking chair by the window, talking to him as if he were a grown-up.

"Are you getting so chubby? Are you fat just like your sisters? Are you my monster baby?" Owen babbled into her face, delighted.

Lydia tapped the doorframe.

"Hallo, Lydia. Supper ready?"

"Did anyone come by this way, Sara?"

Owen's tiny feet pushed against Sara's thighs, kicking excitedly as he tried to stand on his own. "Come in here? No?"

"I mean past the door, down the stairs."

Sara wasn't really paying attention. "Just you, Lydia. Aren't you just the most delicious and enormous baby in the world? You are. You are! Yes, *yes!*"

The girls sprinted across the lawn—first one way, then the other, erratic horseflies. Occasionally they crashed into each other and shouted, and Lydia, watching from the kitchen window, couldn't for the life of her make out what the game was supposed to be. Hide-and-seek, perhaps? They shook the maple trees and slid on their knees underneath the low, spreading branches of the yew.

Dusk fell; sweet plant scents in the sea-salt air. The twins turned into rabbit-fur shadows on the grass. She would have to call them in shortly, but not yet. Let them run wild a little longer, no need to reel them back into this house made gray with tension and fear and exhaustion.

Clover and Tabitha were halfway up the monkey puzzle, their shoes kicked off for better purchase, when Lydia looked again out of the window. They climbed as a pair, boosting each other at the difficult points. And, at the base of the trunk, among the tall grass and blooming dogwood—another child?

A little head, sleek and dark. Their friend, their friend with no name. The head disappeared into the thicket. The twins alighted the first set of branches and then the second, quick as squirrels. Clover's legs and bare feet swung among the foliage, the girls held hands and peered down below to the grass.

Tabitha leaned downward and called out—but Lydia didn't hear what she said. Hands cupped round a mouth, words lost to the wind. They sat with heads cocked, waiting for the reply.

Tabitha kicked her legs. And there, reaching up out of the long, wild grass to begin the journey up the tree—a child's hand, small and white.

"Girls!" Lydia stepped off the patio and shouted. Too far—they couldn't hear, and so she thrashed her arms in the air like a mad person, like a drowning person.

Clover looked up and Lydia waved them in. "Come in, now!" She heard the edge to her own voice. They whispered, heads together, and Tabitha screamed with laughter. She sounded like a bird, Lydia thought, something harsh and mocking. They swung themselves off the branch and clambered down, taking their time. Lydia hated it when they dawdled, which they knew perfectly well.

They met her on the edge of the patio.

"Where are your shoes?" She looked down at their identical heads, summer-tangled hair like yellow thread in plastic barrettes.

Clover yawned. "Don't know. Outside?"

"Who were you playing with?"

Tabitha looked at her sister. "What?"

"In the tree. Who else was with you?"

They replied in unison: "No one."

Lydia pulled on the sleeves of her jumper. "Your friend, he was here. I saw him. Was he in the house? Just now—was he in the house?"

The girls shrugged.

"Who is he? This is just getting silly, now."

"There wasn't anyone, Lydia. Only us." Clover smiled and took Tabitha's hand, and they ambled past her into the orangery.

"What's for supper?" Clover swiped a pear from the bowl on the dresser.

"Dot left a fish pie. Salmon." Lydia rubbed her arms,

unsettled by the lies. The girls might be a handful, but they weren't deceitful, not usually. They had talked about a little boy, before—why not now?

Clover and Tabitha screwed up their matching faces, horrified and disappointed. "We hate fish, Lydia."

"I know. You can have that or bread and butter. It's up to you, I don't have the energy to fall out with you."

"With sugar on?" Tabitha looked hopeful.

So Lydia buttered four slices of brown bread and sprinkled them with golden caster sugar, delivered with severity. "Do *not* tell your mother about this."

They had supper on the sofa in the sitting room, usually forbidden due to crumbs and bad manners, but the framework of the household had buckled under the pressure of Philip's sickness and the girls took full advantage. Owen fell asleep facefirst into his rice pudding and Lydia hauled him up to bed.

She wiped his cheeks, crusted with sweet cream, wriggled him out of his woolen romper, and thought about the head. Small and dark, half-hidden by the grass—she knew it was another child.

He says this is his house.

Lydia sat on the rocking chair and pressed her fingers into her eye sockets. She really hadn't been sleeping all that well, her eyes permanently pink and gritty. Fogged, that's how she felt—steamed up like a warm window on a cool day.

She woke in the night, frequently, always imagining Philip standing next to her bed, drawing rattling breaths, watching her sleep. And then she would put the lamp on and of course he wasn't there—he was far away from her in a strange bed, reaching out for her and finding nothing.

Sara came home the next day with the very last of the light. She unfolded herself from the driver's seat and stood for a long minute beside the car, hands on the roof, staring at the sea. She always needed a moment to gather herself before coming inside. Her shoulders lifted and sagged, wearied by the task of returning to a too-large house full of too few children.

She didn't leave until visiting hours ended at exactly seven o'clock, and she came home smelling of harsh soap and stale coffee. It had been like this for the last week, and although Philip was largely out of the woods, the fever had mutated into pneumonia that blossomed in his lungs and left him weak and tired. They would keep him in until he showed further recovery.

Lydia met her at the front doors. "Drink?"

Sara jerked out of her coat, which fell onto the tiles. She looked at it, sighed, and bent to untie her shoes. "God, yes. Wine?"

"Lovely. Everyone's in bed." Lydia retrieved the coat and hung it on the peg rack.

"Oh, well done. Full marks."

"How's Philip?" Lydia followed Sara into the kitchen, anxious, and fetched a bottle from the pantry.

"Better, today. Could be home in another week, they said. Middle of June."

"Really? That's brilliant."

"They said he can recover here, mostly. Once they've kicked the infection, it'll just be a matter of getting his strength back up. They said it could take six, eight weeks for a full recovery." She sat at the kitchen table and yawned.

"We'll look after him. I'll look after him."

Sara smiled and pulled a box of matches from her handbag. "I know you will."

"Is he missing us?" What Lydia really wanted to ask was, *Is he missing me?* but she thought it might sound selfish.

"What do you think?" Sara laughed and blew a jet of smoke

onto the tabletop. "I've heard no end of it, how much he wants to come home. He's asked after Owen a fair bit—the girls, not so much."

Lydia poured out two large glasses. "And he's still got *Paddington*?"

Sara reached across the table and took Lydia's hand. "Stop worrying. He'll be home soon. Honestly, I think you're more worried than I am."

Privately, Lydia thought this was probably true. "I do worry about Philip. He's lonely up here, he asked me if he could have a friend. I didn't know what to say."

Sara lifted her shoulders and leaned back in the chair. "Plenty of time for that, later. You needn't baby him the way you do—he's almost eight. It's not good for him. He's always been too sensitive."

Lydia tapped her cigarette onto the saucer. "Maybe when he comes home, when he's better, I could sign him up for some of the activities in the village. They do swimming lessons, down at the beach. There's an instructor. Might be good for him?"

"Perhaps. I'd rather keep him close. I like him up here, with me."

Lydia left it alone. Why keep Philip in a house where he was ignored? Sara barely spoke to the children, these days, what harm would it do for Philip to have a little fun? And the girls, they needed other company. They'd become too insular, too tight. Lydia thought it was both cruel and hypocritical of Sara to insist that the children be near her while she shut them out, forcing them to bear witness to their mother's growing disinterest.

"Sara, I wanted to talk to you about—" Lydia hesitated and tugged her hair away from her face.

"Yes?"

"Well, it's probably nothing. I just—there have been a few things, recently, that were a bit odd? Strange. I don't know."

"What?"

"It's nothing bad, I think. I don't know."

Sara stared at her. "I don't understand."

"Right, no, of course not. Okay, so I've just heard a few weird things? Someone singing, in the bathroom. But then it was empty. I saw a woman? I think it was a woman—Dot said she couldn't see. And I found a marble—well, someone gave me a marble."

"Someone gave you a marble?"

"No, not really. I mean, I was downstairs and a marble fell down the stairs. Sorry, I'm not doing a good job of this, am I." Lydia laughed and it sounded like a cry. "I think—Sara, I know how this is going to sound—I think there's something wrong, in the house?"

Sara drained her glass and set it down hard on the table. "Because you found a marble? Lydia, have you heard yourself? You sound cracked. Is this a joke?"

"I've just been hearing strange things—I thought I saw someone in the window, and I know you've heard things, too, you can tell me, I won't—"

Sara held up a hand, cigarette ash fell into her empty glass. "Lydia, stop. I don't know what you're trying to do here, but it's not funny. This isn't the time or the place."

"Sara, I know—I'm trying to make sure we're safe, that's all."

"We're not safe, Lydia. No one is ever *safe*. My husband is dead and my son is in hospital. I brought us here to keep us safe, and look where we are." Sara stood up. "This is ludicrous."

"I'm sorry, Sara—"

"Can I trust you to look after my children, Lydia? Are you going to fill their heads with this stuff?"

"No! Of course not, you know I love the children, I'm trying to protect them."

"From what, Lydia? From a marble? I'm going to bed. Make sure you lock the door. Make sure we're all *safe*."

Lydia wished that Doug was here, but of course if Doug were alive then none of them would be in this house. He'd always filled up spaces with certainty, with an air of authority that Sara relaxed into. Lydia had secretly hated it, how he'd moved through the world as a person beyond reproach, a belief in himself that was founded on nothing more than maleness and rank and the luck of his own birth. But she craved it, now; she would tell Doug about the bad things in this house, the wrongness of it all, and he would tell her what to do. Doug had always known what to do.

But there was no one else: just her. And Lydia was alone here, wasn't she? What use was Sara, now? She either didn't want to see or refused to, and either way it was abandonment. Whatever happened next, only Lydia could protect them.

19

2018

———

ORLA PULLED SAM FROM BENEATH the yew bush, yanked him viciously by the arm. His small, shocked face was white with surprise.

"Sam, who were you talking to? I heard you, I heard you!" She gripped his shoulder, too tight.

He shook his head, terrified. *No one!*

"I don't believe you, I don't believe you, Sam! Who was it? You must tell me, you *must*—" Orla fell back onto her heels. Her hands skidded on the wet grass and Bridie protested.

Sam wrapped his arms round himself, silent mouth opened wide with distress. He pointed to his chest, pointed to the ground.

"Your friends?"

Sam nodded.

"Who are they, Sam? Tell me, sweetheart."

But Sam would not.

He was silent for the rest of the day. Orla kept him inside and occupied him with DVDs. She didn't want him out of her sight, didn't want him in the garden. It wasn't *safe*. Orla thought about his wide-open mouth, the noises coming from his tired little throat. The excitement in his voice as he called out to someone she could not see.

Toby returned and heaved the polythene sacks of compost and slate through the side gate. Orla put Bridie down for a nap. When she came back to the kitchen, Sam was gone, slipped out to join Toby despite his mother's stern face and instruction to *Sit right there and watch the television.*

Orla gathered dirty plates from the table and put them in the sink. She leaned against the countertop and watched her son.

Sam ran along the high back wall, doing rings around the oaks. Occasionally, Toby threw a stick at him, or a small pebble covered in earth, and Sam pretended he'd been shot, and fell to the ground dramatically. He knew to stay away from the dug-out pond—Toby had marched him down and explained the severe consequences of crossing the boundary marked out with stakes and string. Sam, unused to such gravity from his friend, nodded solemnly. They even shook on it.

Bridie cried out in her sleep and Orla went to the hallway to listen. Once more, Bridie called out, and then silence. Orla hoped she would sleep longer, they'd had such a broken night.

When she returned to the kitchen, Sam was a third of the way up the monkey puzzle tree that leaned directly over the pond. As he climbed, he looked upward.

She grabbed hold of the edge of the sink. She had to tell Toby—Toby would get him, he was closer. Orla reached out to the window and found herself fixed to the spot. Her fingers jumped to her chest and felt the lump of the hag stone beneath her shirt; she tugged it out and pressed it to her eye with a hand that trembled.

Sam was halfway up the trunk. When she followed his gaze she saw the other children sitting on the branch above, two sets of short legs swinging. Their bodies were obscured by the tree limbs, but she clearly saw the dangling legs and the white hands on the green leaves. The hem of a dress, cuffs of dark trousers.

Sam, determined, hoisted himself up by a lower branch. The white legs kicked and shuffled over to make room for him on the branch, and Orla caught a glimpse of blond hair. Then Sam was gone, up into the green.

Toby, busy in the flower bed by the east wall, turned just as Sam broke his hold and fell, so beautifully—*gracefully*—down into the trench of the pond.

In his white T-shirt, he looked like a feather.

"Toby!" Her shout left her mouth as a whisper.

But Toby had seen and was already running. He shook off his gloves and they lay like a pair of amputated hands on the grass. He vaulted the string, slid on the loose earth, and fell on his hands and knees in front of Sam, who lay on his back in the damp soil.

Orla slammed the kitchen door behind her and sprinted, hopped the string, and slipped down the crumbling side of the pond, into the deep depression, and knelt next to Toby. She followed Sam's staring eyes upward but saw only branches— no swinging legs, no little white hands. No one else.

"Oh my God, oh my God, I didn't see him start, the tree— how did he get so *high*—" Orla spoke too fast, reached out to touch him. Toby put one large hand underneath Sam's shoulder and the other on his chest and raised her son out of the ground.

"There we go, that's better. Right, let's see what we've got." Toby touched Sam's neck and head. He parted Sam's hair at the back to look for blood. Gently, he took hold of Sam's face by the temples and turned his head from side to side.

"All fine upstairs, no worries here. That arm, though."

Sam's face shone with sweat. Damp hair clung to his forehead and two livid spots of color burned high on his cheeks. He held his arm tight to his body, and his little hand hung limp on the end of an arm that rested against his belly at an unnatural angle.

"Sam, my love, just let me look." He moaned and turned away. "Just quickly, just let me see, I promise I won't touch." Orla took in the bend in his forearm, the palest green bruising already beginning.

Toby crouched in front of Sam. "Well, now, that's a fine break. I expect that hurts." He peered into the child's face. Sam nodded. "Fancy a trip into town? I know someone who can fix that."

A clean crack in his ulna. Orla thought about the white, wet bone and the screaming nerves and the swollen veins. Toby stayed with them while Sam was x-rayed and medicated and fussed over by nurses and wrapped in plaster, and he bounced Bridie around with an amount of cheer that Orla found both exasperating and heartening.

He looked at her over the top of the baby's head. "You all right?"

"I feel terrible."

Toby shrugged and made a face at the baby. "Kids break things, means he was having a good time."

"It shouldn't have happened." Orla felt sick.

"But it did happen, and it's all right. No sense wishing it different. He's a boy, it'll happen again."

"He doesn't usually do things like that. He's not a climber, he doesn't like being dirty."

"It's a big garden, natural for kids to explore."

"He likes to be able to see me. He used to like it, I mean."

"Growing up, though, isn't he. He'll be wanting to go off, see things for himself. He's not a baby, Mrs. McGrath, not like this one here." He blew a fat raspberry into the ambrosia folds of Bridie's neck.

The nurse brought Sam into the room, wielding his plaster arm and grinning. Orla had explained about his speech and they'd been so kind.

"Right, here we are! Mrs. McGrath, you can pick up a prescription for paracetamol at the dispensary, and you'll need to make an appointment for Sam with the GP in about a week."

"Okay, okay, thank you." Sam climbed into Orla's lap and she pulled him close. His broken arm felt weighty, clumsy, where it hung against her thigh. "Can we go?"

"Absolutely, you're all set. Take him into the GP if you notice any redness or swelling above the cast or in the hand, or if the pain is keeping him awake. You should only need paracetamol for the next couple of days. And it goes without saying that you don't want to get the cast wet—so no baths, only showers, and I've found a couple of layers of bin bags usually does the trick." She smiled at Sam, who waved with his other hand.

"Thank you, thank you so much."

Toby stood and swung Bridie onto his hip. "Now then, about time we were getting home. What do you reckon?"

He drove them home. Sam fell asleep in the back, exhausted by the excitement and the attention, and Toby made occasional reference to various limbs he'd injured as a child. Orla knew he was trying to make her feel better, but she didn't. Sam had been lured up there, enticed by something she could neither accept nor rationalize.

Toby parked in front of the house and switched off the engine.

Orla shifted Bridie on her lap, warm and heavy as a dense rye loaf, and felt mildly guilty that the car seat was up in Bristol with Nick. "Thank you, Toby—I can't tell you how much this means to me. You were so great today, I don't know what I would have done if I'd been on my own."

Toby swung his legs out and stretched his hands above his head. "I'm glad I was here—would have been shit trying to do that on your own. And you know I love the kids." He nodded at Sam, who had woken up and was trying to get out of his seat belt with only one hand. Toby opened the door and reached in to help him.

"Come in, have dinner with us." Orla made the offer lightly, knowing she was approaching Toby's invisible line.

"That's really nice of you, Mrs. McGrath, but I can't."

"Please, Toby, I'd love it if you did. I want to say thank you. We'll make pizzas, it'll be great."

Sam bounced on his toes and pulled at Toby's hand to steer him toward the house.

"I can't, I really can't. It's so nice of you. I'm sorry." He dug his hands into the pockets of his fleece.

"Toby—seriously. What's wrong? You've never come in, not even on the shittiest days in the winter for a cup of tea. Do you not feel comfortable? Have we made you feel like we don't want you?" Orla's throat hurt.

"No, no! It's not that—you've been great. You and Nick—you don't know how much I appreciate you giving me this job. I love coming here—"

Sam looked from adult to adult, face twisted in distress.

"Then what *is* it?"

Toby held his car keys so tight that Orla saw the flesh of his hand whiten and then turn livid where the metal dug in. "It's my nan, she made me promise. When I took the job, she made me promise I wouldn't go inside. She's afraid—she didn't even want me up here, but honestly we need the money and I don't see what the problem is."

Orla was surprised; it seemed a disproportionate fear. "Your grandmother said that?"

Toby looked down at the sparse, dirty gravel. "She hates The Reeve, Mrs. McGrath. Most people in the village do. They think there's something bad up here. Water spirits, old gods, all that stuff. My nan said the house attracts all of it, that it's *wrong*. So when I said I'd take on the work up here—she went spare. Dad had to convince her to let me, and she made me promise not to go in."

"And do you believe her?"

"No. No, and neither does my dad. But my grandma, she's always believed in that kind of thing—she reads tarot in the village sometimes, there's a horseshoe over every door in our house. Loads of people here are like that, it's not anything unusual. Dad says she always had an open mind, and too much got in."

"I'm so sorry, Toby. You don't have to come up here, you know, if it's a problem." Orla worried that the distress at being abandoned by Toby, too, was clear in her voice.

Toby smiled and shook his head. "Don't. I like coming. I'll just not come in, if that's all right. It makes my nan feel better."

"That's kind of you."

"You know what I think? It's a load of shit. Honestly, Mrs. McGrath, it's fine. Not everyone thinks like my nan. You can't think like that, you live here."

"I'll take her." Deftly, Nick transferred Bridie from her high chair in the kitchen to the floor in the sitting room, where she immediately took off toward the hallway. She'd become fascinated by the stairs, despite her inability to navigate them successfully, and twice Orla had rescued her from where she'd got herself stuck, halfway up and in tears.

Exasperated, Nick went to retrieve her. He'd been short

ever since he came home after Sam's accident. He had driven from Bristol that night and the recriminations started the minute he slammed his car keys onto the kitchen table.

"For fuck's sake, Orla, how could you let this happen?"

"Nick, can you just be reasonable about this? It was an accident—kids do have them, you know. Toby says he broke loads of stuff when he was little, just running around—"

"I don't give a *fuck* what Toby says."

"Jesus, Nick! I said I'm sorry."

"You don't need my forgiveness, Orla, surely." Nick laughed, a cruel little sound. "Not when you've already forgiven yourself."

"I don't understand why you're being so nasty about this—it was an *accident*." She poured another measure of gin into a glass that was already clouded with fingerprints.

"That's probably enough, don't you think?"

"What?"

Nick picked up the gin bottle and shook it so that the liquid in the bottom sloshed against the sides. A burning, delicious reproach. "Maybe if you laid off the booze a bit, you'd actually notice when your own children were in danger."

"Oh, come on. I don't drink that much, especially not when I'm here on my own with them. Nick, honestly, that's a cheap shot."

"Is it? You get through it pretty fucking quick. I'm always the one who puts the bins out on Monday morning—that recycling fills up fast."

"Fuck off, Nick. You're being awful—I was scared, too, you know. I felt so bad, and you're just making it worse."

"He could have been seriously hurt, much worse than a broken arm."

"I know, I *know* that. You weren't here, you don't know what it was like—I had an eye on him and then Bridie was crying and when I came back he was halfway up the bloody tree and I was so far from him, all the way up here—it was terrifying." Her voice caught, and for a moment Nick looked chastened. "He was following someone, I think, I can't be sure, it was so far—"

"Following who?"

"I don't know. I don't *know* who it was."

"Well, where are they now?"

Orla put her hands to her mouth. "I don't know."

"I told you, Orla, you need to stop it with the drinking, especially in the day, when I'm not here. How can I trust you with them? And you took Bridie in that shitty Land Rover without a car seat?"

"I didn't have much choice, did I? Not when you leave me here without a car every week?"

Nick put the bottle down on the table and picked up the plate of congealing pasta that Orla had put aside for him. "Lucky Toby was there."

"Oh, so now you like Toby again?"

"Don't be obtuse, Orla."

"Well, thanks a lot."

"You know what I mean—you've been really weird lately. Distracted, always in a bad mood. I know you're frustrated because you can't paint"—Orla noted the point he scored with *that* little needle—"but you need to pay more attention. It's your only job, and you're fucking it up. Have you been sleeping?"

"What do you mean?"

"You said on the phone the other day, to Helen, that you're not sleeping properly."

Had she said that? She didn't remember.

"Do you know how hard it is to watch both of them in a house this fucking big? Especially now Bridie's almost walking? It's impossible. You'd know that if you were here."

"Orla, bloody hell. Is that necessary?"

"You don't know what it's like. Seriously, Nick, I was gone for maybe thirty seconds. One minute Sam was just running around the garden and the next thing I knew he was up the tree. You know how quick he is."

"Even so." Nick pursed his mouth, prim.

"What do you mean, *even so*? It's not my fault. It's this house—I can't bear it. We're not the same since we came here—none of us are."

"So, what? You want to move?"

Orla sat down at the kitchen table and spread her fingers on her knees. "Yes. You know I do. I want to *leave*. Don't you? It's been harder than you thought, all the commuting. Hasn't it? You're always complaining about it."

"It's not like I get this brilliant welcome when I come back. The house doesn't exactly feel friendly."

"That's what I'm saying, Nick. To me, the house feels like that all the time. I can't bear it, I can't bear to be here—"

Nick spoke over her, quickly. "I'm really tired of listening to you find fault, Orla. And of course I've noticed you haven't been yourself—you've been annoyed, distracted, short with the kids. Asleep half the bloody time and drunk the other half."

She began to cry; Nick seemed oddly unmoved by her tears, usually a surefire method for reconciliation. "Nick, for God's sake, just be a bit kind."

"We're not moving, Orla. I put everything we have into this house. The kids love it, my parents love it. And Sam is starting to talk, isn't he? That's what you said."

"It was a few words, it's hardly definitive."

"More than he's said in a long time. That was the whole reason we moved here, wasn't it? For that? And now you're saying, what—that it doesn't matter?"

"He wasn't even talking to me, he was just shouting—"

"Then who was he talking to?"

Orla wiped her face with her fingers and put her hands in front of her eyes. "Himself? I don't know, I don't *know*, Nick— and you remember the singing, the tape? I couldn't even find a tape, so I don't even know what I heard. I can't figure it out, he won't say a single word to me, but I hear him, I hear him talking when I'm not there and it makes me feel like I'm failing. I can't keep him safe. I can't keep us safe." She hated to admit that maybe he was right about Sam—maybe she hadn't been paying attention. Or at least, she hadn't been paying attention to the right things. She'd been so fixated on the little legs she thought she'd seen swinging from the tree branch—there one moment and gone as soon as she dropped the hag stone—that she knew in her darkest heart that she hadn't been watching her son as closely as she ought.

That night, when she reached for her husband in the forgiving dark, he turned away. It was always how they'd found their way back to each other, no matter how vicious the fight, and when he retrieved her fingers with an unspoken regret and replaced her hand on the pillow, Orla understood that, for now, she was being put aside: the path to Nick was closed. She wondered what else the house was going to take.

20

1976

———

LYDIA WASN'T PAYING MUCH ATTENTION to the others, happy to sit on the bench and feel the late-afternoon sun on her face and be held by the hum of other voices, other people's lives going on around her. It was easier to be an observer than a joiner—she liked listening to Dot tease Lee and Lee rebuke Freddie for his antiquated ideas about marriage.

She was grateful to be out of the house, even for a few hours. She hated being alone there while Sara was gone, but it was almost worse when Sara was home. The girls mutinied, Owen whined, all of them put on edge by Sara's moods. Lydia was afraid to approach the bathroom, afraid of the trees in the garden. Afraid that something might happen to the children when she wasn't watching, or even if she was. A constant twist of fear lived in her guts, compounded by worry for Philip.

And Sara looked at her now like she was an intruder, an unwelcome surprise that Sara had forgotten inviting. She'd become a nuisance in the house she lived in, ignored by the girls and resented by Sara.

"Yeah, but you wouldn't want a wife that worked, would you?" Freddie sounded whiny, irritated that no one was agreeing with him.

"Fucking hell, Fred, it's not medieval times. And your mum works, doesn't she?" Dot was exasperated.

"Well, yeah, but you should hear my dad complaining about it. Says she's always doing dinner late, house is a state."

Lee sighed. "Then maybe your dad could get a bloody job, or maybe you could help her. She's got you two idiots at home, why aren't you doing dinner?"

"Fuck off, Lee."

Lydia opened her eyes. Freddie folded his arms, scolded into a hurt silence. Dot and Lee laughed.

"Can you even believe the shit he comes out with, Lids?" Dot shook her head.

Lydia smiled. "Good luck to his wife, I say. If he manages to find one."

Lee howled.

Lydia lit another cigarette and watched the smoke climb into the evening air. The garden of the pub filled up with Friday tourists coming for the weekend, seeking out a little bit of Dorset coast to wash away their city lives. Lydia wondered what Danny was doing, back in London. She hadn't tried to phone him again, not since Dot told her off for pining after something so clearly out of reach. And of course he hadn't telephoned her, nor written. He'd probably already put her address in the bin, or covered it up with gig flyers and political leaflets. She marveled, now, that she'd held his attention for as long as she had.

"Lydia?" Sara appeared at the side door of the pub and crossed over to their table with her hands outstretched. The button of her trousers was undone—something that Lydia would always remember. Sara's shirt was untucked on one side, a large stain down the front that looked like tea, or coffee.

"Sara! Hi—do you want a drink? Are the girls with you?" Lydia looked behind her, expecting to see the twins, confused when she didn't.

"Lydia." Sara tripped and fell onto her hands and knees on the grass. A few people looked round, then turned back to their drinks.

"Shit." Lee swung his legs off the bench and pulled Sara up by her arms.

Dot stood up. "Sara? Are you all right? Where are the kids?"

"Lydia." Sara leaned against Lee, face flushed—she looked almost drunk. Lee put his arm round her shoulders.

"Sara—what's going on? Are you okay, seriously?" Lydia worked her cigarette end into the grass with her heel.

Freddie nodded at Dot. "That her, then? The boss? Looks like she's had a lively one."

Sara sat down on the bench and reached out for Lydia's hands. "Philip. Philip is dead."

"What?" Lydia said. "What's happened?" *Sara is wrong, this is a mistake.*

Dot put a hand to her mouth. "Oh, fuck."

"The hospital, they telephoned. I have to go there." Sara grabbed Lydia's nearly full gin and tonic and drank it down. Liquid spilled from the sides of her mouth.

"But he was better?" Lydia said, confused.

"No. No. Not better." Sara hunched forward and put her fists underneath her ribs. "Sepsis. From the pneumonia. They didn't know—they didn't know until later—" She stopped and heaved a dry, bitter sob.

"Okay. Okay." Lydia put her hands over her eyes. "Where are the children?"

"In the house. At home. I have to go to the hospital."

"You left them there alone?"

Sara moaned.

Dot looked at Lydia. "Jesus."

Lee held Sara by the shoulders. "Here's what we'll do. Lydia—Sara can't drive like this. You'll have to take her. Where is it?"

"Poole," Lydia whispered.

"Do you know the way?"

Lydia shook her head. She couldn't speak.

"Shit. All right. Dot, you drive. You take Sara, I'll run Lydia back up to the house."

The twins met her at the front door. Tabitha carried Owen, and Lydia could tell just from looking that he needed to be changed. Lee waved from the car and disappeared back down the hill.

"We're hungry. Where did Mum go?" Clover followed Lydia into the hallway.

"To the hospital." Lydia climbed the stairs to the nursery, trailed by the twins.

"To visit Philip?"

Lydia set the baby on the floor and reached for the bottle of talc, a clean cloth nappy, the cream in the gray plastic tub. "Have you had dinner?"

"No." Clover sat next to her on the floor and made a face at Owen's wet nappy.

"Are you hungry?"

Tabitha picked up Owen's raggedy sheep from the cot and set it down again. "A bit."

"Okay."

The girls followed Lydia down to the kitchen, and she pulled things from the fridge at random. The twins sat quietly at the table, aware that something wasn't right. Half a pork pie, some cheese, sliced ham in its paper packet. Two boiled eggs, the whites faintly blueish. "Eat whatever you want."

"Can we have toast?"

"With jam?"

Lydia put two pieces of bread in the toaster. The wood-effect laminate on the front had begun to peel away from the metal; she picked at it with a fingernail.

Philip, her Philip. She imagined him in his hospital bed, surrounded by white and already so pale. Bruise-blue, suffocating under the weight of his own breath. Not breathing, but barking, scrabbling for air.

The house sat dark and Lydia sat quiet within it. She watched the sun dip below the orangery and then the moon rise from the sitting-room window. The children slept upstairs.

Still Sara didn't come home. Maybe Dot would come back with her—Lydia would like Dot to stay. She thought about being here with just Sara and the children, in the wake of all of this, and her stomach knotted. It would be worse than Doug, so much worse than before. Her mouth and throat were tight with the tears that she would not allow herself to cry.

How could Sara have left the children alone, all three of them? The girls, perhaps—they would have been all right. But to leave them with Owen was incomprehensible. Anything could have happened. Lydia shivered on the sofa.

Wisteria branches clicked against the drawing-room window. The fridge hummed and rattled and then died away.

Do not think about the tapping in Tabitha's room. Do not think about the marble. Do not think about the sound of little feet, running, or the child who doesn't belong here, or anything else that's wrong in this dreadful house. You are the only one left for them now.

Owen wailed above her, thin little cries that bled down the

stairs. Lydia's legs were stiff, aching with cold. Perhaps it was a bad dream, perhaps he would stop.

After a long minute, Owen fell silent and Lydia rose and ascended the stairs. Bright summer moonlight filtered through the glass dome, darkness in the corridors beyond.

At the top of the landing, Sara's bedroom door stood open. White light came in through the open curtains and illuminated the tangle of unmade sheets and various jumpers strewn across the bed.

Lydia should tidy, make it nice for when Sara came back. She turned on the light and shook the sheets out, smoothed down the quilt. She folded Sara's jumpers and put them away in the mahogany bureau. Framed photographs of all the children stood along the top, a little dusty, next to a large portrait of Sara and Doug on their wedding day. Sara wore a high-necked gown in ivory muslin, no veil, just a headband with silk flowers. On the bottom corner, across the hem of Sara's dress, Doug had written *Me and wife* in a decisive, looping scrawl. Lydia averted her eyes from Philip's christening photograph.

As she drew the curtains shut across both windows, she looked down at the garden receding into the darkness of the long wheat fields. The pond shone silver under the moon, the grass rippled and sighed. Owen cried again and Lydia opened the door to the nursery corridor.

The door at the other end stood open, the nursery lit softly with the light from the landing. She couldn't see Owen behind the headboard of the cot, but she heard the mattress shift as he wriggled around in distress. Raggedy sheep lay on the floor.

A woman stood in the half-light, bent over the cot. In blue jeans, men's jeans, not Sara's trousers. Long hair hung down, lighter than Sara's, obscuring the face. The same woman she had seen coming back from the beach.

Lydia stepped into the corridor. "Hello?"

The woman stood up straight, looked down at Owen, and turned and left the room.

"Is she still asleep?" Dot poured the cold tea out of the pot into the kitchen sink and reached for the kettle to fill it.

Lydia put the orange peel and toast crusts from breakfast into the enamel compost pot. "I think so. I haven't heard her get up. Not even for the loo."

Three days—three awful days, the worst of Lydia's life, and still Sara hadn't got out of bed. Dot came every day, came earlier and left later, and Lydia was wretchedly grateful. She hadn't cried, not once. She couldn't—who would be left if she allowed herself to come apart the way she wanted to? Owen needed her, the twins needed her. The girls hadn't seen Sara in days; Lydia took her meals in and out, opened the windows for fresh air. Sara still wore the same clothes from that night at the hospital, and her bedroom smelled awful.

Owen cried, endlessly, through the nights. He felt Sara's disintegration and wailed with fear, twisting and bucking in Sara's arms until she gave up and put him in his cot and walked away, leaving him sobbing and spent. Sometimes Lydia would go in after her and pick him up and swing him back and forth in her arms until he fell asleep. Sometimes she left him.

Owen was so much a child of Sara, still so connected to her in a fundamental, bodily way, nursing sporadically at night, that Lydia didn't feel quite the same affection for him that she did for the others. He was a baby animal, not wholly real to her. She loved him, of course she did, in a practical way that was one step removed. She liked his baby smell and enjoyed his fat, sticky face, but he didn't have her heart the way Philip did. The twins belonged to themselves and Owen belonged to Sara, and Philip had belonged to her.

This was how she drew the lines.

"When's the funeral?"

Lydia rinsed her sticky fingers under the tap. "No idea. Sara's supposed to meet the funeral director tomorrow. A week, maybe?"

Only the second funeral of Lydia's life, already the second for Tabitha and Clover.

"Dot."

Dot bent to put a batch of bread rolls into the range. "Mm?"

"I saw something again."

"Christ, Lydia."

"I know—I know. I'm sorry."

"Don't be sorry, it's just bloody weird, that's all. I can't tell what you think is going on."

Lydia leaned against the sink, felt the cold porcelain through her blouse. "It was when you took Sara to the hospital, that night."

"Right. Go on." Dot swept excess flour from the surface of the table into an open palm.

"I put the kids to bed, waited for you and Sara. Felt like I was waiting for hours."

Sara and Dot hadn't come back until almost midnight. Dot was exhausted, Sara was practically catatonic.

"Yeah. God, yeah, that was a shitty night."

"So I was just in the sitting room, and then I heard Owen crying. So I went upstairs and there was a woman in his room, standing next to his cot."

"What? Who was it?"

"I thought it was Sara—but it wasn't. Different hair. Weird clothes. I think I said, *Hello?* But it was like she couldn't hear me; she just stared at Owen and then she walked out of the nursery, and when I went out to the landing to look, there was no one there."

"Fuck."

"Do you remember, the day at the beach? I thought I saw someone in the house. I *did* see someone in the house. And I've heard weird things before—someone singing upstairs. And that kid I've seen the twins play with, sometimes, out in the garden. A little boy, doesn't have a name, apparently. I don't know where he comes from. I know how it sounds. But it's all too much, I can't handle it, Dot. I feel like we aren't safe here, I can't keep us safe. And now with Philip—" She swallowed. "I tried telling Sara about it, but she didn't want to hear it. She wouldn't take me seriously, so what can I do?"

Dot chewed at her lip, looked down at her nails. "Right, so I was telling my mum about this. About the stuff you saw before, the marble, yeah? And she said the same as Freddie—about The Reeve being weird."

"Haunted?" Lydia felt better for saying the word out loud.

"Didn't want to put it like that."

"What did she say?"

"Just that it's got a reputation, you know. Spooky. She said people used to talk about it being built on a thin place, up here on the cliff. Like—not normal." Dot sighed. "My mum believes in all sorts, she's really superstitious. Lots of people round here are—there's all sorts of stories. Like, fairies and so on."

Lydia laughed, the first laughter the house had heard in days. Dot looked at her, startled.

"Fairies? Fucking *fairies*?" She couldn't stop laughing, she struggled for breath.

"I know how it sounds! But not nice fairies. Not like in films. Bad things, my mum says. You know, curdle the milk, steal the children, all that old shit."

Lydia gulped and swallowed, queasy with laughter. "Right, so, fairies and a thin place?" She felt, suddenly, very untethered to reality.

"So, round here, we have the Midsummer celebration, you know that. I've told you about it. Midsummer is supposed to be when you can cross from one world to the next, when the world is thin. And some places are thin all the time, like up here. Probably less people believe in it all now, but we still have the festival to celebrate, and my mum says there's all sorts of things you can do, you know, for fairies. For protection." She lifted her chin, determined. "Maybe that's what you saw."

"What, a fairy?"

"Maybe?"

"She didn't look like a fairy, Dot, she looked like a normal woman. A human person." Lydia thought, briefly, of pink gauze wings, taut across wire.

"Well, I don't know what they're supposed to look like, do I? Maybe they just look regular. You said you've been hearing all sorts of things. My mum said it didn't surprise her, all of that happening in this house."

"So, what do we do? I need to keep them safe, Dot. I couldn't protect Philip, I couldn't—" She stopped, made voiceless by the grief caught in her throat.

"Come on. I'll help you."

On Dot's instruction, Lydia fetched her sewing kit. The long needles, the spools of colored thread. Assorted homeless buttons, reels of name tape for the girls, lengths of ribbon. The bright, curved scissors, small enough to fit in the palm of a hand and decorated with flowers picked out in brass relief.

Dot took Lydia by the hand, up the stairs and into the nursery. They walked softer past Sara's door; Dot put a finger to her lips.

Above the cot hung Owen's mobile, handed down from Philip. Wooden shapes painted in rainbow colors: stars, clouds, a fat yellow moon. Dot picked a length of orange satin ribbon from the kit and threaded one end through the thumb ring of the little scissors. She fashioned a tight knot, and tied the other end of the ribbon to the apex of the mobile. The silver scissors swung and flashed among the stars and suns.

"Jesus—what if that falls on him?"

Dot tugged on the ribbon, which held fast. "It won't."

"And what's the purpose of this, again?"

"Protection. That's what my mum said. This is where you saw that woman, right? So, this is to protect Owen. Keep him safe. They don't like metal."

"Who, the fairies?" Lydia smiled, she couldn't help it.

Dot folded her arms. "Look, you're the one seeing weird stuff. I'm not the one going nutty. Do you want the help or not?"

Later that evening, when Lydia put Owen to bed in their house silenced by pain, she touched the scissors lightly with her fingers, watched them twist on the end of the ribbon. Owen reached up toward the shapes, babbled something cheerful. This was the least she could do.

On her way to bed, she paused for a moment outside Sara's door, with her ear to the wood. She expected to hear only silence, of course, maybe the same soft weeping that had scored their lives here for the past few days. But Sara was talking, low and urgent. To herself?

I can't. I can't just leave them. Don't make me. Please. Let me love you.

And then silence, and the sweet notes of Sara's grief.

21

2018

———

"HELLO?"

"Orla!"

"Helen!" Orla pushed the fridge door shut with her hip. The wine bottle she had retrieved was heavy and cold and she carried it with her to the sofa. "Hi, hi, it's so nice to hear your voice."

"Just thought I'd check in, see how you are."

"Grand, grand. I'm fine." She removed the cork from the bottle with her teeth and drank straight from the neck.

Helen laughed. "Mother's ruin?"

"No, just wine. Off the hard stuff for a bit."

"Kids in bed?"

"Yup. A cozy night in, just me and the sauce."

"No Nick?"

"Course not."

"He messaged me, you know." Helen paused; Orla heard her breathing. "He said you've not been yourself. You all right?"

Orla smiled. "Not at all."

"What?"

"This house, Helen. It's against me." She upended the bottle again.

"Orla, seriously—"

"What, Helen? Seriously, what? Sam's not himself—you know he had that accident. My poor Sam. And Nick's right, too, although fuck him for texting you. I can't sleep. And I can't keep my children safe."

"Orla, if this is about what I told you, about the history—"

"It's not that."

"But kids have accidents, don't they? And Sam's fine? I don't understand what you think is wrong." Helen sounded distressed and Orla felt a little sorry for her, although not as sorry as she felt for herself.

"I see things. I *hear* things."

"What?"

"A voice, on Bridie's baby monitor."

"You mean like the radio?"

"No—no, not like the radio. A person."

"Well, what did it say?"

"Just a word. *Yes*, I think. Just the word *yes*."

Silence.

"Helen?"

"Orla, that doesn't really sound like anything. Could have been static, could even have been Bridie."

"Maybe. Even Nick hates it here, I know he does, but he pretends it's fine because he can't stand to have made a mistake. He can't possibly admit that this was a bad decision, so instead he just leaves, he leaves all the time."

"Look, why don't you come and stay with me for a bit? Bring the kids, get out for a weekend."

Orla, drunk now, shook her head, although Helen couldn't see. "No. But thank you. I need to be here, I need to work. If I can work, then maybe I can understand."

"Understand what?"

"All of it."

"I don't get it, Orla. Don't you want to leave?"

Orla's throat tightened round the grief that rose. "It would be worse, so much worse, to leave and then have to come back. I couldn't bear it. If we go, we can't return. If I go, I have to stay gone."

Orla dreamed again of the garden, of the magnolia that enveloped her in heavy blooms—silky, creamy petals that obscured her vision and barred her way back to the house. Trapped, she pushed through the branches and the grass and was made weak by the effort. When she finally approached the house, towering and expanded on a vast curve of black lawn, she knew that it was empty, and she was all alone.

She woke, confused, much later.

Whose baby is that?

Faint cries from the passageway. Orla rolled over, but couldn't escape the sound.

Whose baby is that?

Her head was thick with sleep, and still the cries came. Orla sat up.

The door to the passageway was open, a black mouth yawning. When Orla got out of bed to close the door, she saw that the little wooden wedge had been slid out from underneath and was lying almost clear on the other side of the room. The corridor stretched out before her—and at the other end, a hazy square of gray. The door into the nursery stood open. The door that had been stuck fast, locked, resistant, ever since they'd moved in.

Orla put her hands on the doorframe and listened to her baby's sobs. She was needed, she was necessary. She put the light on in the passageway, but the bare bulb only made the nursery door look darker. Only a few short steps to her child.

The sound receded as Orla came toward the nursery; Bridie's

cries faded away to nothing. Bridie's room was still and quiet, and the child in the cot was sound asleep. No tear tracks on those rosy cheeks, not a single sign of distress.

Orla touched her child, lightly, with hands that shook. How could this be? She turned on all the lights in the nursery and the passageway and her own bedroom, and against all sense she took Bridie from her cot and brought her daughter into her own bed. She went back and used one of the wedges under the nursery door and shoved the other under the connecting door to the master bedroom.

Bridie slept against her leg. Orla sat up against the pillows and her eyes flicked ceaselessly from the bedroom door to the connecting door, over and over. Her body was tense and exhausted, straining at every small sound. The house was silent, other than the occasional thump from a pipe beneath the boards, or a beam settling way down on the ground floor.

Nothing to see here, said the house. But Orla knew how it lied.

Morning. *Deliverance.*

Orla woke to the sound of wind. She'd fallen asleep sitting up, vigilant, and her shoulders and neck protested as she stretched. Her head felt thick and slow. Bridie barely slept during the night, whining until Orla put her hands over her ears.

She removed the door wedges and went down the passageway to the nursery, where the door opened freely and revealed an empty room. She opened and closed the door a couple of times, but it didn't stick. Simply, a once-closed door had opened. Orla remembered all the times she had tried to force this door, how many times she had stood in front of it, exasperated, and rattled the handle. She pictured another hand turning the handle in the dark while she slept.

She returned Bridie to her cot and started toward the kitchen, flicking on lamps as she went. No sound from Sam's room: still asleep.

It wasn't until she saw Sam at the kitchen table that she understood that it wasn't early at all, it was very, very late, and Sam had been awake and on his own until almost lunchtime. He was swinging his legs on the chair, staring out into the garden with an intense and querying expression.

"Sam—I'm so sorry! Are you okay? What have you been up to?" Her mouth was dry, sickened by the realization that she had left him utterly alone inside the house. Unforgivable, an unforgivable lapse. She had vowed to watch closer, to do better, and instead the house stole her sleep and made her blind. Her hands shook as she held him close to breathe in the scent of his unwashed hair. She tugged his pajama top down where it had ridden up over his stomach. Sam pointed to the biscuits scattered on the table.

"Oh dear—was that breakfast? Well, I suppose that's all right just this once, since Mummy slept so late. Why didn't you wake me?"

Sam frowned—*I did, I tried.*

Orla thought about her silent son standing over her, watching her sleep. She would have known, wouldn't she, if he'd tried to rouse her? She was a light sleeper, always had been. She pictured him in the half-light, a small shadow, listening to her breathe. Reaching for her, asking for her, while she dreamed and turned away.

They folded into the broken rhythm of summer.

There was no peace to be had in this festive weather. If Orla tried to paint, to make sense of the house around her and the space in which she was condemned to live, Sam was there, watching. When she made lunch, he stood next to her hip and pointed to the sky, to the sun. He even appeared in the kitchen wearing his blue goggles—defiant and demanding.

"Okay, you win! We'll go after lunch, all right?"

Bridie swayed in her high chair, receptive to this jolly mood. At least her children had her; she had no one. Nick hadn't called since he'd left the day before, though he'd sent a few texts. Shorter than usual, but expressing interest in her well-being at least.

As they left the house, all three, with Orla weighed down by various bags of towels and snacks and buckets, she turned and looked back. Sam ran on ahead down the path and Bridie kicked against her pack, livid in captivity.

The cathedral windows shone like mirrors. At the window above the drawing room, something moved behind the glass and slid out of view. Orla set her face to the sea.

Out on the sand, Orla arranged the baby on a blanket and staked an umbrella into the ground. Sam went immediately to the water's edge and stopped, as he'd been told so many times to do. She inflated his rubber armbands and called him back. The cast had finally come off and the limb was pale and dry; it looked almost as if it belonged to another child entirely.

She stripped him and she noted the jut of his hip bones, the way his ribs sat orderly and pale along the narrow barrel of his chest. He swam out of the T-shirt that had grown too large for him these past weeks and pointed impatiently to the sea.

"We're going, just give me a minute!" Orla took his chin between her fingers and wobbled his head back and forth, to make him laugh. Bridie clawed at her sun hat, affronted by the pressure of the elastic strap under her fat chin, and mounted an escape from the blanket onto the sand—Orla dragged her back by her ankles to make her laugh.

She swung Bridie onto her hip and held Sam's hand as

they approached the shallows. Sam hopped and spun, send-ing up exclamation marks of crystal water. Orla went in up to her knees and splashed Bridie, who yelped and wailed. Sam grinned. He ventured farther out, up to his chest, ecstatic. His dark head shone like a seal, Orla watched the white soles of his feet flash under the silver water. The air smelled of ozone, fishy decay, salt. It felt good to be out of the house, as if a pressure had been released. A weight none of them knew they were carrying: the house that sat heavy on their backs. Orla felt safer down here, out of sight of those windows.

They sat on the sandy towels and picked hot grit from be-tween their toes. Bridie fell asleep flat on her back, pink as a cooked lobster. Orla tugged off Sam's armbands.

"I'm going to stay here with Bridie, no more swimming un-til I say it's all right—okay?" Orla stroked her son's damp hair. Sam looked mutinous, but nodded, and took his castle bucket off down the sand.

Orla lay next to her daughter and closed her eyes against the enamel sky. Occasionally, she rolled over to check on Sam, busy on the fierce sand. The drone of an aircraft, faint as an in-sect, in the distance.

Out across the sea, water and sky merged into one shimmer-ing color. Each reflected off the other so that Orla could barely make out the grayish cut of the horizon. Inland from the coast, low cloud hung above the fields and the village, palest cream threading in from the hills. The cloud ended in a hard, straight line on the curve of the cove and bisected the sky with alarm-ing determination. Orla turned from one view to the other, from the bright sea to the shadowed land.

Stand one way, and there is only one path, untroubled by doubt. The sky is clear. Stand another way, and you come to see the clouds gathering unnoticed behind your back, swarm-ing in from a different direction altogether. It occurred to Orla, as she watched the sea eat the sand, that the luck of your life depended entirely on which way you happened to be facing.

When she woke again, the sea still held the clouds at bay, but the light had shifted and dimmed. Her legs were cold under the shade of the umbrella and her hand and arm were reddened where she had flung them out from the towel. Bridie slept on beside her. Sam, who had been digging with vigor—*surely she'd slept no more than five minutes, surely, surely*—was gone from the dune, his bucket abandoned next to deflated armbands and the breeze eroding his wobbly sandcastle in drifts.

Orla sat up, still hazy with sleep, and scanned the beach.

Sam was in the water, up to his neck, arms waving happily, the glint of a rainbow spray in the air. Orla pitched forward and kicked sand over Bridie, who did not wake. As she ran, Sam's head went under. Orla thought about the white feather, falling.

He was far from the beach by the time she reached the sea, and for a long, long moment he was gone from sight. She waded into the water with heavy thighs, feet that dragged. The waves rose to her ribs and she couldn't find him and she was *so slow*, heartbreakingly slow. The sea was rolling and bestial and she was trivial within it.

Sam rose, briefly, about fifteen feet away, and went under again without a sound. As she swam, Orla took in a mouthful of seawater that came back out through her nose and made her retch. She plunged both arms under, felt the sting of the salt on her sunburn, grasped wildly for her child.

When her flesh collided with his, it felt like giving birth. The relief, the fear, the frantic connection from body to body. She heaved him from below the surface and the fear swelled and broke over her and collapsed back in on itself and sucked her down, down, with the force of it.

Bridie shrieked from the shore. Orla staggered back toward

the beach with Sam held tight against her hip, and ignored his coughs that whistled and scraped. He was alive, that was enough, and she was red, red, red from rage. She dropped him onto the sand and left him there, on all fours, spitting between his hands. The necklace swung heavy between her arms as she knelt, wet leather chafed her skin; Alice had promised protection, but there was none. Nobody could help her. In that moment, she hated it, hated what it represented: deviant reality, superstition, fear.

She shoved hats and towels and Tupperware into bags and kicked the umbrella from its stand. Bridie sat quiet, wide-eyed in the face of her mother's madness. When Sam appeared at her side, Orla did not look at his face.

Sam put out his little hand and touched his mother's ankle. *I'm sorry.*

"I said, didn't I say? Not to go into the water unless you were with me. This is the sea, Sam, not a paddling pool. You could have drowned. You could have *died*." She bent over the hot sand, coughed up water and bile.

Sam's face fell, his mouth turned in on itself and he squeezed his eyes closed against the sting of the tears.

The bucket would be left to fade and crack under the sun and, eventually, to be devoured by the shifting sands of the dune. Its little red handle would split and become unmoored from one side, to wave in the air like a crab claw.

Sam, ashamed, wouldn't tell, and neither would Orla. She could not bear the thought of another black mark against her name. Exhausted by failing her children, she felt bitterly the unfairness of such wretched consequences for so small a thing as falling asleep for—*five minutes, surely?* But Orla chose not to consider the angle of the sun, an hour lower in the sky, nor the return of the tide, and held on to the *five minutes, only five minutes*, as a rope to her sanity.

Up the cliff path they go, the storybook family. Mother, daughter, son, lined up and marching beneath the fierce eye of the sun. Sam in his blue hat. Bridie in white, waving fists happily. Orla in her yellow dress with summer-dusted feet and her desperation whipping out behind her. Onward, across seagrass and hot pebbles and husked corpses of worms and butterflies, up the hill to the house that binds them and contains them.

The heavy doors close behind them and the trees in the garden shake out their branches like arms to embrace them. There is no reprieve, there is no leaving. Even down in the sea, where the world shimmers and divides, the house stays with them because they are the house, now, and they carry it everywhere they go. The windows are always watching.

Decay

—

Hush-a-bye, lie still and sleep,
It grieves me sore to see thee weep,
For when thou weep'st thou wearies me,
Hush-a-bye, lie still and *bye.*

English nursery rhyme, traditional

22

2018

———

IMAGINE A THREAD. Palest green cotton, perhaps yellow. The sort of thread that restores buttons and mends a tear and brings ragged edges back together. Soft, nearly invisible—hidden. A thread that binds and loops, a slender current. Something like a vein, perhaps, just a small one. Narrow but vital, miles and miles of the stuff that knits a body together.

And now, picture the thread extending beyond the body— spiraling from the ends of clipped fingernails, running fluid alongside locks of hair, alive yet not alive, and vibrant with the same sort of electricity that makes cells talk to one another and fuels those snapping synapses within a brain.

We reach beyond ourselves. Our threads coil into the world, they unfurl both ahead of us and behind. We are as connected to the past as we are to the future; we are the sliding knot in the middle of a strand that anchors us back as well as forward, bound as much to what has not yet happened as to what cannot be changed.

*

Bridie, trapped in her high chair in the kitchen, screamed, furious, from a baby-blackbird mouth, arching her back and straining against the straps. A couple of crusts lay on the tray, very hard and not fresh. Her face was beetroot, little voice almost gone. The house was full of lavender dark and the open curtains in the drawing room lifted and fell on a night breeze.

Orla considered her daughter. They'd been sitting together for hours, Bridie growing ever more fractious, and Orla was just as tired and bored as the child. Let her tire herself out, just for a bit. She rose and left the kitchen, and Bridie's protests grew faint.

On the stairs, Sam sat in only a pair of shorts and his swimming goggles. Orla passed by her son, headed for her studio, and said, "I can't take you swimming right now, Sam. It's almost bedtime. Why don't you finish your supper with Bridie."

And when Nick arrived home, finally, he came up to her studio with Bridie, sobbing, in his arms and Sam at his side. Orla shifted on the chair and looked at Sam, then up at Nick. She noted that Sam still wore his goggles, and felt vaguely guilty.

Nick spoke low to temper the anger in his voice. "Have they eaten?" Sam slipped his hand into his father's and shook his head, and Orla was annoyed, for a moment, at the small betrayal. "Bridie's soaking. How long have you been up here?"

"It's summer, Nick. So what if the children go to bed a bit later? Does it really matter?"

"Bridie was screaming her head off and you didn't even hear her. And Sam—Sam was out in the garden, Orla, with no fucking clothes on, at ten o'clock at night."

Orla scrubbed at a wooden palette, so furious it made her throat sore. "You're never here; I don't think you've earned the right to give me shit for my parenting." It came out sharper than she'd meant, but she didn't care.

Nick took the children out and she turned back to cleaning

brushes on the trestle table. Among the pots and jars and tubes of thick and fragrant oils, the necklace lay where she had removed it after that day at the beach, after she had so nearly lost her child to an unknown and unknowable pull of horror. Since the moment it had hung round her neck, it had warped reality and invited an aberration into their lives here. Like the shoe, what was meant to protect brought only pain. The stone gathered a little dust and reflected the light in strange patterns, which Orla didn't see.

Very early in the morning, Orla left her bed, although she wasn't aware of it. She descended the stairs, hollow footsteps against the old wood. She moved through her house, in the light of the new day beneath the dome, out through the front doors and toward the water. The salt breeze and the thin, iron light called to mind another world entirely, which Orla inhabited in sleep.

Nick said, later, that he thought she was dead—that her humped shape on the scrubby grass of the front lawn nearly stopped his heart. "That's how I found you, curled up on the ground. You'd been crying, I think, in a dream." He put his head in his hands.

Her sleeping face was set toward the sea, her pale nightshirt dark with dew around the hem and up along her back. Her long hair was wrapped round her neck. Sand and grass coated the soles of her feet, little stones stuck between her toes. The wind caught and lifted strands of her hair, and when Nick knelt to touch her, to wake her, he saw that Orla's face was wet with tears—shining tracks on salt skin.

Orla was sent to the doctor and came home with a blister packet of sleeping tablets, which sat unopened in the drawer of her nightstand. Nick seemed satisfied when she told him about the prescription. He didn't need to know that she wouldn't be taking them. She needed to be alert, watchful.

She'd given him a fright, but Orla was past caring. If she'd woken by herself and crawled back to bed, no one would ever have known. And when Nick said it wasn't the first time, that he'd noticed her getting up more often in the night, all Orla could think was that it hadn't been a problem until he'd been affected by it in a way he didn't like.

The routine of their life in Bristol had been such that, although they'd drifted from each other by small degrees after becoming parents, Orla and Nick remained tethered by the admin of standing dinners with friends, arranging playdate pick-ups and drop-offs, companionable teeth-brushings on weekday mornings, the physical closeness triggered by reaching for the same item in a cramped wardrobe, Nick's hands on her waist as he shifted her gently out of the way to fetch down a clean shirt. Now, out here, Orla realized how little they really spoke to each other about the things that mattered.

She'd made a mistake, she knew, but he didn't help. Orla had forgotten her steps, she hadn't apologized when she was supposed to and they both knew it. So she texted him from the waiting room at the doctor—*I'm sorry. I love you. I don't want to fight*—and he'd returned the sentiment almost immediately. Nick was always happy to apologize, as long as she went first.

Orla heard him on the phone, after she came back from the GP. Nick didn't know she was home; she entered the house silently through the kitchen door to see him perched on the arm of the sofa, forehead resting in his free hand.

"Not really. She says she's fine, but she's not slept the last two nights. I mean, she'll sleep for a bit, but not properly. Just a few minutes at a time—I can tell because she wakes me up. She gets up about fifteen times a night, Mum."

A pause. Nick let out a long breath.

"Well, that's the thing—there's never any noise from Bridie. I've got the monitor on my side, I'd hear if she was crying. But it's like Orla decides she's heard something and then off she goes, she's up and out. But I never hear anything. And even at her worst, Bridie was never up that much during the night."

Orla heard him shift on the sofa, kick off a shoe.

"I know. I *know*, Mum. She's there now and that's a good thing, isn't it?"

She put her handbag on the table, quietly, and moved closer to the doorway.

"You keep saying that, but she's my wife. I'd know if it was that bad. No, it's not like before. I'd say—Mum, I'd *say*. I think, honestly, I just haven't been here enough. It's my fault."

Another silence, longer this time.

"Mum, that's nice of you to say, but it's not really true. Orla's right, I haven't been home enough. And it's not just for her, you know? The kids, too. I miss Sam. I'm blaming her, but I haven't helped. She's alone too much."

Orla returned to the kitchen door and closed it, hard, and heard Nick hang up very quickly.

Nick took the children to the beach—she offered to come, but he shook his head. She supervised as he packed the beach bags and filled bottles with tepid, metallic tap water. She inflated the armbands with her breath and held them out to Sam, who took them and looked up into her face. They exchanged a wordless pact: if he promised to wear his armbands, she promised not to tell his father that he'd almost drowned. Orla allowed him to think that the fault was his, and not hers. A heavy burden for a small child, perhaps, but Orla was tired of being punished herself.

Afternoon stretched on in Orla's silent house. She lay on the sofa, hungry but disinclined to fix it, and listened to the hot wind blow against the doors. Her hair, when it drifted across her face with the breeze, smelled dirty. She'd brought one of her newer pieces down from the studio, still a work in progress, and held it on her lap. Only a little canvas, a few inches square, and as she examined it, she thought about this place in which she found herself.

This house—it had never been hers. She knew that from the beginning and tried to tell herself different when they moved in, but this house would always resist ownership. The patrician face of it, so appealing at first, contained a spite that she should have seen on that first day. She'd thought the house haughty, knew now that it was only ever cruel.

"Hello?" Nick plopped Bridie onto the floor and she immediately made a break for the kitchen. Sam came in behind him, sweaty and damp and covered in sand.

Orla shielded her eyes from the bright light of the hallway. "Hi! Nice afternoon?" She noted Nick's dry hair. "Did you go in?"

He laughed. "Christ, no. Bloody freezing. Sam loved it, though." He pulled Sam close to his side, brown arm round Sam's pale shoulders. Sam put his face against his father's thigh, and it reminded Orla of old-fashioned paintings of faithful hounds.

"Was he good? Did everyone behave?"

Sam looked at his mother.

"They were great, honestly."

She kissed her husband, and although she knew he was still angry with her, his mouth softened against hers. He tasted of apples and salt. Nick swung Sam up into his arms. "I'll fetch Bridie—they both need a bath."

Orla went back into the sitting room and stopped beneath Sam's portrait. Whenever she passed by the painting now, it seemed like she'd painted another child altogether, years ago, in a different life.

But the new work—that was something special. At first it had confused and frustrated her, she hadn't been able to set down exactly what she saw in her head, or on the rare nights when she slept. Gone were the seascapes and landscapes—now she picked holes in her canvases. It wore away at the padding of her fingertips, and she had broken nail after nail, but it was exactly the feeling she was trying to convey. Her nails wore soft, ragged little tears beneath the paint, that absorbed the oil and the light.

Orla propped the new canvas on the sofa, underneath Sam's portrait, and stepped back to admire the contrast.

Nick strolled into the living room, Sam's wet swimming shorts dangled from a finger. "What happened to this, then? Looks like mice—Christ, don't tell me there's mice up there."

"No, no. It's on purpose. What do you think?"

"What do I think of what? I can't tell what it's supposed to be. Looks like a cat's got to it, or something."

She tried to explain. "It's the same as a landscape, really, when you get right down to it. When you think about time— you know, actual *time* with a capital T—it's the place where we live, isn't it? A dimension, right? And it contains everything that's already happened, as well as everything that's going to happen—so I'm collapsing the barrier."

"The barrier?" Nick, distracted, unpacked the beach bag and spilled sand and broken biscuits onto the floorboards, where he looked at them for a second or two, then shrugged and dispersed the crumbs with the toe of his shoe.

Orla took his hand and steered him back toward the sofa. "Between the past and the present, if you like. The future, too. Sort of bringing them together, making a connection. It's what the holes represent—do you see?"

Nick folded his arms across his chest, confused.

She continued, "The canvas is a bit like the present—you know, where we're living now. And through the hole you can see something else, another part of the past. Another window into the future. The idea of time being visible in that way—I want to paint it. Or, at least, my interpretation of it."

"Quite a departure, then, from your usual stuff."

Was it a departure? Not really. To Orla, it felt more like fulfillment. "Sort of, I suppose. And in some ways, no different at all."

And so she came to her canvases with renewed purpose, spent hours in her studio while she scratched and tugged until the fibers gave way. She'd tried using the points of her nail scissors, but the puncture wound was too clean, too artificial. When she picked, little spots of blood marked the canvas and turned brown, and Orla felt that it added to the general effect. These would be even better than her dark seascapes.

Orla sliced tomatoes and listened out for Sam. It had grown later than she'd realized, much past their usual suppertime, and he had fallen asleep on the sofa, waiting. The evening was warm and the view out of the kitchen, down the garden and across the green fields, was hazy with heat. She couldn't remember the last time any of them had worn shoes. Daylight arrived too early and quit too late, stretching out the days into a shape that Orla struggled to contain. She never knew the right time for anything anymore: Bridie's naps were haphazard; Sam's meals came whenever Orla needed a break from plucking holes in canvas, when her worn nails were too sore to continue. But Sam didn't seem to mind. He spent almost no time at all in the playroom, now, and a gritty dust collected on his old drawings of gray people and on the dried-out brushes in pots. He'd pulled away from her, her little shadow gone.

How can a silent child be quieter still? Orla didn't know there could be another layer below silence—but she learned. She realized, too late, that she and Sam had created their own discourse from touch and expression, and found that she'd developed the ability to read his emotions just from the rhythm of his walk. She discovered this only when it became clear that it was lost to her.

Nick had built a fort in the sitting room for Sam, before he left again for the week—just an old fleece blanket strung between the sofa and the armchair and propped up with their camera tripod, but Sam loved it and filled it with his books and his "computer" and several packets of Bridie's vegetable puffs. He slept now in his fort under the open window. His skin goosefleshed in the cool air.

Bridie, asleep in her high chair, had slipped so far down that the shoulder straps dug into her cheeks. Her hot hands flopped over the sides.

Orla ate dinner alone at the table and watched the last of the sun dip behind the orangery and the plum shadows grow on the lawn. She passed Sam's fort on her way to bed, Bridie heavy in her arms, but he wasn't there.

Warm rain arrived and drummed on the glass dome. The long landings lay still and silent; the curtains moved only slightly against the windows in the sitting room, disturbed by a cool draft. A couple of floorboards in the drawing room expanded and cracked. The last of the peony blooms lay scattered along the patio and were lifted by the wind, and the rain stuck the translucent petals to the windows of the orangery. A slow bee knocked against the glass, confused and loud.

Orla put Bridie into her cot. On the shelf, the baby monitor lay on its side, the white plastic gray and furred with dust. Orla stood on the landing outside the nursery, with her hands on the banister, and looked down into the harlequin hallway. Outside, a couple of birds called to each other, frantic and shrill. Orla closed the nursery door behind her and heard only quiet. From room to room she went, but Sam was nowhere.

She stood in the playroom and looked out into the garden—no sign of him. No swaying bushes, no small figure running in among the trees. The playroom was a mess and she felt guilty, briefly. The pad of paper clipped to one side of the easel was empty, all the sheets torn off. She hadn't come in here at all recently, and she thought that Sam hadn't, either. Hardened tubes of acrylic paint lay on the windowsill, used up and dry. A few brushes stood in a jam jar that had once held water, the bristles stiff and dirty.

Between the floorboards under the window, something grew upward, straining toward the light. It was the only thing in the room that wasn't muted by a film of dust, the green leaves extravagantly bright against the old wood. Orla knelt and touched the tiny, delicate plant that sprouted, almost bashful, from under the boards and curled across the floor. Small white berries nestled where the leaves joined the tender stems. She tugged the mistletoe sapling out by the root, left it to wither on the floor, and took the stairs to the attic.

On the stairs, little footsteps in the dust. Orla followed them up.

The boarded-up dormer window cast a low shadow across the expanse of the attic. A deep stain on the floorboards at the end of the attic, covered now in a film of dust, marked where the bird had come in. Rain beaded on the windows and dripped through the frame. The water was turned gritty and orange by the rust on the iron frames.

But the attic was empty, and Orla closed the door behind her, a sick panic rising. *Where is Sam? She must keep him safe.* She lapped the first floor again—nursery, master bedroom, spare room—and when she opened the door to Sam's room and saw the soft mound of his duvet, one pale foot hanging over the edge of the bed, her heart slowed and she put her fingers into her eye sockets and wept with relief. *Be better, Orla. Don't let the house know that you're undone.*

Orla fell asleep on top of the duvet; in the morning, her flesh would be livid from the bite of her clothes.

23

1976

——

LYDIA WAITED FOR SARA TO send her back up to the attic. She slept each night in Philip's bed, his old pajama jacket tucked under the pillow where she could reach it anytime she woke. The room smelled of him, of the very specific scent of his hair and childish sweat. She thought about those last few days in this room with him, how precious he had felt between her arms, with his head on her breastbone. Light and thin with fever, so full of love for her. Sometimes, when she woke in the black, she heard him breathing by the bed. Long, whistling breaths—ragged around the edges with the fluid that filled his lungs. She knew it wasn't real, of course, but she never turned on the lamp; she would never banish him with the light.

Throughout the long nights, Lydia listened to Sara going in and out, in and out to Owen's nursery through the passageway, obsessing over her remaining son. Lydia listened to the doors open and close, first one, then the other, at regular intervals well into the morning. Sometimes, Owen would wake and cry, and Sara sang to him then. Over and over, Sara returned to her child, as though to sleep would be to relinquish him to a danger kept at bay by her watchful, waking eyes. The sound of the nursery doors opening and closing grated on Lydia's nerves—the metallic twist of the handle, the click of the lock, the scrape of the wood against the frame. Lydia took to putting her head under the pillow.

Sara had either forgotten that Lydia slept in Philip's room, or she didn't care. Lydia didn't bring down any of her own things—the room still belonged to Philip, as far as she was concerned, and she wouldn't sully it with underwear and magazines and pots of face cream. Philip wouldn't like it, she thought, if he visited and saw that his animals and books had been moved and his things packed away.

After the funeral, before everyone arrived for tea at the house, she went up to her old attic bedroom and, for the first time since he died, Lydia cried. She lay on the dusty floorboards in her good black shift dress, far too hot in this suffocating June weather, and let the tears slide down her temples to trickle into her ears, tears that stung her sunburned cheeks and coated her hair with salt. Soundless; an uncomplicated grief that needed no enticing.

At Doug's funeral, Lydia had wept a little, and mostly because she felt she ought to. It saddened her to think of the children without a father, of the baby that Sara carried growing up with only one parent. Her throat hurt with the effort of her tears.

But, for Philip—for Philip, she could not cry at all at first. At the funeral, Sara howled and clung to the twins, and Lydia wanted to shake her. It was *indecent*, the way she'd carried on at the church, after all those days of utterly ignoring all of them and weeping alone in her bedroom. *Selfish*. Couldn't she see how her three living children needed her? Leave Philip to Lydia, he belonged to her anyway. *Tend to your flock, Sara.*

Philip was four when Lydia had arrived. Four years old and solemn and curious and ever so slightly officious. Philip was the child of his father, the heir apparent, and Sara left them to it, run ragged by the twins. He shook Lydia's hand when she came to the house for her interview—so pompous—and she'd laughed and laughed until Philip laughed, too. He amused her, this old little boy. If she ever had a child, she thought, she would like them to be like Philip.

It seemed inexplicable that he could be gone. The weight of the absurdity of it, the impossibility of this reality, stifled her. Lydia felt bound in grief, claustrophobic. Her own inability to alter what had happened was shocking.

The coffin was larger than she thought it would be; perhaps she still thought of him as four, and not nearly eight and almost out of short trousers. He would remain this way to her, always: small and serious and beloved.

Dot's head appeared at the connecting door. She tapped softly on the plywood. "You all right, Lids? Sara sent me to find you. People are arriving; she needs a hand with Owen."

"Right. Thanks."

"How's it been? You seen anything else?"

Lydia shrugged. "No. Owen seems fine, the girls are a handful, but that's nothing new. Haven't heard anything."

"That's good then, isn't it? Maybe it's fine, now. Are the scissors still there?"

"Yes. I make sure, every day. I don't think Sara's even seen them."

"She wouldn't notice if you came down to breakfast naked, Lids, not the way she is."

Lydia sat up and brushed off the skirt of her dress. She smoothed her hair. "Tell her I'm coming."

Dot had held Lydia's hand all the way through the church service, on the third pew back from the front. The first two rows were reserved for family, full of Sara and Doug's relatives.

When Lydia tried to sit next to Clover, Sara shook her head and pointed behind.

Doug's parents had telephoned a couple of times, tried to persuade Sara to come back to London for the funeral and have Philip interred next to his father. But Sara held firm and the service took place in the church outside the village. A suitable plot was found under a spreading yew tree. At least Lydia could remain close to him—she didn't like to think of him in a cold cemetery in London, so far away from her.

Such a beautiful day, such perfect weather. Fine and clear and warm, full of sweet air and the music of pretty waves breaking on a summer-holiday beach. The funeral-goers threaded through the town, dark blemishes among the bright tourists in their linen shorts.

The hall and drawing room were full of people sweating in black suits and under black hats, bathed in June sunlight beneath the dome and the tall windows. Dot's mum, Sheila, had come to help, and rows of cups and saucers were lined up on the dining table for the mourners. Sheila stood behind the table and handed out the tea, made gritty by the limescale built up inside the large steel urn loaned from the village hall.

"Lids." Dot touched her elbow and handed her a glass of water.

"Thanks."

They stood together under the stairs. A large photograph of Philip was set on the mahogany occasional table next to a ceramic vase crammed full of fat cream stocks, already drooping in the heat. They smelled too strong indoors, dying in their vase of clouded water.

"Where's Sara?"

Dot pulled at the neck of her black blouse. "Outside, I think. Christ, it's hot in here."

"Lydia?" Tabitha and Clover appeared in matching black worsted pinafores, hair pulled tight into stern French braids and secured with black ribbons. The same dresses they had worn to Doug's funeral, brought out again much too soon.

"Hello, my loves." Lydia put a hand on Tabitha's head and felt the damp heat retained by the thick hair. A small black fly crawled along Tabitha's forehead.

"What is there to eat?"

Dot motioned toward the drawing room. "There's sandwiches, in there. I should help Mum. Come on, I'll show you."

Sara sat in the orangery with the vicar. He had a hand on her knee; Owen writhed on her lap.

"Can I get you anything, Sara?" It was cooler in here, the patio doors open to the garden and the lavender-scented air.

Sara sighed. "Take Owen?" She said it very slowly, as if she was tasting the words in her mouth, like a boiled sweet, or a pebble. Trying out the sounds, unsure what to do next. "Thanks, Lydia."

Lydia left the room with the baby and heard the vicar say, "We must be grateful for the time we *did* have," and the dry noise that came from Sara's throat.

Four days, and the house was silent again. Doug's parents stayed for one night in a bed-and-breakfast in the village and caught the first train back to London the morning after the funeral. Lydia gathered up the shards of a broken teacup from underneath the drawing-room windowsill, left there by a careless guest to topple and smash on the floorboards.

Lydia rose later and later, left the girls to eat breakfast if they liked and to go hungry if they didn't. Sara stayed in her bedroom despite the heat. The house choked them all.

Lydia kept to the patio with Owen; sometimes they played

on the lawn once the sun had moved and the high garden walls
cast a benevolent shadow onto the browning grass.

Dot came on her usual days and made half-hearted meals
and tried to keep the house clean, but fine sand crept in at all
points, strewn across the hall tiles and settling on windowsills.
The house seemed to catch all the wind, all the debris flung up
from the cliff path and the woods. Flies abounded, breeding
among the soft brown bananas in the fruit bowl. Everything
had come loose.

"We want to go in the pond, Lydia."

Lydia looked up from her magazine, wildly out of date, and
yawned. She was very tired, all the time. The twins threw a
double shadow across her legs. "The pond?"

Tabitha pulled a dandelion from the lawn. The milk ran
down the stem onto her wrist and she licked at it with a cat's
tongue, pointed and crimson. "Yes. Mummy said we aren't allowed to go to the beach. It's dangerous."

"Right." Sara had taken Lydia to task for their trip to the
beach with Dot—the trip she had previously thanked them
for—and all Lydia could do was nod and think, *I have no idea
what is happening anymore.*

"But we want to swim." Clover held out her hands. "Because we are too hot."

Lydia stood up. Owen slept on the blanket, pink with heat.
"Okay. But I'll come with you. And you have to be quick."

The girls undressed down at the edge of the pond, among
the long grass that smelled of rotting vegetables and shivered
with insects. The water was mirror-smooth, utterly flat save
for the tiny pockmarks made by beetles landing and taking off.
The cherub turned its stone face toward Heaven.

Tabitha went first, in her old vest and knickers that sagged
at the bum. "Oh, oh! It's muddy, Lydia, it's horrible!"

Lydia laughed. "It's only muddy at the edge, it'll be all right when you're swimming."

Clover followed, up to her knees, and shouted, "There's seaweed in here, Lydia! It's stuck to me!"

"It's not seaweed, it's just pond plants. Honestly, I didn't think you girls were such scaredy-cats!"

Tabitha pulled a face and ducked her head under. They swam out to the middle, touched the cherub, bobbed in the emerald water.

Lydia tugged off her shorts and blouse and stepped in after them. It was cold, shockingly so—she thought it would be like a bath, but the mud between her toes was icy. A few strides out and she was up to her chest, feet no longer touched the bottom. So deep, she'd never realized. No wonder Sara didn't want them down here.

The girls splashed beside her, two otters with slick hair and glittering faces.

"This is good, isn't it!" Tabitha trod water and her pale legs flashed in the murk.

Wind caught the oaks and shook a few green leaves over the pond, rippled the surface. Lydia was very cold. "Okay, I think that's enough." Something slid against her leg.

"But we've barely been in—we haven't even had a swimming race," Clover complained.

"I don't think this is a good idea. Your mum won't like it."

"She won't care."

Tabitha nodded. "She doesn't care about anything."

"Don't be silly." But Lydia knew they were right. She still heard Sara going in to Owen during the night—her endless, restless vigils—but she hardly spoke to Lydia or the twins.

Sara's grief for Doug had been manic, energized. She threw out all his clothes the same night he finally died, whisked away in black plastic sacks. The house sale was another impulsive choice that crackled with a wicked kind of electricity. Change, movement, erasure—Sara grieved her husband with action.

But Philip turned her to treacle. She flowed through the days thick and gasping and so, so slow. When she ate, her jaw moved exactly once per second. She swallowed as an afterthought. Each word she spoke came at the end of a terrible, weighted pause. She didn't cry anymore, not after those first days of raucous wailing. The only thing she'd said to the girls since the funeral was, *I am trying to sleep.* The girls couldn't bear her, and neither could Lydia.

And now, here she came, walking toward them across the lawn in her awful stop-motion way.

Lydia kicked toward the lawn and called out, "Girls. Get out. Get out now, please." They stood on the bank in the hazy afternoon, feet covered in mud and weeds, dripping pond water onto the grass. The twins took Lydia's hands as their mother approached.

Sara bore down upon them, wild-eyed, stinking of cigarettes and unwashed hair. She opened her mouth and it sounded like a siren, an incomprehensible stream of noise, hands flapping, throat working. "*I told you, I told you, how many times, not down here, this is dangerous, anything could happen, Lydia, Lydia, how could you, my girls, my girls.*"

Tabitha and Clover looked at each other and then up at Lydia.

"Sara, please," Lydia tried. "It's fine, I've been with them the whole time. It was just a little paddle, it's so hot today—"

"Stop it—stopitstopit I *said*, why did no one listen? It's a *rule*." She was white with rage.

"Sara, calm down, it's fine. We're all fine, see?" Lydia smiled, seasick.

Sara's mouth twisted, a snail-shell spiral. "I don't give a fuck about *you*."

Tabitha began to cry, then Clover. Sara turned and walked away from them across the lawn toward the house. She passed by Owen, awake now and wriggling on the blanket, and never even noticed him.

Lydia went back up to the attic room that night. She took Philip's pajama jacket and made the bed, nice and neat, just how he would have liked. When she closed the sash window, the room was very quiet.

She didn't want to be near Sara anymore. They hadn't seen her again, not after the pond, and Lydia let the girls eat supper on the sofa, curled up next to her; like new kittens, they sought the comfort of her body and she folded them in.

"Is Mummy still cross with us, Lydia?"

"No, loves, she wasn't cross with you at all. She was cross with me. There's nothing to worry about."

Tabitha tucked her knees under her chin and picked at her socks, pulling at seed-heads stuck to the cotton. "What about the other lady?"

"What lady?"

"The sad lady. Clover saw her in the garden once."

"Clover?"

The child nodded. "She was just sitting on the grass. She was crying."

Tabitha interjected, "She's always crying."

Lydia wanted to be sick. "Where else do you see her?"

The girls looked at each other. "Just, around. Sometimes on the landing. Just walking. Then she goes away. Is she a ghost?" Tabitha sounded interested rather than disturbed.

"What does she look like?"

Clover shrugged and held out her hand for the seeds Tabitha had gathered. "Oh, like a grown-up, I suppose. You know,

Lydia. Like a lady. She's always got a jumper on, and jeans a bit like Daddy used to wear."

Lydia took hold of Clover's shoulders and knelt. "If you see her again, you must tell me, all right?" She worried that her fear might show in her voice, but the twins nodded, turned inward toward each other and closed Lydia out again.

The attic was stifling; she left the door to the steps open to allow for a little cool air, then sat on her quilt and listened to the house settle, to the clicks of bird feet on the roof, so close to her head. How to continue? There was no map for where she was. She thought of Philip, demanding breakfast, backlit by a kinder sun.

She was frightened—very frightened—by what the girls had told her. Ought she to tell Sara? *Yes.* But Lydia knew Sara wouldn't listen. Sara didn't hear anything anymore.

Lydia knelt on the warm floorboards with the camping lamp and found the steel nail file in her makeup bag. She faced the chimney breast that rose through her bedroom and leaned back on her heels. Careful, not wanting to disturb too much of the crumbling plaster, she etched a small, dainty cross, followed by the letters *P R* into the soft surface—low down, just above the floorboards. Such a small thing, but she wanted to leave something of him behind, here in this room. Even if no one else ever saw it, there would be a memory of him here.

The sounds from below reached Lydia even in the depths of her dreams. Grief exhausted her, she slept harder than usual and struggled to wake. For a moment or two, she lay and simply listened, expecting to be reassured by a familiar toilet flush or murmurs from the twins. But when she couldn't place the noise, she slipped out of the attic and toward the rhythmic disturbance that echoed through the night house.

The door to the drawing room stood open, but no lights were on. The sky above was black and flat, as if the glass dome had disappeared altogether and left Lydia exposed and cold in the vast space of the hall.

In the gray shadows of the drawing room, the sound was louder still, and, with her face only an inch past the door, Lydia saw the crouched shape of a person on all fours, moving back and forth across the floor very quickly. Long hair swept the floor. The table and chairs had been pushed, jumbled, in front of the enormous fireplace and the rug was folded over on itself to expose the floorboards.

"Hello?"

The shape whipped round, two wide eyes in a pale face.

"Sara?"

As if she couldn't hear, Sara turned away and bent again to the floor. Lydia saw that she was passing a soft brush back and forth across the wood, working at the boards. A tin of beeswax, lidless, sat just out of reach. Her elbows jerked sharply, too fast, and it made her look like an insect, like a panicked cricket.

"Sara—are you all right? Sara, look at me." Lydia knelt next to a woman she didn't recognize and put her hands over Sara's to take the brush. "What are you doing?"

Sara stared at the floor between her arms. "I'm taking care of it."

"Of what?"

"Of the house. It needs me."

"What?"

Sara smiled. "The floor, we're so rough with it! The children, they don't take care. It needed help." She touched a fingertip to the board beneath her knees.

"It's very late, Sara; won't you come back to bed?" Lydia took her hand.

Sara looked down at their clasped hands. "All right. Yes. All right."

"How long have you been at this, Sara?" Lydia rose to her feet and brought Sara up with her.

"Hours, I think. Or perhaps only a few minutes. I'm not sure. I woke up in the night and I heard it. It asked me to help, it told me to come and love it."

"Who did?"

"The house."

Lydia held Sara's cold hands and felt the tendons of the other woman's fingers, the hard bones at the joints.

"He's here, still." Sara looked past Lydia, through the open doorway to the shadowed hall.

"What?"

"I saw him. Afterward. Only once, but I know it was him. I *know*. I know my own child."

Lydia gripped Sara's wrists. "Philip isn't here, Sara, you know that."

"I followed him. All the way outside." Sara's eyes closed, as if she were remembering a dream. "I called his name. I looked for him. I tried, I tried—" Sara pressed her forehead to Lydia's hands and began to cry. "I tried to find him, to look for him, but he was gone. Under the water. I wanted to follow, but she— she was there and I couldn't see—"

Sobbing, bent in half, Sara wept her grief onto Lydia's skin. She put her face to Lydia's hands; Lydia cupped her palms and held Sara's wet cheeks and saw the bone-white curve of Sara's spine between her bare shoulder blades, disappearing into her nightdress.

24

2018

———

HOPE IN NO SMALL MEASURE is a dangerous thing: intoxicating, seductive. It leads us to places where we don't belong and causes us to knock on doors and unlock gates that would otherwise remain barred. Hope is a breadcrumb trail through a black wood.

Orla phoned Alice after lunch, desperate to talk to someone who didn't judge her like Nick did, didn't make her feel so wrong.

"Orla!" Alice sounded thrilled. "So lovely to hear from you—how are you? Kids okay? You absolutely must come in soon, we've missed you."

"I know, I know—I'm so sorry! I've been busy up here, though, got a few new things on the go." She knew that Alice would be pleased, would encourage her. Nick didn't like this series, but if Alice said she should continue then she could rub his face in that.

"That's brilliant—honestly. I can't wait to see them. Are they much like the last ones?"

Orla laughed. "It's a secret! You can see them when they're done."

"Promise I'll be the first?"

"Promise."

Alice clicked her teeth down the phone. "Now, listen. Will you come down to the village for the solstice? The kids will love it, and it'll be your first."

"The solstice?"

"Yes! You know, Midsummer. The village does a little fete type of thing. Couple of local bands, a cake stall. There's a parade, too."

"Sounds delightful, very countryside," Orla teased.

"It's a big deal around here! People love it, everyone goes. Claude's a stag this year, in the parade—he's got antlers and everything." Alice laughed and sounded proud, too.

"Well, can't miss that then, can we. Sounds grand altogether. When is it?"

"Couple of days, on the twenty-first. Right on Midsummer."

Orla felt buoyed by the phone call. Perhaps some of the work would be finished then, and she could take it to Alice and Claude and allow them to tell her how good it all was.

They were good, her new pieces. Alive under her hands, they sang to her in the same way that Sam's portrait once did.

Around her, the house turned over and shook itself, a waking dog. It was alert, waiting for Orla. Waiting to see what she would do. She knew it, and she couldn't understand how the others didn't. To Nick, and to his parents, and to Alice and Claude, and even Toby, it was stone and plaster and pipes—fixed, dumb. Ordinary.

But Orla—Orla swam through the house, lush as a river. The others saw only the silver surface, but Orla existed down in the cool, deep currents. Tall weeds ribboned her ankles, she bruised her ribs and elbows against slick stones. The house was bigger than any of them had fathomed and Orla lived in all of its dimensions at once.

Orla breathed in and out with the house, a curious symbiosis that sustained her as much as it depleted her. And underneath all of that, down on the riverbed where the water was cold and black and there was no redemption to be found, lay a wanting. Orla knew what it was to be wanted like that, and she'd registered it without knowing.

She knew what the house wanted, but she had only herself to give.

Toby arrived. Orla sat on the lawn with Bridie and Sam on their old picnic rug, bobbled with pollen and crumbs, and watched the two men together. Nick jerked his head toward her, Toby's eyebrows shot up. He turned to them and his face was a question. Nick ran his hands through his hair, the picture of a man exasperated, and Toby shook his head. Orla bent over the baby, desperate with embarrassment. Nick was *telling* on her, as if she were a child, and now she must bear the heaped shame from Toby, as well as from her own husband, for how she'd neglected her children, how she'd failed them.

Bridie sat in the well of Orla's crossed legs and drooled over a slice of apple. Sam lay a few feet away, intently coloring and mostly ignoring his mother. Nick's shadow sliced them all apart.

"I'm heading into the village, pick up a few bits. You going to be okay here?"

"I'm not a child. We'll be fine."

Toby disappeared in and out of the shed to fetch supplies for the day's work: his battered leather gloves for stripping ivy, a heavy-duty pair of pruning shears with loud orange handles for snipping, yellow tubs of fertilizer for the beds. He tugged a faded navy baseball cap from his back pocket. Orla waved from the blanket and Sam sat up.

Toby wandered over. "Well, now, don't you three look comfortable!"

Sam pointed to the pile on the patio.

"Ah, no jobs for you right now, mate, sorry. I'll mostly be up the ladder."

Sam folded his arms—*But I want to help?*

Toby's face was dark under the brim of his cap. "I'll be doing a bit of digging later, down the end; will you give us a hand then?"

Sam gifted Toby a smile, something he had withheld from Orla for days. She looked away from him and down to the oaks when she said, "So you spoke to Nick, then?"

"He said you'd not been well. Sorry. I didn't ask or anything, he just sort of said."

"Sorry. I don't really know why he told you."

Toby cleared his throat and scratched at his forearm. Silverfish flakes of skin swirled away into the summer air. "I think he's just worried? I mean, he seemed worried."

Orla, who had seen the paternalistic set of Nick's face, knew that wasn't true, but was grateful that Toby was kind enough to say so. "I'm fine. He's really blowing this out of proportion."

Toby sweated and looked up at the sky.

Orla let it go.

Morning turned to afternoon and Nick didn't come back. When Bridie was asleep for her mid-afternoon nap, a little roast potato in her cot, and Sam dozed on the sofa in the sitting room, Orla wondered where he might have gone. He'd said the village, but had likely escaped over to Poole, with its big air-conditioned Waitrose and free coffee. A nice little treat for him.

Toby worked steadily on the ivy that grew across Sam's window and made a good deal of noise. Occasionally, she heard the slap of fallen branches on the patio. Twice she heard him swear, when the wire-vines drew blood from a bare arm.

Orla headed upstairs to fetch clean socks for Sam. On the first floor, the grunts of Toby's labor came clear through the open window in Sam's bedroom.

"Going all right, then?"

"Yeah—tough old bugger. Really having to work at it. Sorry about the mess." Little dunes of mortar dust piled up along the windowsill.

Orla reached out a hand. "Is it better if I close the window?"

"No, it's in round the frame and I need to work it out. Sorry. It might need a hoover when I'm done."

Toby met her eyes. And then his gaze slid past her, to the weighted void of the room behind her, and Orla turned and saw the two blond children sitting cross-legged on the carpet, swaying together, hissing like snakes from open mouths, and Toby said, "Oh!" and leaned back and slipped out of sight, and when Orla heard the thump onto the patio she saw that she was still holding out her hand.

Orla sat, alone, in the family room at the hospital. She had been there for a long time, she thought. People passed by the glass strip in the door, but no one came in. The room smelled of disinfectant and warm, dusty carpet. There was a box of tissues on an Ikea coffee table—balsam tissues, which Orla thought was very thoughtful—but she hadn't cried yet.

She hadn't gone in the ambulance, and felt as though she had betrayed Toby terribly by letting him be taken away all alone. Orla had clung to the side gate and felt the wretched pull of the house, the children: she couldn't leave. Only when Nick finally returned was she released.

Toby's father entered with a nurse and Orla stood up very quickly, and felt sick. The nurse handed Mr. Tradgett—Oliver, she'd learned—a piece of paper with numbers on it, and smiled at Orla and left. The dust in the room was very loud.

"I'm sorry." The words were flattened by the weight of their feeling.

He sat down and looked at the paper in his hand. "Thank you."

"Is he—"

"Don't know. Not yet."

"Right." She sat back down. Her thighs in summer shorts stuck to the plastic chair. "What did they say?"

"Not a lot. It's bad, they think. He was awake, but they put him in a coma. They said that's better, but how can it be better?" Wet, red eyes in a pale face, sagged with tomorrow-grief that waited for him.

"I don't know. Maybe so he can rest?" Orla felt the scalpel-edge of her inadequacies.

"Yes. Yes." He looked again at the piece of paper. "Thank you for coming."

"Of course. I'm so sorry, we love Toby, I'm so sorry that this happened at our house, I feel *awful*, I feel so, so awful." Orla put her fingers to her mouth and understood that she had burdened this man with her own leaden guilt. "I'm sorry—I don't mean it like that. Is there anything we can do?" *Let me absolve myself.*

Toby's father put the paper in his pocket and stood up. "That's very kind. No, no there isn't."

Orla wanted to touch him, but knew she shouldn't. "Well, if there is—"

The door swung shut behind him and through the glass she watched him hesitate for a moment, confused about which way he should exit. Oliver was shorter than Toby; she saw the sun-pink skin of his scalp as he left.

The sun was almost down as Orla drove home. She felt

loose, untethered. This was too much, the entire afternoon verged on surreal. Orla laughed aloud with the absurdity of it all, and when she laughed it sounded like a dog, choking. Hoarse and impatient.

Their house atop the hill sat hunkered in the last of the sun. Usually so imposing, it seemed to Orla that this evening it had an air of sly triumph about it, glowering with satisfaction. She rounded the driveway and parked. Surely even the front doors stood a little lower than the day before? The windows were dark and Nick did not come out to greet her.

She found him putting Sam to bed, curiously focused on coaxing their son out of silence. It occurred to her that his usual casual disinterest in Sam's progress was perhaps a little too dismissive, a little forced. How often did he coach Sam like this when she wasn't around to see?

Nick turned as she entered the bedroom. "How did you get on? How's Toby?"

Sam leaned forward in bed with an expression of distress. Orla smiled at her son and said, "He'll be okay, he's being looked after in hospital. His dad is there with him." Sam nodded, relieved, and looked at his father.

Nick smoothed his hands across the duvet. "All right, Sam, come on, just once. I know you can do it, I'll be so proud of you!"

Silence. The room was dim, lit only by the orange night-light.

"Sam, I mean it. It's very important that you show me you can use your words properly. Do you want to talk about what happened today?"

Sam folded his arms across his chest and looked away, turning his face into the pillow. *No.*

Orla moved to tuck him in. "Enough, Nick. It's been a long day. He's fine."

"Orla, seriously. He'll never do it if we don't make him."

"Nick, he's had a serious shock. We all have. Leave him."

When Toby fell and Orla knelt next to him with the phone in her hand, pressing all the wrong buttons in her desperation, Sam had appeared at the door to the orangery with his arms clenched to his sides and his small white face wrenched open in horror. He stood fixed to the spot while Orla wept to the ambulance dispatch, and when Toby had been gathered up and taken away, Sam picked up the abandoned baseball cap and held it to his chest.

Toby was a warning. He had seen what she had seen and Orla felt strangely buoyed by the affirmation of his fall. The house asked too much of her. She had tried to love it, to restore its broken parts and lick its wounds and patch up the damage with her own hair and skin. And yet—not enough. It called for her as a child, needing her as a child, demanding as a child would, and Orla knew that, no matter how much she gave, it would never be enough because she was a mother, and no child is satisfied with anything less than complete consumption. Her children would devour her, if they could; they would eat her up and make her live inside them forever. The house wanted them to live inside it forever.

She had become mother to a monstrous child. The Reeve had spoken to her, whispered, and she had listened.

A mother must sacrifice for her children. Orla knew this and acknowledged the necessity, deep inside. The high keening of a lamb that leads her down to an unlit place.

25

1976

———

SARA HADN'T LOOKED AT THE paper bag of Philip's things from the hospital since the night she'd put it on the chest of drawers in his bedroom. The things he'd taken with him, the things he'd been wearing when he died. A hospital form in pink carbon paper stapled to the front, the handwriting faint. Name, age, effects. Date of birth. Date of death.

Lydia picked up the parcel often, and held it close to her chest. She knew what was inside without having to look. *Paddington*. Philip's pajamas that smelled of harsh soap and sweet child sweat. A comb, half a bag of boiled barley-sugar sweets. His gold christening bracelet. It seemed wrong to unpack the bag, as though dividing up all these precious possessions would be something like a dismantling, a scattering of bodily ashes. Sara didn't mention it, and Lydia didn't ask.

She sat in the dark on the edge of his bed with the bag on her lap and looked at the wall. The rest of the house had gone to bed hours ago, but she couldn't sleep. It wasn't just the heavy heat of the attic, nor Sara's coolness that had set in that day by the pond and never lifted. She missed Philip too much; during the days, she felt as though she could lie right in the middle of the kitchen floor and sleep forever, but the nights would not let her rest.

It had only been ten days since he died, and Lydia knew that none of them would ever return to the lives they were living before. The twins strayed farther and farther from the house each day, and Lydia let them. Sara had laid down a *no farther than the garden* rule, the day after the funeral, as though the fever that had captured Philip might be lurking out of bounds, waiting to snatch Tabitha and Clover once they set foot out of the protective circle of the brick walls.

But Lydia didn't bother to enforce the rule, and when the girls talked about their den in the beech woods on the other side of the cliff, or their tracks in the wheat fields, Sara looked at Lydia and Lydia met her gaze, daring Sara to reproach them all. Sara saw the defiance, saw her hold slipping.

They didn't speak of the night in the drawing room—either Sara didn't remember or pretended not to, and Lydia was too embarrassed to bring it up. Sara had fallen into bed like a stone and Lydia left her there to dream. Who could say what Sara had really seen, or thought she'd seen? The woman was decimated by what had happened to Philip. Worse—she was affronted by it. It was a subversion of all that she had put in place to protect and maintain her children. Brown bread, country air, sustained by nature.

"That's Sara's problem, though," said Dot as she folded towels in the orangery, fresh from the washing line and smelling of grass.

"Her problem?" Lydia sat on the edge of the ratty cane sofa and sucked on the end of a length of cotton to thread it through a needle—more holes in the knees of Tabitha's dungarees.

"She's all city. She thinks everything out here is nice, because it's the countryside. I like Sara, but she's London. She doesn't know what it's like."

Lydia stroked the fabric under her hands. "What's it like, then?"

Dot thought for a moment. "My mum makes me wash the eggs before I bring them up. When they come out, they're all wet, right? So they get stuck all over with chicken shit and feathers. We don't care, really, just give them a rinse before we eat them. But Mum said Sara wouldn't like to see that, the city folk usually don't, so before I bring them up here, I have to scrub them, all clean and nice."

Lydia smiled. "I never knew that."

"Do you know what she said to me, at the funeral? I was helping Mum carry in the boxes of cups from the car and Sara goes, out of nowhere, that she thought her family would be safe here because the sea air would keep them all healthy and that her husband died because of London, but she'd always thought that natural things can't hurt you. It was weird—she was just standing in the drawing room and she said it out loud, but she wasn't looking at us. It was like she was talking to herself."

"You know how she is, about the TV and stuff. Sugar."

Dot shook her head, quickly. "But she smokes so much. Like, all the time."

"I don't think she sees it like that." Lydia shrugged. A bumblebee zipped in through the open patio doors and bumped against Lydia's leg, then flew out again.

"Sara thinks nature has good intentions. I'll tell you what, though, there's all sorts of natural stuff out here that you wouldn't want to touch. Nightshade, baneberry, black bryony." Dot laughed. "Plenty of chicken shit. You remember the business with the tea? Close call, that one. Because she couldn't tell the difference."

"And I suppose scarlet fever is one of those things? Natural, but not nice?"

Dot sighed and smoothed her hands over the pile of neat towels. "My uncle only has one foot—got caught in a thresher. I had an older sister, she died of a fever from bad cow milk before I was born. I could skin a goat, if I had to, I know how to kill geese. Used to help with lambing, out on my brother's farm, when I was a kid. You need small hands; loads of kids round here help with lambing. Sometimes you'll find one that's come too early, though, a sheep that's not been brought in, and the lamb gets stuck and they both die, out in the field. Horrible, but it happens.

"Sara doesn't think about any of that stuff, and why should she have to? She doesn't need to kill a chicken, right, or know what plants she shouldn't eat. My mum had to teach us all that or we'd have run around trying to eat yew berries and shitting our knickers every other day. But for city people, those things aren't important, so they don't know it, and they think living out here is all just, like"—Dot waved her hands, reaching for the words—"like village fetes and scones and jam."

Lydia rested the dungarees on her lap and listened.

"But it's not like that, at least not all the time. And that's why Sara's so weird about what happened to Philip. I'm not saying it's not shit, because it is. Obviously, you don't want your kids to die. But she goes on about it like it's the most unnatural thing to have ever happened, like she doesn't understand it. But there's nothing to understand, it is what it is." Dot took a long breath and looked at Lydia. "I feel sorry for her. She's trying to make nature care about her, and it just doesn't."

Dot pulled another towel from the basket and snapped it open to soften the creases. Something, just a little thing, fell from the folds and bounced hard against the tiles. Dot, frowning, bent to retrieve it. When she picked it up, swinging it in her fingers, Lydia saw only a bright flash of light reflected.

"What is that?"

"Necklace, looks like. Bit chunky, if you ask me—not very stylish."

"Give it here." Lydia held out a hand to take the object. The leather loop was hard, brittle with age, and looked as though it could snap at any moment. It was tied through a hole in the middle of a small green and blue stone, and the colors were vivid even though the surface was dull and scratched. Small flecks of earth had caught in the cracks in the leather strap, as if it had been buried. "Looks really old. Not yours, then?"

Dot made a face. "Not quite my thing, is it, Lids. Sara's, maybe?"

"No, I don't think so. I've never seen it before."

The necklace lay on the sofa where Lydia put it, and was eventually forgotten about in the face of everything that followed. It slipped between the cushions, out of sight, and stayed there.

The days grew hotter and the house relaxed and expanded in the warmth. Windows stayed open and allowed sweet breezes of grass and jasmine. The glass dome caught the changing colors of the day and turned the white tiles to honey, to butter, to violet.

This fragile period of uneasy stasis ended with the words *What the fuck is this?* screamed by Sara from the nursery on a Saturday morning, two weeks after Philip died.

"Sara?" Lydia called up from the bottom of the stairs.

"Was this you? Was this you?" Sara stood on the landing with Owen, who wailed and arched in his mother's arms, straining against her grip.

"What? Sara, what is it?"

The sewing scissors clattered down the wide staircase, trailing their orange ribbon.

"Right, okay, Sara, just give me a minute—it's to help—"

"Have you gone *completely* out of your mind? Do you have any idea how dangerous this is? They could have fallen, taken an eye out, stabbed him in the brain—*Christ*, Lydia, what has got into you?"

Lydia couldn't help it. "They've been there for weeks, Sara, how have you only just noticed?"

Sara stared at her. "What are you implying?"

"You've not noticed much, recently, Sara." Might as well go for it, they were beyond all pretense now.

"I don't know if you remember, Lydia, but my son has just died." Sara's voice was high and thin, imperious.

"Yes, I loved him, too. We all loved him."

"I hope you aren't comparing."

"You weren't doing what was best for him, Sara. We both know that. He wasn't happy here. He missed his school, he missed his old life. You took that from him—you didn't *see* him. You didn't see him." Lydia put a hand to her mouth, shocked at herself.

Sara held Owen tighter, ignored his screams. "I know what's best for my own children."

"No, you don't. You've not said two words to the girls for weeks. You're not listening to Owen right now. You think you fixed everything by stranding yourself out here, but you just made it worse, you were only thinking of yourself. And the way you carried on over Philip, when you'd spent all that time just ignoring him—you know it wasn't right."

"I can't believe I'm listening to this—"

"You pay me to take care of your children because that's what I'm good at, and you didn't even listen to me when I said that Philip wasn't coping, that he needed something different."

Tabitha and Clover came out of the kitchen and stood in the shadow under the stairs, eyes fixed on Lydia.

Sara shifted Owen to the other hip, violently, so that his head swung back on his neck and he yelled. "Are you blaming me for his death? Is that what this is?"

"No!" Lydia rubbed her hands against her cheeks, enraged. "That was bad luck, it was awful, it was no one's fault. But it happened and now we all have to get on, you have three other children alive who *need* you—"

"I'll not be told how to mourn in my own house. This can't go on. I've been watching you, you know. Not sticking to the rules, letting the girls do whatever they want. I had a rule and you let them break it, and if something had happened to them, that would be your fault. Who knows what you let Philip get up to? Where you let him roam? There's a *reason* he got sick. And Owen, those scissors, what on *earth* were you doing? So irresponsible, Lydia." She paused, exhausted by her own spite. "You need to go."

"Fine. I'll go for a walk. I'll take the girls. Give you time to calm down."

"No. You need to leave. Back to London. I'll pay for the train."

Lydia stepped forward, shocked. "What?"

"You're not needed here anymore, Lydia. I'm sending the girls away to school, in September. Boarding. It's what Doug would have wanted. So I won't need you. You are not *required*." She turned and took Owen into her bedroom and closed the door to mute his screams.

Lydia looked at the twins, holding hands in the shadows. Two little girls about to be left alone, about to be forgotten.

"God, Lydia, this is really bad."

"I know."

They sat together in the garden, whispering like adolescents.

Lydia liberated another bottle of wine from the pantry and Dot portioned out a packet of cigarettes.

"And that's not the worst thing." Lydia struck a match.

Dot swilled the wine in the bottle, gulping straight from the neck. She wiped her mouth and left a streak of pink along her cheek. Lydia felt a quick compulsion to smear it clean with a wet thumb. "What do you mean?"

"The girls—they've seen that woman I saw. Out here, in the house. And Sara, she said she's seen Philip? I mean, she was half-asleep, but still, it sounded completely mad. I don't know what to do."

"I don't think there's much you can do. She's sacked you, Lids. You're out on your arse. You can't take the kids with you."

Lydia put her face in her hands, felt the heat of the cigarette against her forehead. "How did it all go to shit like this?"

Dot put an arm round her shoulders, skin that smelled of warm sun and tanning oil and sweat. "Sara's lost it. She can't cope with them on her own—not without you."

"I can't leave them here."

Dot wiped Lydia's face with her fingers. "You have to."

Lydia touched the paper bag on top of Philip's pillow and brought the blanket up to tuck it in. She listened to the sea, distant and pulsing, through the closed window. Out on the landing, the line of bedroom doorways glowered under their prominent lintels, recessed in inky shadow. The debris on the dome shifted in the wind and made a scratching noise against the glass.

Down in the hallway, in the gaping mouth of the house, something moved across the tiles. Lydia leaned over the banister, but the shadow was gone, disappeared into the sitting room. Her hands left clammy prints on the smooth wood.

She wanted to call out, but thought about Sara and Owen sleeping.

She stepped out of her slippers and left them on the landing, went lightly down the stairs. It felt like she was in a dream, as though she was inside someone else's head. The stairs protested beneath her bare feet.

The sitting room was empty, silent. Lydia put her hands out in front of her to touch the armchair, the sofa, the mantel above the fireplace. She didn't want to turn on the lights.

Nothing in the hallway or under the stairs. Philip's photograph remained on the occasional table, although the dying stocks had been taken away long ago. Ahead of her, through the doorway into the kitchen, she saw a small silhouette exit through the orangery. The doors to the patio swung open, pushed by an unseen hand.

Philip.

Of course it was him—who else? He'd come back, he'd come back to the house and to her. Sara was right: Lydia should have listened. She should have waited for him.

She stepped out onto the patio and watched the little figure move across the lawn. Smaller than she remembered, almost as small as he was the first day she met him. She followed him down the length of the garden, his shadow moving in and out of the trees. Her chest ached with love, she opened her mouth but could not speak. But not blond, not any longer. Not Philip with his summer-sun hair: a darker child, a different child, in a bright-yellow shirt that seemed almost to glow in the twilight.

He disappeared in the tall grass at the edge of the pond. Lydia stood, so far away from the house, and listened to the night water and the breeze in the oaks, and felt about in the grass for the child who was Philip but not Philip, pushed aside the long reeds and fell to her hands and knees, searching for him. She beat the grass wildly, crawled right to the water's edge where he'd disappeared. He was not in the shallows, nor gasping for air farther out; no gentle ripples, no cries for help.

Lydia knelt on the muddy bank, brackish slime soaking into her skirt. Her hands were caked in filthy mud, wet up to the wrist. Tears fell, bitter salt to mix with the black water. She had followed him down here—a child who seemed like Philip but could not be, and who had disappeared the moment he reached the water. Perhaps she was seeing things, and that thought no longer seemed so absurd.

When Lydia looked up to stand, he was there again—the boy. On the other side of the pond, on the bank among the tall flowers, Lydia saw his pale face rising above the reeds. Watching, open-mouthed and silent.

26

2018

———

SEE HER NOW, DOWN BY the trees. Kneeling at the bank of a pond that no longer exists, her hands reach out to water but touch only the dry earth. She sways a little, pale fingers pat the grass as she turns round and around like an animal. Sightless eyes in a sleeping face. She sighs, she dreams. Orla returns to her house, finds her bed, falls asleep with palms and feet covered in damp soil and new grass. When she wakes, she'll notice the streaks of mud on the sheets, the green on the pads of her fingers.

Orla woke up to a high, bright sun. All was very still. She heard bees and smelled earth and the white air. Something batted against the window and flew away. She was very hot.

Bridie cried in her bedroom, the sound like the lapping of distant water. Orla still didn't use the nursery corridor; she was afraid of it and continued to enter the nursery from the landing instead.

She heard Nick chatting to Sam downstairs, out of earshot of the baby, so she supposed she would get up. Bridie was pleased to see her, though, and Orla was briefly glad that she'd got out of bed. *See, Nick? I still do the mother-work.*

In the kitchen, her husband and son were drawing at the table, hemmed in by toast crusts scattered over dirty plates.

"Morning." She touched Nick's shoulder.

A clean mug stood on the table, waiting for Orla's coffee, but the coffee pot had been drained and put next to the sink— clearly Nick hadn't thought to refill it for her.

"Hi. Sleep well?" He examined her face. What he meant, of course, was had she taken her tablets.

"Mm." She put Bridie into the high chair and spooned coffee grounds into the pot. Nick headed out to the garden and passed close by his wife, but didn't touch her.

The garden was static in the heat. No trees moved, no insects whispered against the green grass. It looked surreal, flimsy as a stage set. Too bright, too defined.

Orla knew that there was a small, dark stain on the patio slabs beneath Sam's window. Nick had scrubbed at it with washing-up liquid and then baking soda and then, finally, bleach. It had surprised her, how little blood there was. Just a very thin trickle from his ear, and while she knelt over him and waited for the ambulance with the world opening up around her, she had joked to Toby—*please hear this, please hear me*— about how very thick his skull must be.

Faded bunting snapped in the wind coming off the sea, faint strains of accordion music floated above the shouting and laughing and crying and the barking of the dogs. A small stage was set up at one end of the high street; a few old men milled around in front of it, drinking pints of cloudy ale in plastic cups. The band looked hot and jaundiced under the dim shade of the canvas awning.

When they arrived together, with Bridie slung onto Orla's

back and Sam lofty on Nick's shoulders, the streets were already filled with people and dogs and noise and scraps of litter from ice cream wrappers and burger vans. A ketchup-stained napkin blew against Orla's leg.

Nick held her elbow, lightly, and said, "Drink?"

"Yes—thanks. Is there Pimm's?"

"I meant something soft."

"Pimm's, please—if there is." She knew there was; she'd seen the stall.

He looked tired. "Fine. You stay here."

The totem pole of her son atop her husband moved out of sight, lost among other people. Orla stood in the shade of a stall selling painted enamel cups and corn dolls, and jiggled Bridie in her pack.

"Orla!"

"Claude!"

He came toward them through the crowd, sunburn already beginning on his bald head, smelling of warm beer and barbecue smoke.

"Where's Alice?"

Claude pushed his sunglasses up onto his sweaty forehead. "Back at the shop, just closing up. Had a few people in around lunchtime, but we're done for the day."

"We're looking forward to your star turn, later."

He laughed. "Been angling for one of the stags for years. Finally let me do it when Eddie fell out with one of the old buggers and booted him out."

"Eddie?"

"Parish councillor. Organizes this, every year." Claude waved a hand toward the stage and the hot-dog vans. "Where's your men, then?"

"Gone to find me a Pimm's."

"Smart lads."

The sun climbed and sank across the cove. At five o'clock, Claude left them, pink with pride and performance nerves. Alice took the others to the best spot for watching, right on the edge of the high street, where they could see the stags coming with their bright torches. Nick stood behind Orla, who held Sam's hand and realized that he didn't want her to. He tugged and squirmed and eventually she let him go, and he looped his arms round Nick's leg instead. Bridie had fallen asleep; deep welts from the straps of her pack cut into Orla's shoulder blades and stung with sweat.

Nick put his hands on Sam's shoulders and directed him toward the street. "You'll have to watch carefully, see if you can tell which one is Claude!"

Sam nodded, solemn, and concentrated on the empty road.

As the light grew longer, the folk band started up a traditional tune. Lower-pitched, in a minor key, drawn-out screams of violins and something that sounded like a hunting horn. Orla shivered; she didn't like it. Beside her, Alice smiled in the dusk.

Down at the far end of the street, hoots of excitement started. Men hollered and whistled, and soft drumbeats signaled the arrival of the stags. Orla saw the torches, throwing off sparks, before she saw the men holding them aloft.

The stags came, two by two, in tunics of moss-green tied at the waist with old rope. Leather shoes slapped tarmac, a couple of dogs jumped and barked at their heels. Beards had been threaded with ivy vines, and those with bare faces had been daubed in mud. Each man's glory was a set of brownish antlers, tied to the head with hemp rope. Lengths of fresh bindweed, green and violently white, looped round and round. It reminded Orla of a photograph she had once seen in a *National Geographic*, of two stags that had been fighting and had fallen into a river and drowned, locked together in death by their antlers. When the photographer found them, they were nothing more than skeletons; lake weeds had grown around the bones and the horns.

Antlers bobbed and swayed as the men loped down the street. Animal. *Feral.* They dipped their crowns in time with the drumbeat, raised their knees and shouted to the sky, faces lit red in the burning torchlight.

Orla couldn't tell Claude apart, but Alice knew her husband and shrieked and pointed, and Sam jumped up and down and swayed in rhythm with the drums. Orla felt sick. She'd had three Pimm's—one that Nick had bought and two that she'd drunk alone, very quickly, after excusing herself to find a loo.

Behind the men, as they passed by, came other make-believe figures: a court jester in ragged red and yellow; a very drunk woman on a hobbyhorse, in an old-fashioned apron and gown, whose bonnet had gone awry and hung lopsided over one ear. A trio of teenage girls followed, twirling batons American-style, in silver tutus.

And at the end of the procession, a woman dressed all in white, covered head to toe with a lace veil and bearing an enormous bouquet of wildflowers and trailing grasses. Her skirts caught between her legs, her veil whipped in the wind and rose and fell in on itself. She was tall and moved slower than the rest. Orla couldn't see her face.

She tapped Alice's shoulder. "Who's that?"

"What?"

Orla put her mouth closer to Alice's ear. "The woman with the veil."

"Oh! That's the White Lady. The Maiden of the Water."

"What?"

Alice shouted louder. "The Maiden of the Water! Bit of a local thing. She comes from the water—like a spirit. Famous round here. A ghost."

The White Lady turned her faceless head toward Orla and moved on down the road.

And then a shape rose out of the darkness and put its hands on Orla's shoulders and tugged her forward by her T-shirt and slapped her, hard, across the side of her head. Orla stepped back and fell into Alice and the woman was on her then, pushing her down onto the concrete with her knees on Orla's chest. She felt the salt-sting of the woman's tears on her own face.

"You stupid, stupid girl—I told him, I told him not to, and he felt *sorry* for you and it's your fault, it's your *fault*—"

Release. The woman was lifted away, writhing like a marsh eel, and Orla lay on the pavement and looked at the night, felt the fire-blood of her ear.

"Stop it, *stop* it, Mum, you can't—"

Another whip-crack retort of flesh meeting flesh.

"Oh, God, Orla, are you all right?" Alice bent over and took Orla by both hands and pulled her to her feet. Orla felt the back of her head, where an egg hatched.

"Yes, yes, I'm fine. What—"

"It's Toby's grandmother. I'm so sorry."

Orla looked past Alice to the elderly woman who was struggling against Toby's father. She was slender as a bird, pale as wheat under lank silver hair in two braids threaded with fading brown. One of her shoes had come off and the underarms of her blue dress were black with sweat.

Orla put her hands out. "Oliver, I'm so sorry, please tell her, please tell her I'm so sorry." Her voice sounded dry and thin.

Alice took charge. "Get Dorothy out of here, Oliver. She needs to be at home. I'll drive you." She took Orla's hand. "Orla, love, you best be going on, now. Nick—take them home."

Nick lifted Sam, whose astonished face turned again and again from his mother to his father, and started away down the street, leaving Orla to follow.

They came home in the dark, Sam asleep on Nick's shoulder. Orla had Bridie in her pack. The muscles of her shoulders burned. She stumbled on the cliff path and Nick caught her by the upper arm. "Careful. You've got the baby."

"I know." Her head throbbed.

"You okay?"

Orla touched her ear. "No. Not really. I feel like it was my fault."

"What, the woman? Toby's grandma? She's clearly lost it; I feel a bit bad for her."

"No, not her. Toby."

"Don't be stupid, Orla, of course it wasn't your fault. It was a shitty accident, you know that."

"I should have—"

Nick let go of her arm and continued up the path. "There's nothing you could have done. Don't make this about you, Orla. Not like everything else."

A high summer moon washed everything in navy and gray and cast a strange, flat light that made the world seem oddly two-dimensional. Nick looked back every so often, to make sure she was still following him. Still faithful, willing to be led.

The Reeve rose out of the night to meet them. Silver streaks of cloud moved behind the chimney stacks, and the cathedral windows stood black against stone turned white in the moonlight. The jasmine at the front exuded its sweet honey smell.

In the front hallway, Nick turned on a lamp and the rest of the house receded into black, driven back by the light. Orla went upstairs and laid Bridie in her cot.

She wanted a drink, and went back down to the kitchen by way of the sitting room while Nick put Sam to bed. The room was chill; a night breeze swept down the chimney and curled round Orla's feet.

Sam's portrait hung large and seemed, in this light, to bear down upon her. Behind the canvas, creeping out along the cracks in the aging plaster of the wall, slender vines of mistletoe grew. The pale fruit hung heavy and delicate leaves coiled to frame the canvas.

Orla looked at the painting and saw that it had grown away from her, malformed. This was not what she had painted, but it was still the truth. Sam's face, so bright before, was shadowed, as though someone had swept the canvas with a gray brush. His eyes were dimmed, his cheeks sallow. His T-shirt was sickly, jaundiced, no longer the buttercup-yellow Orla had mixed so carefully. His mouth was slack, and bone strained against the skin of his knees. In the rich, full darkness behind him, half-hidden by the black folds of the curtains, a few precise brushstrokes of something ivory, something shining. *Teeth.* And long, thin fingers of honey-colored bone round his shoulders, the same pallid shade as the stone of the house.

"How is it?" Nick reached over in bed and touched the lump on the back of her head, hidden by her hair but still large and tender.

"Sore." A blood blister had sprung up on the outer curve of her ear and it throbbed in time with her heartbeat. "My ear hurts."

"We should lance it."

"Do you know how?"

"Of course. I've done your blisters before, from too much painting."

Although she was turned away from him, she could tell he was smiling. "Okay."

Orla sat on the edge of the bath in their en-suite and watched Nick first rinse the needle, then pass it back and forth above the flame of a match, glinting in the morning light.

"It's going to hurt."

Orla said nothing and pulled her hair into a ponytail. She felt his fingers on her skin and closed her eyes. Then came the sharp, sliding pain of the needle and the break of skin onto the hot flannel. Nick pressed the cloth tight against her ear. He leaned in and their mouths almost touched and for a moment she thought he was going to kiss her, but he didn't.

"Done."

There was a surprising amount of blood on the flannel. He tossed it into the laundry basket.

"Do you think I should go over?" She thought about Toby's white face against the patio, and the lost expression on Oliver's face that day in the hospital.

"Where?"

"Toby's house. To see his family."

Nick stared at his wife. "And why the fuck would you do that, Orla?"

Desperate, she wanted to atone. "To say sorry. I just feel so awful."

"I think you should leave those poor people alone, that's what I think." He left her in the bathroom, where she sat for a long moment, eyes fixed on the bloody flannel.

Downstairs, Bridie raced across the tiles of the hallway on clumsy baby hands and knees, with her father and brother in pursuit. Nick and Bridie shouted with joy and Sam laughed in silence.

Orla stopped on the landing to observe her family. They had changed so much in their short time at The Reeve: Sam almost three inches taller, and Bridie saying clumsy words, and the gray in Nick's stubble blooming in continents rather than islands. Herself, too—so thin now and unsteady on her feet, and eyes that receded in their sockets.

Nick stood and brushed his hands on his shorts. "We need a few things; thought I'd go into the village for a quick trip."

"Okay. Definitely milk—maybe coffee?"

"Sure."

Sam pointed to the front doors, but was rebuffed by his father. Orla suspected Nick wanted an opportunity to drive in peace.

"We'll have breakfast instead, Sam, how about that?" Orla descended the stairs and took her son by the hand. Bridie scooted ahead of them into the sitting room and made a noise that sounded a little like "breakfast." Orla laughed, and Sam smiled.

Sam's portrait was still surrounded by a wreath of mistletoe; no one else had seemed to notice them. In the kitchen, more mistletoe crept across the floor and wound itself round the legs of the table and chairs and across the window into the orangery. Just little tendrils, soft and brightest green, curling and twisting toward the light. Orla stroked the plants and admired their determination to take over her house.

Time was almost up—she knew that. The grace extended by the house was worn thin, its fingers crept closer.

After a little while, bored by her inattention, the children disappeared to make their own amusement. It was the screams that made her drop the tub of yogurt, right there on the kitchen floor.

In the hallway, haloed by the sun streaming in through the cathedral windows, Bridie dangled from the first-floor landing. Her clumsy hands flailed and grabbed at the floorboards; her torso was wedged between the banisters, but her bottom half was suspended over a fatal depth of empty air, over the beautiful black-and-white tiles. Sam knelt on the landing, face twisted and mouth open, pulling at his sister's arms.

Mistletoe grew up the stairs, snaking along the gleaming wood, and white berries fell like snow.

Bridie.

How blind Orla had been, how easily distracted. She'd thought the house only wanted Sam—hadn't it showed her that, over and over? She'd let herself be led astray, but hadn't she always known its capacity for illusion? All along, it had been reaching out for Bridie, too.

On the landing, Orla pushed her son aside and shoved her arm through the banisters up to her shoulder to grab her daughter by the scruff of her little cotton top in jaunty Breton stripes. Orla hauled her baby to safety and Bridie's head banged against the banister and she shrieked, but Orla didn't care. Bridie lay across her lap and sobbed, and Sam's face ran with tears, and Orla's breath whistled through her nose in a thin stream, and when Nick opened the front doors and saw the three of them, saw the abject fear and heard the cries, he dropped the bags and a glass bottle shattered and milk ran across the tiles in a great stream. Orla was glad to see the white pool on the floor, a white that could so easily have been deepest red.

Dazed, she held Bridie out like proof. "She's fine, she's fine."

Nick reached out. She thought he might hit her, but he snatched up the baby and yanked Sam by his T-shirt. "I can't leave you, can I? I can't trust you for one *minute*—"

Orla put her head between her knees to slow the frantic hammering in her chest. "She's all right, Nick."

He didn't see the vines, she realized. He was standing directly on a bunch of leaves and he didn't even notice. How could he not notice?

"I've had enough. We need to go."

"Go where?"

"I'm taking them to Mum and Dad's. You stay here. Just for a few days. You can stay here. I need to be somewhere else."

How cruel, it seemed to her, that she was now to be punished with the very thing she'd begged for—for him to take them all away from here, to be somewhere else.

"Nick, please. Don't—"

But he'd gone. He'd already gone. The house had taken him, in its own way. The way he looked at her, the way he seemed surprised by the lack of his own desire. The house had shown him the truth of who she was, what Orla had known since the moment she and Nick had met—that she was not enough.

He left very soon afterward, with the children and three overnight bags. Orla held Sam tight and told him how much, how very much, she loved him. How she would keep him safe, always. Sam put his hot little hands against her cheeks.

And then she was alone.

27

1976

———

THE ATTIC BEDROOM WAS PACKED UP. Cardboard boxes of books and shoes, suitcases full of dresses and warm woolen jumpers with stout sleeves. Lydia's quilt, rolled up and tied with string.

Lydia and Dot brought everything down to the corner room at the bottom of the attic steps. They affixed paper labels with the address of Lydia's old flat to the two largest trunks—Sara had said she'd send them on, but Lydia didn't trust her to remember, or to care.

Lydia carried a cracked vinyl suitcase, a small overnight case, and a shopping bag full of toiletries. Her dress was damp in the armpits, her feet slid wetly in her moccasins. Tabitha and Clover stood in the doorway and watched, solemn. Sara shut herself in her office with Owen and didn't come out.

"I think that's everything, Lids. Do you want to have a quick check?" Dot stood up and pushed her hands into the small of her back and arched her spine like a cat.

Dust drifted in shafts of sunlight, fell like summer snow onto the floorboards. The room looked so much smaller without her things in it. The windows were coated in grime, stuck to the glass with the sea air that condensed and dried, leaving behind crystal flecks of ocean salt. A couple of old magazines lay splayed open on the floor. The iron bedstead stood sad and skeletal without the colorful quilt. She had stripped the bed; the striped mattress sagged in the middle and looked dirty.

At the far end, Lydia could just make out the little letters she had scratched into the chimney breast. *Something for Philip to find when he comes back*, she thought, madly.

"Nothing left. All fine." She descended the stairs to Dot and the girls.

"What will we do, Lydia?" Clover held Tabitha's hand so tightly that Lydia saw her knuckles whiten. She felt sick.

"Well, there's the woods! You like that. And the wheat is high, you could have a good game in there."

Tabitha shook her head. "Mummy says no. We mustn't leave the garden."

"How about coloring? I left some new books for you in the kitchen. It's meant to rain later, so that might be nice."

"Who will give us our dinner?"

Dot looked at Lydia. "Your mum will do that."

Clover sighed. "I don't think she will."

"Well, I'll be back tomorrow morning to do some cleaning, so, if you've not had dinner, I'll make you an extra-big breakfast, how about that? I'll bring loads of bacon, we'll fry some bread." Dot smiled and put her hands on her hips.

The twins nodded, unconvinced. Clover worried at the button on the waist of her dress.

Sara had left an envelope for Lydia on the telephone table. Her final wages, plus train money. A short, stilted reference, typed in a hurry. A swipe of ink almost obliterated Sara's shaky signature. Lydia counted the money, and felt bad for doing so. Sara might have kicked her out, but she wouldn't stiff her.

"Right," said Dot, lacking all conviction.

"Yes."

They stood in the hall with the twins. Silence from above. Lydia picked up her shopping bag and case. "Well."

Tabitha burst into tears. "Please don't go, Lydia. You don't have to. We want you to stay."

Lydia put her belongings down again and circled her arms round the children. "I promise I'll write. And you can write to me, too; I gave you my address, didn't I? You can send me anything you like, as much as you like."

Clover sniffed into her elbow and streaked thin snot across her cheek. "It's not the same. We don't want you to be gone. Who will look after me and Tabs?"

"Your mum will. She'll look after you. Come on, girls, you know that. Don't be silly." And then Lydia felt guilty, terribly guilty, for calling them "silly," because she knew as well as they did that Sara would do nothing of the sort.

"Come on, before this gets any worse." Dot opened the front doors and picked up Lydia's bags.

"I'll send you some nice things, from London—very soon!" Lydia waved toward the house once she and Dot reached the cliff path, to the two children silhouetted against the dark mouth of the doorway. They didn't wave back.

Lydia stayed for three nights in Dot's crowded home in the middle of the village, on a musty old sofa that smelled of dogs and cooked dinners. Sheila was so kind to her, but it didn't make up for the staggering number of children that climbed all over her the minute the sun rose, or for having to queue for half an hour to use the outside lavatory. Dot told her it was easier to just go in the bushes, but Lydia wouldn't even entertain the notion.

She would stay for the Midsummer festival, to have a short

holiday, then back to London and job-hunting and her flat on the Holborn Road, where the girls had been subletting her room. Her time at The Reeve already seemed like a dream, something that was going to be forgotten too soon, no matter how she tried to hold on to the threads of the memories.

Lydia thought, often, about the woman she had seen inside the house. She wished Sara hadn't spotted the scissors, she hoped Owen was safe. Lydia did not believe in the fairies, or whatever Dot wanted to call them, nor did she believe in ghosts. But she knew what she had seen, what the girls had seen, and she knew that she'd followed her Philip down to the pond that night. Lydia held these contradictions in her mind and never tried to pin them down. Just because those things were impossible did not mean they weren't real.

Dot reported back on the state of the house and the children when she came home each night.

"It's bizarre. I've barely seen her. The girls are holed up in Tabitha's room, drawing all over the walls. Flat-out denied it was them, but I don't know who else would have done it. Bloody weird as well, creepy little faces all over the wallpaper.

"She keeps Owen with her, mostly. I hear him crying all the time. Sometimes she comes out to go to the loo, but she doesn't say much. It's as bad as it was before the funeral. House is filthy, but I'm doing my best."

Sheila handed Dot a cup of tea, and one for Lydia, too.

"Dot, I'm so sorry. I feel like this is my fault." Lydia held the cup tightly in her hands, scalding her palms in penance.

Dot shrugged. "Not your fault."

"If she hadn't found those scissors—"

Dot put her hand up. "It would still have ended up the same, most likely. You know that—she'd have found something else to use. She wanted you gone—she blamed you for what happened to Philip."

Sheila wiped her hands on a tea towel and nudged Dot toward the kitchen table. "Set that for dinner, will you? Listen, Lydia love, grief does strange things to people. Women, especially. Losing a child is something you never get over." She shook her head. "I ought to know. Makes you addled, for a while."

Dot clattered a handful of bone-handled knives onto the table. "Yeah, but you didn't kick us all out of the house, Mum."

"All I'm saying is, give her a bit of time. She'll come round. She can't cope with those kids on her own, she'll need you back soon enough. Stay as long as you like—she'll be down here, begging, you mark my words."

Lydia smiled, but she didn't believe Sheila. She remembered the hard twist of Sara's mouth, how violently she'd thrown the scissors. The scorn, the spite in Sara's voice. No, Sara wouldn't be back. She wasn't the kind of woman who begged.

Midsummer dawned hot and windy. Lydia was to return to London tomorrow, which seemed impossible. London itself seemed an impossible concept after the soft confines of Dorset.

"This an annual thing, then? The festival?" Lydia stood in the kitchen with a cup of very bad coffee. Several rowdy children spilled cornflakes and milk across the table and fought, viciously, over a china bowl of early strawberries.

"Oh, yes. Don't know when it began, really. Some say Saxons, some say French. It's very old." Sheila swiped a child round the back of the head, but with affection.

Lydia raised her eyebrows. "Sounds interesting."

"We're very respectful of that sort of thing, round here. The old ways, the old folk. You have to remember your place—the land belongs to itself, we just take care of it. We give thanks for the soil, for the water. For the spirits that protect." Sheila clasped her hands, solemn.

"Honestly, Mum, you sound cracked." Dot laughed and Sheila reached out to slap her bare arms, brown and freckled in a cheesecloth dress that was practically see-through.

"And what does Lee think of you going out dressed like that?"

Dot licked her lips and made an exaggerated mouth.

The village was busy with locals and tourists, come over from Poole and Lulworth for the festival. Handmade posters flapped in the wind, tied to lampposts and telephone poles with green nylon string. They featured a yellow rising sun behind a blue river and, in big black marker letters, the start time of the parade and FUN FOR ALL THE FAMILY, BRING KIDS. The creator had omitted an exclamation mark, which made the edict to BRING KIDS feel faintly sinister.

Dot handed out coins to her various siblings, who scattered immediately like wood lice under an upturned log.

"Told them to find as much sugar as they can. Little buggers." She watched them go, fondly.

"Thank you, Dot."

"What, for your ice cream? Don't worry, you can get me a pint later."

"No, for having me. And your mum. I don't know where I'd have gone—"

"Ah, don't worry about it. Mum's always taking in strays."

"Seriously—I don't know anyone else here. It would have been really, really awful."

Dot pulled at her belt, fastened it tighter round her billowing dress. "It's all right, Lids. It all went very bad, there. I'm glad I could help you."

They sat on a low stone wall outside the post office and watched the men wander by with dogs on bits of rope, the women in long, bright skirts towing sticky children bare from the waist up. Lots of hippies came out this way for the festival, parked their scrappy old camper vans down by the cove and complained when the police came to move them along.

"I'm glad you're still going back up to the house. At least someone is keeping an eye on the children. How is Sara, really?" Lydia wiped a dribble of ice cream from her forearm and winced where it had dried and caught in the hairs.

Dot swallowed the last of her cone. "Honestly? Not great. It's all a bit—well, weird. Like I said. I've only seen her once. She asked me to leave food outside the door, so I am. That's all she said to me, really. Girls asked her, yesterday, could I take them to the beach and she said no. Of course. Told her about this, too"—Dot waved toward the surrounding crowds—"but she said it sounded *unhygienic*. Rich, coming from her, given the state of the place. I'm trying to feed the girls best I can. They don't ever talk about Philip, but they ask after you a lot. I told them you're having a holiday with me, then you'd be back to London tomorrow."

Lydia thought of them running in a silent house, up and down stairs powdered with dust, rooting in an empty fridge. Falling, exhausted, into unmade beds, pulling on trousers with holes at the knee. Little castaway children, fending for themselves in a castle from which there would be no rescue.

The afternoon stretched and deepened into dusk. Lydia and Dot were tipsy on warm cider, chaperoned around the various stalls by Lee, who held Dot's hand and paid for Lydia's roll from the hog-roast man. She watched the pig's head rotate, sightless, toffee and soot.

Dot shoved through the crowd to find a good place to stand for the parade—the highlight of the event, apparently, although Lydia couldn't summon the interest. Her mind was up at The Reeve, roaming the landings and corridors, searching for the children.

A little hand slipped into hers, sticky and warm.

"Lydia?"

She turned and looked down and there they were, as though her errant mind had summoned them and brought them to her, down from the house on the hill. Tabitha and Clover, bewitched in front of her.

"Jesus." Dot took Clover's hand. Lee looked confused.

"We came to find you." Tabitha smiled up at Lydia.

"How did you get down here? Where's your mum?"

They shrugged in unison. "Don't know. We walked."

"Dot said there was a party." Tabitha looked around, eager.

Clover nodded. "We wanted to come to the party."

Lydia bent down and held Clover by the shoulders. "Where's your mum? Does she know you're here?"

"She's asleep. We saw her yesterday. And we haven't seen her again."

Dot looked at Lydia. "Shit."

"Yeah. Shit. I should get up there. Will you keep the girls?"

"Sure, sure. Of course."

Lydia handed Dot a pound note. "This should keep them going. Get them something to eat. I'll be back when I can. I'll go back to your mum's house."

The sun sighed down into the sea as Lydia took the road out of the village and away to the cliff. The noise of the festival faded behind her as she walked. Night fell, properly, and Lydia thought she heard something like hunting horns, high and wavering, in the distance.

The lane was very quiet, heavy with waving pink valerian and wild garlic, and the cliff path was even quieter. Waves broke languid on the beach, beaten down by the heat that had not eased.

Lydia heard her own breath, very loud in the still dark.

Long shadows, the color of deep heather, crept ahead as she walked the path up to the house. The front doors were open, left like that by two little girls who escaped. Wisteria blooms sagged against the drawing-room window. The broken body of a magpie lay off to one side, almost hidden in the leaves that had fallen onto the gravel.

"Sara?"

The house returned only silence. All of the doors and windows were open, as though a hurricane had blown through and no one was left to notice.

Inside, Lydia stared. The great glass dome was entirely obscured by a huge growth of some kind of plant that extended up the stairs, up the banisters, climbing the walls of the hall and swaying from the ceiling. Wreaths of vines wrapped round the doorframes and snaked across the black-and-white tiles. She followed the trailing tendrils into the sitting room, where more mistletoe grew. White berries lay scattered across the floor and popped under her shoes as she walked.

Bunches of leaves and berries hung from the mantelpiece and slid under the sofa. Beneath the outrageous plants, a little drift of sand lay under the sitting-room window, piled up against the wall. The sofa had a large streak of chocolate on one of the cushions.

More mistletoe grew along the walls of the kitchen, hanging in garlands over the stove and winding round and round the brass taps of the sink. Lydia couldn't even tell where it was coming from, so thick was the mass of twisting vines and leaves. Beneath the lush, strange plants the kitchen was squalid. Flies hovered above an old ham sandwich on the table, its edges curled up in the heat. The bread had been sliced crudely, clearly by the girls. Crisped orange peel was strewn on the floor, a half-empty bottle of milk stood out on the counter. It had curdled, and smelled awful. Lydia tipped it down the sink.

She tore away a branch that blocked the kitchen door to the orangery and left it sagging against the floor.

"Hello?"

She strained, listening for Owen. Nothing.

The garden was enormous under the rising moon. Sara's sandals lay abandoned on the patio. The elderberry tree moved in the breeze and whispered against the brick wall. A wine bottle lay on its side at the ledge where the patio met the grass; a line of ants marched out of the neck and across the pale slabs.

"Sara? It's just me! It's Lydia! Are you all right?"

Owen's answering cry from the open bedroom window made her turn, and, as she did so, she noticed the trail of clothes leading down to the pond—a pair of trousers, something that might be a vest or a shirt. A pair of silk knickers, torn at the side. Owen wailed above.

Lydia followed the trail. Another empty bottle, blue glass against the yellowing grass. Gin.

"Sara!"

At the edge of the pond, where she herself had knelt and wept only a few nights before, an area of tall grass was flattened and broken, as if a dog had turned circles round and round. As if someone had come here to follow, and search, and had been denied.

The moon cast long light across the garden. The oaks swayed, silver. The monkey puzzle, black as ink, rose into the night. The pond lapped at Lydia's feet, soft music to entice her in. A few fallen leaves drifted on the surface, gold on black silk. "*Feuilles mortes*," thought Lydia.

Out in the middle of the pond, Sara's nude body bumped

against the cherub, rocking so gently with the movement of the water in the wind. She was facedown, and her long hair streamed out. *A beautiful ribbon, shining against a chartreuse velvet dress.*

Next to Sara, a sodden paper parcel floated, a scrap of pink paper stapled to the front. Half a bag of boiled barley sweets bobbed in the water. Lydia imagined the white pages of *Paddington* sinking into the green darkness, telling a story forever and ever.

On the far side of the pond, where the sweet and poisonous meadow flowers grew to waist height and frogs basked in the cool earth, the long grass parted and Lydia watched as a pale foot stepped out from the foliage and into the water. Two slender legs followed, wrapped in white. The woman moved quickly and with purpose, sinking herself deeper into the water as she approached. Her head and face were obscured by a veil the color of summer clouds, turning gray as it soaked up pond water. Behind the fabric, Lydia saw the faint outline of a face—hollowed eye sockets and an open mouth. The woman was tall, up to her neck now and still walking, hands trailing behind her like the wake of a ship. Water filled the cavernous mouth and, as the woman reached Sara's body, the water closed over the top of her head and then she was gone altogether, entombed beneath the surface of the pond.

28

2018

——

EVERY STORY IS A GHOST STORY. All houses are haunted houses; each person is the specter at their own feast, the wraith dogging their own footsteps.

How blissful to believe that our lives are fresh and new— the truth, Orla knew, is that every life has been lived before. We leave nothing behind but ourselves; we take everything forward.

She considered the house, the husband, the children. The life lived at the behest of others, or even at the behest of a different Orla. A diminished person, an Orla that wanted less and strived for less and allowed less, even with herself.

In the breathless breadth of the world, what cages we make for ourselves.

The holes in the canvases grew larger, ringed with old brown and fresh maroon. Orla wanted to know what was behind them, what lay through them, and from time to time would put her bloody fingers in her lap and press the hag stone against her eye sockets, searching the surface of her paintings through the hole. But they didn't speak to her. Sometimes she looked at the wall, sometimes out into the garden. She tried with her left eye, but the views were the same.

There was no one to ask why she wasn't in bed, why she lapped the landings and descended the stairs and opened and closed the doors to the sitting room and drawing room and covered every floorboard of her house with penitent feet. And so she allowed The Reeve to swallow her the way it had always wanted, the process against which she had kicked and fought for so long. Would it have helped, if she'd understood before what was needed? Likely not, and she may never have produced these abstract paintings, the best work of her career. The house had permitted her to continue until they were finished, and then it would put out its hand for the payment. The house had given, and the house would take.

Orla missed Bridie a little, and Sam a lot, and she missed Nick because he was familiar and regular and the last link to a life she'd enjoyed, mostly. She would miss the way he smelled and how his eyebrows went up when he laughed, as though everything was a surprise waiting to be sprung.

And Toby—she missed him, too. He had looked after them all and, when it counted, Orla was unable to look after him in return. She'd let the house fell him, and added that to her score of guilt. Perhaps he would be all right. She thought her atonement might yet be enough to save him.

As she worked late into the night, she listened. Orla and the house hummed in conversation, in velvet sympathy. She heard the unknown feet pace the landing, murmurs in the nursery passage. Sometimes the passageway doors opened and closed, very softly, and Orla turned her head in bed to look. It didn't frighten her anymore, not really. Occasionally, from the studio, she would hear the inexplicable but unmistakable sound of a glass marble plinking down the stairs and skittering across the hall tiles. She never found any marbles, but she heard them just the same. Sometimes children's voices floated up from the ground floor, which Orla liked to think was Sam and Bridie—a faded signal from a far-off future.

Round the banisters and through the boards on each and every floor, mistletoe flourished. When Orla sat to paint, she felt the tickle of the growing plants between her bare toes, the curling vines that reached out to bind her to the house.

Her final canvases were stacked in the studio, marked with Post-it notes for Claude and Alice. She wouldn't see them hung, but she had ideas about which should stay together, and which pieces stood alone. They were her testament to what had happened here, what had happened to her in this house. They showed all the houses it had ever been, ever might be.

Alice called after Nick had been gone two days. "I didn't realize you were up there on your own, Orla. You all right?"

"Fine. Yes, fine. It's so I can work. A holiday."

Alice spoke very gently. "Are you working or having a holiday, Orla?"

"Oh, yes! Work for me, holiday for them."

"Ah, that's good. You getting a lot done? Don't work too hard."

Orla smiled and shook her head. "It doesn't feel like work. It feels like I'm discovering something. Finding something out."

"That's great—that's great, Orla."

"All the holes."

"What?"

"Did you know, Alice, that there are holes everywhere? And sometimes we can see through them—see things we aren't supposed to."

Alice laughed, but she sounded worried, Orla thought. "You're not talking about the house again, are you?"

"Of course I am. The house is the biggest hole. That's why I'm painting it."

"Right. Look, do you want me to come up? Might be nice, have a coffee. I'll bring something from the café."

"That would be lovely. Lemon?" Orla thought about the first time she'd met Claude, how large Sam's piece of yellow cake had looked next to his face. "How about Friday?"

You're supposed to share yourself with the people you've chosen to love, your inner workings and sorrows and victories, but Orla had carried her life mostly alone and was content with that. Even with her husband, she retained a slight detachment that at once frustrated and beguiled him. Perhaps he thought she did it on purpose, but the truth was that Orla was never sure how much people wanted to hear her speak, and so she was generally at ease within silence.

What people needed of her and from her was specific and almost impersonal: the mothering and the housework and the stoic agreement to the terms of their life as dictated by Nick. At times, it felt as though she could be replaced by anyone, any other woman, and as long as children were fed and sheets were cleaned and tax returns were filed, her family might never notice, might never realize the facsimile in her place. As though her labor equals her love, and is replaceable. She was glad of it now, glad to have spent a lifetime practicing the art of disappearing, of removing herself in such a way that those left behind almost never noticed, and only later wondered if perhaps they'd been abandoned. But, to Orla, freedom and abandonment looked pretty much the same. And so, for those she loved, she slipped loose the knots of her affection and drifted until she no longer saw them.

The hag stone lay, useless, on the trestle table. It had never shown her what she'd needed to see. By the next morning, it was gone, disappeared within the house, but Orla never noticed.

Orla didn't sleep that last night. Sleep seemed beyond her, a precious thing she mustn't touch. She worried it might distract her, that if she slept she would wake with a changed mind and undo all the work that had gone before. So she paced the house, up and down, and picked tirelessly at her canvases and noted, often, how strange it was that she didn't seem tired at all.

When the dawn came, Orla left her house on the hill for the last time. She didn't take shoes, no need, and wore only her summer shorts and linen T-shirt from the day before.

Ropes of mistletoe hung across the front doors; Orla parted the curtain as she left, crushing berries with her hands. Juice coated her fingers and tasted bitter where she licked. They were everywhere now, the vines—even her bed had become a blanket of soft, pulsing branches. Beams creaked and settled with their new weight, windows were blinded by masses of leaves. The light in the house was dim and murky and turned her skin to green, as if she was underwater.

She left the front doors open. She wanted Nick and the children to feel welcome when they came home, and there's nothing so welcoming as an open door.

Tall marram and blowsy cow parsley lined the cliff path, fragrant under a sun that was already coming up hot. Bright clumps of sea pink shuddered in the wind that stroked the clifftop, and out toward the fields a carpet of sea campion, pale as a bride, hummed with hoverflies. A couple of wasps clicked in the air next to her face.

Empty snails broke under her feet. She thought of the jar in

Sam's room, full of gritty seashells turning green in the damp at the bottom of the glass. Orla put a shell in her pocket, for Sam, and then turned it out again and let it fall onto the sand. She tucked her hair behind her ears and put a hand to her eyes to look out over the water. A still day, clear on the horizon.

Early, only a few lone figures on the beach, picking across the pebbles, curved as commas. When she finally descended, she was mostly—but not quite—alone on the sand. She thought of Alice and Claude, yawning in dressing gowns and stepping around each other with sleep-murmurs, romantic and still half-tied to bed.

Orla will meet the sea and she will let it take her, and then she will come back to the house. She will be there, waiting, when her husband and children come home, and she will never, ever leave; she will live with them forever.

And what will it be like, to live side by side? To live parallel but unseen? Perhaps it will be something like the dreams she's had ever since they first arrived—a slow, underwater existence, distorted and suspended in her own river of time.

The first three inches of water were bath-warm and cooled rapidly toward Orla's feet. She imagined herself to be an apple on an ocean: carried by the waves, unable to set her own course, but oddly unsinkable. She'd bob and float until the rot set in.

Shallow water lapped at Orla's knees.

The house had wanted them all, in the beginning, she knew that. It had watched them. It opened itself up and lifted that thin veil and showed her the future, the cycle to which they were all bound. The house would have to make do with Orla. She came to it willingly, a sweeter meat.

Neck-deep now, Orla steadied herself against the tide and watched the sunlight turn the surface to mercury. Ocean weighted her hair. From the shore, she heard someone shouting, someone who sounded like Toby, but of course it couldn't be. She heard the glottal thump of feet pounding water. Someone was coming for her, but she didn't want it, she didn't need the rescue. Wasn't she rescuing herself? The voice sounded again, closer, but Orla didn't look back.

She stared down at her silvered flesh beneath the sea and felt a swift joy in the certainty of her decision. The certainty of the release. My God, what a life, to enter the world bowed already with the burden of living. Brought mewling into the light to endure the demand of I am, I am—the endless throb and pulse of it. The child will shout, later, *I didn't ask to be born!* And you'll have no answer, you benevolent and milk-sodden bitch, because they're right. You've condemned them to breathing in and out, over and again, and how the days pile up when the in and out is just too much to ask of anyone.

Orla thought, *I have passed my own burden down to you.* And she was sorry.

A hand closed around her hair, white under the green sea.

Arriving

—

29

2023

———

PAUL SET THEIR BAGS DOWN on the black-and-white tiles. "It amazes me, still, every time we come here."

Jenny laughed. "Every time? This is only the third time we've set foot in this house, you make it sound like we've been coming here for years."

"It does feel familiar, though, doesn't it?" He put his hands on his hips and tilted his head to look up through the glass cupola. "You said so yourself, when we came to look—that it already felt like home."

"I know. Weird, isn't it." Jenny rubbed her arms, too hot under the fire-eye of the dome, lit up with summer sun. Small heaps of soft sand piled up under the lip of the front doors, driven in by the breeze. "Like I'd been here before."

Out on the driveway, two moving vans had spilled half their load onto the patchy gravel, and a wiry young man carrying stacked plastic boxes full of kitchen implements cut through the hallway between Paul and his wife.

"Sorry." Jenny stepped back, into shadow.

Paul rubbed his chin. "Sadie still sleeping?"

"Last I checked. She's passed out on the back seat; I opened all the windows."

Poor darling Sadie had cried all the way from Reading, mashing a plush rabbit tight between her hot hands and ignoring Jenny's attempts to distract her with countryside views. She wept when they packed up her pink bedroom, wept when Jenny brought iced biscuits to Brownies for Sadie's final meeting, wept as Jenny buckled her into the car for the journey to Dorset. Such a sensitive child, Sadie cried over the smallest, strangest things: a dried-out worm on the pavement, the last slice of bread in the packet ("He is very lonely, Mummy. He has no more bread friends"), a too-small jumper removed from the rotation and put into the charity-shop bag. Jenny worried about her daughter, who felt things so deeply and adored the whole world.

Reading was intended to be a brief stopping place in the journey of their marriage, but rising house prices and one redundancy had kept them tethered there, impatient in their narrow terraced house and straining for better. Sadie's arrival compounded the frustration, penned in cramped rooms strewn with plastic nonsense and infinite loads of laundry half-drying on cheap metal clothes racks.

So when Paul's very elderly parents finally died and Jenny discovered she was pregnant again, they took the inheritance and struck out toward the life they'd always dreamed of. They had just enough for the minimum required deposit on The Reeve, and a mortgage was made possible by Paul picking up some extra part-time consultancy work for a remote firm. A good chunk of their remaining cash would go toward replacing the existing broadband with fiber—cables would need to be laid out to the house; Jenny had moaned out loud when the quote came back from BT.

But it would be worth it, the sacrifices and the rigorous

budgeting and shopping from the generic-brand shelves in the supermarket. Worth it for Sadie, who could grow up with space and freedom by the sea. Worth it for the new baby, due imminently, who would never hear his parents hiss at each other in a dark bedroom. Worth it for their marriage.

Jenny put her hands in the small of her back and stretched. Paul made a sympathetic face. "Sore?"

"Mm. I'm so big now, it's hard to get comfortable." She bent to retrieve her overnight bag.

"I'll get that." He picked up the bag, took her hand, and led her up the grand staircase to the master bedroom that opened out from the first landing. Their bed frame leaned against the far wall, wooden bones of a skeleton stacked in haphazard pieces.

Jenny pointed to it. "Right, that's your first job—put that thing together so I can have a bloody nap."

Paul laughed and squeezed her hand. "Still glad we're doing this?"

"Very." She smiled at her husband, felt the catch of excitement behind her breastbone. This wonderful house, all hers, to do with as she pleased. *Heaven.*

"I'll fetch Sadie in—don't want her to sleep too long." He set off down the stairs; Jenny noted how the light fell on the bald patch starting at his crown.

The long lawn of the back garden was browned by weeks of too much sun and too little rain. Jenny crossed to the first set of windows on the north wall of the master bedroom and raised the sash. These old windows would have to go; the wood looked almost rotted through and the panes were only single-glazed.

The estate agent had warned them that it needed work, but they didn't mind. On their very first visit, Paul went from room to room and made a detailed list of everything that had to be fixed and updated. Then they'd sat together over a takeaway curry and prioritized the list into sections.

"It just needs a firm hand, that's all. Restore some order, tackle it properly." He ran a finger down the Excel sheet on the screen.

"You make it sound like a horse, or something. Like a dog. A firm hand!" Jenny laughed, and spilled yogurt onto her rounded belly.

The previous owners had made a good start, but sold up before the work was finished. According to the estate agent, the house was in better condition than the last time it went on the market, but conceded that some of the bigger jobs had been left undone.

Jenny was enchanted by the adjoining nursery, although the connecting door to the baby's room seemed to be stuck, or locked. But Paul could deal with that; likely a new handle was needed. It seemed such a romantic notion, to have a separate nursery. Sadie had slept in their room for the first year and it was hell. Paul, who had grown up in comfort, was amused by her appreciation for all this space. Jenny, who had grown up in a tiny terrace in Leeds, privately resented the kind but patronizing way he'd looked at her when she declared the master bedroom large enough to include an armchair with a footstool, something she'd always wanted.

Gratitude for the house bloomed, heady, and she leaned out of the bedroom window to take in the scope of the garden and the scent of the lavender hedge. She hoped she would never stop feeling lucky to be here, that she would never take it as her due, the way Paul did. She rested her bump on the windowsill, closed her eyes and put her face to the sun. The sea sounded so wonderful in the distance, rhythmic and inviting. Perhaps she would take Sadie to the beach later, to cheer her up. Poor baby, having to leave all her friends behind. But she was only six, she'd be fine. Soon enough, she'd forget her old friends and her pink bedroom and come to love this house the way Jenny already did.

Jenny surveyed the sweep of overgrown lawn, the beautiful oaks wreathed in pretty mistletoe, the lacy elderflower that sprang up all along the high brick walls. A large patch of earth had been turned over and flattened out beneath the oaks, shadowed by the stern monkey puzzle. The estate agent said something about the previous owners recovering the original pond, but never completing the job before they left; faded orange string marked out the abandoned perimeter and the soil was rich with dandelions that had taken hold. Jenny thought it would be quite a nice idea, really. She'd like a water feature.

Leggy yarrow and thick clumps of goosegrass waved along the string markers, threatening to envelope the wooden stakes made almost invisible by a carpet of weeds.

And there—movement in the tall grass. The plants swayed, as if pushed apart by hands. The turn of a browned shoulder, pale fabric that could be a blouse, or a dress? Jenny leaned forward, held tight to the window frame. She saw sunlight reflecting off wet hair, but couldn't tell the color. Too far away to see.

"Mummy! I'm hungry. I want orange juice. Can I sleep in your bed tonight?"

Jenny turned to embrace her daughter, who smelled of hot skin and sea-salt air, and, when she came back to the window, the grass was still and the garden lay flat and bright under the sun, and there was no woman. There was no one, just Jenny and her child and her not-yet child, and the house.

She closed the sash and left the room. Her footsteps died away down the staircase, faint shouts from the movers lifted and fell on the wind. In the warm silence of the bedroom, the door to the nursery corridor opened, very quietly, and after a moment closed itself again.

Author's Note

—

IN JUNE 2014, I took a short holiday in Dorset with my friend, Carolyn. Our intention was to walk part of the Dorset Coast Path and eat pounds of crab along the way, which I'm pleased to say we managed. On the stretch from Lulworth Cove out toward Weymouth, just after a couple of "hands-and-knees-job" hills, we passed an old house, all by itself, right on the cliff edge and bordered by a sandy path. There was nothing else around for what seemed like miles—just this house, with boarded-up windows and a high-walled garden. It looked sort of Victorian, architecture-wise, all brick and slate, and was in quite good shape, aside from the boarded windows—presumably for weather protection, given its position on the cliff. It struck me as quite sad, and quite spooky, to have this grand house all alone in such a vulnerable and isolated place, and for it to be entirely empty. I loved it completely and began writing this book in my head at that moment, although it took a while to come to the page.

The Reeve is not quite that house—I took a few liberties with reality—but it's not far off. I remember the feeling of being alone, and a little scared, and also being caught by the magnificent views, enchanted by the cliffs and the sea and how the house stood austere in the face of the elements. I hope I have captured some of that feeling in this book.

For anyone who is from Dorset, or thereabouts—my apologies for the things I have missed, or got wrong entirely, geographically or otherwise. The village and the bay in this story are inspired by Lulworth Cove, although again I have taken a few liberties.

"Reeve," by the way, is the old Dorset word for "unravel." Make of that what you will.

Acknowledgments

———

TO MY EDITOR, LEONORA CRAIG COHEN, for loving this book and shaping it into the greatest version of itself. You have looked after it so well, and the opportunity to work with someone just as creepy as me has been a profound pleasure. Thank you for holding my hand!

To everyone at Serpent's Tail who has taken such care of this book and of me: Hannah Westland, Anna-Marie Fitzgerald, Emily Frisella, Georgina Difford, Ali Nadal, Linden Lawson, and to Mark Swan for the fabulous, eerie cover for the UK edition. Thank you.

To my agent, Hayley Steed, who took a notion for a very new writer, years ago, and signed her up. You have been a steady source of encouragement, inspiration, and good, sensible advice when I have run away with myself. Your faith in my writing, and that I could make a career of it, has been life-altering; how lucky I am to have found you.

To everyone at the Madeleine Milburn agency, for being so collectively supportive and providing me with a truly exceptional start in the industry. In particular, Georgia McVeigh, who read this novel in its infancy and gave such wonderful feedback.

To my wonderful team at Mariner Books in the US, specifically to Kate Nintzel for acquiring the book and having such enthusiasm for it. I am extremely lucky to have had input from such an experienced and skillful editor.

To Lucy Carson, for finding the perfect home for me across the (haunted) pond.

To every marvelous friend who read my early writing and told me to continue: Henry Cockburn, Rebecca Reddecliffe, Jessica Richardson, Charlotte King, Laura Buchan, Kathleen Sargeant, Emily Cockburn, and Rachel Sené-Todd.

To the friends who remained steadfast supporters as this book went on its publishing journey and I grew increasingly unhinged, who continued to provide strong drinks and suppers and understood when plans were canceled, or when I was absent from the fun: Michael and Emma Bailey, Abby and Liam O'Looney, Chris Wright, Aarish Pandiya, Megan Webb, Sophie and Brian O'Radcliffe, Damilola Odimayo, Amanda Mason and Harry Jenkins, Lisa Williams, Victoria Beadle, Della Wolfe, and Sharon Ridge.

To Abi Strevens, without whom this book would not have been written. Thank you.

To Fiona Whitehouse, who gave me generous and useful advice on how artists earn a living, among other things. Thank you for your kindness.

To Caoimhe Ní Dhónaill, who read this manuscript before anyone else, provided solid notes, and was so frightened that she almost didn't finish it—you have been an excellent barometer for fear and a generous reader.

To Carolyn Ramsay, who once took a walk with me in Dorset. That trip inspired this novel and also delivered outstanding crab sandwiches. Thank you.

To my dearest friend, Heather S. Wright, whom I love so much. My primary editor, my greatest source of amusement, the person upon whom I call when the ideas (or the motivation) run out, and who never fails to inspire. The best sort of friend a person could have, only much more like a chicken.

To my family, large and lively and ever proud, ever supportive: Mike, Chris, Jessie, Genevieve, James, Emily, Jamie, Sarah, Andy, and Bonnie. To the other half: Helen, James, Jane, Simon, and Doreen. Thank you.

To those who will never read this: Bill McKellar, Harry and Valerie Cuming, and Shirley and Phil Crabb, none of whom ever underestimated the restorative power of a gin and tonic.

Finally, and crucially, thank you to my husband, Tim. For his unshakable belief in my abilities, for his unwavering commitment to helping me realize a dream. For a multitude of dinners, delivered to the desk of a woman who was too busy to say thank you (but he knew she meant it). For understanding the difficult days and celebrating the good ones. Without you, my life as I know it would not—could not—exist. Without you, this novel would not exist—nor the next one, nor the next. I am indebted to you, and I love you.

About the Author

———

KATE COLLINS was born in Cork, Ireland, and has spent her career in trade and academic publishing. She studied literature and medieval history at Lancaster University and stayed there to complete a master's degree in contemporary literary theory.

She now lives and works in Oxfordshire, in a falling-down old house that is, sadly, not haunted (despite her best efforts).